Roberta Kray was born in Southport. In early 1996 she met Reggie Kray and they married the following year; they were together until his death in 2000. Through her marriage to Reggie, Roberta has a unique insight into the world of the London gangland.

NOTHING BUT TROUBLE

ROBERTA KRAY

sphere

SPHERE

First published in Great Britain in 2012 by Sphere
This paperback edition published in 2012 by Sphere

10

A CIP catalogue record for this book
is available from the British Library.

ISBN 978-0-7515-4479-4

Typeset in Garamond by M Rules
Printed and bound in Great Britain by
Clays Ltd, Elcograf S.p.A.

Papers used by Sphere are from well-managed forests
and other responsible sources.

MIX
Paper from
responsible sources
FSC® C104740
www.fsc.org

Sphere
An imprint of
Little, Brown Book Group
Carmelite House
50 Victoria Embankment
London EC4Y 0DZ

An Hachette UK Company
www.hachette.co.uk

www.littlebrown.co.uk

For my great friends Marcelle and Stuart Garratt and their lovely daughters Tanya, Kirsty, Sian and Narika.

Prologue

On the surface there was nothing different about that dull August day in 1998, and yet it was to change all our lives for ever. Shall I tell you about it? There's a part of me that wants to, that longs to, but another part that's simply too afraid. I've kept it hidden for so long, and if I open the box all kinds of demons might fly out. I'm not sure if I can cope with that. There's something else I'm worried about too, another fear that can't be pushed aside: I'm terrified of being judged. Even as I write these words I'm aware of how cowardly they sound. But that's who I am. I'm a coward and a liar, and because of me a ten-year-old girl died.

Well, there it is. I've taken the first step, admitted it, and there's no point in trying to backtrack now. So I'll tell you what I know. It may not be the whole truth, the *exact* truth, but I'll do my best. Time plays tricks with the memory, and my account may not be completely accurate.

This is a story about six ten-year-old girls. On the day we're talking about, five of them ate their breakfasts, left their respective homes and met up at the rusting gates of the Mansfield Estate. Becky Hibbert was the first to arrive, closely followed by Kirsten Roberts, Lynda Choi and Sam

Kendall. Paige Fielding, as always, was the last on the scene; she was the self-proclaimed leader of the gang, the tallest and the loudest, and she liked to exert her authority by keeping everyone waiting.

Alley cats was what the neighbours called them, kids with too much time on their hands and nothing better to do in the school holidays than aimlessly roam the East End streets of Kellston. On that particular Wednesday the sky was a gloomy shade of grey, but the air was mild enough and the rain had stopped falling. The five girls, dressed in jeans and T-shirts, flip-flopped down the high street with boredom tugging at their heels. With less than a quid between them, they were on the lookout for anything that could be easily lifted.

After being thrown out of Woolworth's – they'd raided that store too many times before – they headed for the market, where there were usually easy pickings. Keeping their eyes peeled for careless shoppers who left their purses too close to the top of their shopping bags, they strolled casually up and down between the rows of brightly coloured stalls, their quick hands swiping what they could. Small, easily hidden items were what they were after. The jewellery stalls were their favoured sites, with their heaps of rings and bracelets and dangly earrings. The girls had little idea of the value of what they took but, like jackdaws, were drawn to anything that glittered.

After they'd accumulated as much as they safely could, the next stage was to find a quiet place to survey the haul. This was always somewhere in the confusing maze of alleyways that criss-crossed the dingier parts of Kellston. On that

Wednesday morning they went round the back of Albert Street, haunt of the local toms – although none were working at that time of day – and hunkered down by a pile of old crates. The ground was littered with discarded condoms, used needles and empty plastic cider bottles.

It was Paige who gathered the spoils together, making sure the others didn't hold anything back. She had a sixth sense for when someone was lying to her and the ability to inflict the worst Chinese burns in living memory. Paige was, to put it mildly, a Class A bitch.

'Gimme,' she ordered, holding out her hand, palm up, to each girl in turn.

Everyone did as they were told.

Paige would examine the stolen goods, sneering if she thought they weren't up to scratch. Everyone had to contribute something or they wouldn't eat that lunchtime. Those were the rules and everyone stuck to them. Most of what they lifted was cheap costume jewellery, but occasionally they struck gold with a purse or a wallet. When that was the case the cash was divided equally between them, but the credit cards went straight into Paige's back pocket.

That Wednesday, however, the pickings were slim. A few rings, a silver chain and a selection of bangles was the sum total of the morning's activity. As midday approached and their stomachs started to rumble, the gang drifted down to the Hope and Anchor, where old Johnny Lucker, a lifelong fence, would be sitting hunched over his pint of bitter. Paige put her head round the door, frantically flapping her hand until she got his attention. Then it was off to the staff entrance at the side. There, beside the bins and out of sight of prying eyes, Lucker's nicotine-stained fingers furtively examined the goods. His mouth turned down at the corners as he saw what was on offer.

'Barely worth leaving me pint for,' he grumbled.

'Aw, come on,' Paige said, flicking back her long brown ponytail. 'That chain's worth summat. You know it is.'

'I'll give you five quid for the lot.'

'Ten,' Paige said.

'Five,' he repeated firmly. 'And that's being bleedin' generous.' He rummaged in his pockets and came up with four pound coins and a quid's worth of change. 'Here. Take it or leave it. It's the best I can do.'

Paige pulled a face but reluctantly accepted the cash on offer.

And perhaps that was why it happened.

Paige wasn't happy, and when she wasn't happy she always found a way to vent her frustration.

It was hardly the first time the girls had been disappointed. Sometimes they got lucky, sometimes they didn't. So there was nothing particularly different about that day, apart from one essential fact. As they wandered back in the direction of the chip shop, Minnie Bright appeared from nowhere and tagged along behind them. She was the type of kid who no one wanted to be friends with, small and spindly, with a colourless face and strange pale eyes. In fact everything about her was vapid, as if she'd been put through the washing machine as many times as her ragged clothes. She had an odd smell too, a faintly metallic odour.

'Fuck off,' Paige said.

But Minnie didn't. As if oblivious to the demand – she

was probably used to similar ones at home – she continued to saunter behind them. One of the buckles on her cheap plastic sandals was broken, and it made a small clinking sound as she put one foot in front of the other.

Becky Hibbert turned, placed her hands on her hips and glared at her. 'Are you deaf or what?' Becky saw herself as Paige's lieutenant, the second in command, and as such was always out to try and impress. 'Fuck off, okay?'

Minnie lifted a hand, scratched hard at her scalp and gazed blankly back.

'Yer not wanted,' Becky said. Leaning forward, she gave the girl a shove. 'Clear off! Don't you understand bloody English?'

Minnie stumbled back a step, bit down on her lower lip, but didn't say a word.

None of the others intervened. Although not cruel by nature, Kirsten, Sam and Lynda all had the same instinct for self-preservation. They knew that as long as Becky and Paige were busy tormenting Minnie, they themselves were safe from similar treatment.

Suddenly, glancing to her left, Becky was distracted. Momentarily forgetting about her victim, she gave Paige a nudge with her elbow. Her voice was a hushed combination of awe and excitement. 'Look who it is. It's him, it's him!'

'What are you talking about?'

'At the bus stop.'

'Who?'

'The Beast,' Becky whispered.

All six of them simultaneously looked across the road towards the man in jeans and a dark jacket. He was in his fifties, an average sort of height and with sandy-coloured hair receding from a large domed forehead. His mouth, wide and fleshy, tugged impatiently on a cigarette. All the kids knew Donald Peck, or at least knew of him. He was the local bogeyman, the flasher, the weirdo who liked to unzip his flies and show his floppy cock to unsuspecting children.

'See that man, Minnie?' Paige said, grinning. 'The one with the black sports bag, yeah? Well, he kills bad girls like you and chops them into little pieces.'

Minnie shrank back, her pale eyes widening.

'See that bag he's got? It's full of arms and legs and tiny hands.' Paige reached out and grasped Minnie by her skinny wrist. 'Shall I give him a shout and tell him to come over here? Shall I tell him how bad you've been?'

Minnie frantically shook her head, her startled eyes darting between Paige and the man across the street.

'What?' Paige said. 'I can't hear you.'

'N-no,' Minnie eventually squeaked out.

The bus arrived and temporarily obscured their view. After a while they saw Donald Peck walk towards the rear and settle down in a seat, placing the bag beside him. Paige waited until the bus had moved off before resuming her torment of Minnie.

'Okay, I'll let you come with us. But you'd better do exactly as I say, or I'll be giving the Beast a bell and telling him where you live.' The corners of her mouth curled into a cruel smile. 'He'll come round in the middle of the night and snatch you away, and you'll never be heard of again. You got it?'

Minnie's head bobbed up and down like a manic nodding dog.

'Okay, let's go.'

The others, realising Paige was up to something, exchanged a quick series of looks.

'Where are we going?' Kirsten said.

'You'll see,' Paige replied.

She led them back along Station Road with her hands in her pockets and a new swagger in her step. From time to time she leaned in towards Becky and whispered in her ear. The two of them giggled together, glancing over their shoulders at the others. Even at that tender age, Paige had discovered the ancient art of divide and rule.

After five more minutes she swung a left on to Morton Grove, with its long row of dilapidated terraced houses. A few England stickers were still pasted on to windows, along with some red and white flags, symbols of a hope that had long since died. France had won the World Cup, and England had lost to Argentina. Beckham had been sent off after mistaking an opponent for a football.

'Where are we going?' Kirsten asked again.

'Almost there,' Paige said, turning in to the alley that ran behind the Grove. It was empty, as most of the alleyways usually were. They were known as a mugger's paradise and all sensible people avoided them. A high red-brick wall lay to their right, and to their left were the mean backyards, the majority concreted over and used as dumping grounds for unwanted household items.

'Here it is,' Paige said triumphantly, flourishing a hand as she stopped outside one of the houses. They all stood and stared at it. There was nothing special about it; in fact the total opposite. The building was a wreck. Part of the guttering hung down from the roof, mortar was crumbling from between the bricks and the blue paintwork was peeling off in strips to reveal a lighter shade beneath. The windows, opaque with grime, didn't need the grey net curtains to keep out prying eyes. The backyard was flanked by two tall rickety fences and was littered with debris; an old broken bicycle, a fridge and a heap of rotting bin bags took up most of the available space.

For a while nobody spoke.

It was Paige who eventually broke the silence. 'Do you know who this house belongs to, Minnie?'

Minnie shook her head.

Paige grinned, clearly enjoying herself. 'Course you don't. You know fuck all. Well, it belongs to a queen, a very rich and beautiful queen, and she allows anyone who can get inside to choose what they want from her collection of jewels.'

Minnie's eyes widened again. 'A queen?'

Becky sniggered. 'Yeah, you could be dripping in gold, Minnie. You could have a tiara and everything. You'd look like a princess.'

'Why don't you try the back door, Minnie, and see if it's open?' Paige urged. She gave the girl a push. 'Go on, go and see. You might be the lucky one.'

'Don't be daft,' Lynda Choi said.

Paige spun around and hissed at her. 'Who are you calling daft?'

Lynda gave her a wary look. 'I only meant—'

Paige glared. 'Just keep yer Chinkie gob shut, all right?' She paused for a second, waiting to see if anyone would challenge her over the comment – no one did – before looking smugly back at Minnie. 'What did I tell you earlier about doing what you're told?'

Minnie, after a short hesitation, began to walk down the narrow backyard. Every couple of steps she glanced back at the other girls.

'Go on,' Paige urged. 'Don't hang about. Just see if the door's open and then come straight back here.'

Once Minnie was out of earshot, Kirsten said softly, 'This is *his* house, ain't it?'

Paige pulled a face. 'What if it is? I bet he keeps all sorts in there. Probably got thousands hidden under the mattress.'

'You reckon?' Kirsten said.

'Yeah, pervs like him don't keep their dosh in a bank. They don't do nothin' normal. And he's on the bus, so he's well gone.'

Minnie reached tentatively towards the metal door handle, but withdrew her fingers again and turned, her pale eyes focusing on Paige. Then, as if the potential wrath of the bigger girl outweighed all other considerations, she turned back, quickly gripped the handle in her grubby hand and pressed it down. There was a distinct rattling sound, but the door didn't open.

'Shit,' Paige murmured.

Minnie rushed back, her thin cotton dress flapping round her legs.

Sam Kendall heard Lynda expel an audible sigh of relief.

9

She tried to catch her eye but her friend looked away. Sam felt guilty about earlier, that she hadn't defended Lynda. She knew that name-calling was bad, that it was hurtful, but her fear of Paige was greater than her sense of right and wrong. 'I'm starving,' she said. 'Let's go and get some chips.'

But Paige had other ideas. So far as she was concerned, this wasn't over yet. Her expression grew tight and determined. To walk away empty-handed would be to admit defeat, to lose face in front of her troops. 'There must be another way in.'

'There isn't,' Sam insisted. 'Come on, it doesn't matter. Let's go to the chippie.'

'What about that window?' Becky said, pointing. 'The little one on the left. It's not shut properly.'

Paige, with Becky and Kirsten on one side and Minnie on the other, strolled down the yard and peered up. The frosted window, probably leading into the bathroom, had been propped open a couple of inches. It was way too small for any adult to get through, too small even for most of the girls – but there was one person who might just manage to wriggle in.

'You know what, Minnie, I think this could be your lucky day.'

Lynda Choi remained with Sam by the gate. She hopped from foot to foot, her anxiety growing. It was all very well nicking a few odds and sods from the market, but breaking in to a house was something else entirely. You could end up down the cop shop for that. She could imagine her mother's face, her mother's *shame*, if she did get caught. The thought was enough to propel her into action.

'I'm gonna go,' she whispered to Sam. 'Are you coming?'

Sam dithered for a second, aware that they'd be punished for their desertion but as eager as Lynda to get away. She didn't like being near this house. Its blank grey windows gave her the creeps. And although she knew that Paige had made up the story about the chopped-off arms and legs and tiny hands, she still had a scary mental image of them scattered around the dingy rooms inside.

'Yeah, okay.'

As they sped off down the alley, Paige was crouching down and Minnie was climbing clumsily on to her shoulders.

It was a few minutes before their absence was noted. By then Minnie had made two failed attempts at getting through the window. Even with the help of Paige's extra height, she hadn't quite been able to reach. It was Becky who looked round and realised the other girls were missing. She walked to the gate and peered both ways along the alley. It was empty. She hurried back and reported the news. 'They've gone.'

'What d'ya mean?' Paige said, her dark brows crunching together in a frown.

'Sam and Lynda. They've scarpered, done a runner. What you gonna do about it?'

Paige heard the challenge in her voice – Becky always liked to stir things – and was in two minds as to whether to go after them. She glanced rapidly from the gateway to the house and back again. They couldn't have got far, and if she was quick she could catch them up. Yeah, she could grab the treacherous little cows and teach them a lesson they'd never forget. But appealing as this prospect was, it would mean abandoning the break-in. She was furious but determined not to show it. Instead she gave a casual kind of shrug. 'So, who cares? All the more for us when we get inside.'

Becky, hoping for a more vehement response, looked disappointed. 'I suppose.'

'I suppose, I suppose,' Paige mimicked in an exaggerated high-pitched voice.

Kirsten giggled.

Becky's lips tightened into a thin straight line. She didn't like being on the receiving end of Paige's mockery. 'Maybe I'll piss off too,' she said sulkily.

'Go on then. We don't care.'

Becky scowled but stayed where she was. It was that 'we' that was troubling her. Leaving Kirsten alone with Paige – Minnie didn't count – was too risky. By this time tomorrow the two of them could be best mates and she'd be left out in the cold.

Paige glared for a while. When she was satisfied that Becky wasn't going to give her any further trouble, she returned her attention to the trickier problem of getting into the house. It was only on the third attempt that Minnie finally managed to grab the edge of the window. Paige took hold of her ankles and pushed her further up. With an effort, Minnie got her head through, and then her shoulders. She hung suspended for a moment, half in, half out, with her legs flailing and her grubby knickers on display, before eventually slithering through the gap and disappearing from view.

'Minnie?' Paige called out softly.

There was a clattering sound from inside.

'Minnie? You okay?'

Nothing.

'Minnie?'

'Yeah,' she finally replied in her small whiny voice. 'I banged me leg.'

'Come on, don't hang about. We ain't got all bleeding day.'

Paige stood back, well pleased with herself. Now all they had to do was to wait. Minnie was under strict instructions to go straight to the back door and open it. She'd been told three times and asked to repeat it. Even a moron like Minnie should be able to manage that. Earlier, Paige had got down on her hands and knees and peered closely at the lock: there had been no light coming through it, so the key must still be in there. Once they were inside, she decided, she'd make the others stay downstairs while she went up to the bedroom. Creeps like Peck always kept their cash under the mattress. How much was there likely to be? Hundreds, she thought, maybe even more.

The sky had grown darker, large grey clouds gathering overhead, and now a few drops of rain began to fall. A couple more minutes passed but Minnie still didn't appear. Paige banged on the door with the flat of her hand. 'Minnie? What are you doing? Stop messing about and open up.'

There was no reply.

'Bitch,' Paige muttered, growing increasingly impatient. 'I bet she's filling her pockets with all sorts.' Dragging an old metal bin across the yard, she clambered on top and put her face to the open window. 'Minnie? Get yer thieving arse back here or I'll fuckin' kill you.'

But still Minnie didn't respond.

Paige had had enough. The silly cow was making her look like a fool. The rain was falling harder now, one of those freak summer showers that could drench you in moments. Shaking the water from her ponytail, she leaned in towards the window again. 'Minnie? Minnie, you've got to get out of there now! The Beast's coming! Quick! He's coming to get you.'

Paige jumped off the bin and without a backward glance made for the gateway. The two other girls followed her automatically, and the three of them ran down the alley whooping and screaming with laughter.

That was the last time any of them saw Minnie Bright. It was forty-eight hours before her crack-addicted mother reported her missing, and a few hours more before the police entered the house and found her small twisted body hidden under a bed.

1

Harry Lind sat back, put his feet up on the desk and cast a critical eye over his new surroundings. The room, freshly whitewashed, still smelled of paint despite the open windows, but he wasn't about to complain. The office was twice the size of the last one and half the rent. The trade-off was that they'd had to relocate the business to the East End, a move that his business partner Mac remained distinctly dubious about. Had it been the right decision? He hoped so.

Harry slowly took in the row of filing cabinets, the wooden floor, the slatted blinds – pulled up now to let the spring air flood in – and his old oak desk. The walls needed some pictures to soften the starkness of the white, but as yet he hadn't decided exactly what he wanted. He looked through the open door to the reception area beyond. A wine-coloured leather sofa, along with a couple of matching easy chairs, had replaced the uncomfortable seating of the previous office. There was even a new desk for their receptionist and PA, Lorna Green. Today, Friday, was her last day at the Strand. She and Mac would be joining him on Monday morning.

Harry knew that they were taking a chance. The West End had a prestige that was missing from the mean streets of Kellston, and although their overheads may have been reduced, that wouldn't make a difference if they didn't get the clients. Having spent the last nine months twisting Mac's arm about the move, Harry was starting to feel the pressure. What if it all went wrong? But no sooner had the thought entered his head than he pushed it aside. Kellston was one of those up-and-coming areas, close to the City, and the office was near the station. There was no reason why the business shouldn't flourish.

The sound of traffic drifted up from the road. Harry's gaze, still on the reception area, alighted on the sign on the wall: MACKENZIE, LIND, and underneath, PRIVATE INVESTIGATORS. His mouth slid into a smile. It still gave him a kick to see his name in print. For the first time in years he actually felt optimistic about the future. Yes, signing the partnership deal had been the right move. After he'd been invalided out of the police force, there had been a long period when he'd had trouble getting up in the morning, never mind looking to the future. Now, at forty-three, he was, perhaps, finally managing that closure the shrinks were always banging on about.

Harry was still contemplating this notion when he heard the buzzer go, an indication that someone had come through the main door downstairs. He swung his legs off the desk, stood up and put his jacket on. Strictly speaking, the office wasn't open for business until Monday, but he wasn't about to turn any potential clients away.

The woman who strolled into reception was in her early

16

thirties, wearing jeans, a white shirt and a faded denim jacket. Her oval face, although not conventionally beautiful, was open and expressive. It was framed by a bob of shiny pale brown hair, and from underneath her fringe a pair of grey eyes crinkled at the corners. 'How are you doing, Harry?'

'My God,' he said, placing his hands on his hips and shaking his head in surprise. 'Jessica Vaughan. To what do I owe the pleasure?'

'Good to see you too,' she said, smiling. 'I was just passing by and thought I'd pop in and say hello.'

Harry stared at her for a moment. She'd lost a bit of weight but still had curves in all the right places, curves that had drawn his attention a few years back when they'd met for the first time in the Whistle. Quickly he focused his attention back on her face. 'It must be . . . God, how long is it?'

'A while,' she said. 'So do you have time for a chat, or are you too important to mix with the hoi polloi now that you've gone up in the world? I noticed the sign on the door. Mackenzie, Lind, huh? So you finally took the plunge.'

'I guess that makes me a grown-up. It had to happen one day.'

'So now all you have to do is deal with those commitment problems of yours and you'll be a fully rounded human being.'

Harry grinned. 'You haven't changed.'

'Nor you. Well, except for the hair.'

Harry touched his head self-consciously. His father had been completely grey by the time he'd hit forty-five, and

17

already his own black hair was generously streaked with silver. 'Thanks for that.'

'Don't worry. It suits you. It gives you a look of statesmanlike distinction.'

'Yeah, right,' he said, instantly spotting a line when he heard it. 'So what are you really doing here, Vaughan? And none of that I-was-just-passing-by nonsense. Don't forget you're talking to a trained detective.'

Jess perched on the corner of Lorna's desk and lifted her eyebrows in mock offence. 'Heavens, can't a girl look up an old friend without her motives being questioned?'

'Most girls, perhaps, but not the ones who do what you do. How's it going on the journalism front?'

'Moderate to good. I'm getting by.' She paused, her mouth curling into a smile again. 'But this has nothing to do with my brilliant career. As it happens, I do have a friend who needs some help. Trouble is, she's not exactly well off, so I was wondering . . .'

Harry folded his arms across his chest and tilted his head. 'You were wondering?'

Jess gave a tentative lift of her shoulders. 'Mates' rates, perhaps?'

'I'm suspecting that's a euphemism for no charge at all. You know, believe it or not, I am actually trying to run a business here. I can't afford to—'

'No, she'll pay you. I promise. Only . . . er, it might have to be in instalments. But hey, money's money even if it doesn't come in all at once.'

Harry grinned again. 'Is that what you say to yourself when *you* don't get paid?'

'Ah, come on. You owe me.'

Harry barked out a laugh. 'And how do you figure that out?'

'The last time we worked together, I got shot.'

'Winged, actually. And how was that in any way my fault? In fact, if my memory serves me correctly, it was your idea to go there in the first place.'

'But after it was all over and I wrote up the story, I kept my mouth shut about how involved you were with Ellen Shaw.'

At the mention of her name, Harry felt a familiar pang. It was always the ones who got away, the might-have-beens, who lingered in your thoughts. He still hadn't figured out how Ellen had got so completely under his skin. Small, dark and fragile, she hadn't even been his type, or at least not his physical type – he preferred tall, leggy, confident blondes – but her memory continued to haunt him. 'You trying to blackmail me, Vaughan?'

'Absolutely,' she said, 'but only for the greater good.'

'Glad to hear it. And, just to put the record straight, Ellen and I were never involved. We were just ...' But just what they had been continued to elude him. 'Nothing happened.'

Jess's grey eyes widened as she placed her hand dramatically over her heart. 'God forbid.'

Harry gave up and waved towards his office. 'Okay, grab a seat and I'll get some coffee.'

Jess jumped up off the desk and gave him a quick peck on the cheek. 'Thanks, Harry. You're a star.'

'I'm not promising anything.'

She gave him one of her knowing smiles. 'Course not.'

Harry went through to the kitchen. There was coffee in the percolator, still hot from when he'd made it earlier. He poured it into two mugs and carried them through to his office, along with a bowl of sugar and a spoon. He put the bowl down in front of her. 'Do you take sugar? I can't remember.'

Jess, who'd sat down in one of the new chairs, was busily testing its swivelling abilities. Like a kid with a new toy, she swung left and right and left again. Then, putting her feet back on the floor, she stopped and gazed up at him. 'Boy, you really know how to flatter a girl. I can see I must have made a major impact.'

'It's been what, three, four years? Do you remember if I take sugar or not?'

'You could have stayed in touch.'

'So could you.'

Harry wondered why they hadn't. He and Jess had always got on, give or take the odd disagreement, but his life back then had been complicated. When they'd last seen other, their paths crossing on a difficult case, he'd still been trying to come to terms with the fact that he'd never be a cop again. His head had been all over the place, his long-term relationship with Valerie Middleton on the rocks, his emotions in freefall. 'You want to tell me what this is all about?'

'Take a seat,' she said, 'and I'll reveal all.'

Harry walked around his desk, sat down and peered at her over the rim of his mug.

'Well?'

Jess smiled again, but this time it was more tentative. She let a few seconds pass before she glanced down at the floor and then up at him again. 'You remember the Minnie Bright case?'

Harry's face instantly grew serious. 'The Kellston girl, the poor kid who was murdered.'

'That's the one.'

The lines between his brows grew deeper. No cop, no matter how hard they tried, ever forgot a case where a kid was involved. And Minnie's had been a particularly tragic one. 'That was years ago.'

'Fourteen,' she said.

Harry ran his fingers through his hair. 'Jesus, is it really that long?' He'd been a DS back then, one of the officers who'd gone in to search the terraced house on Morton Grove. Minnie's lifeless ten-year-old body, found stuffed under the bed in the spare room, was a horrifying discovery that would never leave him. 'That sick bastard Peck, yeah?'

'That's right, Donald Peck. He hanged himself in prison a few years after he was convicted. Always swore he was innocent.'

'Don't they all,' Harry said.

Jess placed her elbows on the desk and put her chin in her hands. 'Except, I mean, Minnie wasn't ... er ... interfered with in any way, was she? She wasn't raped or sexually assaulted.'

'He killed her,' Harry said. 'He broke her neck and then hid the body.'

'But why leave her in the house? The body was there for over forty-eight hours, wasn't it? He had plenty of time to move her, and he must have realised that someone would come looking eventually.'

21

Harry's blue eyes narrowed. 'What's this all about, Jess? What's going on?'

'Don't look like that. I'm not here to screw anyone over. You know me better than that. But maybe what happened wasn't as straightforward as everyone thinks.'

'Meaning?'

'Meaning exactly that. This mate of mine, the one I want you to see, was one of the girls who were hanging out with Minnie that day. Sam Kendall. Do you remember her?'

'Vaguely,' he said. Minnie's five friends had all been interviewed by female officers. He had an impression of a group of small pale-faced girls, their eyes full of panic and fear. They'd come forward after Minnie had eventually been reported missing by her mother. Hannah Bright, a crack-addicted tom, had failed to notice her daughter's absence for two whole days.

'Sam's a cabbie. That's how I got to know her. She works for one of those all-women taxi firms in Hackney. Anyway, we got talking one night and she told me about the murder and about how a year or so ago one of the other girls, Lynda Choi, had drowned in the River Lea. The coroner reported a verdict of accidental death, but Sam thought it might have been suicide. She reckoned Lynda couldn't get over what had happened. And that got me thinking about how some people find a way of coping with these kinds of trauma and others don't. I thought it might be an interesting subject for an article.'

'Hang on,' Harry said, leaning forward. 'So you're writing a story about this?'

Jess gave a sigh. 'You've got that expression on your face

again. Look, I'm not writing about the original investigation, only about what happened after. There's not a problem with that, is there?'

Harry considered it for a moment. 'Except you said earlier that you thought the cops might have got it wrong.'

'I did *not* say that.'

'Not in so many words, perhaps, but—'

'I didn't say Donald Peck was innocent. I merely mentioned that there could, possibly, have been more to the case than came out at the time.'

'Peck had form. He was a known sex offender.'

'Okay, okay, but forget about that for now. Sam agreed to be interviewed and she also pointed me in the direction of the other girls who were there that day. Lynda was the only one she'd kept in touch with, but two of the others, Paige Fielding and Becky Hibbert, are still living locally.'

'And I bet they were simply overjoyed to hear that the past was going to be raked up again.'

Jess frowned. 'I didn't put any pressure on them, if that's what you're thinking. I do have a few scruples.'

'Now who's the one being defensive?'

Her forehead quickly cleared and she smiled again. 'Okay, point taken. Anyway, as it happens, they were both more than willing to talk to me. Paige especially. She was mad keen on the idea of having her picture in a magazine. I made arrangements to interview them, one in the morning, one in the afternoon – this was about two weeks ago – but the night before we were due to meet they suddenly pulled out. Paige called me, said they'd changed their minds and weren't prepared to go through with it.'

'So they had a change of heart.' Harry shrugged. 'It's not that surprising. Maybe they thought it through, decided not to open old wounds.'

'Or maybe someone warned them off.'

'That's a bit of a leap. You got any evidence?'

Jess delved into the pocket of her jacket and took out her phone. She scrolled through the menu, found what she wanted and passed the mobile over to him. 'Here, take a look at this.'

Harry stared down at the photo on the screen. It was of a dark blue minicab parked in a street. 'What am I looking at exactly?'

'It's Sam's car. The tyres have all been slashed and some-one's run a key along the paintwork. It was done a couple of days ago. She found it like that when she got up in the morning.'

'Could have been yobs.'

'Except it's the second time in a fortnight.'

Harry still wasn't convinced. 'Or a disgruntled customer. Maybe she overcharged someone or nicked a neighbour's parking space.'

'Sure,' Jess said, going into her pocket again, 'and maybe a disgruntled customer sent these too.' She pulled out two folded sheets of A4 paper. 'These are only photocopies. The police have the originals. They were sent through the mail to her home address. The envelopes were typed and they were posted in Kellston.'

Harry reached out, took the sheets, unfolded them and flattened them on the desk. The first one read: *Keep yer mouth shut BITCH*, and the second: *YOU killed Minnie*

Bright. They'd been put together from words cut from a tabloid – the *Sun*, he guessed, although he couldn't swear to it. In this world of high-tech communication there was a curiously dated feel to the messages, as if the perpetrator had seen something similar done on an old TV crime show and believed it was the obligatory way to send threats. Or maybe they just had an overly heightened sense of drama. 'Very nice,' he murmured.

'Aren't they just.'

'But she has reported it?'

Jess gave a nod. 'Yes, but what can the cops do? They've put it all on record, but a few slashed tyres and a couple of poison-pen letters hardly make her a priority. Sam's scared, and she's not the type who scares easily. Someone wants to shut her up, and the question is why?'

Harry gazed down at the sheets again. 'It could just be a crank.'

'But how did they even know that she was speaking to me? And why should they accuse her of killing Minnie? That's what's so weird. It's freaking Sam out. She's had a few odd phone calls too, the sort where the person leaves a long, unpleasant silence and then hangs up. The number was always unidentified.'

'I'm still not sure what you want me to do about it.'

Jess gave him one of her wide-eyed, pleading looks. 'Just have a chat with her. *Please.* You can do that, can't you? I don't see why anyone should be this concerned about Sam talking unless they're frightened of something incriminating coming out.'

Harry pulled a face, aware that he could be treading on

sensitive toes if this all led back to the original investigation. DCI Saul Redding, now Detective Superintendent Redding, had been the officer in charge of the case. Although Harry was convinced that Peck's conviction had been a safe one, he also knew that even the cleanest of cops could get antsy when their judgement was called into question. 'What about the other girl? You've mentioned Paige and Becky and Lynda, but there were five in all, weren't there?'

'Kirsten Cope,' Jess said. 'Or Kirsten Roberts as she was back then. She's an actress in one of those minor TV soaps, lives out in Essex now. She refused point blank to see me.'

'Maybe she didn't fancy the publicity.'

Jess gave a snort. 'That would be a first. She spends most of her time falling in and out of nightclubs trying to be noticed. Barely a week goes by when she isn't in the gossip column of one magazine or another.'

'Yeah, but there's publicity and publicity. Perhaps she doesn't want to be reminded of the Minnie Bright murder. What happened back then must have been pretty traumatic for all those girls.'

'I guess,' Jess said. 'Maybe that's why she changed her name. But there's something more going on here, I'm sure of it.'

'Anyone else know about this article you're intending to write?'

She shook her head. 'If they do, it's not come from me or Sam, but I've no idea who the others might have told. Look, I wouldn't have come here unless I thought it was serious. I'm genuinely worried for Sam. I've got a bad feeling about all this.'

Harry picked up a biro off the desk and tapped his teeth with it. He was silent for a while. Unlike Jess, he was more inclined towards the view that the threats against Sam Kendall were malicious rather than dangerous, but it wouldn't do any harm to hear the girl out. 'Okay. How about if I see her tomorrow?'

Jess's face lit up. 'You mean it?'

'But like I said earlier, no promises, right?'

'No promises. I get it.' She glanced at her watch, pushed back the chair and rose to her feet. 'I've got to go, but thanks, Harry. I really appreciate it. Sam works late on Friday nights, but she could be here by . . . say, one o'clock?'

'That's fine.'

Jess took a business card from her bag and put it on his desk. 'We should get together sometime, go for a drink and have a proper catch-up.'

'Yeah, that sounds good.'

'Are you on the same number?'

'Same number,' he said.

Jess turned to go, then stopped. 'Oh, I meant to tell you. I think you may have a more profitable client loitering outside. I noticed him on the way in, middle-aged geezer, grey hair, smart suit and tie. He was pacing up and down the street, kept stopping to stare at the door and then walking on again.'

'You probably scared him off.'

'Yeah, I tend to do that to men.' She grinned, raised a hand and gave him a wave. 'Thanks again, Harry. I'll call you tomorrow.'

After she'd gone, Harry went to the open window and

gazed down. The office was on the first floor, above a newsagent's. He couldn't see anyone matching her description hanging around. After a minute Jess appeared and began walking towards the station. He stared at the top of her head for a moment, wondering if she'd glance up. She didn't.

He took off his jacket and sat back down at his desk. So, the first client of the new business, if he agreed to take the case, was probably one who'd still be paying the bill five years down the line. Still, it could be worse. They could have no clients at all.

2

It was another half-hour before Harry heard the buzzer again. Going through the same procedure as he had with Jess, he got up from his desk, put his jacket back on, went into the reception area and waited. There was a long delay, as if whoever had come in had stopped on the stairs and was in two minds as to whether to proceed. Harry had to fight against the temptation to put his head round the door and give them some friendly encouragement.

The man who finally entered the room was in his early fifties, almost as tall as Harry, with cropped steel-grey hair, a squarish face, a strong jaw and a pair of piercing dark eyes. He had the kind of upright stance that suggested he might once have been in the army – maybe even still was – and was sporting an authentic deep tan. His grey suit, perfectly tailored, had probably been made in Savile Row.

'Are you Mackenzie?' The voice was gruff, with a hint of a southern Irish accent.

'The other one.' Harry put his hand out. 'Lind, Harry Lind.'

'Martin Locke.'

As they shook hands, Harry noticed the gold Rolex watch on the other man's wrist. 'Come on through to my office. Would you like a tea or a coffee?'

'No,' replied Locke brusquely. 'Let's just get on with it, shall we.'

As Locke pulled out the chair and sat down, Harry was already aware of what the problem was. He'd seen plenty of husbands and wives over the past few years, all desperate to find out if their spouses were cheating on them. Of course, deep down, most of them already knew the answer, but they still felt the need to see the evidence in black and white. Harry watched while Martin Locke crossed his legs, stared down at the floor and began to twist the gold band on the third finger of his left hand. 'So, how can I help?'

'It's a delicate matter.'

'I understand.' Harry waited patiently. It was the first few steps that were always the hardest, saying it out loud. There was no point in pushing for the information; it was better to let people take their time.

Locke lifted his head and looked him straight in the eye. 'I can rely on your discretion?'

Harry gave a nod. 'Naturally.'

Locke thought about it for a while longer. 'It's my wife, Aimee. I think she may be seeing someone else.' As if it was a relief to finally say the words, he heaved out a breath. 'We've been married five years. We've had our ups and downs, what couple doesn't, but I thought we were all right. Only recently . . .'

Harry nodded again. 'Recently?'

'I could be wrong, I don't know.' He glanced quickly

30

towards the window and then back at Harry. 'It's just a feeling.'

In Harry's experience, it was rarely just a feeling. There were usually more practical reasons why people suspected their partners. 'She's been acting differently?'

Locke's face tightened. 'I need to know the truth. She's younger than me, you see, and ... Well, no man likes to be made a fool of, does he? I want to know where she goes, who she sees.'

'You'd like us to mount a surveillance operation. That's no problem.' Harry opened the top drawer of his desk and pulled out a form. He passed it over to Locke along with a biro. 'If you could fill this out. I'll need your address and a contact number. Does your wife work?'

Locke ignored the biro and took a gold fountain pen out of his inside jacket pocket. 'Only on Wednesday and Friday nights. At a club called Selene's. I presume you know it.'

'Yes,' Harry said, although he'd never actually been inside. The club was in the West End and hadn't been open that long. About ten months or so, he thought. He remembered reading an article about it in a magazine. It was one of those exclusive joints where the glitterati hung out, ordering cocktails at a hundred quid a pop and partying until they dropped.

'There's a casino there too. That's where my wife works. She's a croupier.'

Harry was surprised.

Locke must have seen the expression on his face, because he said, 'I don't keep her on a leash, Mr Lind. She's free to work where she wants – and to do what she wants. Within reason, naturally. She was a croupier when I met her and she enjoys it, so why not?'

'You've got a photograph?'

Locke dived into his pocket again. He took out a small head-and-shoulders shot and passed it over. 'This was taken a few months ago.'

Harry gazed down at the picture. Aimee Locke was an attractive woman in her late twenties, with wide grey-green eyes, a full mouth and shoulder-length blonde hair. There was, however, something forced about her smile, as if she hadn't really wanted to have the photo taken.

'I'm away on business next week,' Locke continued. 'I'll be gone from Monday morning until Friday night. What I want is a full report of what she does, where she goes and who she sees.' Now his voice was more forceful, the earlier uncertainty gone. This was suddenly a different man, one who was used to giving orders and having them obeyed. He glanced up from the form and stared hard at Harry. 'You think you can manage that?'

There was an edge to his tone that Harry didn't like. Martin Locke, he decided, probably wasn't the nicest guy in the world. But that didn't matter. He wasn't paid to like his clients, only to do the best job he could for them. 'Yes,' he replied shortly.

Locke finished filling out the form, signed it with a flourish and pushed it back across the desk. Harry noted the address: 6 Walpole Close. The street was on the south side of Kellston, part of an exclusive enclave of detached modern houses with the kind of security – high walls, electric gates and multiple alarms – that discouraged the local riff-raff from even attempting a break-in. His eyes scanned down the page. Aimee Locke was twenty-nine and drove a white Ford Mustang. Lucky Aimee. 'So you want us to start first thing Monday morning.'

'No, I want you to start this evening.' He paused briefly, his lips thinning into a tight straight line. 'She told me she was working, but I know she's meeting someone at a restaurant. Adriano's on the high street. I heard her making the arrangements on the phone.'

Harry had been planning on doing his unpacking tonight – the upstairs flat, overflowing with boxes, looked like it had been hit by a bomb – but it could wait. He gave a nod. 'That's no problem.'

'I'll book a table for two in your name. For eight o'clock. She should be there by half past.' He paused again. 'It'll be on expenses, naturally.' Reaching back into his pocket, he retrieved his wallet, flipped it open and took out a folded piece of paper. 'Here, this is a banker's draft. I presume it'll be enough for now.'

Harry took the cheque from his hand and opened it. It was for two thousand pounds. He had to fight against the impulse to raise his eyebrows. Most of their clients, and especially the wealthier ones, had a tendency to wrangle over even the most moderate of retainers. They wanted results, but rarely wanted to pay for them. He kept his voice neutral as his gaze flicked up towards Locke again. 'That's fine. I'll write you out a receipt.'

Martin Locke shook his head. 'No need.' His eyes narrowed a little, his mouth crawling into a smile. 'It's not as though I don't know where you are.'

Was he joking? Harry thought not.

'After tonight,' Locke continued, 'you can leave off until Monday morning. We're spending the weekend together, so there's no point you being there.'

'Monday morning, then,' Harry said.

Locke rose to his feet and stared grimly down. 'Oh, and I'd rather you didn't call. I'll come and see you when I get back. You can update me then.'

'As you like,' Harry said as he stood up too, and the pair of them shook hands across the desk.

Harry watched as the older man left the office. It was only when he heard the front door close that he sat down again. He picked up the photograph and stared appreciatively at Aimee Locke. She was certainly a looker, the kind of woman who could turn any man's head. But was she a cheat? Only time would tell. He didn't enjoy sneaking around after adulterous wives, or husbands – it all made him feel faintly dirty – but a job was a job, and in the present economic climate he couldn't afford to be fussy. At least Mac would be pleased. The office wasn't strictly open yet and already there was money coming in.

Harry glanced at his watch. It was almost three o'clock. He'd better organise some company for tonight or he'd be eating dinner alone. Grabbing his phone, he called a couple of the part-timers who worked for Mackenzie, Lind, first Debbie and then Elaine, but both of them were busy. He wondered if Valerie was free, but instantly dismissed the idea. As a copper, she wouldn't be too keen on taking part in one of his undercover operations. No, he'd better ask someone else. As he ran through the possibilities, his eyes alighted on the card Jess had left him. Why not? He'd just agreed to help her out; maybe she'd return the favour.

She answered after a couple of rings. 'Hello?'

'Hey, Vaughan. It's me, Harry.'

She sighed down the line. 'Oh, please tell me you haven't changed your mind about seeing Sam Kendall.'

'No, of course not, but how do you fancy dinner tonight?'

There was a distinct hesitation. 'Dinner?'

'Don't worry,' he said quickly. 'I'm not trying to get into your pants. It's purely business, a surveillance job. I need someone to share the table with so I don't stand out like a sore thumb.'

Jess laughed. 'Jeez, you really know how to make a girl feel special.'

Harry smiled down the phone. 'Years of practice, hun. I know this is short notice, but you'd really be helping me out. Would it be any more tempting if I said it was dinner at Adriano's?'

'That fancy Italian on the high street?'

'That's the one.'

'And you'll be paying?'

'I'll be paying.'

Jess thought about it for a moment. 'Well, I did have plans, but seeing as you've asked so nicely, I suppose I could change them. Okay, you've got yourself a date. When do you want me there?'

'Better make it eight. She's due at eight thirty, and I'd rather we were there before she arrives.'

'Eight it is. I'll see you then.'

'Thanks. You're a pal.' Harry put the phone down, leaned back, laced his hands behind his head and stared up at the ceiling. His gaze slowly dropped to focus on the picture of Aimee Locke. Innocent or guilty? In a few hours, he could be finding out.

3

At six o'clock Harry left the office and drove his slightly battered silver-grey Vauxhall down the high street. The lull between the departure of the shoppers and the arrival of the Friday-night crowd provided a good opportunity to grab a parking space near the restaurant. He needed to be prepared in case Aimee Locke and her dinner companion went on somewhere else after eating.

After locking the car, he strolled slowly back to Station Road. It was only the beginning of May, and what remained of the afternoon's spring sunshine fell weakly against his face. He felt a slight ache in his right leg, but it was nothing serious. After endless sessions of physiotherapy, and multiple hours in the gym, his limp was now barely noticeable. The flashbacks had become rarer too, although occasionally that terrible day still crept into his dreams.

Harry pushed the thought to the back of his mind. He wanted to look to the future, not the past. He might not be a cop any more – the blast at the crack factory had put an end to that career – but he was still alive, still healthy and well beyond the tedious stage of feeling sorry for himself. Part of him would always miss the police force, but that was something he was learning to live with.

There was a crush of people around the station, commuters returning from their day's work. They spilled out across the pavement and formed untidy queues around the row of bus stops. He weaved through the crowd until he reached the office door. Before going up to the flat, he nipped into the newsagent's and bought a pint of milk and an evening paper. A pile of unpacked crates awaited his attention, but first he'd make himself a brew and have a quick read through the news.

On the first floor he checked again that the office was locked and then went back along the landing and up the next flight of stairs. He sniffed as he opened the door. The flat had an unpleasant musty smell, as if it had been empty for a long time. He sidled past the crates and opened the two double-glazed windows. The roar of traffic poured in, along with a blast of exhaust fumes.

Harry took a moment to re-examine his new home. The living room was a decent size, although it was sorely in need of redecoration: the walls were a bilious shade of green, the ceiling had been Artexed – probably at some point back in the seventies – and the cream paintwork on the doors and skirting boards was badly chipped. There were two bedrooms, a bathroom with just enough room for a shower, basin and toilet, and a narrow galley-style kitchen. It was hardly the height of luxury, but it would do for now. He had a roof over his head and that was all that mattered.

Showered and shaved, Harry was back at Adriano's by ten to eight. He wore a bland dark blue suit, a white shirt and blue

38

tie. Nothing fancy, nothing to make him stand out. He needed to blend into the background and make sure he didn't draw attention to himself.

Martin Locke, true to his word, had made the booking and Harry was shown to a table in the centre of the room. It was an excellent vantage point and he wondered if that was down to luck or if Locke had specifically requested the position. He sat down and ordered a bottle of still water.

While he was waiting for his drink to arrive, he took a leisurely look around. The restaurant, one of the best in Kellston, was almost full. There was only one other man sitting on his own, over by the window. The guy was in his mid-twenties, slimly built, with a thin face and a mop of curly brown hair. He was casually dressed in jeans and a jacket and kept glancing down at his watch. Yes, he was certainly waiting for someone, but was that someone Aimée Locke?

Jess arrived at the same time as the waiter turned up with the water. She ordered a beer, then pulled out a chair and sat down opposite Harry. 'Hey,' she said. 'Twice in one day. People will start to talk.'

'Thanks for coming. I know it was short notice.'

'A free dinner,' she said, grinning. 'What self-respecting freelancer could refuse an offer like that?'

'I like to do my bit for the poor and needy.'

'And very grateful we are for it too.' She gestured towards her clothes. 'Sorry, I meant to get changed but I didn't have time to go home.'

'Don't worry. You look fine.'

Jess lowered her voice as her grey eyes swept the room. 'So is she here yet?'

Harry shook his head, resisting the urge to glance towards the man by the window. 'She's not due until half past.'

'The poor woman's going to wish she hadn't come at all.'

He heard the note of censure in her voice. 'You don't approve.'

Jess raised her eyebrows. 'Of adulterous wives, or the men who spy on them?'

'What do you think?'

'Come on, you're not that keen on all this sneaking around yourself. You hate doing this kind of work.'

He shrugged. She was right, although he wasn't prepared to admit it. 'Hate's a strong word. I can't claim it's my favourite part of the job, but it goes with the territory. And anyway, when it comes to poking your nose into other people's business, you're hardly whiter than white.'

Jess laughed. 'True enough. So what's he like, the cuckolded husband?'

'I can't tell you that.'

'Why not?'

'Client confidentiality.'

'Boring,' she said.

'And what happened to innocent until proven guilty? We don't even know that she is playing away yet.'

'I bet he's older than her.'

Harry knew that she was waiting for a reaction. He didn't give her one. Jess was used to digging – she'd made a career out of it – but he wasn't going to spill the beans about Martin Locke. Instead he said, 'I hope you're hungry. We could be here for a while.'

Jess refused to be sidetracked. 'If he's so certain that she's coming here tonight with her bit on the side, why doesn't he just turn up himself? Why bother paying you? He could save himself a few bob.'

'Hey, it's this job that's paying for your free meal, remember. I wouldn't be too quick to recommend the DIY approach.'

Jess laughed again. 'Good point.' She picked up the menu and began to read through it. 'God, I'm starving. I haven't eaten since breakfast.'

'And if he did turn up, it would be game over, wouldn't it? She'd know she'd been rumbled.'

Jess glanced up. 'So he catches her in the act. What's the problem with that?'

'In the act of what, though? Having dinner with a man who's not your husband doesn't qualify as grounds for divorce. She could claim he was an old friend or a mate from work. And what if it *is* perfectly innocent? He could end up looking like a fool.' Harry thought about Locke for a moment. 'I think he wants to get his facts straight before he starts hurling any accusations around.'

Jess opened her mouth, about to say something, but promptly shut it again as her beer arrived.

'Ready to order?' the waiter asked, notepad at the ready.

They both picked the crab ravioli as a starter. For the mains, Jess chose the tagliatelle porcini and Harry went for grilled lemon sole with a side salad. He'd been living off takeaways for the last few days and felt in need of something healthy.

'Would you like a glass of wine?' Harry asked.

'No, I'll stick with the beer.'

After the waiter had gone, Jess leaned forward and put her elbows on the starched white tablecloth. She stared across the table at Harry.

'What?' he said.

'Nothing.' She sighed. 'I'm just wondering where all the time has gone. Its ages since I last saw you.'

'About six hours, actually.'

'You know what I mean. *Before* this afternoon.'

'You'll be telling me next that you've missed me.'

Jess's mouth curled up at the corners. 'Let's not get carried away, Mr Wonderful. I'll tell you what I do miss, though: having a decent story to work on. I feel like I've been treading water for the past few years.'

He picked up his glass and took a sip of water. 'But all that's about to change now you've got the Minnie Bright case to tear apart.'

She left a short pause, her eyes peering intently into his. 'You're not still stressing over that, are you? I've already told you what I'm writing about. It's nothing to do with the original investigation.'

'Except that what you journalists say and what you do can be two entirely different things.'

'Have I ever lied to you?'

Harry couldn't put his hand on his heart and say yes, but there was a difference between lying and being economical with the truth. Jessica Vaughan, as he recalled, was an expert in the latter. 'Not exactly.'

'Well then.'

Out of the corner of his eye, Harry saw some movement.

He glanced over towards the window. The thin-faced guy had stood up and was greeting a redhead who bore no resemblance to Aimee Locke. So much for that theory. He looked back at Jess. It was probably time to change the subject. 'Are you still living in Hackney?'

'Yes, same old flat. And you? Still in Kentish Town?'

'No, we sold that place. I've just moved in above the office.'

'No excuse for being late for work, then. What made you decide to shift the business?'

'Money, basically. The rent and rates are getting way too expensive up West. Actually, it was Val who suggested Kellston.'

Jess looked surprised. 'Valerie Middleton?'

'The very same.'

'Oh, I didn't realise you two were back together again.'

'We're not,' he said. 'But we keep in touch.'

She pulled a face. 'That's nice.'

'What's with the attitude? You don't think exes can be friends?'

'Not really. At least not in my experience. *Are* you just friends?'

Harry, who only last week had stayed over at Valerie's flat, left a short hesitation before replying. 'What is this, twenty questions? Since when did my love life become so fascinating?'

Her mouth twitched with amusement. 'And since when did you become so prickly? Actually, don't bother answering that. You always were touchy when it came to talking about your love life.'

'Not touchy,' he protested. 'Merely protective of my own private business.'

'Which is ironic, don't you think, bearing in mind what you do for a living?'

Harry smiled back at her. 'Are you having a go at me, Vaughan?'

'As if.'

He was saved from any further interrogation by the arrival of the starters. As they both tucked into the ravioli, they fell silent – Jess because she was hungry and was concentrating on the food, Harry because he was pondering on what the future held. If history had a habit of repeating itself, then he'd better watch out: the last time he'd become involved in one of Jess's investigations he'd almost got a bullet through his brain. Jessica Vaughan and a quiet life didn't go together.

4

It was twenty-five past eight when Aimee Locke walked into Adriano's with her companion. Heads turned as the two women were shown to their table, but all eyes were firmly fixed on only one of them. Aimee Locke's photo, Harry rapidly acknowledged, didn't come close to doing her justice. The flesh-and-blood version was ten times more stunning than the picture.

'That's her,' he murmured. 'The blonde.'

His gaze took in her face before travelling down the rest of her body. The high cheekbones, wide grey-green eyes and generous mouth were framed by waves of shoulder-length fair hair. She was wearing a black dress, short enough to reveal a pair of shapely tanned legs but not short enough to make her look slutty. She was tall and slim, with curves in all the right places.

'Are you supposed to be leering like that?'

His eyes slowly swivelled back to Jess. 'Can you spot any man who *isn't* staring at her? Or any woman, come to that. It would look more suspicious if I wasn't showing an interest.'

Jess gave a snort. 'Interest? You've virtually got your tongue hanging out.'

Harry grinned before glancing back at his client's wife. Even the way she walked was remarkable, a smooth gliding motion that drew attention to her hips. She was poised and graceful, the epitome of elegance. Aimee Locke was the centre of attention and there was no doubt that she knew it.

'Quite an entrance,' Jess said.

A waiter seated the two of them a few tables away. It wasn't close enough for Harry to eavesdrop, but it was near enough to have a good view. For the first time he focused on the other woman. A slim, dark-haired Asian girl, she wasn't a loser in the looks department either. It was only her proximity to Aimee Locke that made her features seem ordinary.

'So, no secret lover,' Jess said, with what sounded like a hint of satisfaction. 'Perhaps he got it wrong. Are you sure he's not just paranoid?'

'I can see why he might be. Having a wife like that would make even the most confident of men insecure. Although perhaps we shouldn't jump to any premature conclusions.'

'Meaning?' Jess said.

Harry took a bite of his lemon sole, taking a moment to savour the taste. 'Meaning she could be going on somewhere else after dinner.'

'Or she's just enjoying a pleasant evening out with a friend.'

'So why lie about it? She told him she was working.'

Jess, in the process of twisting ribbons of pasta round her fork, looked up. 'Perhaps it's because he employs private detectives to spy on her. Constant suspicion can get a bit wearing after a while.'

'That sounds like the voice of experience talking.'

She shrugged. 'Are you telling me you've never had a jealous girlfriend?'

'I can't remember the last time I met a woman who was interested enough to *be* jealous.'

Jess laughed. 'Ah, poor you. Perhaps you need to work on that work/life balance. All work and no play and the rest of it . . .'

'Which is rich coming from a fully signed-up workaholic.'

While they bantered, Harry kept a surreptitious eye on Aimee Locke. She'd ordered a couple of martinis that had arrived in half the time it had taken for his water to be delivered. Occasionally she smiled, reached out and touched the arm of her companion. Her fingers, long and slim, were adorned with a number of rings, although none of them were as bright or as shining as the sparkling diamond on the third finger of her left hand. 'Perhaps it's not another man he needs to be worried about.'

'What, you think they might be . . .?' Jess glanced over. 'No, no way. There's no body language there.'

'They seem pretty friendly to me.'

'Yes, friendly,' Jess said. 'But nothing more.'

'They're in a public place. Maybe they're being careful.'

Jess shook her head. 'No one can be *that* careful. There's always something that gives you away.' She gave the two women another glance before looking back at Harry. 'I hate to think what's going on in your head at the moment.'

'Pardon me?'

'Two lovely women, a hotel room, the slow removal of clothing . . . Do I need to go on?'

'No,' he said. 'But if you'd like to, I wouldn't make any forceful objections.'

She raised her eyes to the ceiling. 'Spare me.'

'You're the one who brought the subject up, so to speak.'

'Well, consider it closed.'

Aimee Locke was ordering her meal. The waiter's smile, barely at forty watts when he'd been serving Harry, was now at full brightness. Harry got the feeling that she could have ordered beans on toast and the man would still have enthused about the wisdom of her choice. Still, he could hardly blame the guy; in his position he would probably have been equally fawning. There was something about a beautiful woman that made all rational behaviour fly out of the window.

Half an hour later, Harry and Jess were drinking coffee while Aimee Locke and her girlfriend ate their pasta. The two women had skipped the starters and gone straight to the mains. Their conversation had suddenly grown serious. The smiles were gone, replaced by more solemn expressions. It was the dark-haired woman who was doing most of the talking. Aimee, who was only picking at her food, looked pensive as she listened.

'Whatever it is, it's not good news,' Harry said.

Jess peered at him over the top of her cup, her eyes bright with amusement. 'Maybe they're breaking up.'

'Very funny.'

'I thought so.'

Aimee Locke's companion pushed her plate to one side,

stood up and made her way across the room towards the Ladies'. After a moment Jess rose to her feet too. 'Excuse me,' she said. While she was gone, Harry let his gaze wander back to Aimee, but made sure it didn't linger there. The last thing he wanted was to inadvertently catch her eye. She seemed preoccupied, worrying on her lower lip and staring absently into space. There was definitely something on her mind. Then, as if she'd reached a decision, she quickly raised a hand, caught the attention of the waiter and asked him for the bill. Harry, who'd already paid, realised that he and Jess had better leave soon or they'd end up following the two women out.

When Jess got back, he immediately stood up. 'You ready?'

'Sure.'

Once they were out on the street, he offered to pay for a cab. 'I'd give you a lift home, but I've no idea where she's going or how long it's going to take.'

Jess stopped and put her hands on her hips, looking indignant. 'Hey, you can't just dump me now.'

'I'm not dumping you. I didn't think you'd want to—'

'Of course I do,' she interrupted. 'You figure she's cheating. I figure she isn't. Let's see who's right.'

There was no arguing with Jess when she was in this kind of mood, so he didn't bother trying. 'Okay, if that's what you want.'

They walked up the road until they came to where the car was parked. Jess looked at the battered silver Vauxhall and grinned. 'I see your taste in motors hasn't improved.'

'My other car's a Porsche,' he said.

'In your dreams.'

Harry unlocked the doors and they both climbed in. As Jess pulled her seat belt across she said, 'So, do you want to know the name of the other woman?'

'Pardon?'

'I found out who she is.'

Harry drew a breath and stared at her through the darkness. 'You asked that woman her name? Please tell me you're kidding.'

'No, I'm being perfectly serious.'

'Jesus,' he murmured. 'You do realise that the whole point of surveillance is *not* to draw attention to yourself?'

'Don't worry,' she said, smiling. 'I didn't mention that I was in the company of a hotshot private detective spying on her mate. It was just Ladies' chit-chat, nothing out of the ordinary. She'd have forgotten all about it, and me, by the time she got back to her table. I pretended that I recognised her, that we'd met before, and suggested that it might have been at the recent Women in Business conference. She looks the professional type, so I reckoned it was worth a punt.'

It occurred to Harry that Jess had paid a lot more attention to the dark-haired woman than he had. 'And?'

'And I was right. Her name's Vita Howard. She's a local solicitor.'

Harry's ears pricked up. 'A solicitor?'

'Yeah, interesting, isn't it? Maybe your client isn't the only one seeking professional help. Or the only one looking for a divorce. Could be the wife's going to get in there first.'

Harry kept his eyes on the door of the restaurant while

he thought about it. 'Could be,' he agreed. 'And maybe she's already lined up husband number two.'

'Not necessarily.'

'She doesn't strike me as the type who's likely to be on her own for long.'

'By that I take it you mean that she looks like the type who prefers someone else to keep her.'

He shrugged. 'You think I'm being overly judgemental?'

'It's a big conclusion to jump to after less than an hour's observation. It could be that her husband is a bore or a brute and she's simply had enough of him.'

Harry thought back to his afternoon meeting with Martin Locke. 'That's not beyond the realms of possibility.'

'So, did I do well getting Vita Howard's name?'

'I still think it was risky,' he said.

'Yes, Jessica, thank you very much for that useful bit of information. That's all right, Harry, it was a pleasure.'

He grinned. 'Thank you very much, Jessica. I appreciate your input.'

5

It was another five minutes before a smart minicab, a dark green Toyota, pulled up in front of Adriano's. Shortly afterwards, the two women came out of the restaurant and got into the back of the car. The driver set off, indicating left after he'd gone a couple of hundred yards. Harry followed, keeping a safe distance.

The cab made a short journey through the back streets of Kellston until it came to Lemon Road, a row of small but neat terraced houses. Harry drove past as the cabbie stopped, then slowed down and pulled in a little further along. They watched as Vita Howard got out, leaned in to say a few final words to Aimee, then gave a wave and closed the door.

'No steamy girl-on-girl action, then,' Jess said. 'I hope you're not *too* disappointed.'

'I'll try and live with it.'

The cab set off again, returning to the high street before heading west. Well, if there was one place Aimee Locke wasn't going, it was home. Harry let a couple of cars get between them. He doubted if the cabbie would notice the tail, but he wasn't prepared to take any chances. Blowing his cover on the first night of the job wouldn't be too impressive.

The Friday-night traffic grew denser as they approached the West End, the roads clogged up with black cabs and slow-moving buses. By now it was getting on for ten o'clock.

'Perhaps she *is* going to work,' he murmured, talking as much to himself as he was to Jess.

'Where's that, then?'

Harry hesitated, but then decided that there wasn't any real harm in telling her. If he was right, she'd find out soon enough anyway. 'Selene's,' he said.

'In Mayfair?'

He gave a nod. 'You know it?'

'I know who owns it.'

He thought back to that article he'd read in the magazine. 'Some aristocrat, isn't it? Lord someone or another?'

'James Harley-Cunningham. Yes, he's the front man, but he's got a partner behind the scenes – an old friend of yours, as it happens.'

Harry gave her a sidelong glance and frowned. 'Why do I get the feeling that I'm not going to like this?'

'Because you're not.'

He waited a few seconds but she didn't say any more. 'Come on, Vaughan. Don't keep me in suspense.'

She took a quick breath. 'It's Ray Stagg.'

'Shit, you're kidding?'

'I said you wouldn't like it.'

Harry didn't. Ray Stagg was an East End villain. Not a gangster exactly, but a lowlife all the same. He was involved in drugs, prostitution, loan-sharking and any other dodgy deal he could dip his grubby fingers into. 'How the hell did he get involved with a place like Selene's?'

'Because he knows where the money is, and it's not in a sleazy lap-dancing joint in Shoreditch. He sold his old club to some Russian geezer and then teamed up with one of England's bluebloods. Stagg has the money and Harley-Cunningham has the connections. It's a marriage made in heaven.'

Harry slapped the palms of his hands against the wheel. Stagg was one of those Teflon criminals who through either good luck or good management – perhaps a combination of the two – had always managed to evade the law. He'd been arrested on more than one occasion, but no charges had ever stuck. It had been a few years since their paths had last crossed, and Harry wasn't in a hurry to renew the acquaintance. 'That bastard should be in jail.'

'Maybe he's seen the error of his ways and decided to go straight,' Jess said drily.

'That'll be the day. He's just found a more lucrative outlet for all the lousy gear he peddles.'

Mayfair was busy, the streets humming with activity. Harry concentrated on his driving as they went down Park Lane, skirting the shadowy tree-filled expanse of Hyde Park. Selene's, which was just around the corner from the Dorchester, had a long queue outside. The taxi drew up beside the door and Aimee Locke got out. She stopped briefly to have a word with one of the doormen and then went into the club.

Jess undid her seat belt. 'I guess this is goodbye, then.'

'What are you doing?'

'Well, I'm presuming you'll want to follow her inside.' She pointed towards her jeans. 'They'll never let me in dressed like this, so I'd better leave you to it. It's not a problem. I can easily get a black cab.'

Harry nodded towards the Toyota, which still hadn't moved off. 'You don't need to. Unless the driver's picking up someone else, I think she may be coming back.'

'Oh, okay,' Jess said, settling back in her seat. 'So what is it that this woman does? What's her name, by the way? I can't keep calling her *this woman*.'

'She's a croupier,' he said. 'She works in the casino.'

'And?'

'And?' he echoed.

'Come on, Harry. You know I won't blab to anyone. Cross my heart and hope to die. At least tell me her Christian name.'

Harry pulled a face, unsure as to whether he should or not.

'Ah, come on,' Jess said again, her voice more wheedling now. 'If it wasn't for me, you still wouldn't have a clue as to who she had dinner with tonight.'

'No, but it wouldn't have taken me long to find out. I have her address, remember? I only had to check the electoral register to find out the rest.'

'So I saved you the bother.'

'What does it matter what her name is?'

Jess gave a light shrug. 'I don't know. I'm just curious.' She glanced at him, her grey eyes widening. 'You do trust me, don't you?'

'Don't pull that one on me, Vaughan.'

'You're getting very cynical in your old age.'

'Just being discreet.'

'And you think I can't do discretion?'

'I didn't say that.'

They watched as the long queue outside Selene's shifted slowly forward. Unlike the VIP guests, who turned up in limos and waltzed straight in, the lesser mortals had to endure the chill evening air. Harry couldn't recall the last time he'd been in a nightclub. It must have been years ago.

'So?' Jess said. 'Are you going to tell me her name or not?'

Harry, knowing from past experience that Jess wouldn't stop until she got what she wanted, finally decided that it would be less of a hassle to give in gracefully. 'It goes no further, right?'

'Naturally.'

'Okay, her name's Aimee, Aimee Locke.'

'There,' Jess said triumphantly, 'that wasn't too difficult, was it?'

He heaved out a sigh. 'Just make sure that—'

Jess lifted a hand and made a fleeting flat-palmed gesture across her mouth. 'My lips are zipped, hun. Your secret's safe with me.'

'Good.'

It was fifteen minutes before Aimee reappeared. She didn't look any happier than she had in the restaurant, but even an unhappy Aimee Locke, Harry noted, still made heads turn. It was more than just beauty; she was one of those women who had an aura about them, a charisma that went beyond the physical.

'So, she isn't working,' he said. 'I wonder what was so important that she had to come all the way over here.'

'To pick up her wages, perhaps?'

Harry, remembering Martin Locke's address, his expensive clothes and the flashy gold watch he'd been wearing, shook his head. 'I can't believe she's that desperate for cash. And anyway, don't most people's wages go straight into their bank account these days?'

'I guess. And she doesn't exactly look destitute. Maybe she needed to speak to someone.'

That was what Harry was worried about, especially if that person was Ray Stagg. There was no particular reason why it should be – the club must employ lots of people – but he had one of those uneasy feelings in his guts. Somehow, whenever there was trouble Stagg was never too far from the centre of it. 'That's what phones are for.'

'She might have left something at work, something she needs.'

'Perhaps,' he said, although he wondered what could be so urgent that it couldn't wait until her next shift.

Aimee got back into the taxi and they set off again. It didn't take long to realise that they were heading back in the same direction that they'd come.

'Ever had that déjà vu feeling?' Jess asked as they approached the outskirts of Kellston.

'Looks like she's going home.' He wondered what Aimee was going to tell her husband. Her shift, he presumed, wouldn't normally finish until the early hours, and so she'd need a good reason for being back at this time.

The cab veered south and wound its way into the more exclusive part of the district. The streets were brightly lit, illuminating the fancy houses beyond the high security gates. Jess peered out of the window. 'God, not much evidence of a credit crunch here. Your client must be rolling in it. If I'd known, I'd have ordered the lobster.'

'I'm sure that would have gone down well on the expenses claim.'

The cab indicated right, turned into Walpole Close and drew up outside number 6. Harry drove past and pulled in further up the road. He watched in the rear-view mirror as Aimee Locke got out, walked up to the tall wrought-iron gates and punched in a code on the security pad. A second later the gates swung smoothly open. The driver waited until they'd closed again before taking off. Harry didn't move until the cab was out of sight, then he did a U-turn and cruised slowly back.

The house was a large white two-storey ranch-style construction with a steep roof, shuttered windows and a covered veranda running the length of the building. In front of the house the path split into two, with the left half winding around to the back. The floodlit front garden, awash with pink and white rhododendron blossoms, was empty. There was no sign of Aimee; she'd already disappeared inside.

'Very nice,' Jess said. 'Do you reckon there's a pool?'

'Why? Are you thinking of moving in?'

Jess flicked back her hair and smiled. 'Well, if your client's after a divorce, he could be looking for a replacement soon. I'm not proud. If it means getting my bank balance out of the red, I'd be more than happy to fill the vacancy.'

Harry laughed. 'So much for independent women. Drop your CV off at the office and I'll be sure to pass it on to him.'

'I may just do that.'

Harry didn't hang about outside the house. There were cameras fixed to the pillars either side of the gates, and so after a quick look he took off and accelerated down the street. 'Right, let's get you home.'

'Aren't you going to wait to see if she goes out again?'

'No, I reckon that's it for tonight. She's been drinking so she can't drive herself, and she's just let the cab go.'

Jess leaned her head against the back of the seat and yawned. 'So I was right after all. She isn't playing away.'

'Hey, just because she didn't do anything tonight doesn't mean she's Little Miss Innocent. It's early days yet.'

'You say that like you *want* her to be cheating on him.'

'That's not what I meant. All I'm saying is that if someone's not being truthful, you have to wonder why. She told her husband she was working, but instead she went and had dinner with a solicitor. That's suspicious in anyone's book.'

'We don't know that Vita Howard is *her* solicitor. They could just be mates.'

'So why lie about meeting her?'

'But did she actually lie?' Jess said. 'Perhaps she just forgot to mention it.'

'Hang on, Vaughan. Wasn't it you who suggested earlier that she could be the one getting in first with the divorce proceedings?'

'I'm always suggesting things. It doesn't mean they're right.' She inclined her head and smiled at him again. 'Although it doesn't mean they're wrong either.'

Harry put his foot down and set off towards Jess's flat in Hackney. He wasn't sure how much he'd learned tonight, other than that Aimee Locke was a stunner and that she'd been less than honest with her husband. That, however, didn't make her a cheat. Oh, and there had been that one other revelation: Ray Stagg was the power behind the throne at Selene's. That single fact, however, was more than enough to set alarm bells ringing.

6

It was shortly after six when Harry was woken by the thin morning light filtering through the flimsy curtains. He had a moment of confusion, of disorientation, as his eyes flickered open and he peered at the unfamiliar green walls. It took a few seconds for his brain to register where he was; not at his old flat in Kentish Town but in the new one in Kellston. This, in turn, reminded him that he still had a pile of unopened crates awaiting his attention. With a groan, he rolled out of bed and padded through to the bathroom.

Twenty minutes later, showered, shaved and dressed, he was standing by the living room window eating a slice of toast and sipping from a mug of coffee while he gazed idly down on the street. Nothing much was happening. The shops weren't open yet and even the station was quiet. There were only a few people passing by, on their way to work perhaps, or going home after a night shift.

He lifted his eyes to the pale blue sky. It was going to be another nice day, but only nice, he suspected, in the meteorological sense; he wasn't looking forward to his appointment with Sam Kendall or the memories it was bound to revive about the tragic Minnie Bright case. Before the prospect could cast too great a shadow, he pushed it to the back of his mind. He'd agreed to the meeting and there was no point in stressing over things he couldn't change.

Turning, he walked across the room, put his mug down on the table and surveyed the surrounding chaos. His heart sank. Just how much stuff did one human being need? He'd had a major clear-out before leaving Kentish Town, but he still appeared to be in possession of enough for a family of five.

For the next few hours he worked methodically, unpacking the crates one at a time and finding a place for everything before moving on to the next. As he filled cupboards, wardrobes and drawers, his thoughts drifted to the previous night and his first sight of the lovely Aimee Locke. He had a weakness for beautiful women, especially tall, cool blondes, and he wondered if her personality was as seductive as her appearance. Not that it was any of his business. His only business was in finding out whether she was a faithful wife or not.

From Monday, one of their full-time employees, Warren James, would be doing the surveillance during the day. Harry would take over the watch in the evening. Usually these jobs were the height of tedium, with endless hours spent doing nothing more interesting than sitting in the van twiddling one's thumbs and waiting for something to happen. He wondered if Martin Locke had really needed to go away this week, or if he was simply giving Aimee enough rope to hang herself with.

Harry's thoughts were still fixed on the long, shapely legs of his client's wife as he dug into one of the crates and came across two framed photographs: one was of his father taken a few Christmases ago, the other of himself and Valerie. Both of the pictures, for different reasons, made demands on his conscience.

It was over a fortnight since he'd last phoned his dad, and he knew that a call was overdue. He'd been putting it off, the way he put off anything uncomfortable. Their conversations were always strained. His father, a firm believer in repression over expression, was of the stiff-upper-lip school of thought: bad stuff was to be swept under the carpet, feelings never discussed. Harry still couldn't work out whether this had been the cause or the result of his mother's desertion. Whatever the reason, she had walked out when Harry was five and had never – as far as he knew – been in touch since.

He glanced at his phone, thought about it, then decided to ring later. It usually helped to have a glass of whisky to hand when he made these calls, and it was too early to start drinking. As a salve to his conscience, however, he placed the photograph in a prominent position on top of the bookcase.

Walking back across the room, he picked up the second picture and sighed. Valerie's smiling face could not be so easily dealt with. Over the past few months they'd been seeing more and more of each other, sliding back into a relationship that if not exactly passionate was certainly easy and comfortable. They knew each other inside out, too well perhaps, and it was only a matter of time before a decision would have to be made about their future. Did she want them to get back together on a permanent basis? Did he?

They were questions he didn't have any answers to at the moment. Harry stared down at the photo before opening the top left-hand drawer of the dresser and slipping it inside.

By half past twelve the unpacking was finished. He took the empty crates out to the corridor and stacked them against the wall for the delivery company to collect next week. Then he went downstairs and unlocked the office. The pungent smell of paint was still in the air and so he opened the windows again.

Sam Kendall arrived punctually at one o'clock. She was a small, slender girl, about five foot two in height, with an elfin face, short, spiky brown hair and brown eyes. There was a smattering of freckles across her turned-up nose. She was wearing a pair of grey jeans and a long-sleeved black-and-grey-striped T-shirt.

'Thanks for seeing me,' she said, shaking his hand. 'I really appreciate it.'

Harry took her through to his office and gestured towards the chair. 'Would you like a coffee?'

'No thanks,' she said, sitting down and crossing her legs. 'I'm fine.'

He walked around the desk and sat down too. 'Jess has explained what's been going on, but why don't you go through it again for me.'

Sam gave a nod, took a few seconds to gather her thoughts together and then started. As she recited the details, pretty well repeating everything that Jess had said, Harry listened closely, absorbing not only her words but the careful way in which she delivered them. Quickly he began to form an impression. She seemed intelligent and thoughtful, certainly not the type who was prone to hysteria, attention-seeking or exaggeration.

When she got to the end, Sam delved into the pocket of her jeans and pulled out an envelope. 'Here,' she said. 'I got another of those notes. This one wasn't posted; it was pushed through the door to my flat. It was there when I got home last night.'

Harry reached across and took it from her. He sat back, pulled the sheet of paper from the envelope and stared at it. Like the others, it had been compiled of cut-out letters from a newspaper. *YOU GONNA DIE LIKE MINNIE YOU BITCH*. Glancing up, he saw the worry in Sam's eyes. 'Did you talk to the neighbours, ask if they noticed anything?'

'Only the woman upstairs, and she didn't see anyone. But it would have been dark. And it's a busy street; people are passing by all the time. I went to work at seven so it must have been delivered after that.'

Harry leaned forward again, folded the note and laid it on the desk. 'So who do *you* think is responsible?'

'I've no idea,' she said, looking slightly startled. 'That's why I'm here.'

'But what was your first instinctive thought?'

Sam gave a shrug, frowning briefly before her brow cleared again. 'I don't know. Someone connected to Minnie, I guess. Her mother or some other member of the family?'

'But why should they blame *you* for Minnie's death?'

Sam worried at her lower lip, gazing down at the floor for a moment before looking up again. Her voice had a slight tremor in it. 'Because we *were* to blame, partly at least.' She hesitated before continuing. 'Do you know what happened that day?'

Harry didn't divulge that he was one of the officers who had found the body. He was careful to keep his voice neutral. 'You were with Minnie Bright, yes? You and four other girls.'

Her face twisted a little. 'We should never have let her go inside that house. We should have stopped her.'

Harry found himself wondering what it was like to carry that sense of guilt around. It was a burden, he suspected, that would never be lifted. 'You were just kids. You couldn't have known what was going to happen.'

Sam gave a small, dismissive wave of her hand, as if that was an argument she'd heard before, and one that didn't sit well with her conscience. 'We were old enough to know that Minnie wasn't ... well, that she wasn't like the rest of us. She was kind of young for her age, a bit odd, the kind who never really fitted in.' She paused again. 'In all honesty, we weren't very nice to her.'

'Kids are often cruel to each other.'

'I know,' she sighed. 'But I was mean *and* cowardly. I knew it was wrong, what she was being asked to do, but I didn't have the guts to try and stop it. I was too scared of being picked on myself.'

He could understand what she was saying. He still recalled his own daily panic at school, the constant fear of doing or saying the wrong thing. Although he already knew the answer to his next question, he asked it anyway. He wanted to see how she'd respond. 'So one of the other girls dared her to go inside?'

Sam's face flushed red and her hands briefly wrestled in

her lap. 'Yeah, that was when me and Lynda legged it. We could have taken Minnie with us, but we didn't. We left her there and . . .'

She didn't need to finish the sentence. Both of them were aware of what had happened next.

Harry left a short silence and then tapped his fingers on the note. 'So do you know if any of the other girls have received threats like these?'

Sam shook her head. 'I haven't seen them for years. My mum moved us to Hackney after the court case. Lynda was the only one I kept in touch with, and she . . . she passed away last year.'

'Yes,' he said. 'I heard. I'm sorry.'

Sam suddenly sat forward, putting her elbows on the desk. 'I think Lynda had found out something, or remembered something. She called me on the night she died. I was working and had the phone turned off, so I didn't get her message until after I arrived home. That was about two o'clock, and I didn't want to ring at that time, but when I called her later that morning she didn't pick up . . .' She raked her fingers through her hair and rubbed at her face. 'I was too late.'

'What did she say in the message exactly?'

Sam wrinkled her brow. 'It wasn't very clear. I think she'd been drinking and she sounded upset. She said she had to talk to me about *that day*. That's what she always called it. She thought about it a lot, even after all these years.' She paused. 'I think about it too, of course I do, but for Lynda it was like a great dark shadow that was always hanging over her.'

'And that's all she said, that she had to talk to you?'

'No, there was more. She said that it was important, that it *changed things*. I think those were her words. I didn't keep the message. I was going to ring her back, so I deleted it.' Her face twisted, her eyes becoming bright with tears. 'I know it doesn't sound like much, but I've got this feeling that whatever it was might have been the final straw, the thing that pushed her over the edge.'

'You don't believe it was an accident?'

'I don't know what to believe. She'd been depressed, I mean *really* depressed, and back then I thought she might have ... I know what the police thought, and what the coroner said, but ...'

'You suspected suicide?'

She bowed her head before slowly lifting it again. 'No ... yes ... Christ, I don't know. Yes, I suppose I did. She'd been drinking heavily, that's what they said at the inquest, so I thought she might have decided to end it all. And she might have wanted to make it look like an accident so her family wouldn't feel so guilty. I mean, people always do feel guilty, don't they? How can they feel anything else? But now, with these threats and everything, I'm starting to wonder if it was something else, if someone might have ...'

Harry could see where she was going without her having to spell it out. Not an accident, not suicide, but murder.

Sam gazed at him pleadingly. 'Please help me, Mr Lind. You probably don't think I'm in any real danger, but I can't think straight with all this going on. I can't eat. I can't sleep. I'm always looking over my shoulder, wondering what's going to happen next. I have to find out who's doing this. I have to make them stop.'

Harry, although he didn't entirely buy into the murder theory, could see how upset she was. Lynda's death must have knocked her for six, and now she was the target of a malicious campaign. He didn't have the heart to refuse, even though he still had reservations. If he started digging around in the Minnie Bright case, he was likely to upset the Kellston police, and that was hardly smart when Mackenzie, Lind had only just moved into the area. On the other hand, the wrath of the local constabulary was nothing compared to the grief Jessica Vaughan would inflict on him if he refused to help. 'Okay,' he said. 'I'll make some enquiries, see what I can find out.'

Relief instantly spread across Sam Kendall's face. 'You will? Thank you. Thank you *so* much.' She rose to her feet and shook his hand again. 'I'm so grateful. I really am.'

After she'd gone, Harry wondered if he'd made the right decision. It was all very well doing favours for a friend, but this one could land him in a heap of trouble. Lynda's death, no matter how it had happened, was inextricably linked to the murder of Minnie Bright. He swivelled the chair round and gazed dolefully out of the window. The sun was out, the sky was blue and everything seemed peaceful. A good omen, or simply the calm before the storm?

7

The plane touched down at twelve thirty, and within half an hour he had gone through passport control, retrieved his suit-case and strolled through customs without so much as a second glance from the uniformed officials who were standing there. He'd expected nothing less. In all his travels through Europe – and they'd been wide and varied – he had never once been stopped. In the early years he had viewed this as a sign from above, a symbol of his strength and his invulnerability, but now he wondered if that had simply been the arrogance of youth. A more likely explanation perhaps was that he'd had the good fortune to be born with the kind of face that did not invite suspicion.

As he walked through the terminal, he paused by a book-shop, pretending to examine the rows of novels displayed in the window. His eyes quickly sought out the reflections of the travellers behind him. Was he being followed? It was unlikely, but in his line of work you could never be too careful. When he was as sure as he could be that there was no one on his tail, he refocused his gaze on himself.

He was a commonplace middle-aged guy of average height and average build. His eyes were grey, as was his thinning hair.

He was neither handsome nor ugly, but perfectly ordinary. The word bland could have been invented to describe him. For some men this objective evaluation of their looks might have been disheartening, but for him it provided a solid reassurance. His features were so mundane that they attracted no attention whatsoever – and that was exactly how he liked it.

Turning, he strode towards the train station. In his left hand he carried a black nylon suitcase, not too large, not too small. Under his beige raincoat he was wearing an off-the-peg navy suit, a white shirt and a blue-and-white-striped tie. As he walked, he lifted his right hand and patted the upper left pocket of his jacket. Fake passports didn't come cheap, and he needed to keep this one safe. He had many identities, but on this occasion he was travelling as Ian English, a retired expat home to visit his family.

As he stepped on to the station platform, mingling with the crowd, he thought of his real family back in Cadiz. He looked up at the clock, knocking off an hour for Spanish time. The lunchtime rush at the bar he owned would be in full swing now. His wife, Anna, would be serving the food and drink, clearing the tables, stacking the dirty plates and glasses on the counter and looking forward to a sit-down. He could imagine her smiling as she wiped her forehead with the back of her hand, a fondly remembered gesture that made the breath catch in the back of his throat. Immediately he brushed the image aside. He was no longer a husband. He was another man, with another man's responsibilities.

From Gatwick there was a service every fifteen minutes to Victoria, and he didn't have long to wait for a train. As he made his way through the compartments, he took note, as always, of the people around him. He could sniff out a copper at a hundred paces, but it wasn't just the filth he had to worry about. If there had been a leak – and he prayed to God that there hadn't been – then his shadow could be much harder to spot.

He lifted his suitcase on to the overhead rack after choosing a seat beside a pretty blonde girl with an iPod round her neck. She glanced sideways, instantly dismissing him as of no significant sexual interest before shifting a fraction of an inch closer to the window. He was certain, even if pressed, that the only facts she'd be able to recall about him were that he was old and that he was male. Girls of her age – what was she? – nineteen? twenty? – viewed most men over forty as being in their dotage.

Before settling down, he glanced casually over his shoulder to see if anyone, especially anyone without luggage, was taking a seat behind him. He was instinctively more wary of the male passengers, but fought against the prejudice; there were plenty of female cops these days, plenty of women involved in all kinds of undercover work. It was best not to make any assumptions.

He passed the half-hour journey staring at a paper he had picked up at the airport. War, famine, political scheming. He flicked over the pages, but he wasn't really reading. It was all bad news and he didn't need reminding of the dire state of the world. He had problems of his own. It was these more personal problems that he dwelled on as the train rattled towards its destination.

Knowing when to quit was the trick to his game, and he'd made that decision years ago. Being back on the job made him uneasy. It was over a decade since his last assignment, and had he been given the choice he would not have come out of retirement, but a favour had been called in, and it was the kind of favour that couldn't be refused.

What if something went wrong? Past mistakes – made more notable by their rarity – rose into his mind. He felt a shifting in his chest, a spasm of anxiety. But no, he had learned by those mistakes. They would not happen again.

He took slow deep breaths, trying to free his mind of all the niggling doubts. Clarity was what he needed now, clarity, discipline and focus. As he breathed in, he caught a subtle hint of perfume from the girl sitting beside him. The smell, redolent of blowsy old-fashioned roses, triggered something in his subconscious, a disturbing reminder of the past. He quickly turned his head away.

The journey felt like a long one, but eventually they arrived at Victoria. He got off the train, strolled along the platform and entered the busy main forecourt. Here he bent down by his suitcase, unzipping a side pocket while he surreptitiously took stock of the faces around him. Did he have company? He didn't think so.

There was a café to his right, and he considered getting a coffee, but decided to push on. He had to find the offices of the car rental company, and then make his way to the East End. For the first time in years he was going back to where he'd been born. He felt a shiver of revulsion roll down his spine. Would it have changed much? On the surface perhaps, but not underneath. It had been rotten when he lived there and would still be rotten now.

8

Jess answered the phone and smiled broadly as Harry Lind gave her the news. 'That's great,' she said. 'You're a star. So what shall we do first?'

There was a short hesitation. 'What's with the *we*?'

'Well, there's no point in us working separately. We may as well pool our resources. Sam's absolutely fine about it, so you don't have to worry about client confidentiality.'

'Maybe that's not what I'm worried about.'

She snorted. 'Oh, charming as always. Are you trying to say that I'm difficult to work with?'

'As if,' he murmured.

'So what's the problem?' She didn't give him time to answer before pleading her case. 'Look, I've already got a file on this, a heap of papers. Why don't I just bring them round? Or even better, why don't we meet at the market. Paige Fielding has a stall there. Perhaps we can find out what made her change her mind about talking to me.'

'You mean right now?'

'Sorry, are you busy?'

There was another brief hesitation. 'No, but—'

'Okay,' she said, before he could think of something he'd

rather be doing. 'That's good. Let's meet by the monument in half an hour. See you in a bit.' She hung up quickly, reached for her jacket and pulled it on.

Neil was lying on the sofa, drinking from a can and watching the TV. On it two teams of burly rugby players were throwing a ball around. He looked over at her. 'I take it you're deserting me, then?'

She walked across the room and bent down to kiss the top of his head. 'Sorry, hun. There's something I've got to do. It's important. But I won't be long, only a couple of hours.'

'And I'm *not* important?'

Jess grinned, knowing that he wasn't being serious. One of the things she liked about Neil was that he never complained when her job took priority. She didn't work nine to five, five days a week, but had to chase her stories whenever and wherever they arose. 'Of course you are. Your importance goes beyond mere words.'

'Prove it,' he said, reaching up and pulling her down so he could kiss her on the lips.

'I will,' she replied as she reluctantly broke away from his embrace. 'Later.'

'Promises, promises.' He lay back, gazing into her eyes. 'So what's the emergency? What's so pressing that you have to sacrifice a Saturday afternoon with the man of your dreams?'

She turned away and grabbed her bag, a brown folder and the car keys. 'For one, the man of my dreams doesn't taste of lager and cheese and onion crisps. And for two, it's a matter of striking while the iron's hot. If I don't grab

Harry Lind's attention now, this whole thing could go off the boil.' Jess knew that Harry had at least one other case he was currently involved with – finding out how faithful or otherwise Aimee Locke was – and she didn't want him to get so completely sidetracked that he lost all interest in Sam's problems. Thinking of Aimee reminded her of the woman she'd been having dinner with. 'Hey, I don't suppose you've ever come across a lawyer called Vita Howard?'

Neil was a senior barristers' clerk for a large law firm in Lincoln's Inn. He worked half as many hours as Jess and earned three times as much. 'The lovely Kavita? Yes, I know her.'

Jess raised her brows. 'Lovely, eh?'

He grinned. 'Well, not as lovely as you, naturally. But were I a free man of good health and natural appetites, I might just be tempted to give her a second glance. Why do you ask?'

'I met her last night, briefly. Does she do divorce work?'

'No, that's not her bag. She's into criminal law, dealing with all the lowlifes of Kellston who regularly walk through the doors of Patterson, Hoylake and Co. She's a smart cookie, though. She's wasted with that firm.'

'So why does she stay there?'

Neil put his can down on the coffee table, shifted on the sofa and rearranged a couple of cushions. 'Rumour has it that her old man has something of a record. She fell into the trap of mixing business with pleasure and ended up married to one of her clients. That kind of connection doesn't go down too well with some firms.' He picked up the can again. 'So why do you want to know? Are you after some good prenup advice in case I pop the question?'

She laughed. 'Yeah, that's it. I'm planning ahead. So if you're intending to take me for every penny I've got, think again.'

He pulled a face. 'So much for my master plan.'

'Okay, I'd better go. See you later.' Jess stepped into the hall, then put her head back round the door. 'Oh, and what we just discussed about Vita Howard, it's off the record, right?'

'Who?' he said.

She gave a nod. 'You're smarter than you look, babe.'

'Love you too, honeybun.'

Outside, Jess got into her cherry-red Mini Cooper, threw her bag and the file on to the passenger seat and set off for Kellston. Her mouth widened into a smile as she drove along Victoria Park Road. She'd been seeing Neil Stafford for almost a year now, and had never been happier. He was smart, attractive and funny. He was also amicably divorced with no kids and – as far as she could make out – no seriously bad habits. Just for once, she appeared to have struck gold.

They weren't actually living together – he had his own flat in Pimlico – but they spent most weekends and a couple of nights in the week together at either his place or hers. This arrangement suited Jess just fine. She liked spending time with him, but she liked her own space too. There would come a point, she supposed, when he might want something more, but thankfully it hadn't yet been reached.

Putting the radio on, she hummed along to an old song she could only vaguely remember the words to. She thought about what Neil had told her regarding Vita Howard. She'd been hoping to get some useful information to pass on to Harry, a kind of thank-you for taking on Sam's case, but her original theory that Aimee Locke could be thinking of beating her husband to the punch seemed unlikely in the light of what she'd learned. Although maybe not. Just because Vita didn't specialise in divorce didn't mean she couldn't give advice about it. But then again, with the kind of money Aimee had, wasn't she more likely to consult one of those flash City lawyers?

Jess continued to weigh up the arguments as she negotiated the weekend traffic. She tapped her fingers against the wheel as her mind wandered on to the Minnie Bright case. Despite what she'd told Harry about being interested in the legacy of the crime rather than the crime itself, she wasn't convinced that the original investigation had been that thorough. The cops had found the poor kid's body in Donald Peck's house, and from that point on it was case closed. But if it had all been so clear-cut, then why was someone trying so hard to stop Sam from talking about it? The more Jess thought about this, the less it added up.

9

When Jess reached Kellston, she drove along the high street before turning into Station Road and swinging a right into the car park of the Fox. It was after three o'clock and there were plenty of spaces. The lunchtime rush was over and it wouldn't get really busy again until the evening.

She leaned over and slid the file under the passenger seat where it couldn't be seen. Then she picked up her bag, got out of the Mini and locked it. A couple of signs warned in large red letters that parking was for clients only and that any other vehicles would be clamped. Jess wasn't worried. She knew the landlady, Maggie McConnell, and had permission to park there whenever she wanted. However, for courtesy's sake she nipped into the pub to let Maggie know that she wouldn't be long.

The Fox was Jess's favourite pub in Kellston, a free house with excellent beer, good food and a pleasant atmosphere. And she wasn't alone in her preference. Even at this time of day, although it wasn't exactly heaving, there were still a fair few customers spread out through the interconnecting rooms. They were mainly locals, she guessed, who had walked here and left the car at home. With so many pubs closing down, it was to Maggie's credit that she managed to maintain a thriving business.

Jess walked through the pub until she found the landlady sitting at a table near the back. She had a heap of papers to her left and a glass of her usual tipple, gin and tonic, to her right. Maggie McConnell was a well-preserved woman in her mid-fifties, small and slim, with a heart-shaped face and a pair of twinkling blue eyes. Her naturally blonde hair was cut short and generously streaked with silver. She looked up as Jess approached, and smiled.

'Hello, stranger. Haven't seen you for a while.'

Jess smiled back. 'Oh, you know what it's like, all work and no play. Anyway, you're looking well. I just popped in to let you know I've left the car outside. I shouldn't be longer than half an hour or so. Is that okay?'

'You don't need to ask, love. You're always welcome.'

'Thanks. I appreciate it.' Jess had first made Maggie's acquaintance through her former mentor, Len Curzon, when she'd been working at the *Hackney Herald* several years back. Len had been familiar with all the pubs in north and east London, although his preference had been for the spit-and-sawdust dives. That was where the small-time villains hung out and where he could, if he was lucky, pick up useful snippets of information. The Fox, however, had been an exception. 'So,' she said. 'Business seems good.'

'Not bad,' Maggie agreed.

Jess glanced down at the table. 'Catching up on the paperwork?'

'VAT, rotas, orders,' Maggie said, wrinkling her nose. 'It never seems to end.'

'Rather you than me.'

Maggie lifted her glass and took a sip. 'That's why I need this. It helps to numb the pain.' She gestured towards the chair beside her. 'Come on, take the weight off your feet. I haven't seen you in ages. You can spare five minutes for a chat, can't you?'

Jess glanced at her watch. She didn't want to keep Harry waiting, but it suddenly occurred to her that Maggie could be just the person to ask about the Minnie Bright murder. She'd been running the Fox for over twenty years and there wasn't much that went on in Kellston without her knowing all the ins and outs of it. Jess pulled out the chair and sat down. 'Actually, there was something I wanted to ask you.'

'Ask away. But have a drink while you're here. What would you like?'

'Oh, okay. Just an orange juice, thanks.'

'Shelley?' Maggie called out to the girl behind the bar. 'Be a love and bring an orange juice over, will you. And I'll have another G and T.'

While she waited for her juice to arrive, Jess took a moment to study the woman beside her. Despite her size and her placid demeanour, Maggie McConnell was a force to be reckoned with. Nobody messed with her. Everyone in the neighbourhood, from the cops through the villains to the local toms, was welcome in her pub so long as they obeyed the four basic rules: no scrapping, no soliciting, no thieving and no drugs. Anyone caught breaking those rules would be out on their ear, no second chances.

Shelley delivered the two glasses, put them down and headed back to the bar.

'Thanks,' Jess said.

Maggie put her elbow on the table, cupped her chin with the palm of her hand and said, 'So what's on your mind?'

Jess hesitated. Although Maggie knew her well enough by now to be aware that she wouldn't be planning on writing some sensationalist piece of tabloid journalism, she was still unsure as to how to broach the subject. Crimes as terrible as this one always left deep scars on the local community, and even though it had occurred more than fourteen years ago, there were obviously some people – as Sam Kendall could testify – who didn't want the past raked up again.

'Come on, love,' Maggie urged. 'Spit it out. You can tell me, whatever it is.'

Jess looked back at her, still trying to formulate the right words in her head. She quickly came to the conclusion that there was no easy way to enquire about this particular subject, so she took a deep breath and began. 'Well, I've been working on an article about the Minnie Bright murder. Actually, not so much about the murder itself as the impact it had on the other girls – you know, the ones who were with her on the day it happened. Do you remember much about the case?'

A shadow passed across Maggie's face. 'Remember? Who could forget it, love. That poor little girl. A dreadful business, that was.' She reached for her glass, took a gulp of gin and stared into the middle distance for a few seconds before refocusing her gaze on Jess. 'So what is it you want to know?'

'I'm not really sure,' Jess replied honestly. 'It's just that ... that some things don't seem quite right.'

'You mean about Donald Peck?'

Jess had actually been thinking about Sam Kendall and the threatening messages she'd received, but decided to ride the wave. Go with the flow, Len had always insisted, you might learn something useful. 'Did you know him?'

'Oh, everyone round here knew him, love. He wasn't right in the head. I mean, it ain't normal, is it, always wanting to get your bits out, but no one thought of him as dangerous. He'd been at it for years, ever since he was a kid. I'm not saying it's right what he did, but he never went any further, never tried to touch or nothin'.' She paused, looking thoughtful again, before adding, 'Jesus, no one expected him to . . .'

'He always denied it though, didn't he?'

Maggie raised her eyes to the ceiling. 'Well, he wasn't the sharpest knife in the drawer. Probably thought that if he kept on saying he was innocent, someone might finally believe him. That's what people round here do, love. Even when they're bang to rights.'

Jess took a sip of her orange juice. 'So you never doubted that he *was* guilty?'

'Who else could it have been? It was his house they found the poor kid in.'

Jess gave a nod. 'I suppose. But if that's the case, why is someone so determined to stop me writing about it?'

Maggie frowned back. 'You been having trouble, love?'

Jess hesitated, but decided she could trust her. Maggie wasn't a gossip, and she was sure it wouldn't go any further. 'No, not me. This is in confidence, right, but one of the girls who was with Minnie that day agreed to talk about it and next thing she's being warned off and her car's being trashed. A couple of the others said they'd talk too and now they've suddenly pulled out and won't tell me why.'

'Same reason perhaps,' Maggie said.

'I'm not so sure.' Somehow Jess couldn't see Paige Fielding as the type to be intimidated by a few anonymous threats made of cut-out letters from a newspaper, or even the vandalising of her car. Sam Kendall wasn't a pushover either – she couldn't be with the job she did – but she was a more thoughtful and sensitive type. And on top of being riddled with guilt about what had happened in the past, she'd also had the tragic death of Lynda Choi to deal with.

'Well it can't be Stella, that's for sure,' Maggie said. 'She never leaves the house from one month to the next. Poor cow don't know what day of the week it is.'

'Stella?' Jess asked. She hadn't heard the name before.

'She's got dementia.' Maggie reached for her glass and took another large gulp of gin. 'Christ, if I ever lose my marbles, promise to shoot me, love. Can't think of anything worse. It's a living death, ain't it? And she's only my age.' She gave a visible shudder, as if someone had just walked over her grave. 'Still, it's hardly surprising with everything she's had to put up with. Be enough to send anyone over the edge.'

'Who's Stella?'

Maggie, as if expecting her to know, looked surprised. 'Stella Towney, of course. Donald's sister.'

'Oh, right.' Jess hadn't really looked into Donald Peck's family background. On the whole she'd been concentrating on the girls' story rather than his. 'So she still lives around here, then?'

'Palmer Street, just down the road. They moved away for a while after the trial, went to ... Devon, Dorset?' She shook her head. 'I can't remember. Some place on the south coast. But Stella was back within the year. She was born here, you see, lived here all her life. She couldn't settle anywhere else.'

Jess nodded. Stella Towney, all things considered, didn't seem a likely candidate for Sam's mystery tormentor. 'That can't have been easy for her, coming back here. I don't suppose she was welcomed with open arms.'

Maggie pursed her lips. 'Well, it was hardly her fault, was it? *She* didn't do anything.'

'Of course not,' Jess said quickly, seeing the flash of anger in the older woman's eyes. 'All I meant was that people have a tendency to vent their rage on whoever's to hand. It's not fair or just, but it is what happens.'

'Sorry,' Maggie said, reaching out to touch Jess lightly on the arm. 'I didn't mean to snap, love. And you're right. It was those stupid morons who drove her out in the first place. What that poor woman went through – bricks through the windows, dog shit through the letter box, abuse being screamed at her in the street ... As if *she* was the one who'd killed that little girl. God, there are some ignorant pigs in the world.'

'It must have been awful.'

'And for Clare,' Maggie said. 'She was just a kid back then, only a few years older than Minnie Bright. Imagine having to deal with all that at her age. Stella tried to protect her, but there was only so much she could do.'

Jess's ears pricked up. Someone else she didn't know

about, not to mention someone who might have a motive for not wanting the story of the killing revived. 'That's Stella's daughter?'

'Yeah, she came back with Stella, stayed for a while, but then took off again as soon as she was old enough. Can't say I blame her. She went back to Devon or wherever and got herself a job.'

'So she doesn't live here now?'

Maggie hesitated. 'Well, yes, she's come back now to take care of Stella, but she wouldn't be involved in any of the stuff that you've been talking about. I'm sure of that. She's a nice girl, quiet. She just wants to be left alone to get on with her life.'

Jess gave a reassuring nod while in her head she carefully filed the information away. 'Has she been back for long?'

'Only a few months. She works in that Asda on the high street.'

'Really?' Becky Hibbert, another of the girls who'd been with Minnie Bright on that fateful day, worked at the same supermarket. Now that had to be more than a coincidence. Had Becky told Clare about the article Jess was writing? It was a possibility.

'Like I said, though,' Maggie insisted firmly, 'she's not the type to go causing trouble.'

But she could be the type who would try to prevent it, Jess thought, as she finished her orange juice and rose to her feet. 'I'd better shift, Maggie. Thanks for the drink and the chat. It's been good to get some background on the case.'

'No problem, love. You take care of yourself.'

'I will. And thanks again.'

As she left the pub, Jess looked at her watch and pulled a face. She was going to be late for her meeting with Harry, but it had been worth it. Maggie had just given her an unexpected lead. Clare Towney could well be in the frame. The girl might be nice, might be decent, but she wouldn't want the Minnie Bright murder coming back to haunt her – or her mother. Yes, all in all it had been a profitable stop-off. She had some new information and a possible suspect. Hopefully it would be enough to keep Harry interested.

10

It was warm outside, and as she strode along the high street, Jess could feel the heat of the sun on her face. She shed her denim jacket and flung it over her shoulder. Summer had come early. The sky was clear blue and cloudless, and the temperature must have been up in the seventies.

The market was its usual riot of noise and colour. Quickly weaving her way between the stalls, her senses were assailed from all directions. The smell of spices, of curries, of frying onions vied with the stinks and scents of the crowd. While her eyes drank in the rainbow shades, she heard bursts of music, rap and reggae, along with brief snatches of conversation.

By the time she managed to reach the monument, a memorial to the dead of two world wars, she was wondering if Harry would still be waiting. But there he was, standing just to the left of the obelisk with his arms folded across his chest. Hurrying towards him, she saw that he was wearing a stylish grey summer suit with a crisp white shirt open at the neck. Her gaze took in his austere, almost gaunt face, his wide thin lips and the two deep lines that seemed engraved forever between his brows. A pair of Ray-Bans hid his piercing blue eyes, but she could see the impatience in his stance if not his face.

He caught sight of her as she approached and deliberately looked down at his watch.

'I know, I know,' she said, trotting the last few steps and lifting her arms in a gesture of apology. 'I'm late. I'm really sorry. I got held up.'

'You didn't think about calling?'

'It's only ten minutes.'

'More like twenty,' he said, glancing down at his watch again.

'Is it?' she said, all wide-eyed innocence. 'I didn't realise. Sorry. But I did find out something interesting.' She linked her arm through his. 'Come on, I'll tell you while we walk.'

Paige Fielding's stall was at the far end of the market. As they jostled their way through the densely packed crowds, Jess revealed what Maggie had told her about Stella Towney and her daughter Clare. When she came to the end of her story she looked up at Harry. 'Quite a coincidence, don't you think, Clare coming back to Kellston just as all this bad stuff starts happening to Sam.'

'So now you've got her down as your number-one suspect.'

She could hear the cynicism in his voice and frowned. 'As *a* suspect,' she corrected him. 'I mean, it makes sense, doesn't it? She works in the same place as Becky Hibbert, which is how she could have found out about the article. And after what happened to her mum post-trial, she could be worried about history repeating itself.'

'But why pick on Sam Kendall to warn off? Why not Becky or Paige?'

Jess thought about it for a moment. 'Maybe Becky told her that Sam was my main contact. After all, Sam was the one who put me in touch with the other two, so perhaps Clare thought if she could scare her into keeping quiet the others might follow suit.'

'Sounds pretty thin to me.'

Jess, disappointed by his negative reaction, gave a light shrug. 'I still think it's worth pursuing.'

'You should be careful. You can't start hassling her without any evidence.'

'No one said anything about *hassling*,' she replied indignantly. 'What do you take me for?' She didn't wait for an answer before adding, 'But you've got to admit that she does have a motive.'

Harry gave a small lift of his eyebrows as if to imply that he didn't have to admit anything of the sort. 'All I'm suggesting is that you tread carefully. From the sound of it she's had a rough ride. You don't want to go making matters worse.'

'I don't intend to,' she said. Although disappointed by Harry's lack of enthusiasm, she wasn't deterred. She was still convinced that she was on the right track. Once she'd worked out the best approach, she'd go round to Palmer Street and put some questions directly to Clare Towney. Jess had a nose for the truth, and if the girl *was* guilty it wouldn't take her long to discover it.

Eventually they fought their way through to Paige Fielding's pitch. Her stall was on a corner and was covered with a blue-and-white-striped awning. From it she flogged a multitude of cheap kitchen goods: pots and pans, cutlery, crockery, colanders, sieves and plastic food containers.

'That's her,' Jess said to Harry, pulling him aside for a moment. 'The one in the turquoise vest.'

She couldn't see his eyes – they were still hidden behind the dark lenses – but she was pretty certain that he was making a rapid assessment of the woman she had pointed out. Paige was a tall, big-breasted girl with sharp features and long brown hair. There was a heavy gold chain around her neck, a jangle of gold bracelets encircling her wrist and several gold rings on her fingers. She was sporting a deep, artificial-looking tan that had probably come out of a spray can.

'Okay,' Harry said. 'Let's do it.'

Paige was serving an elderly lady as they walked up to the stall, packing a selection of items into a carrier bag and totting up the price as she went along. When payment had been made and the customer had left, she turned her head to smile at Jess. As recognition dawned, the smile instantly vanished.

'Oh, it's you,' Paige said coldly. 'What the hell do you want?'

'A word,' Jess said.

'I'm busy.'

Jess made a show of looking around. There was no one waiting to be served, no one even browsing. 'It won't take long.'

'I've already told you. I ain't interested. Just leave me alone.'

'Five minutes,' Jess said. 'That's all I'm asking. I only want to know why you changed your mind about the article.'

Paige put her hands on her hips and glared at her. 'Got a right to do what I like, ain't I? It's a free country.'

'Sure,' Jess agreed. 'But a few weeks ago you were well up for it, couldn't wait to get started, and now ... Come on, Paige, you could at least tell me why. It's not too much to ask, is it?'

For a few seconds Paige appeared to be thinking about it, but then she leaned across the stall towards Jess, her eyes hard, her lips tight and grim. She barely opened her mouth as she hissed out the words. 'Look, you bitch, what don't you understand about *leave me alone*? Get the fuck out of my face or you'll be sorry you ever met me!'

'Hey,' Harry said. 'Cool it, yeah? There's no need for that kind of talk.'

As if only just realising that he was with Jess, Paige's eyes flicked warily in Harry's direction. 'And who the hell are you?'

'My name's Harry Lind.'

Paige looked him up and down before saying sneeringly, 'You the filth? You look like the filth.'

Jess wondered what it was that so readily identified him to Paige as a policeman – albeit an ex-one. If she herself hadn't already known about his former career, it would never have occurred to her. Maybe it was some sort of aura that was only obvious to those who made it their business to be able to spot a copper at a hundred paces.

'Actually,' Harry said, 'I'm a private investigator.'

As if this was barely one step removed from the law, Paige gave a contemptuous grunt. 'Stay out of it. This is none of your business.'

'Someone's made it my business.'

'Oh yeah? And who would that be, then?'

Harry gave her a thin smile. 'Look, you don't want us here. We don't want to be here. So why don't you do us all a favour and tell us why you've decided to pull out. That way we can all get on with our lives.'

'I changed my mind,' Paige said stubbornly.

'Did you?' Harry said. 'Or did someone change it for you?'

'I dunno what you're talking about.'

Jess had noticed the tiniest of hesitations before Paige's response. It wasn't marked, but it was enough for her to be sure that the girl was lying. 'Do you really want to be an accessory to death threats, to criminal damage?'

'And what's that supposed to mean?' Paige snarled. 'I ain't done nothin'. Whatever you're trying to pin on me . . .' She shook her head. 'I'm not having it, right?'

'If you're covering something up, it's going to come out eventually. You can count on it.'

Paige's expression grew even darker. 'Just fuck off,' she said. 'Fuck off and leave me alone.'

Jess might have stayed and tried to push her further, but she felt the pressure of Harry's hand on her arm.

'Let's go,' he said. 'We're wasting our time here.'

Reluctantly, Jess allowed him to pull her away. As they moved back into the crowd, she gave one last glance over her shoulder. Paige already had her phone pressed to her ear.

The girl's left hand was bunched into a fist and she had a face like thunder.

'Well,' Harry said, 'that went well.'

'She's lying.'

'Of course she is, but the question is why.'

'Because she's up to her neck in it. She's either been threatened or bribed and my money's on the latter. Did you notice all the bling she was wearing? You don't get that from flogging pots and pans twice a week on Kellston market.'

'Maybe she's got a rich boyfriend.'

Jess gave a snort. 'She hasn't. She's shacked up with a lowlife called Micky Higgs. He's a small-time dealer who works at the Lincoln Pool Hall. No, I reckon she's been paid off.'

'So what are you thinking? That Clare Towney has been flashing the cash, making sure that no one opens their mouths about what happened in the past?'

She looked at him. 'Who mentioned Clare Towney?'

Harry gave her a sidelong glance. 'That's who you're thinking, though, isn't it? Except it doesn't quite add up. From the tone of the notes sent to Sam, the perp sounds more like someone who's angry about what happened to Minnie, someone who's got a personal interest.'

'Clare's got a personal interest.'

'You know what I mean,' Harry said. 'Someone closer to Minnie. Towney may be less than happy to have the subject raised again, but why would she accuse Sam of being responsible for Minnie's death?'

Jess let the question roll around in her mind for a while before she came up with a suitable answer. 'Maybe it's because she's trying to shift some of the blame from her uncle. I mean, the girls were the ones who encouraged Minnie to go into the house in the first place. If they hadn't done that, then ...' She gave a shrug. 'I suppose it would never have happened.'

They were silent for a while as they negotiated the rest of the market. The stallholders were packing up, the noise subsiding and the crowd thinning out. Trade was coming to a close for the day. Jess was the first to speak again.

'Becky Hibbert may be a better bet. She's not as tough as Paige. A bit of pressure and she might cave in.'

'If she knows anything.'

'She must do,' Jess insisted. 'Both of them are involved in this – one way or another. They have to be. Why else would they suddenly decide not to talk?' In frustration she slapped the palm of her hand against her thigh. 'Someone's got to them, and I'm going to find out who it is.'

Harry gave her another glance and grinned. 'You journalists don't give up without a fight, do you?'

Jess shook her head. 'It's not just about the article. It's more than that. Sam's a friend, a decent person, and she doesn't deserve any of this. Who's going to help her if I don't? The police, no offence, are doing sod all about it. She's out there on her own and worried sick about what's going to happen next.'

'Yeah, I understand.'

Jess wasn't sure if he really did, but she gave him a nod all the same. She wasn't sure either if her vehement response was quite as truthful as she'd been trying to make it sound. Since her major scoop with the Grace Harper story – a child

95

who everyone thought had been murdered, but who had later reappeared under the name of Ellen Shaw – her reputation had soared, slipped down a few notches and then gradually plateaued out. Now, all these years later, she was aware that she needed something good, something better than good, to boost her name and get her back in the game.

They turned into the high street and strolled slowly back to the car park of the Fox.

'So what next?' Harry said when they were standing beside the Mini.

She opened the passenger door, bent down and pulled the folder from under the seat. 'Here,' she said, handing it to him. 'This is a copy of everything I've gathered to date. Have a read through and let me know what you think.'

Harry took the file and put it under his arm. 'You're going to see her, aren't you?'

'Who?'

'Clare Towney,' he said.

'Probably,' she replied. 'At some point.'

'Well, when you reach that point, give me a call and I'll come along with you.'

'What's the matter? Don't you trust me on my own?'

'I thought we were in this together,' he said.

'We are.'

'Well then.'

Jess gave in gracefully. She'd have preferred to go solo, but was prepared to compromise if it meant Harry committing to the cause. 'Okay, you've got a deal. But in the meantime, why don't you have a word with Kirsten Cope?'

'I thought she'd refused to see you.'

'She has. But that doesn't stop you having a go. She may be more inclined to talk to a private investigator than a member of the press. Her address and phone number are in the file.'

'I'll see what I can do. You fancy a coffee, or do you need to get off?'

'No, I'd better go,' she said. 'But thanks for the offer, and thanks for coming along today.'

'No problem.' He waved the file in a gesture of goodbye, then turned and strolled towards the road.

Jess walked around the car but didn't immediately get in. For a while she leaned her elbows on the warm metal of the roof and watched as Harry Lind headed towards his new flat. She had a feeling about this case, a gut instinct. There was a can of worms waiting to be opened, and she was about to start prising off the lid.

11

Ray Stagg slammed the skinny youth against the wall, hearing the satisfying thud as his body made contact with the brickwork. 'What have I told you, asshole? You don't peddle your shit here!'

The boy's nose was bleeding profusely – it was probably broken – and one of his eyes was almost closed. He stared wildly out through the other one, a desperate pleading look that only increased Stagg's determination to finish the job. He put his right hand tightly around the young man's throat and squeezed. Leaning into his face, he spat out a warning. 'No one, d'ya hear me, *no one* deals in my club. Do you get that? And in case you forget—'

Unexpectedly, the door to the storeroom opened and James Harley-Cunningham walked in. At the sight that met him, his face paled and his lips parted in shock. He looked from Stagg to the kid and back at Stagg again. Then he quickly closed the door behind him. 'For God's sake, Ray. What's going on?'

Stagg retained his grip on the youth's throat as he glanced over his shoulder. 'I caught this toerag here trying to deal smack to the punters.'

'Let him go. That's enough!'

'Enough?' Stagg said. 'Christ, I've barely started.' He could have carried on, but he preferred to do his dirty work in private. Regretfully, he released his victim, and the youth slid down to the floor, the breath hissing out of his lungs like a deflating tyre.

With his arms hanging limply by his sides, James gazed down at the dealer, his hands slowly clenching and unclenching. His voice, when he spoke again, was hoarse with fear. 'Jesus, what have you done?'

'Nothing more than he deserved.'

'Is he okay?'

'Let's hope not,' Stagg said. 'Otherwise I've just wasted the last ten minutes.'

A low groan came from the floor. At this point Stagg would usually have put the boot in. Instead, he leaned down, yanked the beaten youth up by his lapels, dragged him over to the back door and hurled him out into the yard. 'No second chances,' he called after him. 'Next time you'll be leaving in a fuckin' box.'

When he turned, he saw that James was standing very still with his shoulders slumped. His jaw was slack, his mouth wide enough to catch flies.

'I didn't have any choice,' Stagg said.

'You could have just kicked him out. You didn't have to . . .'

Stagg gave a shrug. 'Yeah, I could have – but what kind of lesson would that have been? By this time next week he'd have been back again with half the scumbag dealers in London in his wake. You let them think you're a soft touch and that's just the beginning. Before you know it, the big boys will have moved in and this place will be swimming in gear. Is that what you want?'

James shook his head. 'No, but—'

'But nothing,' Stagg insisted firmly. 'This is the only language these bastards understand.' In fact the club was already swimming in gear, but it was *his* gear and nobody else's – his coke, his E, his dope, his crack. The profits were his and he intended to keep it that way.

'What if he goes to the law?' James said anxiously, already baulking at the prospect of his licence being taken away. 'He could do you for assault.'

Stagg brushed down his suit whilst mentally raising his eyes to the ceiling. James Harley-Cunningham, his business partner, moved in the blue-blooded circles of London and the Home Counties. He was a nice enough guy, but about as streetwise as a pedigree poodle. 'Yeah, and what exactly is he going to tell them? That he was just dealing a little bit of the white stuff and along came the big bad man and beat the shit out of him? Hardly likely, is it? Nah, you don't have to worry, mate. He'll crawl back under whatever stone he came from. We won't be seeing him or hearing from him again.'

'You think?'

'I'm sure.'

As if he'd been temporarily paralysed, James finally began to move again, shifting restlessly from one Gucci-clad foot to the other. He stuck his hands deep in the pockets of his tailored jacket and pursed his lips. Stagg looked over at him, aware from his stance and from the expression on his face that he was still shocked by what he'd witnessed. It was

100

unfortunate that he'd walked in when he had. Next time Stagg would remember to lock the door.

'You all right, mate?'

James gave a nod, but his eyes told a different story.

Stagg felt irritated by the younger man's ignorance of the realities of the club world, but he was simultaneously aware that it was this naivety that enabled him to make a packet on the side. The legitimate end of the business brought in good profits, but they were split straight down the middle. It was the lucrative extras, the junk, the dope, the white stuff, that really swelled the coffers of his personal bank account. He had this side running like a well-oiled machine, and the last thing he needed was a spanner in the works.

'Look,' he said, walking over and laying a hand genially on James's shoulder. 'No one likes this kind of thing. It's ugly. It's nasty. But it has to be done. You do see that, don't you? There are plenty of firms out there who'd like a piece of Selene's. You either stamp on it now, or you sit back and watch until we're drowning in the shit. At that point there'll be no going back, word will get around and we'll end up with the law on our backs.'

'I suppose,' James said dubiously.

Stagg squeezed his shoulder. 'Believe me, it's a fact. This way we send out a clear message and we keep control.'

James managed a tentative smile. 'I just don't like—'

'I know, I know. I don't like it either. But it's over now. Finished. You don't need to stress about it. You just do what you do best – keeping the punters entertained – and I'll sort out the rest.'

101

James opened his mouth as if about to say something, but swiftly closed it again.

'Good man,' Stagg said, patting him on the back.

Together they left the storeroom and walked silently along the corridor. They parted at the corner, James heading in the direction of the music and the main area of the club, Stagg pausing for a moment to watch him. He frowned as his partner strode quickly away, hoping that he'd done enough to smooth things over. He didn't need Harley-Cunningham taking the moral high ground or poking his nose into things that didn't concern him.

After a while Stagg moved off too. He unlocked the door to his office, went through to the private bathroom and took a slash. As he was washing his hands, he peered at his face in the mirror. Yeah, not a mark on him. Looking good. In fact, better than good. He might be forty-seven, but he could pass for ten years younger. And when push came to shove, he was still fit enough and strong enough to get the better of any dirty little scrote who trespassed on his territory.

Stagg dried his hands and went back to the office. There he poured himself a large brandy before sitting down behind the wide glass desk. He lit a cigarette and inhaled the smoke, the act made ten times more enjoyable by the knowledge that it was illegal to smoke on the premises. Well, the law could go fuck itself! It was his office and he'd do what he damn well liked.

He picked up the phone, hesitated for a second and then punched in the number. It was answered after a couple of rings. 'It's me,' he said. 'You okay?'

'What are you doing? I told you not to call.'

Stagg swept his sleek fair hair back from his forehead. 'Sorry, babe. I was worried about you.'

'And you'll have good reason if he catches me talking to you.'

From the other end of the line he heard the sudden click of a door closing and then the tapping of heels on a wooden floor.

'Just tell me you're all right.'

Her voice softened a fraction. 'I'm fine. Really, I am.'

'I want to see you. Can you get away? Can you come to the club?'

'Are you crazy?' she said.

'Yeah, I'm crazy. I'm crazy about you.'

She whispered her reply. 'Don't.'

'Everything's in place. Just tell me that you haven't changed your mind, because once the ball starts rolling—'

'I haven't,' she said. 'Why should I? Look, I have to go. I'll call you Monday.'

'Take care of yourself,' Stagg said. But he was talking into emptiness. She'd already hung up. He replaced the phone in its cradle and sighed. Sitting back in his chair, he linked his hands behind his head and gazed at the wall. She was trouble, he knew she was, but that was the appeal: it was what made her so completely irresistible.

12

At seven o'clock on Sunday morning, Harry's sleep was abruptly interrupted by a series of loud clattering noises coming from the floor beneath. Worried that someone was breaking in, he leapt out of bed, pulled on his jeans and a T-shirt and dashed out of the flat. It was only as he was taking the stairs two at a time that he realised that he hadn't grabbed anything that could be used as a weapon – or even thought about picking up his phone. Well, it was too late to do anything about that now.

As he rounded the corner of the stairwell, his heart pumping at the prospect of interrupting a burglary, he came across two middle-aged men huffing and puffing as they heaved an old metal filing cabinet along the corridor. It took his brain a second to register that they were taking it *into* the office of Mackenzie, Lind rather than out.

Squeezing past them, he padded along the landing and found Lorna Green standing in the main reception area waving her arms, barking out orders and conducting what looked like a military operation. 'Over in the corner. Not there, *there!* To the left. No, not right up against the wall.'

Lorna was their PA and receptionist, as well as Mac's

other half. She was forty-six, a prettily plump woman with an apple-cheeked face and shoulder-length wavy fair hair. Usually more the sympathetic than the strident sort, today she was revealing her inner steel. She stopped mid-orders when she saw Harry, and smiled.

'Hi' she said, glancing down at his bare feet. 'Sorry, we didn't disturb you, did we?'

He gazed back at her, confused. 'I thought you were coming on Monday.'

'That was the original plan, but I told Mac it was a bad idea. We'd never get the van parked outside, not with all the morning traffic. I mean, we're supposed to be opening tomorrow and I don't want to have to spend half the day organising things. No, it makes more sense to get it done now.'

'You want a hand with anything?'

Lorna seemed about to make a suggestion when she was distracted by one of the removal men trying to dump a tall potted palm in an inconvenient or perhaps visually undesirable spot. Quickly she hurried over to take control of the situation.

Harry walked through reception in search of Mac. He found his partner lurking in his new office, standing by the window and peering down on to the street.

'Keeping your head down?'

'I had to cancel my game for this,' Mac said with a sigh. 'I don't see what was wrong with the original arrangements.'

Since being forced to give up his two favourite pursuits – heavy drinking and reckless gambling – Mac had begun playing golf. It was a game he'd previously viewed with contempt, the pastime of boring bank managers and senior police officers, but he had now taken it up with enthusiasm. Harry suspected this was more to do with the crafty Scotch at the nineteenth hole than any real appreciation of the fresh air and exercise.

Mac left the window, pushed his hands into his pockets and perched on the corner of his desk. He was an ex-cop like Harry, a large man knocking on sixty with wide shoulders and a receding hairline. What was left of his grey hair was shaved close to his skull.

'I don't understand what the rush is. We could have done all this tomorrow.'

Harry knew, despite the grumbling, that Mac and Lorna were tight. If it hadn't been for her, Mac would have ended up in the gutter. She'd saved him from himself – or at least from his self-destructive habits – and got his life back on track.

'Well, if it makes her happy. After all, she's the one who keeps things running smoothly. Best to let her do it her way.'

Mac shot him a look, as if to suggest that a little more loyalty to the male cause might be in order. 'You're not the one who was dragged out of bed at the crack of dawn.'

'Not far off,' he replied, glancing at the clock on the wall. 'How on earth did she manage to get that lot on the job at this time of day?'

'You know Lorna. If she makes up her mind about something, there's no stopping her.'

'I need a shower,' Harry said, 'and some breakfast. Have you eaten yet?'

'Good idea,' Mac said, pulling himself upright. 'Let's get out of here. You got any bacon, any eggs?' He rubbed his hands together, instantly cheered by the prospect of food. 'I can throw something together while you take a shower.'

'There's eggs, but if you want anything else you'll have to get it from the newsagent's. You could grab some milk while you're there; I'm sure the removal guys will be expecting a brew before too long.'

'I'll do that,' Mac said.

'What about Lorna?'

'She won't mind. She'll prefer us out of the way.'

They went back through to the reception area, already half filled with crates and boxes.

'Ten minutes,' Mac said to Lorna. 'Just nipping upstairs to get some fuel. Do you want anything?'

She shook her head, preoccupied by the job in hand. 'No, I'm fine. I'll grab a sandwich later.'

'Okay, I'll bring you back a coffee.'

But Lorna was no longer listening. Another filing cabinet was being lugged through the door, and it demanded her immediate attention.

By the time Harry had taken a shower, shaved and got dressed, the pungent smell of frying food was drifting through the flat. He went into the kitchen, where two hefty portions of sausage, bacon, eggs, mushrooms, fried bread and beans were sitting on the counter. He stared at the plates.

'God, Mac, what is this? Some kind of suicide attempt?'

Mac made a huffing noise. 'There's nothing wrong with a decent breakfast.'

'Sorry, my sincere apologies. Thanks very much for clogging up my arteries.'

'It's a pleasure. Now stop whining and grab a plate before it goes cold.'

Harry cleared a space on the living room table and they both pulled out chairs and sat down. Mac took a large mouthful of his food and grunted appreciatively. 'Ah, you can't beat a good fry-up.' He glanced at Harry. 'Oh, and if Lorna asks, we had scrambled eggs on toast.'

'Like she's going to believe that. She's not stupid. She's going to have you on lettuce for the rest of the week.'

Mac was quiet for a while, digging into his breakfast with all the eagerness of a half-starved man. When the plate was almost cleared, he looked up at Harry and said, 'So, have you thought any more about what I suggested?'

'You mean the honeytrap idea?'

'There's money in it. Women want to know whether their partners can be trusted or not. We're missing a trick if we don't get on board.'

'I don't know,' Harry said. 'It still makes me feel uncomfortable. You take some ordinary Joe, a guy who's basically the faithful type, he has a few drinks too many, gets propositioned by the sort of girl who wouldn't normally look twice at him and suddenly all his judgement flies out of the window.'

'A cheat's a cheat. It doesn't matter what the circumstances are.'

'Says the man who's been divorced three times.'

Mac grinned. 'So I know what I'm talking about.'

'Yeah, but this honeytrap stuff is just a form of

108

entrapment, isn't it? That guy could have gone on and been faithful to his wife until death did them part if he hadn't been set up.'

'I don't see what you're stressing about,' Mac said, waving his fork in the air. 'The woman wants to know if her man's open to temptation, half-cut or not. If he does it once, he'll do it again.'

'But that's my point. Maybe he *wouldn't* have done it, or rather agreed to do it – I'm presuming these girls make their excuses and leave before the serious fumbling begins – if it hadn't been presented to him on a plate.'

Mac huffed out a breath. 'Perhaps you're taking this too personally. Just because *you* wouldn't refuse a beautiful blonde offering to make herself at home on your lap doesn't mean that no one else would.'

The image of Aimee Locke sprang suddenly into Harry's head. He could visualise her long legs, her languid walk across the restaurant. 'Yeah, but I'm not about to be married. All beautiful blondes are welcome on my lap.'

Mac laughed, but then swiftly returned to plugging the idea. 'All I'm saying is that there's a demand. And if we don't respond to it, there are plenty of others who will. Plenty who already have, come to that. You checked out the competition recently? It's market demand, Harry. We either go with it or we get left behind.'

Harry could see that Mac had already made up his mind, and suspected that no amount of reasoning would make him change it. Having won the argument on the move to Kellston, he decided to be diplomatic and give in gracefully on this one. 'Well, if it's what you want.'

'Good, that's decided then.'

'So long as I get to sit in when you interview the girls.'

'It's a deal,' Mac said. 'I'll get Lorna to place an ad in the paper.'

Harry took the dirty plates through to the kitchen and dropped them in the sink for later. He made a strong brew for Mac and a coffee for Lorna, and carried the two mugs back to the living room. 'Here, you'd better get downstairs before she sends up a search party.'

Mac hauled himself out of the chair with a groan. 'Why do I get the feeling that today's going to be a long one?'

'Because it is, for you at least.'

Mac narrowed his eyes as he took hold of the two mugs. 'Tell me you're not doing a runner?'

'Got it in one.' Harry picked up Jess's brown folder from the corner of the table and waved it at him. 'Things to do, people to see and all that. And I've already done my fair share when it comes to this move. I sorted out all the stuff that came over last week, remember?' He knew that if he hung around, Lorna would find something for him to do, a something that would probably involve rearranging every piece of furniture as soon as the removal firm had left.

'What's so important that it can't wait?'

'Nothing,' Harry said, 'but you even think about telling Lorna that and I'll tell her all the gruesome details of what you just shovelled down your throat. I know whose shoes I'd rather be in.'

Mac took a slurp of tea and stared gloomily over the rim of the mug. 'Deserter,' he murmured.

Harry grabbed his jacket off the back of the chair. He'd

been intending to have a lazy Sunday, but now that prospect was out of the window he might as well follow up on the Sam Kendall case. A nice drive over to Chigwell should blow the cobwebs away. The soap actress, Kirsten Cope, was about to have the pleasure of his company.

13

The Sunday traffic was light and it took less than forty minutes for Harry to make it to Chigwell. The morning sunshine glittered on the windscreen as he cruised along Manor Road, peering at the numbers until he found the flats he wanted. He pulled in and let the engine idle while he gazed across the road. The three-storey building was new, probably only built in the last year or so, and had tall, narrow windows, an arched doorway and a steeply slanting roof. It had been constructed of red brick faced with sections of vertical timber panelling. It wasn't to his taste – a cross between mock-gothic and an alpine chalet – but then he didn't have to live in it.

Harry wondered if it was still too early to call. The clock on the dashboard was nudging on 8.30. Perhaps he should try and find a café, and sit down and sip on a cappuccino for a while, but then again, if Kirsten Cope had fallen out of a nightclub at three in the morning, the combination of a hangover and lack of sleep might just give him the edge.

He killed the engine, but didn't immediately get out of the car. Instead he flicked through Jess's file until he came to the relevant pages. There was a brief summary – name, date of birth, address, phone number, etc. – and then a bunch of press cuttings, a few pertaining to Kirsten's acting career but the majority from the gossip columns of the tabloids.

Kirsten Cope was clearly the kind of girl who liked to court publicity. In the past she'd been romantically linked to a couple of actors, a pop star and a TV presenter, but she was now dating a Premier League footballer called Nico Polvani. Harry pondered on what was so alluring about men who kicked footballs around. The money must be part of it, of course, the bulging weekly pay packet, but he guessed it was as much about the exposure. Once a girl had bagged a player, she'd also booked her slot in the publicity machine. Harry was still hoping for the time when it would be fashionable for every young starlet to have a private eye on her arm.

He turned over the pages, examining the numerous photographs. Cope was attractive in a mundane sort of way – slim, long fair hair, blue eyes. Or at least he presumed they were blue. The pictures were all in black and white so he couldn't be sure. Yes, she was pretty enough, but nothing outstanding, nothing to blow your socks off. He'd have had a problem picking her out from a line-up of similar-looking wannabes.

Harry shoved the file under the seat and got out of the car. He strode across the road, walked up the short drive to the flats and stepped inside the porch. He tried the glass door, but it was, unsurprisingly, locked. Next he checked out the names on the bells. There were six flats in all, and the name *Cope* was on the third one down.

He pressed the buzzer and waited.

It was answered after about thirty seconds. 'Hello?'

From the briefness of the greeting he couldn't work out if he'd woken her up or not. He leaned in towards the speaker on the wall. 'Kirsten Cope?'

'Yeah?'

'I wonder if I could have a word. My name's Harry Lind. I'm a private investigator.'

'What do you want?'

Harry wondered if she ended every sentence with a question mark. 'It's about the Minnie Bright case.'

'No comment,' she said brusquely, as if responding to some tabloid hack trying to get the lowdown on her love life.

He heard the click as she terminated the connection. He pressed the buzzer again, but didn't have time to say anything before she snapped down the line, 'Just leave me alone or I'll call the police.'

'You won't need to,' Harry lied. 'That's where I'm heading next if you won't talk to me.'

There was a long pause while she thought about it. Too long, Harry thought, for someone who had nothing to fear.

'What's that supposed to mean?' she said eventually.

'Do you want to have this discussion over the intercom – I'm sure your neighbours will be fascinated – or can I come in? Ten minutes, that's all it will take.'

There was another pause, this one slightly shorter than the last, before the buzzer finally went and he was able to push open the door. Inside, the foyer was clean and tidy, smelling faintly of disinfectant, as though someone had recently mopped the floor. Sunlight streamed through the narrow windows and fell against the tiles in mote-filled stripes. He climbed the stairs, walked along the landing and tapped lightly on the door to number three.

Even though she was expecting him, she didn't respond immediately. Getting dressed, perhaps, or just deliberately making him wait. When she finally deigned to open up, it wasn't with a smile. She gave him a look that would have made Medusa proud before stretching out a hand. 'Got any ID?'

'Sure,' he said, taking his wallet from his jacket pocket, removing a business card and passing it over to her.

'Anyone could have one of these printed,' she said, frowning hard at it.

'I'm sure you're right,' he said. 'But who'd bother?'

Kirsten gave him another nasty glare before turning on her heel and heading back inside the flat. She left him to close the door behind him. It wasn't the most effusive welcome he'd ever received, but at least he'd managed to get over the threshold.

The living room was airy and spacious, an open-plan area with a well-equipped kitchen to the rear. It was painted in one of those rose-tinted shades of white. Long pink drapes framed the windows and dropped to the polished-wood floor in swirling pools. There was a large pink rug, two white sofas with pastel scatter cushions and a glass coffee table covered with the latest gossip magazines and a cluster of Sunday tabloids. Harry absorbed the decor in a matter of seconds. It was no more to his taste than the outside of the building.

Kirsten Cope stood waiting in the middle of the room

with her arms folded firmly across her chest. If she had been out on the razz last night, there was no visible sign of it. The girl looked wide awake and ready for battle. She was small, no more than five two, and was wearing a pair of very short denim cut-offs and a baby-pink shirt tied under her breasts. Her navel was pierced and studded with what might have been a diamond. Closer examination, he thought, would have settled the matter one way or another, but it would hardly have been gentlemanly. He wondered vaguely whether she coordinated her clothes to match the room.

'What did you mean about the cops?' she said crossly.

As she hadn't offered him a seat, Harry remained standing too. 'Death threats, criminal damage. It's serious stuff. If I can't get to the bottom of it, the police will have to be involved.'

'It's got nothing to do with me.'

'It appears to be connected to the Minnie Bright case.'

'So?'

'So you were one of the girls who were there that day.'

Kirsten flicked back her long fair hair and gave a shrug. 'Maybe someone's just got it in for Sam.'

'So you do know it's Sam Kendall that I'm talking about?'

Kirsten's body stiffened, as if she'd inadvertently let something slip. He could almost see her brain ticking over while she thought about it. Then she gradually relaxed again. 'It's no big secret, is it?'

'I'm just curious as to who told you.'

Her mouth took on a sulky expression. 'It was Paige as it happens, Paige Fielding.'

'So you two are still friends?'

She gave another of her lazy shrugs. 'I wouldn't say that exactly. We haven't got much in common any more, but we stay in touch. She gives me a bell from time to time.'

He noted the way she stressed that Paige was always the caller. 'You've moved on.'

'What's that supposed to mean?'

Harry glanced around the living room. 'It's a far cry from the Mansfield Estate.'

'So? No law against trying to better yourself, is there?'

'No law at all,' he agreed.

'I still don't see what you're doing here. What do you want exactly?'

'I want to know why someone is trying to intimidate Sam. I want to know what they're afraid of.' He left a short pause before adding, 'And when people are reluctant to talk to me about it, I have to wonder why.'

'Maybe they just value their privacy.'

Harry recalled the press cuttings he'd just been leafing through. Not much sign of an overwhelming desire for privacy there. 'Maybe,' he echoed.

A sly look passed over her face. A second later it was gone again. She dropped the frosty attitude and broke out a smile. 'Well, I suppose as you're here you'd better sit down. Would you like a coffee? It won't take a minute.'

Harry was in little doubt about the reason for the sudden change of attitude. She'd tried the cool approach and that had got her nowhere, so now she was embarking on a charm offensive. Plenty of men, he was sure, would be more than happy to be twisted round her little finger, but he wasn't one of them. That, however, was something she had yet to learn. 'Thanks,' he said amiably. 'That's very kind of you. Milk, no sugar.'

'It's no bother.' She flashed him that smile again. 'Make yourself comfortable.'

Harry lowered himself carefully on to the white sofa closest to the coffee table. Why anyone chose to have white sofas was beyond him. They seemed an almost masochistic purchase. How much time was spent worrying over whether visitors might spill a drop of red wine or leave their mucky paw prints on the pristine upholstery?

While Kirsten bustled about in the kitchen, he made another quick survey of the room. Yeah, it was just as pink as when he'd last looked at it. There was even a pink vase on the window ledge containing a flashy display of pink and white roses. He wondered if the flat was rented or owned. Either way, she must be earning a decent wage.

He turned his attention to the coffee table, pushed the tabloids aside and checked out the magazines. In amongst the weekly gossip rags was a lads' mag with Kirsten's name emblazoned on the front. He picked it up, went to the list of contents and flicked to the relevant pages. His eyebrows shifted up a notch as he gazed down on the glossy double-page spread – Kirsten Cope, in all her glory, lying face down on a shaggy white rug. The only thing she was wearing was a come-hither smile and a bucketful of slap. He let his gaze roam the length of her spine until it came to rest on her peach of a backside.

It was at that point that she came back with two mugs in her hands and saw what he was viewing. 'Oh,' she said, feigning a coyness that didn't say much for her acting ability. 'I didn't realise I'd left that out.'

Harry closed the magazine and placed it back on the coffee table. He wasn't sure if he was supposed to make a comment. *Nice arse* didn't seem entirely professional. He considered several options, but settled for the uncontroversial. 'Thanks for the coffee.'

'So,' Kirsten said, settling herself down on the other end of the sofa. Her perfume, a scent that was too heavy and too musky for the morning, mingled with the more aromatic smell of the coffee. She smiled again, displaying a row of very white, very even teeth. 'What did you want to ask me?'

Harry smiled back. 'Well, as I said earlier I'm here about the threats that have been made against Sam Kendall. It strikes me that someone's got upset, scared even, in regard to what she might reveal about the Minnie Bright case. And the thing is, I can't figure out why that should be.'

He waited for a response, but Kirsten stared blankly back at him.

Harry gave her a prompt. 'You got any ideas?'

'Me?' she said, raising a hand to her chest in sham astonishment. 'Why on earth would I know anything?'

'I didn't ask if you knew anything, only if you had any ideas. Could you hazard a guess as to why she's the only one of you who's been targeted? I mean, there were five of you with Minnie that day. Lynda, of course, is no longer with us, but that still leaves four. Why pick on Sam and nobody else?'

As if she was thinking hard, Kirsten frowned. Her forehead puckered briefly before quickly clearing again. 'I suppose it's to do with that article. She was the only one who agreed to be interviewed, wasn't she?'

'Well, that's not strictly true. Paige and Becky agreed too, but then they pulled out. Do you know why that was?'

'You'd have to ask them that.'

'You haven't discussed it with either of them? With Paige, for instance?'

'No,' she said. It was snapped out so sharply that he was sure she was lying.

Harry allowed a short silence to settle. Eventually, as he'd known she would, Kirsten felt obliged to fill it.

'It's not right, is it, poking around in all that old stuff again. It's history, or it should be. The poor kid's dead and buried. Why can't they leave her in peace?'

Harry suspected that it was more her own peace she was bothered about, but he gave a sympathetic nod. 'Go on.'

'That's all, really. But it's why I didn't want to talk to that reporter woman. I haven't got a clue why the others pulled out, honestly I haven't. Perhaps they thought about it some more and realised that . . . that it just wasn't the right thing to do.' Her eyes dropped briefly to the floor, and when she raised them again, there was a glistening hint of tears. 'Jesus, when I think about what happened to Minnie . . . It was awful, just terrible. I still have nightmares about it.' Leaning forward, she plucked a lemon-coloured tissue from a square box on the table and dabbed at her eyes.

'I understand,' he said, noting that he'd been right about her eyes. They were blue, a very pale shade of cornflower blue.

'Do you?' she murmured. Her lower lip quivered a little.

She reached out and touched him lightly on the arm. 'People don't always get how hard it is, how painful, how it never goes away. But I think you do. I think you really *do* understand.'

Harry had seen the performance a thousand times before – a pretty girl who thought a display of vulnerability, of wide-eyed innocence, would enable her to wriggle out of any tight corner – and this particular version wasn't going to win any Oscars.

'I try my best.'

'Yes,' she said softly. Her hand continued to rest on his sleeve. Her fingernails were long and pink, and she was wearing several silver rings. 'You come over all tough, Mr Lind, but I reckon you're the sensitive sort at heart.'

Harry gave her his most sensitive smile before subtly moving his arm. He picked up the mug and took a sip of coffee. It was good and strong, with a faint aftertaste of vanilla. 'Don't be fooled,' he said. 'I really am as tough as I look.'

'I believe you,' she said. She gave him one of those up-from-under glances and batted her eyelashes. 'I bet you have to deal with all sorts in your job. Perhaps we should go for a drink sometime and you can tell me all about it. I like a man who can take care of himself.'

Harry's gaze shifted from her face to the coffee table and briefly settled on the magazine. Had he been the type who liked his girls served up on a plate, he might have been tempted, but obvious had never really done it for him. He preferred the cool, aloof sort of woman, the sort who made him chase further than a foot across the sofa. 'Well,' he said, being careful to come across as duly flattered, 'that sounds like a plan. Perhaps when this case is over . . .'

He let the sentence hang in the air while he put the mug back down. Then he moved swiftly on. 'So, getting back to Sam Kendall. I'm presuming nothing similar has been happening to you? No threats, no odd phone calls?'

'No, nothing.' Her blue eyes suddenly widened. She worried on her lower lip for a second and faked a small shudder. 'God, do you think I could be in danger too?'

He didn't fall for this act either. It was all too stagy, as if she'd rehearsed the routine while she'd been grinding the beans in the kitchen. 'I shouldn't think so. It all seems to be connected to the article, and since you refused to talk to the journalist, I don't see why you should be a target.'

'Bloody reporters,' she said.

Harry thought it was interesting how celebrities, even minor ones like Kirsten Cope, spent half of their lives desperate to get into the papers and the other half squealing like babies when they got the kind of attention they didn't want. He thought about Jess and suppressed a grin. 'I got the impression that this one was trying to write a serious piece about the aftermath of Minnie Bright's murder, how it affected the people who were caught up in it, the enduring legacy . . . that type of thing.'

'That's what she might have *said*,' Kirsten almost hissed, 'but all those damned journos are the same. They're devious bastards. They're not interested in the truth. They only want to dig the dirt.'

'And is there any dirt to dig?'

Kirsten's expression instantly changed, her face growing hard, her blue eyes blazing with anger. She spat out the words before she had time to think. 'And what the fuck is that supposed to mean?'

'Only asking,' he said, but he'd already got the answer he needed. She was hiding something. He'd seen the flash of panic, the instant recoil of her body. She'd had a knee-jerk reaction that no amount of acting lessons could have disguised.

As if realising her mistake, Kirsten quickly forced out a smile. 'Sorry, I didn't mean to snap. It's just that all this ... all this ...' She flapped a hand vaguely in the air. 'It brings back a lot of bad memories.'

'If there's something about that day you'd like to tell me ...'

She was wary now, on edge. 'What day?'

Harry stared patiently back at her. 'The day Minnie Bright was murdered.'

Kirsten gave a tiny start, but then suddenly and unexpectedly relaxed. She leaned back against the sofa, her lips parting as she expelled a breath. 'Oh, I know what's going on here. You've been talking to David, haven't you? Well, I wouldn't believe a word *he* says; he's an out-and-out nutter. In fact, if I was looking for a suspect, he'd be at the very top of my list.'

Harry had no idea who this David was – perhaps he should have looked through Jess's file more thoroughly – but decided not to display his ignorance in public. 'I'll bear that in mind.'

'So what did he say to you?'

He gave a shake of his head. 'I can't tell you that, any more than I'd repeat what you've said to me.'

'He's got a screw loose,' Kirsten said tartly. Quickly she moderated her tone. 'I mean, I guess it's not his fault, what with what's happened and all, but he can't go around making crazy accusations.'

'What kind of accusations?'

Kirsten narrowed her eyes. She wasn't the sharpest knife in the drawer, but she wasn't completely stupid either. 'You've talked to him, you should know.'

'People say a lot of things. Some of it's the truth and some of it isn't.'

She took a moment to think about this statement, her brows pinching together with the effort. She opened her mouth and then closed it again. Having made one mistake already, she wasn't prepared to make another.

After the unforeseen detour, Harry returned to his original line of enquiry. 'So nothing else happened that day, nothing the police weren't told about?'

'How many times?' she said, her mouth growing sulky again. 'I don't know what you're getting at.'

'Why do I have the feeling that you're not being straight with me?'

That hard look came back into her eyes. Her voice, taut with anger, was barely more than a whisper. 'Are you calling me a liar?'

'I'm not calling you anything. I'm simply offering you the opportunity to put your side of the story, to come clean before this all gets out of control.'

'Shit,' she said through clenched teeth. 'I've had enough of this. I want you to leave.'

'But—'

'Now!' she insisted, her voice growing shrill. 'Get out! Get out of my flat!'

Harry could see that he'd come to the end of the line. Knowing when to quit was as important as knowing when to stick. He got to his feet and gazed down at her.

'What are you staring at?' she growled.

'See you around,' he said. 'You've got my number if you need it.'

She glared at him, her mouth twisting into a sneer. 'You'll be a long time waiting.'

At the door Harry glanced back over his shoulder. Kirsten was still sitting on the sofa, but she had drawn up her knees. The knuckles of her right hand were pressed hard against her mouth. He threw her one last parting shot. 'The past always catches up with you in the end.' It was a corny line and he knew it, but he didn't care. She was a two-bit actress in a TV soap opera. Corny lines were probably what she understood best.

14

Back in the car, Harry didn't set off immediately. He sat for a while drumming his fingers against the steering wheel while he mentally reviewed his encounter with Kirsten Cope. It had left a bad taste in his mouth. She was lying and he knew it, but he didn't know why.

Reaching down, he retrieved Jess's file from under the seat and quickly flicked through the pages. There was no mention of a David so far as he could see, but a large pile of press cuttings – cuttings relating to the original trial of Donald Peck – were stacked up in the back, and the name could be buried in any one of them.

He picked up his phone and immediately it started to bleep. *Battery low* flashed up on the screen. He swore softly under his breath. He'd forgotten to recharge it. Still, he should be able to squeeze out one short call. He punched in the number and waited. It was answered after several rings by a sleepy-sounding voice that murmured an incomprehensible greeting.

'Jess? Is that you?'

'Huh?'

'It's Harry. Sorry, did I wake you?'

There was a short pause, and then a long expelled breath that was somewhere between a groan and a sigh. 'What time is it?'

He glanced at his watch. 'Almost nine.'

A more distinct groan floated down the line. 'Hold on a sec.'

'I haven't got a sec,' he said. 'My phone's almost out of juice. I'm in Chigwell. I've just been to see the delightful Kirsten, but I'll tell you about that later. I was wondering if the name David meant anything to you. I don't have a surname, but he must be connected to the Minnie Bright case in some way.'

Jess paused while she thought about it, or maybe she was just trying to get her sleep-dazed brain into gear. 'Er, no, I don't think so. It doesn't ring any bells.'

'Could you ring Sam and see if she knows him?'

'You mean now?'

Harry could hear movement in the background, and then a male voice saying something that he couldn't catch. Jess obviously had company. 'Why, don't you hotshot reporters work on Sundays?'

'Ha ha,' she said. 'Okay, I'll give her a call.'

His mobile began bleeping again, this time more insistently. 'Damn, my phone's about to die. Look, I'm on my way home. I'll call you back in an hour or so.'

Harry plugged the phone into the charger connected to the car's cigarette lighter, switched on the engine and headed back towards Kellston. While he drove, he went over his conversation with Kirsten again. He recalled her reaction when he'd raised the subject of what had happened on that fateful day fourteen years ago. He'd got her rattled, if only for a moment, and that didn't make him happy. On the contrary, it worried the hell out of him. It meant that Jess's hunch could be right, that not all the truth had come out about the murder of Minnie Bright – and that could mean trouble from all kinds of quarters.

Harry dwelled on this uncomfortable thought all the way back to Kellston. It was too early to go jumping to any rash conclusions, but not so early that he couldn't toss a few ideas around in his head. Kirsten Cope was lying. So too was Paige Fielding. Perhaps something else had happened, something the girls had omitted to mention to the police, or even deliberately covered up. Now the past was coming back to haunt them. Although he was still convinced that Donald Peck's conviction was safe – along with all the circumstantial evidence, his DNA had been found on Minnie's clothing – there could be more to the case than he'd previously thought.

He wasn't in a rush to return home. Doubtless Lorna would still be trying to create order out of chaos in the office. On reaching the northern end of the high street, he veered off to the left instead of driving south towards the station, went half a mile past the high-rise towers of the Mansfield and drove on to the industrial estate. Already it was busy, the local DIY enthusiasts, the compulsive shoppers and the eager gardeners all out in force.

He parked the Vauxhall and went into B&Q. After grabbing a trolley, he wheeled it through the aisles until he reached the painting and decorating section. There was only so much time a man could live with bilious green walls. He didn't spend any time dwelling on a colour scheme – white would do just fine. He dumped three large tins of matt white paint into the trolley, then added a couple of rollers with plastic trays, two tins of white gloss, sandpaper, a brush and a bottle of turps. Did he need anything else? He decided not, went to the checkout, joined the short queue and paid.

After placing his purchases in the boot, Harry got into the car and checked his watch. It was ten past ten. He'd better get back and make that call to Jess. As he moved off, he lowered the window and leaned his elbow on its base. The car park smelled of old dust, exhaust fumes and something more acrid that maybe came from one of the factories on the estate. He breathed in the warm tainted air and wrinkled his nose. Some smells, no matter how old, never went away.

At Station Road the removal van had disappeared, but Mac's dark blue Freelander was still parked outside with two of its wheels up on the kerb. Harry disconnected the phone and slipped it in his pocket. He put Jess's brown folder under his arm, retrieved the carrier bags from the boot, unlocked the front door and went quietly up the stairs. Even before he reached the top he could hear Lorna issuing instructions, only now they were directed solely towards Mac.

Harry peered cautiously around the corner of the stairwell. The landing was empty, but the door to the office was wide open. There was no one in his line of sight, so he quickly made his move. As he headed up the second flight, he heard the soft repetitive whoosh of the photocopying machine.

He opened and closed the door to the flat as quietly as possible, and walked carefully across the room, grateful now for the dark green carpet. Shabby and threadbare as it was, it would hopefully disguise his footsteps. He felt a tiny twinge of guilt, but nothing persuasive enough to make him change his mind about helping out downstairs. Lorna was a detail person, and if past history was anything to go by, she'd still be fretting over those details when the sun went down.

After putting the carrier bags on the table, he went through to the kitchen and got a cold beer out of the fridge. He leaned against the door jamb and took a few long pulls from the bottle. Looking out at the living room, he wondered how long it would be before he felt at home. It was probably a mistake, financially speaking at least, to opt out of the property market, but needs must. Anyway, it was too late to start stressing over that now. He'd already sold the flat in Kentish Town, given some of the profits to Valerie and used the rest to buy into the business.

Harry took a couple more swigs of beer and then picked up the landline phone and dialled Jess's number. She answered quickly.

'Hi.'

'Hi, it's Harry.'

'Good,' she said. 'I'm glad you're back. I've got some news for you. I rang Sam, and guess what?' She didn't wait for an answer before carrying on. 'Lynda Choi's older brother is called David. I'm presuming he's the person

130

Kirsten was talking about. Sam gave him a call and he's agreed to meet us in Connolly's at half twelve. Is that okay with you?'

'What, today?' he said.

'Why, don't you hotshot investigators work on Sundays?'

Harry grinned. 'And who was it slogging over to Chigwell while you were still wrapped in your duvet this morning?'

'I'll take that as a yes, then.'

'I'll see you there.'

Harry hung up. With a couple of hours to spare before the meeting, there was time for him to make a start on the decorating. He went into the bedroom, stripped off his clothes and put on an ancient pair of jeans and a T-shirt. Then he dug out some old sheets from the bottom of the bathroom cupboard and laid them over the living room floor. He unhooked the curtains and shifted the furniture into the middle of the room. After opening the windows, he prised the lid off the first can of paint, poured a quarter of it smoothly into the tray and set to work.

An hour and a half later, it was clear that the green wasn't going to give up without a fight. He'd finished the first coat on the wall opposite the windows and started on one of the adjacent walls, but he could see now that he'd need two coats and maybe even three to hide the darker colour underneath. He dropped the roller into the tray and stood with his hands on his hips, studying his handiwork. Well, it might not qualify for *Ideal Home*, but at least there was a part of the room that didn't make him wince every time he looked at it. The rest would have to wait.

He went through to the kitchen and washed his hands and arms. Then he got changed again, putting on a clean blue shirt, cream chinos and a pair of trainers. Connolly's was only round the corner, so it wouldn't take him long to walk there. As he crept downstairs with the same care as when he'd arrived, the painting and the Minnie Bright case mingled together in his thoughts. The word *whitewash* sprang into his head, and the corners of his mouth turned down.

15

Harry arrived fifteen minutes early. Connolly's was quiet and there were plenty of tables to choose from. He picked a four-seater by the window, a good place to watch the world go by, and when the waitress came over he ordered a chicken salad sandwich on wholemeal and a cold bottle of water. Another beer would have gone down well, but the café wasn't licensed.

While he waited for his sandwich, Harry looked around. Connolly's had been trading in Kellston for over thirty years, a family-run business that had inevitably changed with the times. It had started life as a typical greasy spoon serving up hot strong tea and heart-attack fry-ups in a permanent fug of cigarette smoke. Now it had adapted to suit the changing tastes of the local population. The killer breakfasts hadn't been abandoned, but now the café catered for the lunchtime trade as well, office workers and shoppers who wanted pert little salads with rocket leaves and healthy dressings. Not to mention the usual selection of lattes, mochas and Americanos.

Connolly's, he thought, was like a chameleon, cleverly changing its menu and its atmosphere to suit the time of day. It was the only all-night café in the district, and in the early hours, while others slept, the local toms would gather to warm themselves up and exchange gossip over a hot cup of tea. Cab drivers, doormen, clubbers and cops all frequented the place too.

Jess arrived when he was halfway through his sandwich. She gave him a breezy wave before going to the counter and ordering a black coffee. As she stood with her back to him, her elbows on the counter, he had a flashback to that cold rainy night when they'd first met. He remembered her leaning on the bar at the Whistle, her tight cashmere jumper accentuating her curves. She'd been mad at Len Curzon – an old hack from the *Herald*, who'd earlier plonked himself down beside Harry and spent the next half-hour bending his ear – and not the slightest bit shy in showing that displeasure. While Jess had been doing unpaid overtime, working on the Grace Harper story, Len had disappeared to the pub.

Harry had liked her feistiness, her confidence, liked it enough in fact to take her on to a jazz club in the West End. They'd talked until the early hours, drunk too much and even indulged in a reckless snog in the back of a black cab. A thin sigh escaped from between his lips. There'd been a lot of water under the bridge since then.

Jess put her cup down on the table and slid in opposite him. 'What are you looking so pensive about?'

He almost told her, but then thought better of it. He nodded towards the black coffee. 'Heavy night?'

'You could say that. We went for dinner with a couple of

Neil's friends.' She pulled a face. 'Turned out to be a boozy one. We didn't make it home till three.'

'So this Neil, he's the new man, is he?'

Jess grinned. 'You make it sound like I change them every five minutes. He's not that new as it happens. We've been together for almost a year now.'

'It must be love,' he said drily.

She scrutinised him with her wide grey eyes. 'You're in an odd mood.'

'Am I? Yeah, maybe I am.'

Jess lifted the cup and blew gently on the surface of the coffee. 'So come on, we've got five minutes before David's due. Let's have the lowdown on your meeting with Kirsten.'

Harry gave her a quick synopsis of the conversation he'd had that morning. Jess listened intently, sipping her coffee, until he'd finished.

'You see?' she said. 'There's something not right about that day, about what happened with Minnie Bright.' She put the coffee down, placed her right elbow on the table and cupped her chin in the palm of her hand. 'They're definitely hiding something.'

'Yeah, but whatever it is, it didn't originally bother Paige or Becky. That's what I don't get. If they're covering up, and they want to keep whatever it is hidden, then why would they agree to talk to you in the first place? It doesn't make sense. Surely they'd run a mile?'

'Perhaps it's because I stressed that the article wasn't about the murder but the effect it had on other people. I was concentrating on the present rather than the past. They might not have seen that as any kind of threat. So long as I didn't go digging into the original case . . .' She frowned as she thought about it, her pale brows knitting together. 'Kirsten must have been the one who made them change their minds. She's had more experience of the press than the other two. She's bound to be more cautious.'

'More aware, you mean, that journalists can be a touch economical with the truth.'

'*Some* journalists,' Jess retorted smartly.

'Apologies,' he said. 'I stand corrected.'

'And how on earth did you manage to get her to talk to you? She just kept slamming the phone down on me.'

Harry sat back, trying not to look too smug. 'Ah, now that would be down to the famous Lind charm.'

'Really?'

'There's no need to sound so surprised.'

'And was it that famous Lind charm that also got you thrown out of her flat?'

He grinned. 'Only after I'd found out what I wanted. And I wasn't thrown out exactly, more . . . encouraged to leave.'

'Right,' she said, smiling back. 'That's one way of putting it.'

He glanced at his watch and then towards the door. It was almost twelve thirty. 'So what do we know about David Choi?'

'Not much. Sam met him occasionally when she and Lynda were kids, but he was three or four years older so their paths didn't cross that often.'

'Choi. Is that a Chinese name?'

'No, the family was originally from South Korea, but Lynda and her brother were born here. The Chois have a dry-cleaning business over on the industrial estate, quite a successful one by all accounts. They've got a few City hotels and restaurants on their books now, but things were pretty tough while Lynda was growing up.'

'Hence the Mansfield,' he said.

Jess nodded. 'Not the greatest place to raise your kids. Anyway, according to Sam, David called her a few weeks after Lynda's death – he got her number from Lynda's phone – and asked if Sam'd talked to his sister on the night she died. She said he was very softly spoken, very polite. She told him about the message, expressed her condolences and that was the last time she heard from him.'

'So he could have called some or all of the other girls too.'

'Seems likely, although from what Kirsten said, it sounds like her conversation with him wasn't quite so amicable. Didn't she mention him making accusations? I wonder what all that was about.'

'Well,' Harry said, seeing the door to Connolly's open and a young guy of Asian appearance walk in. 'Now's our chance to find out.'

David Choi was a thin man in his late twenties, his short black hair slicked down with gel. He was wearing a pair of beige trousers, a white shirt and a worried expression. His dark eyes darted nervously around the café before eventually coming to rest on Jess and Harry. Harry gave him a nod and he quickly approached the table.

Jess stood up and shook his hand, making the introductions at the same time. 'Hi, David, thanks for coming. I'm

Jess, Jessica Vaughan, and this is Harry Lind, the private investigator Sam told you about.'

David Choi leaned forward and shook Harry's hand too, but he didn't sit down. His gaze jumped from the window to the table and then back to the window again. His mouth twitched at the corners. He slipped his hands into his pockets and immediately took them out again.

Harry, seeing his anxiety, rose smartly to his feet. Realising that their position was in full view of any passers-by on the high street, and that for some reason David Choi was unhappy about this, he said, 'Let's find somewhere less public, shall we.' He picked up his glass and the plate with the remains of the sandwich and headed towards the back of the room. Here, hidden by the long steel counter, was a small alcove with two empty bench-seat tables. He chose the one closest to the wall. Jess slid in beside him and Choi took the seat opposite.

'Would you like a coffee?' Jess asked.

Choi shook his head. 'I can't stay long. I've got to get back to work.' He glanced warily over his shoulder, as if someone might be eavesdropping. Although no one was within listening distance, he still dropped his voice to something barely above a whisper. 'I shouldn't even be talking to you.'

'Why's that?' Harry said.

Choi looked at him, met his eyes for a second and then abruptly dropped his gaze. 'I was told, wasn't I?'

'Told what?'

'To keep my mouth shut.'

Harry felt Jess tense beside him. She was remembering

perhaps the note that had been sent to Sam. *Keep yer mouth shut BITCH.* She leaned forward, her eyes gleaming with that singularly intense look that journalists get when they think they're about to make a breakthrough.

'You've been warned off?' she said.

'In your own time,' Harry said softly, concerned that the guy was about to take fright and do a runner. He was clearly scared, his chest heaving and falling, his hands twisting restively on the tabletop.

Choi took a few deep breaths before he spoke. Slowly he raised his gaze to look at the two of them again. 'This is just between us, right?'

'Of course,' Jess said quickly. 'You've got our word on it.'

Harry, unwilling to make any reckless promises, wasn't quite so fast with the reassurances. If what Choi said turned out to have a bearing on the original Minnie Bright investigation, it might be impossible to keep quiet about it. 'So long as it isn't evidence of a crime being committed.'

Jess nudged her knee against his and threw him a what-the-hell-are-you-doing type of glance.

Harry ignored her. 'But we're not here to cause problems for anyone. Your name won't be mentioned unless it's absolutely essential. We're just trying to get at the truth. I'm sure that's what you want too.'

'Yes,' Choi said, giving a terse nod of his head. 'Okay, I understand.'

'You said you were told you to keep quiet,' Jess prompted. 'Quiet about what?'

There was a short pause while his eyes darted over to the

139

counter and back again. 'It was the phone calls,' Choi said eventually. 'The calls Lynda made on the night she died.'

'So it wasn't just Sam Kendall that she rang,' Jess said.

'She called all of them, all the girls who were with Minnie Bright that day.' David Choi raked his fingers through his hair, the pain clearly visible on his face. 'I wanted to know what Lynda had said to them. I was trying to understand, to make some sense of what she did.'

'You don't think her death was an accident?' Harry said, recalling Sam Kendall's thoughts on the subject.

'She'd have wanted to make it look like one,' Choi said. 'For our parents' sake. Lynda never got over what happened. She couldn't move on. She couldn't build a proper life for herself. She blamed herself for leaving Minnie there. They gave her counselling, therapy and all that, but … it didn't make any difference. She lived with the guilt every single day of her life.'

'It must have been tough,' Harry said. 'Tough on all of you.'

Choi took another deep breath. 'She was a good girl, kind, but she was always sad. As she got older, the doctors called it depression. They gave her pills, lots of them, but nothing helped. It was like a disease inside her, like a cancer that just kept on growing. In the end …'

There was a short, gloomy silence, broken only by the persistent hiss of the coffee machine and the clatter of cutlery.

'So you called the other girls,' Jess eventually prompted gently.

Choi briefly closed his eyes, and when he opened them again, he had a more determined look on his face. 'Yes. A few weeks after she died, Lynda's mobile phone bill arrived. I went through it carefully and checked all the calls that she'd made that night. I thought . . . I thought that if she'd talked to someone, they might have an idea as to what it was that finally pushed her over the edge. I was just trying to get some answers, but the more I asked . . . I don't know, it was like they were hiding something, that they were worried about what I might find out.'

'What makes you say that?' Harry asked.

'Because they lied to me.' His dark eyes suddenly flashed bright, his right hand clenching into a fist. 'Apart from Sam Kendall, they all claimed that they hadn't heard from her.'

Harry frowned, beginning to wish that he'd had this information before his visit to Kirsten Cope. 'But the phone records said otherwise.'

Choi's face twisted with anger and disgust. He reached into his pocket and took out a sheet of paper. 'You see this,' he said, placing it on the table and jabbing at it with a finger. 'It shows that she made four calls, one to each of them.'

Harry pulled the phone bill towards him and he and Jess stared down at it. Choi had written the names next to the numbers in small neat print. The call to Sam was short, only a few minutes, and the one to Becky wasn't much longer. But the call to Paige had lasted nine minutes and the one to Kirsten Cope, made just after eight o'clock, for forty-three.

Choi poked a finger towards the bill again. 'You see. That Cope woman swore to me that she hadn't talked to Lynda, but she must have. It's there in black and white.'

'So you confronted her?' Jess said.

'I found out where she lived and went to her flat, but she wouldn't let me in. She said she'd call the police if I didn't go away, that she'd have me arrested for harassment. She called me a stalker, but it wasn't like that. I was only trying to find out the truth. I wasn't—'

'Hey, it's okay,' Harry said, seeing how distressed Choi was getting. He stretched out a hand and placed it gently on the younger man's wrist. 'It's okay. We get it.'

Choi waited until Harry had removed his hand before speaking again. 'And then, two days later, I was threatened by a man. He grabbed me on my way home from work and put a knife to my throat. He told me to lay off, to stop asking questions or he'd shut me up for good.'

'Did you report it?' Harry asked. An incredulous look appeared on Choi's face. 'I've got a wife,' he said. 'Two small kids. He swore it wouldn't just be me he went after next time.' A visible shudder ran through his body and his dark eyes widened. 'What if he finds out that I've talked to you? What if—'

'I don't think he'll come after you again,' Harry said, hoping that he was right. 'Things have moved on since you went to see Kirsten Cope. If anyone's going to be in the firing line, it's more likely to be me or Jess.'

Choi worried on his lower lip, his hands starting their restless dance again.

'This guy – what did he look like?' Harry asked.

'It was after eleven, dark. I couldn't see his face too well. He was wearing a hood.'

'Tall, short, black, white? How old was he?'

'White,' Choi said. 'About the same height as you.' He paused and then added, 'But much younger, I think.'

Harry heard Jess make a tiny noise in the back of her throat, probably the result of having to swallow one of her wisecracks. 'And what about his voice? Was it local?'

'Yes, I think so.'

'And there was nothing distinctive about him?'

Choi began to shake his head but then stopped. 'Only the rings,' he said. 'There were gold rings on his fingers, lots of them. Those coin ones.'

'Sovereigns,' Jess said.

Before any more questions could be asked, Choi rose abruptly to his feet. His face was drawn, his voice tight and strained. 'I'm sorry, but I can't tell you any more. I have to go now.'

'Okay,' Harry said. He touched the phone bill. 'Is it all right if I hang on this?'

'Sure.'

'Thanks for coming to see us. We'll let you know if—'

But Choi had already turned his back and was heading for the exit.

'That's one scared guy,' Jess said.

'Well, when some crazy goon puts a knife to your throat, it doesn't do much for the nervous system.'

'Some crazy *young* goon,' Jess said with just the hint of a snigger.

Harry picked up the remains of his sandwich, decided

143

that he wasn't that hungry any more and put it back down. 'One day you'll be old and grey, Vaughan, and then you'll regret your ageist attitudes.'

Jess laughed, but suddenly her face grew serious again. 'You know, I reckon the guy who attacked David could have been Micky Higgs – Paige Fielding's other half. He wears those rings on his fingers.'

'Him and plenty of others.'

'Yeah, but it makes sense, doesn't it? Kirsten tells Paige that David Choi has been harassing her about that call, and Paige sends out her own personal storm trooper to scare him off.' She lifted the cup to her lips and took a few fast gulps of the black coffee. 'What the hell are they all so worried about?'

Harry idly drummed out a beat on the table with his fingertips. 'I believe that's what they call the million-dollar question.'

'And why did Lynda Choi even have their numbers on her phone? It wasn't as if she was friendly with them. She didn't have anything to do with the others after the trial. Sam reckoned she was the only one Lynda kept in touch with.' She paused and glared hard at his hand. 'Do you have to keep doing that?'

Harry stopped his fingers mid-beat, his hand poised in the air. 'What's the matter? Is it aggravating your hangover?'

'It's aggravating every part of me.'

'I never realised you were so highly strung.'

'I'm not,' she said. 'But my head is.' She carefully rubbed her temples and gave a low groan. 'God, remind me never to go out and enjoy myself again.'

'So what happened to the girl who could party until dawn?'

Jess narrowed her eyes and gave him one of her dry looks. 'Hey, I can still do the partying – it's just the day after I have the problem with.'

'Okay,' Harry said. 'I've got a theory, if your addled brain can take it.'

'Fire away.'

'Right. We know that Lynda Choi made a call to Sam and that Sam's phone was turned off. But there was obviously something on her mind, something that was bugging her about the day Minnie Bright died and which she felt the need to share. With Sam not around to talk to, who would she turn to next?'

Jess frowned while she thought about it. 'Well, it wouldn't be Paige. She was a bully back then and she hasn't changed much now. And Becky was always the brainless sidekick, so I guess that leaves Kirsten Cope. Yeah, I suppose of the three, Kirsten was the one she would have disliked the least.'

'But in order to get her number,' Harry continued, 'Lynda might have had to contact the other two.' He slid the bill across the table so that it was sitting in front of Jess. 'You see, she called Becky first – her number's probably in the phone book so it wouldn't have been difficult to get hold of – and got Paige's number off her. Then, five minutes later, she rang Paige.'

'But why call Paige at all? Wouldn't Becky have had Kirsten's number?'

Harry shook his head. 'I don't think so. Kirsten told me

145

this morning that she occasionally hears from Paige, but I doubt she keeps in touch with Becky Hibbert. I get the distinct impression that Ms Cope, now that her naked body adorns the glossy lads' mags, has pretty much turned her back on all things Kellston.'

'Naked?' Jess said.

'We detectives pride ourselves on our powers of observation.'

'I can believe it.'

'So what do you reckon? A feasible theory as regards the phone calls?'

'Up to a point,' Jess said. 'But if Kirsten Cope doesn't give out her number to all and sundry, surely Paige would be aware of that. Why would she give it to Lynda?'

'Maybe she just wanted to get rid of her. Sam did say that Lynda sounded drunk, a bit rambling when she left the message. Or Paige could have realised that Lynda had cottoned on to something important about that day and the only way to find out was to let her talk to Kirsten.'

'Okay,' Jess said. 'I'll buy that. It's not beyond the realms of possibility.'

Harry sat back, folding his arms across his chest. 'Of course the girls could have had a perfectly innocent reason for lying to David Choi about the calls.'

'Such as?'

'Such as not wanting to be dragged into an inquiry about Lynda's death. Perhaps they simply didn't want to get involved.'

Jess huffed out a cynical breath. 'Like you believe a word

146

of that. Those girls are up to their necks in it and you know it.'

Harry did know it. He knew it with every bone in his body – but that didn't mean he had to like it.

It was Monday morning and the call came shortly after nine o'clock. A package had arrived for him and was available to collect at reception. He went down in the lift, sharing it with a middle-aged couple in matching Pringle sweaters. Their eyes met briefly and nods were exchanged. There was a typically British silence and an awkward shuffling of feet as the lift descended to the ground floor.

The hotel, a high-rise warren of right-angle corridors, was white and sterile and about as devoid of character as any place could be. Hundreds of people came and went on a daily basis, there to see the city or make deals, to visit friends or simply be invisible for a while. He smiled vaguely at the receptionist, gave her his name, signed for the DHL package and immediately returned to the lift.

His room was on the sixteenth floor. He went back up in the lift alone and strolled along the corridor, the package held securely under his arm, until he came to the right number. He slipped the card in, opened the door, closed it again and then leaned back, taking a moment to absorb the cold anonymity of what lay before him. How many rooms had he slept in like this one? Too many. The carpet was utilitarian beige, with curtains to match. There was a double bed flanked by two small bedside tables with lamps, a closet, a dressing table with a mirror, a TV, a kettle, two cups and saucers and the usual array of tea bags, coffee sachets, sugar and UHT milk. To his left was a tiny bathroom with a shower, toilet and washbasin. Straight ahead lay a pair of doors that led out on to a skinny balcony with metal railings. He gazed out through the glass. From this height there was a good view; in the distance he could see the gleaming dome of St Paul's Cathedral.

He shouldn't be in London. He knew this with every atom, every nerve end of his body. But there was no going back now. A promise had been made, a promise that could not be broken. He found himself wondering what would happen if he were to drop down dead in this bleak, sterile room, if he were to suffer a sudden heart attack or stroke. The police would be called and they would check his identity and would find a man who did not exist.

And what would Anna do? In Cadiz, she would report a husband with another name who had not returned from a trip to Bonn. The Spanish police, if they ever got around to it, would check the flights and find no passenger bearing his name. Would the connection be made with the corpse in London? And if it was, would that be better or worse for her? A relief, he supposed, but a tainted one. She would struggle to understand what he was doing here in this cheap, anonymous hotel on the edge of Kellston. Perhaps she would suspect that he'd been conducting a sordid affair, a week-long fling with another woman. Why else would he have lied to her?

'Jesus,' he murmured softly.

Quickly he pushed the thoughts aside. They were morbid

and distressing, not worth dwelling on. Stepping away from the door, he went over to the bed and sat down, laying the package carefully on the duvet next to him. It was an innocuous-looking parcel, wrapped in brown paper, with the name and address of a Munich bookshop stamped across the front. He cut through the tape with a penknife and opened the flaps. Inside was a thick hardback German dictionary.

Opening the book, he found, as expected, a hollowed-out centre. Nestled within this space were a .22 Ruger MKII, bullets and a silencer.

'Thank you, Munich,' he said grimly.

He took the gun out and weighed it gently in his palm. He gazed down at the bright red logo on the pistol grip, the symbol of a dragon with its wings outstretched. It looked rather like a phoenix rising from the flames. He took a moment to consider the appropriateness of the symbol, his lips sliding into a wry smile, before returning the gun to its hiding place. He wrapped the paper around the book, put the package in his suitcase, locked the suitcase and placed it in the back of the closet.

'Soon,' he said quietly to himself. 'It will soon be over.'

As he walked back across the room, he caught sight of himself in the mirror. He looked tired, almost haggard. There were bags under his eyes and his skin was grey. For the last couple of nights he hadn't slept well, and even when he had managed to drop off his dreams had been full of fear and panic, of being trapped, of turning into blind alleys where there was no escape.

'Don't go there,' he whispered into the silence of the room. 'Don't even think about it.'

He pushed back his shoulders, shrugged on his jacket and picked up the car keys for the Peugeot rental. He would spend most of the day going over his route, checking out the back streets, the one-way systems, the traffic lights and CCTV cameras. With a job like this, you couldn't afford to leave anything to chance.

But first he had something else to do.

Fifteen minutes later, he was driving through the wide cemetery gates. He went slowly up the main thoroughfare, swung a left by the majestic weeping willow and pulled the car neatly in to the side. He did not get out immediately, but sat hunched forward with his hands on the wheel. He looked from side to side and gave a small nod. Yes, it was all exactly as he remembered it.

He glanced automatically at his watch even though he had nowhere to be, at least nowhere to be in a hurry. The cemetery, so far as he could tell with so many trees and bushes in the way, was deserted. It was only him and the dead and a few grey squirrels. He got out of the car and shut the door quietly even though there was no one to disturb.

With his hands deep in his pockets, he strolled up the gentle slope and started to head across the grass. Here, in the older part of the cemetery, many of the graves were cracked and broken, tilted sideways, with weeds poking up through the gaps. Thin rays of morning sunshine broke through the clouds, warming the back of his neck. They were not strong enough, however, to prevent the growing chill in his bones.

When he came to the place he wanted, he stopped and quickly lit a cigarette. He drew the smoke deep into his lungs, as if it could provide some form of protection, a shield against his anger and disgust. Through the years he had trained himself to feel nothing, to create a barrier to the past that could not be breached. But now a slow, steady drip of rage was leaking down his spine.

He pondered on what it was that influenced a man the most. Nature or nurture? Had he been born as he was, his genes already programmed, or had he been moulded? Not that it really mattered. His eyes blazed with hatred and contempt as he stared down at the writing on the weathered grey headstone. Then, without another thought, he leaned forward and spat on the grave, before turning his back and striding away.

Job done.

As he drove back towards the gates, he noticed a bright red Mini parked on the main thoroughfare. Glancing over to his right, he saw a young woman in a faded denim jacket standing very still with a bunch of daffodils clutched to her breast. There was something about her stance that touched him. He only caught a fleeting glimpse, a snapshot of pale brown hair, of wide eyes, of curved and slightly parted lips. It wasn't a beautiful face, but rather a pleasant, thoughtful one. It was the kind of face, he thought, that you would like a daughter to have.

Daughter. He rolled the word around in his mouth, savouring it, tasting it. But its sweetness had a sour edge too. He'd had a daughter once, but that had been a long time ago. She was gone. She was lost. At some point all the good things were taken away. It was only a matter of time.

17

Jess lifted her eyes as the Peugeot passed smoothly by, surprised to find that she was not alone. Usually at this hour of the day she had the cemetery to herself. She caught a glimpse of a grey-haired, middle-aged man wearing sunglasses behind the wheel. He was there and then gone, so she thought no more about him.

She sighed into the daffodils as she gazed down at Len Curzon's grave. It was four years now since he'd been murdered whilst in pursuit of that great final scoop. She still thought about him, still missed him, despite all his dreadful habits. He'd been more than a mentor to her; he'd been a friend and an inspiration. Even though his glory days had been behind him, the good stories so thin on the ground as to be virtually invisible, he'd still had the old hack's nose for a decent lead. He'd taught her to follow her hunches, to be relentless, to hit the trail like a sniffer dog until it led to the truth. And now here she was chasing another big exclusive.

'So,' she said out loud. 'How am I doing? Am I on the right track?'

Kneeling down, she removed the papery dead flowers

from the urn and laid them on the grass beside the headstone. There was no sign of anyone else having been there since her last visit at Christmas. Len's wife Jean had predeceased him, and the two of them lay buried together. They'd had no kids to grieve for them, and she wondered if their childlessness had been a decision or a disappointment. Maybe Len had focused all his attention on the job instead. There were a lot of questions she hadn't asked while he was alive, and now it was too late.

Jess emptied the stagnant water out on to the ground and filled the urn with fresh water from a bottle in her bag. Then she took the cellophane off the daffodils, peeled off the elastic band at the base of the stems and arranged the flowers as nicely as she could. As she placed the urn back in front of the headstone, she wondered if she'd got her own work/life balance right. Sometimes it was all too easy to get caught up in the thrill of the chase and to forget about the people who really mattered. Neil was a good man, an understanding man, but even he might run out of patience eventually.

After wrapping the dead flowers in the cellophane, she rose slowly to her feet. As she gazed down, she felt that familiar pang of sorrow and loss. 'Well, I can't hang around here all day,' she murmured. 'People to see. Things to do.' But still she lingered for a while, drinking in the peace of the cemetery before returning to the faster pace of life outside the gates.

By 10.30, Jess was on the Mansfield Estate in search of Becky Hibbert. It was another nice day, so she'd left the

Mini at the Fox and strolled up the high street in the sunshine. She never parked on the estate if she could help it — you left a decent car for five minutes and you'd come back to find it either stripped or gone. With its three bleak crumbling towers, its dark passages and graffiti-covered walls, the estate was the local hotbed of crime. There was nothing, so far as she could see, to recommend it. Dirt and despair seeped out from every corner.

She thought about the Chois and how they'd finally managed to escape, but not before the damage had already been done. Lynda had teamed up with four other Mansfield kids, all of them bored and restless, with too much time on their hands. That single summer's day fourteen years ago had probably sealed her fate as well as Minnie Bright's.

Jess frowned as she walked along the litter-strewn path. What could it have been that Lynda had remembered after all this time? Something that had put the wind up Kirsten, that was for sure, and something worrying enough for her to persuade Paige to unleash her thug of a boyfriend on the unsuspecting David Choi. But whatever it was, it must have happened before Minnie Bright went into the house. By the time the poor kid had got through the window, Lynda and Sam had taken to their heels.

At the fork in the path Jess veered to the left, stopping outside the entrance to Haslow House and gazing up at the endless rows of rusting balconies. Here and there, like tiny pinpricks of hope, lay a gleaming window or a freshly glossed front door, but the majority of the occupants had long since ceased to care. Neither Becky nor Paige had travelled far from their roots. They'd grown up on the Mansfield and lived there still.

She walked into the cool foyer, wrinkling her nose at the smell. It was a combination of bad odours, but the most pervasive was the stink of urine. Jess had never understood why people chose to pollute their own environment. A kick against the lousy cards they'd been dealt, or some kind of tomcat mentality that compelled them to mark their own territory? Or maybe they just didn't give a damn.

She found a lift that was working and stepped inside. The smell was even worse within the confines of the small metal box, but she jabbed at the buttons anyway. Ten floors was a long way to walk, and Becky Hibbert might not even be in. Jess knew that she worked the afternoon shift at the supermarket and was hoping to catch her before she went out.

The lift jerked slowly upwards, heaving and groaning like an old man with a sack of rocks on his back. Jess took short shallow breaths, hoping to avoid the worst of the stench. To distract herself, she tried to figure out what she would say to Becky. There were times when you only got a single shot, and this could be one of them. She couldn't afford to waste the opportunity. David Choi had given them a lead and it was up to her to exploit it.

When the lift finally reached the tenth floor, she stepped out with relief and took a few quick gulps of air. She went to the corner and checked the arrows on the wall to see which direction she should be going, then set off in search of Becky's flat. It didn't take her long to find it. Only five doors to the right and she was there.

There was no bell, and so Jess knocked on the door. She waited, but there was no response. After thirty seconds she banged a little harder, but this yielded no result either. Leaning her head close to the door jamb, she listened for any sound coming from inside. There was only silence. Was Becky really out or was she just ignoring her? For many of the residents on the Mansfield Estate a knock on the door meant only one thing – the loan shark was here to collect his weekly interest.

There was a square window to the side of the door, but the curtains were three-quarters closed. Jess put her hands to the grimy glass and peered through the remaining slice. She could see an untidy living room with a worn-looking sofa and toys scattered across a threadbare carpet. But no sign of any life. 'Sod it,' she said under her breath. There was nothing worse than getting hyped up for an important meeting and then having the rug pulled from under your feet.

Should she wait, or would she just be wasting her time?

Turning around, Jess took a couple of steps forward and gazed down from the iron railings. From here she had a good view of the estate, but there was no sign of Becky. Five minutes, she decided, and then she'd be off.

It was more like ten before her eyes finally made out the familiar figure plodding through the main gates. She was pushing a pram with one hand and had a toddler attached to the other. Jess quickly took a step back in case Becky looked up and saw her. With the kids and the pram she was bound to take the lift, and once she was on the tenth floor there was nowhere else she could go in a hurry.

It was another few minutes before Jess heard a dull

grinding noise coming from the shaft. Then the sound of doors creaking open. Shortly after that, Becky appeared from around the corner. She was a short, heavyset girl with big boobs and hips. Strands of lank brown hair, in need of a wash, hung limply around a plain, sullen face. She was wearing a pair of grey joggers and her green hooded top had sweat stains under the arms. Preoccupied by the toddler's whingeing, it wasn't until she was almost at the door that she glanced up and saw Jess standing there. Her brows crunched together in a full-on scowl.

'What do you want?'

'I've just got a couple of questions, if you don't mind.'

That Becky did mind was perfectly clear from her expression. 'I've got nothin' to say to you. How many times do you need to be told? I'm not gonna do it, right?'

The kid stopped snivelling and stared up at Jess, temporarily distracted by this sudden turn of events. A small ball of snot nestled in his left nostril. Jess looked down at him, and then at the sleeping baby. It was at that very moment that she noticed the two carrier bags attached to the arms of the pram. She thought at first that it was grocery shopping, but suddenly realised that Becky had been indulging in a more expensive form of retail therapy.

'Emily's,' Jess said, tilting her head to read the name on the front of the bags. 'That's a pricey kind of shop. Designer, isn't it? They must be paying well at the supermarket these days.'

She could see that Becky was flustered. Lying was probably second nature to her, but that didn't mean she did it well.

'I've been working extra shifts, ain't I? Anyway, it's none of your business what I spend me money on.'

'It is if you're being paid to keep quiet. The police take a dim view of people deliberately covering up a crime.'

'And what crime would that be, then?'

'Threats, criminal damage. I presume you've heard what's been happening to Sam Kendall.'

Becky gave a shrug of her heavy shoulders. 'I don't know nothin' about that.'

Jess decided that now was the moment to play her ace card. 'But you do know about the phone calls Lynda made on the night she killed herself. She called you, didn't she? She was in a state and she wanted Paige's number.'

'How did you—' Becky stopped short, her mouth still open. But it was too late to take it back. She'd already confirmed part of Harry's theory.

Now was the moment for Jess to start sowing the seeds of suspicion. 'What you have to ask yourself is why you should keep quiet when others aren't. I mean, it's going to look bad for you when the truth comes out.' Then, not wanting any of this to lead back to David Choi, she quickly added, 'There's a private investigator working on Sam's case now. If you have the right contacts, it isn't too hard to get hold of old phone records. Perhaps Paige told you about him. His name's Harry Lind.'

Becky shook her head. 'Paige ain't told me nothin'.' And then, as if her brain had only just caught up with what Jess had mentioned earlier, she said, 'What do you mean about other people talking?'

Jess smiled thinly back at her. 'Sorry, I can't tell you that.

159

Let's just say that not everybody is being quite as tight-lipped as you.'

Becky's face twisted a little, and she shifted from one foot to the other. Finally she seemed to make up her mind. She dug into her pocket and pulled out a key. 'I've gotta go. The kids need feeding.'

Jess, inwardly cursing, sensed that her best opportunity was slipping away. 'And then there are Social Services to consider. I don't suppose they'll take too kindly to your involvement in all this.' It was a low blow and she knew it, but desperate times called for desperate measures. If she wanted Becky to come clean, then she was going to have to force her hand.

Becky's gaze darted down towards her children before moving up to settle on Jess again. 'This ain't got nothin' to do with them.'

'Think about it,' Jess said. 'Do you really want to be the scapegoat in all this, Becky?' She got her purse out of her bag and took out one of her business cards. Quickly, she scribbled Harry's name and number on the back. 'If you don't want to talk to me, you can give the private detective a call – in confidence, naturally. Only I'd make it soon, because the longer you wait, the worse it's going to get.'

Jess thrust the card into Becky's reluctant hand and walked away. When she reached the corner she glanced back over her shoulder, but the other woman had already gone inside. Had she done enough? She hoped so. She'd lit the fuse and now all she could do was stand back and wait for the bomb to go off.

18

Harry put his elbows on the desk, opened his mouth and yawned. He'd been up since the crack of dawn, making sure that the van was ready and all its equipment in proper working order. Today was the start of the Aimee Locke surveillance. He could have done the checks the night before but had spent some of the evening slapping another coat of paint on the walls of the flat and the rest sharing a bottle of wine with Valerie at Wilder's.

He frowned as he thought back over the evening. She'd been more distant with him than usual, less relaxed. Just the pressures of the job, or something more? He didn't want to dwell on the something more. He wasn't sure how he'd feel if she hooked up with another man. Their partnership may have died, but it hadn't quite been buried. She was a free agent and had every right to pursue a new relationship, but a part of him still baulked at the idea. She'd had boyfriends since him, of course she had, but none of them had been serious. And when she'd almost been killed by the Whisperer a couple of years back, he was the person she'd turned to.

He pondered on this for a while before switching his

thoughts to the events of the morning. The Lockes' side of the street had double yellow lines, but there had been plenty of space on the other side. The local residents kept their expensive motors behind secure iron gates, and so the only people who parked on the close were those who either worked at the southern end of the high street or shopped there. It had been too early for either to be out in force.

He had chosen a spot with a clear view of the Lockes' house, but not directly opposite. The white van, despite its hi-tech interior, looked like the kind any workman might use, a bland sort of vehicle that blended effortlessly into the background. He had turned off the engine, waited and had a quick scan around. When he was sure that no one was watching, he had climbed into the back. For the next couple of hours, long, fruitless and predictably tedious hours, he'd sat peering through a camera lens until Warren James had come to take over the surveillance.

In that time, nothing had happened. No one had come. No one had left.

Although he had a mountain of paperwork to get through, Harry's mind continued to drift. With his fingers poised on the computer keyboard, he started to think about Valerie again. She'd asked him what he was working on, but he hadn't mentioned the Minnie Bright case. He told himself that this was because he hadn't wanted to put her in an awkward position. She hadn't been involved in the original investigation, but she was still a cop, and all cops got defensive when old cases came under scrutiny – especially when those old cases had been headed by their current boss. Had she sensed that he was being evasive, or had her mind been elsewhere?

At ten past eleven he'd walked her back to Silverstone Heights, but this time there had been no invitation to come up for coffee. Just a quick peck on the cheek, a vague excuse about having an early start, a promise to call him and then she was gone.

Harry was still mulling this over when the internal phone started to ring. He picked it up. 'Yes?'

'There's a call for you,' Lorna said. 'A woman. She won't give her name but she says it's urgent.'

'Okay, put her through.' Harry waited until he heard the click. 'Hello, this is Harry Lind speaking.'

There was a rustling on the other end of the phone, an edgy clearing of a throat.

'Hello?' Harry said again.

And then the line went dead.

Harry gave a shrug and replaced the phone in its cradle. He was used to nervous clients. Whoever it was would think about it some more and then they'd call back or they wouldn't. Either way there was nothing he could do about it.

Shortly afterwards the phone rang again. He expected it to be his mystery caller but instead it was Mac.

'You got a minute?'

'Sure,' Harry said. He walked out to reception, gave Lorna a nod and went into the room next door. Mac glanced up and waved towards the empty chair.

'That was quick,' he said, as if Harry had sprinted from the other side of Kellston. 'Grab a pew. I won't be long.'

163

Harry sat down, stretched out his legs and made himself comfortable. His partner's office was a little larger than his own and had the same view over Station Road. The left side of the room contained a solid bank of metal filing cabinets, the right a couple of bookcases filled with volumes on law and criminal procedure. A tall potted palm – the one that Lorna had been fussing about yesterday – stood proudly in the corner. The surface of Mac's desk, even though he'd only been in for a few hours, was already invisible, covered by a chaotic heap of files, folders and overflowing plastic trays. His large mottled hands were busily sifting through the writs that needed serving. It was the bread-and-butter part of the business, tedious but a steady earner.

After a while, Mac stopped his sorting, picked up a white form that had been lying to his left and skimmed through the details. 'So,' he said. 'Sam Kendall. One of the Minnie Bright girls, huh?'

Harry gave a nod. 'Threats and criminal damage.'

'And you think it's connected to the original case?'

'Well, someone wants to shut her up, and that's never a good sign.'

Mac placed the form carefully on his desk. He sat back, folded his arms across his chest and stared at Harry. 'You'd better make sure of your facts before you start pissing off the high and mighty at Cowan Road.'

'I'm not intending to piss anyone off.'

'Pretty cut-and-dried, the way I remember it.' He left a short pause. 'But then I wasn't there. Didn't you work on that investigation?'

Harry shook his head. 'No, I was part of the team that

went into the house, but I was pulled off the case shortly after. We had a spate of armed robberies in the area, banks and building societies. It was pretty violent stuff. I got assigned to that instead.'

'Who was running the Bright case?'

'Saul Redding,' Harry said. 'He was a DCI back then. But I'm sure it was all by the book. He's got nothing to worry about.'

'He's got plenty to worry about if he sent the wrong man down.'

'He didn't,' Harry insisted. 'Peck did it all right. His DNA was all over her. I think this is something else entirely, something to do with the girls and the story they told the police.'

'I hope you're right, Harry. This could be a bloody minefield. Just tread carefully, right.' Mac glanced down at the form again. 'Jessica Vaughan. So she's back on the scene, is she?'

Harry could hear the disapproval in his voice. He grinned. 'Mad, bad and dangerous to know.'

'Yeah, well, you can joke about it, but last time you got mixed up with that lunatic journalist you almost got your brains blown out.'

'I'll be sure to pass on your best regards.'

'Don't bother,' Mac said. 'Just keep me posted.'

'Will do.'

'And watch your back.'

'I'll do that too.'

Harry had only just returned to his office when the internal phone started ringing. He perched on the edge of the desk with one foot on the floor. 'Hey, Lorna.'

'Your shy lady friend is on the line again.'

'Okay, put her through.' He waited for the click, for the sound of life on the other end. 'Hello, Harry Lind.'

Again there was silence. Not complete silence, but nothing in the way of actual words.

Harry kept his tone soft and reassuring. 'How can I help?'

There was a small intake of breath, a gathering of courage. And then finally she spoke. 'She said I could talk to you – on the quiet, like.'

The accent was local, the voice tense and agitated.

'Of course,' Harry said. 'In complete confidence.'

Another pause. 'And she won't go to Social Services, right? I ain't done nothin' wrong. They're not taking me kids away from me.'

Harry frowned, not catching her drift. He'd thought at first that she'd been referring to Lorna, but now he was starting to realise otherwise. 'Er, when you say *she* . . .'

'You know.'

Harry didn't know. He tapped his heel against the edge of the desk, suspecting that they could be here all morning if he didn't cut to the chase. 'Do you have a name for this woman?'

'*Her*,' she snapped, as if he was being deliberately obtuse. 'From the magazine.'

The light suddenly dawned. Harry rose smartly to his feet, interest flashing in his eyes. 'Ah, you mean Jessica Vaughan.'

'That's it. She said I could talk to you.'

'Okay,' Harry said. 'What is it that you'd like to tell me?'

166

There was another short silence. The woman hadn't given her name and he knew she wasn't going to. All he'd have to do was ring Jess and ask who she'd given his number to, but in the meantime he quickly ran through the list of possible suspects. It had to be one of the Minnie Bright girls. Definitely not Kirsten Cope, unless her acting abilities had improved drastically. And not Paige Fielding; he'd heard her voice at the market and it didn't sound like this one. Which, by a matter of elimination, left Becky Hibbert – the one Jess had pinpointed as the weakest link. It seemed like she'd been right.

'I ain't done nothin' wrong,' the voice whined again.

'I'm sure you haven't. You just want to get things straight, yes? That's completely understandable.'

Her voice tipped up a pitch. 'And you won't tell the others? You mustn't tell the others. This is just between you and me, yeah?'

'You and me,' he repeated. His heart was beginning to beat a little faster as he waited for the revelation. Something else had happened that fateful day fourteen years ago, and possibly, just possibly, he was about to find out what.

'Lynda Choi did call me.'

'Yes,' Harry said.

'She wanted Kirsten's number.'

'But you didn't have it,' Harry said, trying to help things along. 'So you . . . what? Put her in touch with Paige?'

'I might have done,' she said cautiously.

Harry's eyes flicked up towards the ceiling. This was like getting blood from a stone. 'And how did Lynda sound that night? Was she calm, upset, confused?'

There was a hesitation, as if Becky was rolling these three options around in her mind. 'I dunno,' she said eventually. 'A bit . . .'

Another long pause.

'A bit?' Harry prompted.

'She was kind of weird,' she said finally. 'Rude. I dunno. Maybe she was pissed. She wasn't very friendly, didn't ask how I was or what I'd been doing. After I told her I wasn't in touch with Kirsten no more, she said I had to give her Paige's number. Just like that. No please or nothin'.'

Harry walked over to the window, separated two slats of the blind and gazed down on the street beneath. 'And that's it? That's all she said to you?'

'Yeah.'

'She didn't mention why she wanted to get in touch with Kirsten Cope?'

'Nah.'

Harry swallowed a sigh. So far nothing new, but he still lived in hope. He stared at the people passing by. 'But she told Paige, right?'

There was a distinct hesitation. 'Er . . .'

'And you're good mates with Paige, so I'm presuming that *she* told *you*.'

Becky paused again, clearly battling between the desire to say as little as possible and the urge to dodge any trouble that could be heading in her direction. The latter impulse won. 'It were about that day, you know, with Minnie Bright and all. Lynda took off with Sam Kendall, yeah, but then later she changed her mind and went back.'

Harry could feel the hairs start to rise on the back of his

neck. He let the slats of the blind drop back into place and turned away from the window. 'Lynda went back to the house on Morton Grove? Are you sure?'

'That's what I said, weren't it?'

'How much later?'

'I dunno. Not that long. It was after we'd legged it, though. We didn't see her. She told Paige she felt bad, leaving Minnie there like that. We didn't know nothin' about it, not till the phone call. She didn't tell no one back then, not even the filth.'

'Why do you think that was?'

Harry could almost hear her brain ticking over as she tried to come up with an answer. In the end she resorted to her familiar response.

'I dunno.'

'Okay,' he said patiently. 'So she went back to the house. What happened next? What did she remember or what was so important that she suddenly felt the need to contact people she'd barely talked to in fourteen years?'

'Well she didn't tell *me,* did she?'

'Come on, Becky,' Harry said firmly, using her name for the first time. 'It is Becky, isn't it? Half a story isn't any use. If we're going to sort this out and keep you out of trouble, I need to know everything.'

There was another of Becky's by now familiar pauses. For a moment Harry thought she was about to hang up on him, but instead she began to speak again.

'Okay, okay, I'm doing my best. But I only know what Paige told me, right? She said Lynda was crying on the phone, going on and on about how bad she felt, that she'd known Minnie was still in the house and she should have done more to get her out.'

'Hang on,' Harry said. 'How did she know?'

'What?'

Harry reckoned he'd have more joy talking to a brick wall. 'How did Lynda know that Minnie was still inside? Did she see her, speak to her?'

'No, she didn't see her. I don't think so. But she saw a light or somethin'. Yeah, that was it. It had gone a bit dark and it was raining, which was why she didn't hang about. But she reckoned she'd seen a light go on and off in the upstairs window, just quickly like, and it was too soon for *him* to be back so she'd known Minnie must still be inside. She called out to her and banged on the back door but Minnie wouldn't answer. So she just left. That's what she was stressing over. She felt bad about it, that she hadn't stayed and tried harder to get her out.'

Harry frowned. 'Right,' he said. There was nothing in this information that changed anything. He could understand why Lynda would feel bad, would feel guilty, but he still didn't get why she'd felt the sudden need, after all this time, to share the information with Kirsten Cope. Just the burden of a guilty conscience, or something more? He tried again with a question he'd already asked. Sometimes if you asked often enough you finally got the answer you needed. 'Why do you think she wanted to talk to Kirsten especially?'

'How would I know? Paige just wanted to get rid of her, that's why she gave her the number. Said she was going on and on and none of it made any sense.'

170

'Okay,' Harry said, 'but that doesn't explain why you all decided to keep quiet about the calls. Why is everyone so bothered about them? And what's with all the threats to Sam Kendall, the damage to her car?'

Becky's voice turned instantly defensive. 'I don't know nothin' about that.'

'Okay, I believe you,' Harry said quickly. 'But come on, why did you all lie about the calls Lynda made? Why didn't you just tell the truth?'

''Cause we'll get the blame, won't we?' she snapped back. 'For what happened to Lynda, to Minnie, for everything. That magazine woman will write all kinds of lies about us and she'll say it was our fault for making ... for letting Minnie go inside in the first place.'

'No one blames you,' Harry said. 'You were kids. You had no idea of what would happen. No one blamed you back then and they won't now.'

'Yeah, but people twist things, don't they, put words in yer mouth. Paige said that—' She stopped suddenly, as if she'd let slip something that she shouldn't.

'Paige said?' Harry prompted.

But Becky refused to be drawn. 'It doesn't matter. That's all I can tell you. I don't know nothin' else.'

'Okay.'

'And she'll leave me alone now, yeah? That woman? She won't come hassling me no more?'

'I'm sure she won't,' Harry said. 'Not if you've told me everything.'

'I have. I swear I have.'

'But if you remember anything else, anything at all, no

171

matter how unimportant it seems, you can call me at any time. Will you do that, Becky?'

'Sure,' she said. 'I've got to go now.'

Before Harry could say another word, she hung up. He put the phone down, stared at it for a long moment, and then picked it up again.

19

Jess answered straight away. He could hear the sound of a radio in the background, the faint chatter of a DJ. 'Hi, Harry. What's the news?'

'I just got a call from Becky Hibbert.'

'Great. That was quick. What did she say?'

Harry perched on the edge of his desk again. 'Tell me you didn't threaten her with Social Services.'

There was a short hesitation. 'I didn't threaten her with anything. Not exactly. I just mentioned in passing that being involved in criminal activities might bring her some unwanted attention from certain quarters.'

'So you tried to scare her into talking.'

Jess drew in an audible breath. 'Oh come on, don't get all holier-than-thou with me. I bet you did much worse when you were a cop. Are you telling me that you never put any pressure on a suspect?'

Harry frowned. 'There's a difference between a bit of pressure and threatening to have someone's kids taken off them.'

'I didn't do that,' Jess said impatiently. 'But let's face it, if she is completely innocent as regards what's been happening

173

to Sam, she wouldn't have been worried enough to call you. It proves that I was right about them hiding something. Anyway, spill. What did she have to say for herself?'

Harry wasn't entirely comfortable with Jess's methods – methods that, if they became public, could adversely affect the reputation of Mackenzie, Lind – but decided to drop the subject. He knew that whatever he said would be like water off a duck's back. Jessica Vaughan was immune to criticism, and the more you pushed her, the more stubborn she became. He gave a quick sigh before providing her with a rundown of what Becky had told him.

'So Lynda went back to the house,' Jess said after an extended pause.

'It appears so. You'd better give Sam Kendall a call and find out what she knows about it.'

'She doesn't know anything. If she had, she'd have told me.'

'Are you sure?'

'What's that supposed to mean?'

Harry could hear the defensiveness in her voice. 'Well, the two of them left together, didn't they? So how come Sam never mentioned anything about Lynda going back?'

'Because she wasn't aware of it.'

'Except she didn't mention them splitting up and going their separate ways either. Lynda must have made the decision five or ten minutes after they'd run off together. Why didn't Sam tell you about it?'

'Maybe she didn't think it was important.'

'Maybe,' Harry echoed softly.

'Okay,' Jess said. 'I'll ask her about it. But putting that

aside for the moment, I still don't get why the other girls are so worried. There's nothing new here, is there? We already knew that Minnie was still in the house, so the fact that Lynda went back doesn't actually change anything.'

'Becky reckoned that you were going to blame them for Minnie's murder. I guess that's reason enough to be worried.'

Jess gave a snort. 'No, I don't buy that. There's something else, something they're still keeping quiet about. Why go to all that bother with David Choi? It's a complete overreaction. All they had to do was refuse to talk to me and I wouldn't have a story.'

'True enough, but people don't always act in a rational way. And Kirsten Cope has a lot to lose. She's in the public eye, and any bad publicity could mean the end of her career. Maybe she did overreact, maybe she did ask Paige to unleash her pet goon, but that doesn't mean there's any great mystery.'

Jess didn't sound convinced. 'Do you think Becky was being straight with you?'

'Yeah, I think so. She was pretty wound up. And she didn't want the others to know that she'd been talking.'

'Mm,' Jess murmured thoughtfully. 'But maybe Paige didn't tell Becky everything. Just enough to explain Lynda's weird phone calls but not the whole story. She might have guessed that Becky wouldn't keep her mouth shut.'

'And she was right.'

'I wonder why Lynda didn't tell the police that she went back to the house. I mean, back then, when it all happened.'

175

Harry gave a shrug. 'She was only a kid. She was probably scared – and feeling bad about being the last one there, the last one who could have got Minnie out before Donald Peck came home.'

'So you think the phone calls were just some kind of guilt trip, an unburdening of what she'd been feeling for the past fourteen years?'

'It's possible.'

There was a silence that went on for several seconds.

'What are you thinking?' Jess said.

'I'm starting to wonder if it was more than a light that Lynda saw.'

'For example?'

'I don't know. Maybe something she didn't think was important at the time, something that only clicked into place on the night she rang the other girls.'

'Something that the others don't want to come out.'

'It would explain why they denied ever having heard from her.'

'So what next?' Jess said.

'Give me David Choi's number. I'll call and see if he knows anything. And you can ring Sam and find out what happened after she and Lynda left.'

'Do you think David will talk to you?'

'There's only one way to find out.'

Harry scribbled down the number, said his goodbyes and hung up. He didn't ring David Choi straight away. Instead, he walked around his desk and sat down, frowning. Immediately, he stood up again. He was too restless to stay still. What had Lynda remembered, or believed she'd remembered? It wasn't just about the light. It couldn't be. As he began to pace the office, he thought back to that day fourteen years ago when he'd been part of the team who'd searched the house in Morton Grove.

Stopping by the window, he flipped open the slats of the blind and gazed down on the street. But he didn't see the station or the pavement or the people hurrying by. He was back in those rooms with the shabby furniture and the thin frayed carpets, the unwashed mugs and the overflowing ashtrays. The whole place had stunk of dirt and decay.

Harry's stomach twisted as he thought of that climb up the stairs, of the horror that had been waiting for them. One foot in front of the other until the landing was reached. Grey light coming through a small window. A brief pause before the turning of a handle, the push of a door . . . and then the sudden wafting stench of death. A soft groan escaped from between his lips. There was nothing that could prepare you for *that*.

The breath caught in Harry's throat. He turned away and slumped down in his chair. Then he leaned over the desk, put his head in his hands and rubbed at his eyes. But it didn't matter how hard he rubbed or how hard he tried to forget. Some images would remain engraved upon his mind for ever.

20

Kirsten Cope paced from one side of the room to the other with the phone pressed hard to her ear. Her face, already pinched, grew increasingly tighter. She slapped her left hand angrily against her thigh.

'For fuck's sake, Paige, we had a deal. What are you playing at?'

'Don't have a go at me. It's not my bleeding fault, is it? I can't be with her twenty-four hours a day. Anyway, you don't have to worry. She didn't say nothin'.'

'Oh yeah, and you know that for sure, do you? That silly cow doesn't know the meaning of keeping her trap shut. If Becky has been—'

'She hasn't. The only thing she told the bitch was to piss off out of it and leave her alone. That was all.'

'And you believe her?'

'She wouldn't lie to me. She wouldn't dare.'

Kirsten stopped pacing and glared at the wall. 'You'd better be right. If she talks, if she lets something slip, then—'

'She won't. Will you stop stressing. Becky knows what's good for her. She won't be blabbing. *You'll* be the one who blows it, Kirsten, if you don't calm down.'

'Yeah, well, you haven't got a private detective on your back. He came round here, for Christ's sake. He was going on about that day.'

'So what? He came to see me at the market. He hasn't got a clue. He's whistling in the wind, hun. How's he gonna find out anything? I'm not gonna tell him, you're not gonna tell him and Becky's gonna keep her big gob shut too. So what's the problem?'

Kirsten's hand bunched into a fist, her fingernails digging into her palm. 'You know what the bloody problem is.'

'Well don't take it out on me. I've stuck to my side of the deal, so if you're even thinking of asking for the cash back ...'

'Did I say that?'

A brittle silence fell between the two women.

Paige was the first to speak again, her tone more conciliatory. 'Look, I get why you're freaking out, but you don't need to. I'm taking care of things, aren't I?'

'I suppose.'

'So we're okay then, you and me?'

Kirsten briefly shut her eyes, trying to keep her anger at bay. She didn't trust Paige, but she couldn't afford to get on the wrong side of her either. 'I suppose,' she said eventually, through gritted teeth. 'So long as you keep Becky in check.'

'I've already said, ain't I? She won't be any trouble.'

'Okay, but let me know if anything else happens.'

'Nothing's gonna happen, hun. We're safe as houses. All that stuff, it's in the past, finished with. They'll soon get tired of asking questions – especially when they're not getting any answers.'

'They know we're hiding something.'

'So what?' Paige said, impatience creeping into her voice again. 'They can dig as much as they like, they're not going to find anything. Look, I've got to go. Micky's waiting for me. I'll call you in a few days, right?'

'But—'

But Paige had already hung up.

Kirsten hung up too, scowled at the mobile phone for a few seconds and then hurled it across the room. It bounced off the wall, skidded across the wooden boards and came to rest against the base of the sofa. 'Fuck it!'

The man who was sitting there stared at her. 'That make you feel better, babe?'

'That bloody reporter, that Vaughan woman, has been round to see Becky again.'

'Has Becky said anything?'

'Paige reckons she hasn't.'

'So?'

Kirsten stamped her foot like a five-year-old. 'So what the hell does Paige know? She takes the cash and then does sod all. What if that private detective finds out something? Maybe he's already on to us, maybe—'

'And getting hysterical is going to help how, exactly?'

'I'm not getting bloody hysterical!'

'Just listen to yourself.'

Kirsten put her hands on her hips, two thin strips of colour appearing on her cheeks. 'Why is no one taking this seriously? This isn't just a reporter we're talking about. There's a detective sniffing around, a bloody peeper. He's not going to stop until he's found what he's being paid to find out.'

'And how's he going to do that? For God's sake, stop acting like a bloody drama queen and start using your brains. The more you panic, the more mistakes you're going to make. You don't have to worry about Harry Lind.'

'And how do you figure that out?'

'Because he's an ex-cop.'

'What?' Her eyes widened with new alarm. 'He's the filth. He's the bloody filth?'

'I said *ex*-cop. And he isn't going to want to cause any trouble for his old mates in the force. All he's investigating is the damage to Sam Kendall's car and the threats that have been made against her.'

Kirsten shook her head in frustration. 'For God's sake, don't you see? That's the whole bloody point! Those threats are all about the past, and that's where he's going to be digging.'

The man gave a casual shrug. 'Nah, I know his type. He's just going through the motions. He'll talk to the people who were connected to the case, tick all the right boxes and then put in his bill. Give it a few weeks and this will all be forgotten.'

'I wouldn't be so sure.'

'Trust me, babe. I know what I'm talking about. Coppers don't like people interfering in old cases. It makes them look bad, like they might have got something wrong. And this Harry Lind, he's not going to want to piss off the law, is he? Start doing that and you're inviting the kind of attention that you'd rather avoid.' He leaned back against the sofa, his expression irritatingly smug. 'The past is dead and buried, babe. You don't need to worry.'

Kirsten felt a cold shiver run through her body. *Dead and buried.* That was what Minnie Bright was. Gone and never coming back. 'And what if Becky shoots her mouth off? What then?'

'She won't. I'll sort it.'

'Oh yeah, like you sorted Lynda?'

No sooner had she uttered the words than she instantly regretted them. She saw his jaw tighten, his expression change. Instinctively, she took a step back, but already it was too late. He leapt up from the sofa, his arms snaking out, his hands grasping her tightly around the throat. He pushed her back against the wall, slamming her with so much force that she felt a sickening jolt of pain run down her spine.

'Are you accusing me of something, babe?'

His hot breath was in her face and his eyes were wild with anger. Kirsten parted her lips to try and speak, to try and appease him, but his fingers were already choking her, pressing hard into the soft flesh around her windpipe. Her arms flailed weakly, her fingers clawing uselessly at his wrists. She spluttered out a sound, a stifled cry.

'What was that? I can't hear you properly, darlin'. You trying to apologise?'

He glared down at her, his face a mask of cruelty.

Like a dying fish on a line, Kirsten's mouth gulped open and closed as she gasped for oxygen. He was going to kill her. She was sure of it. *Please*, she pleaded with her eyes.

She felt his fingers tighten, saw tiny black spots dancing in front of her. His body, taller and stronger than hers, had her firmly pinned against the wall. There was no escape, nothing she could do. She tried to nod, to say *yes, yes, yes,* but even that was impossible.

'You think I pushed her into the river, babe? Is that what you think?'

Kirsten used the last fragments of her energy to try and struggle free. It was no good. And she had no hope of a reprieve. He was beyond reach, beyond any human feelings of pity or forgiveness. Silently she prayed to a God she had never believed in. Then, just as she was sure that her life on this earth was about to end, he released his grasp and shoved her brutally down on to the floor.

She lay there panting, her chest heaving at the sudden rush of air into her lungs. Then, instinctively, she rolled up into a ball. All she could see was his feet, his ankles, and she was sure that the kick would come before long, the boot in her ribs, in her face, in her groin. She closed her eyes, waiting for the killer blows, but instead, incredibly, he started laughing.

'What's wrong with you, babe? Look at me.' He leaned down, took her by the shoulders and gave her a shake. 'I'm talking to you. Don't just ignore me.'

Kirsten blinked open her eyes. Her throat felt tight and sore and her chest was still heaving. She stared up at him, still afraid, still unsure of what was going to happen next.

'Now you don't want to be starting any nasty rumours, do you?'

'No,' she mumbled.

'I can't hear you.'

'No,' she said again. It came out as more of a squeak than a word.

His mouth slid into an unpleasant smile. 'Good girl. Because when it comes to rumours ... well, I'm sure our little journalist friend would be more interested in your sick little secret than anything I might or might not have done.'

'I didn't mean it,' she said quickly. 'I'm sorry.'

He grabbed hold of her chin and tilted it up. 'Who takes care of you, Kirsten?'

'Y-you do,' she stammered.

'Yes, *I* do. And don't you ever forget it.' He let go of her chin, stood upright again and placed his hands on his hips. Gloatingly, he gazed down at her. 'You're mine, Kirsten Roberts, mine until the day you bloody die!'

She raised a hand to her mouth and bit on her knuckles. Tears began to roll down her cheeks. One mistake, one lousy mistake, and she would have to pay for it for the rest of her life.

21

Harry had spent the last hour in Hackney making enquiries about the damage to Sam Kendall's car. She lived in the ground-floor flat of a three-storey house in Chelling Road, and that had been his first port of call. There had been no reply when he'd tried the doorbell, and her phone had gone straight to voicemail. There had been no sign of her cab either. He presumed that she was working, on the day shift rather than the night. Even before he'd started asking around he had known that it was a long shot, but it had to be done. Sometimes, just occasionally, the long shots paid off. Not on this occasion, however.

After trying the bells of the two flats above her – again, no joy – he had worked his way methodically along the road, stopping at every house that had a view of the parking space outside Sam's flat. The results had been much as he'd expected. Even those who'd answered the door – and they had been few and far between – had given him short shrift. Not getting involved seemed to be their main priority. He was met with responses ranging from the indifferent to the outright hostile. If anyone had seen anything suspicious they weren't prepared to tell him.

Harry was reminded of those door-to-door enquiries he had made as a copper. It all seemed such a long time ago. Then he'd been ringing on bells trying to get information on murders, on assaults, on missing children. Most of the kids were eventually found safe and well and duly returned to their frantic parents, but some were not so fortunate. The memories of the few stayed with him like small trembling ghosts in the back of his mind. Minnie Bright was one of the unlucky ones, a little girl who had never gone home.

Harry frowned as he gazed along the length of the road. He'd been hoping to come across one of those useful neighbours, elderly perhaps, or just incurably inquisitive, who spent large amounts of their time looking out of the window. Unfortunately, they appeared to be in short supply round here. He glanced at his watch, saw that it was 2.25 and decided to call it a day. He'd made a note of the properties where he'd got no reply and would try again one evening when people were more likely to be back from work.

Walking round the corner, he got into his car and wondered if he should stop by Jess's place. She was only a five-minute drive away. He took out his phone, intending to give her a call, but then changed his mind. Mac was none too pleased with his involvement in this case, and his continued absence from the office would only provide further cause for complaint.

Instead, Harry returned to Kellston and began making background checks on a shortlist of prospective employees for one of their regular clients, a large finance company in the West End. He wasn't overly fond of such deskbound employment – he'd had enough paperwork in the force – but it had to be done. The window was open and a fly buzzed relentlessly around his ear as he ploughed through the list.

It wasn't until after four that David Choi returned his call. He sounded tentative and wary. Harry suspected it taken him a while to pluck up the courage to ring.

'Thanks for getting back to me. I just wanted to run something by you. Do you think it's possible that Lynda went back to the house on the day that Minnie Bright died? I mean, after she and Sam had left the other girls.'

'Back to Morton Grove? Why would she do that?'

'Maybe to check that Minnie was okay? She never said anything to you about it?'

'No, nothing. Do you think she did?'

'I don't know,' Harry answered honestly. 'Look, can you remember anything Lynda might have said, might have mentioned, in those last few weeks? No matter how trivial it may seem.'

There was a long pause on the other end of the line. And then an elongated sigh. 'She wouldn't talk to me, Mr Lind, not about what happened. But I know that she was dwelling on it.'

'When you say dwelling . . .'

'She'd started going over things, the whole case, the trial, everything. She was even collecting copies of newspaper reports from the library. She had hundreds of them, and every night she'd read through them again and again.'

Harry wondered if that had been down to Lynda's inability to come to terms with what had happened, or if she'd been searching for something specific. If the latter was the case, then on the night she died, the night she'd made all the phone calls, she might have found what she was looking for.

'Hold on,' David Choi said. There were some voices in the background, a faint burble of conversation. The sound of footsteps followed and then the distinctive click of a door being closed. 'Sorry about that. I'm at work.'

'It's okay, I won't keep you. If I find out anything else, I'll let you know.'

There was another short pause, and then David said quickly, 'Are you sure she went back to the house?'

'No, I'm not sure of anything at the moment.'

'Was it one of the other girls who told you? Was that what Lynda called them about? Is that what they're trying to cover up, her going back there? It must be. Why else would they—'

'Hey, hey, slow down,' Harry said. 'Don't start jumping to conclusions. People lie for all kinds of reasons. It doesn't always mean that they've got anything to hide.'

David's voice tipped up an octave. 'So why threaten me? Why put a knife to my throat? Tell me which one it was.'

But Harry had no intention of going there. David Choi, despite his fears for his family, might be tempted to take matters into his own hands. 'I can't tell you that. Just stay away from the girls, keep your head down and trust me, okay?'

There was a short silence.

'David?'

'Okay,' he replied eventually, somewhat grudgingly.

'I'll be in touch.' Harry put the phone down, hoping that

he hadn't said too much. The last thing he wanted was for David Choi to start ruffling feathers again. If Micky Higgs had been responsible for the last attack, he might not stop at mere threats this time. And then there was Becky Hibbert to think about. If the other girls thought she'd grassed them up, she'd be none too popular either.

Harry sat back, linked his fingers behind his neck and gazed up at the ceiling. He still didn't buy into Jess's big cover-up theory, but something was wrong. There were things coming out now that should have been revealed fourteen years ago. Thinking of Jess reminded him that there had been no news from her yet on the Sam Kendall front. Should he call? No, she'd get in touch if and when she had some information.

For the next half-hour Harry carried on with the background checks he'd been making before David Choi rang. At twenty to five, he switched off the computer, put on his jacket, picked up Jess's file and went through to reception. Lorna was standing in the centre of the room, making a three-hundred-and-sixty-degree turn with her hands on her hips. She tilted her chin and looked at him.

'Do you think the sofa would look better against the wall?'

'I think it looks just fine where it is.'

Lorna narrowed her eyes. 'Are you humouring me?'

'As if,' he said, grinning.

'It matters, you know. First impressions are important. I want the office to look right.'

'And it does,' Harry said. 'You've done a great job.'

'Yeah, sure. You two wouldn't notice if I painted the

whole place pink and hung a chandelier from the ceiling.' She walked back behind her desk and sat down. 'Are you off to Walpole Close?'

'Yes, I told Warren I'd take over at five.'

Lorna nodded towards a sturdy carrier bag on the table beside the water machine. 'There's a flask of coffee for you there, and some sandwiches.'

'Ah, you're an angel,' he said, leaning over the desk to give her a peck on the cheek. 'What would I do without you?'

'Fall asleep most probably. Now push off and leave me in peace.'

Harry picked up the bag, gave her a wave and headed for the door. Once outside, he was in two minds as to whether to take the car or not. In the end he decided not. It was only a fifteen-minute walk, and it was still warm; he might as well make the most of the sunshine. As he crossed the road and passed the station. The commuters were already streaming out. They had a tired, slightly bedraggled look about them. The term *rush hour*, he thought, was a complete misnomer; in London the crush seemed to have been extended to include most of the day and half the evening too.

As he squeezed his way through the crowd, Harry turned his attention back to David Choi's phone call and what it had revealed about Lynda's preoccupation with the Donald Peck trial. A part of him – the part that didn't want to upset the applecart – considered that it was simply a reflection of her disturbed state of mind, an attempt to reconcile her actions with the facts of the case. When she'd made the calls to the other girls, there had been no suggestion that she'd

190

thought Peck was innocent – at least not to Harry's knowledge. So surely there was nothing to suggest that the law had got it wrong. And yet that conclusion didn't sit comfortably with him. He had one of those uneasy feelings shifting around in his guts.

Harry took a left and strode along the high street. As he walked past Wilder's, the door opened and a young couple emerged. A few bars of jazz drifted out with them into the evening air and he was suddenly reminded of Valerie. What was she doing now? Still at Cowan Road, perhaps, or on her way home, or heading for the pub with some of the guys from work. Maybe he would give her a ring later.

He headed south and started to wind through the back streets. After a further ten minutes he found himself in the more exclusive part of Kellston. The houses set back off the road lay behind high walls, but he caught glimpses of them, along with their large manicured gardens, as he passed the gates. It was quieter here, and the air smelled cleaner, as if the atmosphere, like the fancy cars and the exotic plants, had been especially imported.

Harry, even if he had the money, doubted that he'd choose to live in a place like this; it seemed cut off from the realities of city life, from the very things that had always made London so appealing to him – the cultural and economic mix, the hustle and bustle, the sheer unpredictability of it all. There was something artificial about this exclusive enclave, something that left a bad taste in his mouth.

As he turned the corner into Walpole Close, he took out his phone and let Warren James know that he was almost there.

'Good timing,' Warren said. 'I was just dreaming of a nice cold beer. The door's open. Come on in and make yourself comfortable.'

Harry took a good look around as he approached the white van. There was no one else on his side of the road. Across the other side, however, coming from the opposite direction, there was a smartly dressed middle-aged woman walking a pedigree pooch. She stared quite blatantly at him, her expression stern and accusing, trying to judge perhaps if he was the sort of man likely to break into her house while her back was turned. He gave her a neighbourly nod, but she ignored him.

He slowed down, waiting until she'd passed and gone a little way down the road before striding up to the van, sliding open the door and quickly stepping inside. Warren James, a slim black guy, was sitting at the table with a laptop in front of him. He was the resident computer expert at Mackenzie, Lind – able to dig out a fraud from the most meagre evidence – but he doubled up on surveillance when things were quiet.

'Bang on time,' Warren said.

Harry closed the door. The van was warm inside and littered with the debris of hours of surveillance – breadcrumbs, chocolate wrappers, empty Styrofoam cups and a couple of newspapers. 'We aim to please.'

Warren stretched his arms up over his head and yawned. 'God, I'll be glad to get out of here. It's like the land of the living dead.'

'Not much action, then?'

'She hasn't been out all day. She has had a couple of

192

visitors, though, a woman in her late forties who arrived on foot at ten o'clock this morning and left at twelve – I think she was the cleaner – and a guy who turned up at two and left around three thirty.'

Harry raised his eyebrows. 'An hour and a half?'

'I wouldn't get too excited about it. I checked out the car and it's licensed to an Aidan Russell.' Warren hit on a few keys and a series of photos came up on the laptop. 'Here, there are some pretty clear shots of him arriving and leaving.'

Harry leaned over Warren's shoulder and examined the snaps. The car was a pale blue Jaguar and the man was in his early thirties with brown hair and a neatly trimmed beard.

'So what shouldn't I be getting excited about? They were alone together, right?'

'The guy's a hairdresser. He could have been here to snip the lady's tresses.'

'Do hairdressers usually make house calls?'

'I should think it depends on how rich the client is. I doubt our Mrs Locke is short of a bob or two.' Warren picked up some A4 sheets of printed paper and handed them over. 'Russell owns a couple of salons, one in Chelsea and one in Covent Garden. He's got a Facebook page for the business.'

Harry flicked through the publicity, which was mainly pictures of beautiful women with desirable haircuts. 'I don't suppose it mentions if he's gay or straight?'

Warren stood up and shrugged into his leather jacket. 'Well, he drives a powder-blue Jag. I know where I'd put my money.'

'I'm not sure if that counts as definitive evidence of his sexuality.'

'Powder-blue?' Warren said again, pulling a face. 'That's a crime against motoring, man.'

Harry laughed and took Warren's place in front of the laptop. A second computer to the right was screening live footage of the space in front of the Locke gates. 'See you tomorrow, then. Have a good evening.'

'Good luck.'

Harry watched him leave. Warren James was ten years his junior, happily married with a couple of kids and another on the way. It probably wasn't all sunshine and roses – nothing ever was – but he seemed to have his personal life sorted in a way that Harry could barely envisage. The older he got, the more distant the possibility of playing happy families became. His on–off relationship with Valerie had placed him in a kind of limbo he seemed incapable of escaping from.

With relationships on his mind, Harry sat back and glanced through Warren's notes again. Could Aimee Locke be cheating on her husband with her hairdresser? Even with Martin Locke away, she would be playing a risky game by entertaining him in her own home. But then people weren't always smart when it came to having affairs.

'Aimee,' he murmured. 'What are you doing?'

The traffic increased a little over the next hour. He watched as people returned from work, executive cars purring past the van, but the Locke gates – no matter how hard he stared at the computer screen – remained firmly closed. Perhaps she would go out later. Perhaps that was why she'd had her hair done.

At six o'clock Harry took the Tupperware box out of the carrier bag and peered inside. There were four large sandwiches, two cheese and pickle, two ham salad, an apple, some grapes and a Mars bar. When he'd first started working for Mac, Lorna's attempts to mother him had driven him crazy, but these days he appreciated her efforts. He picked up one of the ham sandwiches, bit off a corner and gave a grunt of pleasure.

While he ate, he continued to focus on the wrought-iron gates. The only movement came from the rhododendron blossoms swaying in the breeze. He finished his sandwich and poured a cup of coffee. He sensed it was going to be a long night. Settling back in his chair, he pulled over Jess's file on the Minnie Bright case and started from the beginning.

22

At ten past seven Jess walked down to the corner shop and bought a pint of milk, a microwaveable meal for one and a bottle of wine. Neil, who normally did the cooking, was on his way to a legal seminar in Edinburgh and she had no desire to spend any more time than was necessary in the kitchen. Her plan for this evening was to make a thorough trawl through her notes on the Minnie Bright case and see if there was anything she'd missed.

It was when she was almost back at the small block of flats that she began to feel it, a weird tingling sensation on the back of her neck. Someone was watching her. She glanced quickly over her shoulder. There were plenty of people around, but none, so far as she could tell, who were showing any particular interest. But still the prickling continued, a sixth-sense feeling that couldn't be ignored.

She scanned the cars parked along the side of the road, lifted her gaze to the windows of the surrounding houses and finally looked over at the green expanse of Victoria Park before wondering if she was just imagining it. Even so, she hurried the final few yards, reaching for her keys as she went.

Once inside the communal hallway, she walked smartly along the corridor, unlocked her front door and bolted it behind her. She went into the living room and peered out through the window. From here she had a clear view of the main road and watched as two young guys, a man in a grey suit and then a blonde girl walked past. None of them paid any attention to the flats.

'Where are you?' she murmured. '*Who* are you?'

Jess continued to stand there, watching. After a while she frowned and turned away, wondering if her instincts had been wrong. It was easy to get paranoid when you were involved with secrets and lies – and the Minnie Bright case had plenty of those. She had almost persuaded herself that she'd been mistaken when the phone suddenly rang and she jumped half out of her skin. She gazed at it for a moment, her heart beating faster, before snatching it up off the coffee table and looking at the screen. It was only Sam Kendall. With a sigh of relief she answered the call and passed on the information Harry had received about Lynda returning to the house.

'She never said anything to you about it?'

'No, not a word,' Sam replied. 'We split up when we got back to the Mansfield. She went off in the direction of Haslow House and I went to Carlton. That was the last I saw of her.' She paused for a moment. 'So you really think she went back?'

'Do *you* think she could've?'

'It's possible, I suppose. She might have felt bad about leaving Minnie alone with the others. Lynda was that kind of person. But why would she keep quiet about it?'

'We're still trying to figure that one out. She didn't tell the police. She didn't tell her family. She didn't even tell you.'

Sam thought about this for a few seconds. 'It might have been because she didn't want to get into any more trouble. Back then, I mean. Lynda's parents were pretty strict. She wasn't even supposed to be out with us that day. Her parents had enrolled her in one of those summer schools, but she hated it and never went.' She left another short pause, cleared her throat and added, 'When she spoke to the cops, she must have been terrified – I know I was – and just wanting to get the whole thing over and done with. If her interview was anything like mine, it would have been pretty clear from the start that they were more interested in the girls who were actually with Minnie when she went inside the house. All they wanted from me was to make sure that my story, up to the point where we left, tallied with everyone else's.'

Jess gave a nod. 'Lynda might have realised that admitting to going back meant she would have been the last one on the scene, and so she simply kept quiet about it.'

'I'm sure she wouldn't have lied – she wasn't the type – but if the cops didn't ask the right questions . . .'

'She would have let them go on believing that when she returned to the Mansfield with you, she actually stayed there.'

'I guess,' Sam said. 'I mean, if there wasn't any extra information she could give them, she might have figured that it was better to keep her mouth shut.'

Jess gave another nod, understanding how easily a ten-year-old Lynda could have made that decision. 'Thanks, Sam. I'll let you know if we hear anything else.' She said her goodbyes, put the phone down and wandered back over to the window. Her eyes automatically scanned the street again, left and right, before she headed for the kitchen to put her lasagne in the microwave.

Two hours later, Jess was on her third glass of wine. Her copious notes, including trial reports, a huge pile of press cuttings and all the information she'd gleaned from Sam Kendall, were strewn across the table. She'd decided to go back to basics and to try and create a timeline for the day. So far she had:

Donald Peck gets on bus to Bethnal Green at around 12.15 to visit Ralph Masterson, a retired probation officer. Arrives at 12.35. Stays for about 20 minutes.

The five girls walk to Morton Grove.

Sam and Lynda leave (12.30). Back at Mansfield by 12.45?

Minnie Bright enters the house (12.35?).

Paige, Becky & Kirsten leave (12.45?).

Lynda returns to Morton Grove (13.00?). Sees light go on briefly in upstairs room. Bangs on door but gets no reply. Goes away.

Donald Peck leaves Masterson's at around 13.00.

Peck returns to Morton Grove. Depending on traffic, back by 13.30? Finds Minnie inside the house.

And that was that, Jess thought, flinching at the knowledge of what had happened next. By the time Peck returned, Minnie would have been in the house for about an hour. What had she been doing for all that time? Still searching for the queen's treasure, perhaps. Still hoping to become the princess she had never been in real life.

Jess took a sip of wine, pulled one of the trial reports towards her and began to read. Donald Peck had insisted that he'd gone for a long walk after leaving Masterson's and hadn't got back to Morton Grove until after five. There was no one to corroborate this fact, and he was vague about where he had been. 'Just around,' he'd replied when the barrister had pressed him. 'I don't remember where exactly.' When he *had* got home, he said, he hadn't noticed anything amiss. The door to the upstairs spare bedroom had been closed, as it always was. He hadn't gone inside, and claimed to know nothing about the body that was lying under the bed. When pressed about the smell that had been present in the house when the police had entered two days later, he'd replied, 'I thought it was the drains.'

The story hadn't gone down well with the jury. Although the DNA evidence was inconclusive – Peck's hairs were found on Minnie's clothes, but they could have come from the carpet she was lying on – they found him guilty of murder and the judge passed down a sentence of life.

Jess chewed on the end of her pen, wondering why Peck hadn't shifted the body. Surely he'd have wanted to get it out of the house as quickly as possible. Even if he'd believed that no one else knew where Minnie was, it would still have been risky to keep her there. Of course, he didn't have a car, which would have made things trickier, but he could have removed the body in the dead of night and dumped it in one of the many alleyways that twisted around the back streets of Kellston. So why hadn't he? It could have been, she supposed, a kind of paralysis, or an inner denial as to what had happened. Or perhaps he'd simply been too scared of being seen.

She scribbled down Ralph Masterson's name on a fresh sheet of paper. Would he still be alive if he'd been retired fourteen years ago? She'd make a few calls in the morning and see if she could find out. Under his name she added those of Clare Towney, Peck's niece, and Hannah Bright, Minnie's mother. It could have been Paige or Kirsten who had sent the anonymous notes to Sam, but somehow she didn't see it as their style. Paige was more likely to unleash her pet goon of a boyfriend – as she'd done with David Choi – than to waste her time snipping up tabloid newspapers. And why would Paige or Kirsten accuse Sam of being responsible for Minnie's death? When it came to blame, they were much higher up the list themselves. They were the ones, after all, who'd encouraged the girl to go into the house in the first place.

Jess let out a sigh and then remembered that she hadn't called Harry yet. She picked up the phone, ran through the menu and pressed his number. He answered on the first ring.

'Hey,' she said. 'It's only me.'

'Got any news?'

'Yeah, I talked to Sam Kendall, but it's like I thought, she didn't know anything about Lynda going back. But she didn't dismiss it out of hand. And she reckons that Lynda may have kept quiet about it because she didn't want to get in any more trouble.'

'Right,' Harry said. 'So we still can't be sure one way or the other, although I can't see any reason for Becky to lie about it.'

'No, me neither. I think it's true, but we still don't know what she saw when she did go back. Apart from that light going on and off.'

'Which must have been Minnie. And we already knew she was still there.'

Jess played with the glass of wine, turning the stem around in her fingers. 'I've been going through the notes on the trial. Don't you think it's odd that Peck didn't try to dispose of the body?'

'I'm sure he meant to, only the police got there first.'

'But two days? Why would he wait that long? A child goes missing, there's going to be a search for her. He's a known sex offender who likes flashing at kids. He must have realised that the cops were going to come banging on his door before too long.'

'Well, it's not that easy to get rid of a body. She may have been small but she wasn't *that* small. Perhaps he was still planning how to do it. And don't forget, he didn't know about the other girls or that they were going to report what had happened. He probably assumed that Minnie had got into the house on her own. And as he didn't have any kind of record for actually abducting children, he might have reckoned that he was safe for a few more days.'

Jess pulled a face. 'Taking a bit of a chance, wasn't he?'

'And one that didn't pay off.'

'Mm,' Jess said. 'Unless he was telling the truth. Maybe he didn't know she was there.'

'Unlikely.'

'Well, it may be unlikely, but there's something going on here, something that Paige and co. want to keep covered up.'

'It's a big leap to go from there to claiming that Donald Peck was innocent.'

'Maybe. I don't suppose you know if Ralph Masterson is still around, do you? The retired probation officer? He was the guy that Peck went to visit that day.'

'I've no idea. What do you want to know for?'

'I just thought it might be interesting to talk to him, to hear his take on things. He must have known Peck pretty well. I was going to try the probation service, but I don't suppose they'd give me his number even if they did have it.'

'No, they probably wouldn't.'

'So if you have any contacts . . .'

Harry heaved out a sigh. 'Okay, I'll see what I can do.'

Jess knew he wasn't happy about the direction this investigation was taking, but she couldn't see what other choice they had. If they were going to discover the truth about the past, then any bit of information, from any source, could be useful. 'Thanks. I appreciate it.'

'Talk to you tomorrow, then.'

'Yeah, talk to you then. Good night.'

Jess put the phone down and yawned. She'd been staring at small print for most of the evening and her eyes felt tired and scratchy. Should she call it a night? But she was sure that somewhere in the piles of paper lay a clue that had been missed. Wearily, she pulled the trial reports towards her and started reading again.

23

It was almost three o'clock when Jess was abruptly woken up by a strident, high-pitched beeping sound. For a moment she lay there squinting into the darkness, before finally realising that it was the smoke alarm going off. Groaning, she pulled a pillow over her head, pressing it against her ears. 'Damn thing,' she muttered. It was the third time in a month that it had gone off for no apparent reason.

Eventually, knowing that she had to do something before it disturbed everyone else in the block, she threw off the duvet, forced herself out of bed and padded barefoot across the floor. It was only as she was opening the door to the living room that she became aware of the smell, the thick, acrid odour of something burning. What? Her brain, still fuzzy with sleep, couldn't process the information her senses were giving her. Her fingers fumbled for the light switch, but when she clicked it on, nothing happened.

Jess stood still, peering into the gloom. Everything seemed grey, as if the room was filled with a dense cloud of fog. She tried the switch again – on, off, on, off – but the electrics were clearly dead. Suddenly she heard a splintering noise, a crackling, before a lick of orange appeared by the far wall. It was followed by another, and another, until the licks turned into flames and the heat hit her in the face. It was only then that she fully woke up.

'Oh, Christ! No, no, no!' she yelped.

Quickly, Jess retreated into the bedroom, slamming the door behind her. She leaned against it, breathing heavily. Her heart was pounding in her chest, her pulse racing. *Try and stay calm*, she told herself. *Whatever you do, don't lose the plot.* With the living room alight, and the fire coming from the direction of the halls, there was no way she could get out that way. She would have to make her escape through the bedroom window. Luckily, she was on the ground floor.

A thin stream of smoke had started creeping under the door. She jumped away and raced across the room. It was only as she reached the window and pulled back the curtains that she recognised the fundamental flaw in her plan. With burglaries being what they were in London, her landlord had installed a sturdy set of iron bars. The grille could be opened with a key, but in the five years that she'd lived here, Jess had never used it. Where was the key? *Where was the bloody key?* She looked around, but couldn't remember where she'd put it. Frantically, she pulled at the bars, but they were too solid to budge. She reached between them to try and open the window – at least she could shout for help – but even though it was unlocked, that refused to budge too. She pushed and shoved at the handle, but the window wouldn't shift. What the hell was going on?

Jess glanced over her shoulder. There was more smoke coming into the bedroom. She had to call the fire service. Why hadn't she thought of that before? But her phone was on the table in the living room. God, she should have tried to grab it. Maybe she still could. Backtracking to the door, she opened it an inch but was met with an almighty wave of heat. By now the fire had really taken hold and the whole room was ablaze. She swiftly closed the door again. Her stomach lurched with fear and there were tears in her eyes, tears of fright and confusion. What next? *Think, think!*

Her brain stalled for a moment but then kicked into gear again. The first thing she had to do was to stall the encroaching smoke. Flinging open the wardrobe, she pulled a load of clothes off their hangers and laid them at the foot of the door. How long would that give her? A few minutes, perhaps. There was only one sure way out of this nightmare – she had to get through that damn window!

Stumbling back across the room, she tried the handle again, but although it turned, the window still wouldn't budge. She hammered on the glass with her fists. Would anybody hear her? The bedroom was set to the side of the flats, away from the street, and the next building was over twenty yards away, separated by a square of grass. There were no lights on in that house. Of course there weren't. It was the middle of the night.

The alarm had stopped screeching, silenced by the fire. She could imagine it there on the ceiling, a melted, dripping blob of plastic. But surely someone in her block would have been roused by the noise, would have realised what was going on? Surely someone would have made that 999 call?

The grey smoke was leaking in again, sliding between the sweaters and the shirts and the coats. Real panic was sweeping over her now. Sheer black fright, tight as a shroud, was squeezing out her last drops of courage. She crouched down by the door, desperately trying to stem the flow. It was useless. She could feel the smoke sliding into her throat, her lungs, eating away at her oxygen. Leaping up, she fled back to the window.

She'd have to break the glass. That was her only chance. At least then she might be able to grab some air. But what could she smash it with? What could she use? With her breath coming in short, fast pants, she picked up the small high-backed chair by the bed and slammed it against the wall. She felt a jarring run the length of her arm, but the chair remained in one piece. She swung it again, harder this time, and finally it broke, two of the legs splintering off and landing on the floor.

She bent down and grabbed one of the legs. Shoving it between the bars, she tried desperately to smash the pane. But the glass was thick, double-glazed, and no matter how hard she tried, it still refused to give. Something came into her head about going for the corners. She made a few final thrusts, but it was no good. She had no power left in her arms. Her strength was ebbing away, her body too weak to carry on.

Smoke was filling the room now, making her cough and

choke. *Get down on the floor*, her brain was telling her. *Smoke rises. Your only chance is to get down low.* She crumpled to her knees, fell sideways and curled into a ball. *Please God*, she prayed as she gasped for air. *Please God ...*

24

By the time Harry got to the hospital, it was twenty past five. Dawn was just beginning to break, the dark sky thinning to silver. A few light drops of rain pattered against the windscreen. He parked the car in a space near the entrance and went inside. As he strode through the maze of almost empty corridors, there was an eerie silence, relieved only by the occasional snore, the odd murmur or the light trilling of a phone. He couldn't help but remember the last time he'd been here, the time Ellen Shaw had been brought in after deliberately stepping out into the road. He had watched her from the window of the old office, watched her look carefully to the left, to the right and then . . .

He screwed up his face. Ellen had lived, and Jess would too. She was one of life's survivors. But a fire, a bloody fire! He knew the kind of damage that could cause. He had seen it when he'd been a cop. Quickly he tried to push those images out of his head. She must be conscious or she wouldn't have been able to give them his number to call. Unless they had found it in her wallet or her phone. The woman who had rung him had given only the barest of details.

He turned a corner and saw the sign that he'd been looking for: Highfield Ward. Hurrying forward, he pushed open the doors and peered through the semi-gloom. It only took a moment for him to spot her. Jess was perched on the side of a bed in the corner, dressed in a large white T-shirt and an untied flowery hospital gown. Her head was bowed, her eyes fixed on the floor as she gently swung her legs to and fro. He felt a wave of relief run through him.

She glanced up as he approached and gave a rueful smile. 'Sorry, I didn't know who else to call. I haven't got any money on me, and Neil's in Edinburgh and ... Well, I suppose I could have tried Sam, she might still have been working, but—'

'Hey, it's no problem,' he said, laying his hand lightly on her shoulder. He could see how shaken she was, even though she was trying hard not to show it. 'I'm glad you did. Are you okay? What happened?'

She shook her head. 'God knows. I woke up and the whole place was on fire. Apparently the guy across the hall raised the alarm.'

A nurse, a small blonde girl, came over and looked up at Harry. 'She's lucky to be alive. I was talking to one of the crew who brought her in, and they said that if it had been another five minutes—'

'Well, it wasn't,' Jess interrupted swiftly. 'And I'm fine. I didn't even lose consciousness. The doctor says I'm okay, so I may as well get off.'

'What the doctor said was that he'd like to keep you under observation for twenty-four hours.'

'There's no point,' Jess replied wearily. 'I haven't got any dizziness or nausea. And if I do start to feel ill I can always come back. No offence, but all I want to do is get out of here.'

'Well, you can't leave like that,' the nurse said, glancing down at Jess's bare feet. 'You can't walk through the hospital without any shoes on.'

Harry, who could see that Jess was adamant about leaving, flashed a smile at the nurse. 'Perhaps you have a pair we could borrow, just until she's in the car, then I'll bring them straight back.'

'I'm not sure if—'

'Five minutes,' Harry said. 'And I'll take good care of her, I promise. Like she said, we can always come back if she starts to feel unwell.'

The nurse put her hands on her hips and thought about it for a moment. Then, with the kind of sigh that suggested that she wasn't going to waste any further breath on trying to prevent the inevitable, she said, 'Okay, if you're absolutely sure. Wait here and I'll see what I can find.'

'Thanks,' Jess said to Harry as soon as the nurse had gone.

'Are you sure you shouldn't hang on for a while?'

She gave him a look. 'Oh please, not you as well. I'm fine. Anyway, the NHS is supposed to be short of beds. They should be glad to get rid of me.'

'I don't think it quite works like that. Still, if you've made up your mind ...'

'I have.'

Harry took off his jacket and passed it over to her. 'Then you'd better put this on. It's chilly outside.'

'You're a gent,' she said, taking off the gown and shrugging on the jacket over the smoke-stained T-shirt.

After a couple of minutes the nurse returned with a pair of yellow plastic shower shoes. 'Sorry,' she said. 'This was all I could find.'

'No problem,' Jess said, quickly standing up and slipping her feet into them. 'Thanks. I appreciate it.'

'You can drop them off at the main desk,' the nurse said to Harry. 'There's no need to come all the way back.'

'Thanks for your help. I'll do that.'

When they got to the car, Harry opened the passenger door for Jess and then switched on the engine and the heat before nipping back through the main doors of the hospital. On his return he opened the boot and rummaged around in his sports bag until he came up with a pair of white socks.

'Here,' he said, as he got in behind the wheel and handed the socks to her. 'And don't worry, they're clean.'

'Now you're spoiling me,' Jess said.

'Yeah, that's true, but I'm a sucker for a damsel in distress.' He drove out of the car park and headed for the main road. 'I'll take you back to my place and you can get your head down for a few hours.'

'I haven't got time to sleep,' she said. 'There's too much to do. I need to get to the bank, and call the insurance company. I have to pick up my car and buy some new clothes and sort out a computer and ...' As the full impact of what she had lost began to sink in, Jess leaned back and groaned. 'Jesus, everything's gone. I haven't even got a phone.'

'All of which we can sort out,' Harry said. 'After you've

had a shower and a sleep. It's still early. There's nothing you can do yet.'

Jess thought about this for a moment and then turned to look at him. 'Are you trying to tell me I smell, Mr Lind?'

He admired her attempt at levity, even if the lightness didn't quite reach her eyes. 'Eau de Smoke,' he said. 'Personally, I find it very appealing, but I'm not sure if it would be to everyone's taste.'

'You certainly know how to make a girl feel better when she's just lost all her worldly possessions.'

'I pride myself on it.' Harry gave her a wry smile. 'Look, all that really matters is that you're alive. All that other business ... well, they're just things, and most of them can be replaced. I can help you with that. It's just practical stuff. From what that nurse was saying, you're lucky to still be with us.'

'I think she may have been exaggerating.'

'Do you?'

Jess gave a light shrug. 'Always look on the bright side, right?'

'I wasn't being dismissive,' he said. 'I know it must be a complete nightmare. But it could have been a damn sight worse. All I'm trying to say in my cack-handed way is that you *can* deal with this.'

'Let's hope so,' she said softly.

She was quiet for a while, and Harry left her to her thoughts. The traffic was light, and it wasn't long before they were approaching Kellston. When they reached the high street, he glanced at her and asked, 'So, have you any idea how it happened?'

'Not a clue. Like I said, I woke up and the flat was on fire.' She paused, and when she spoke again her voice wavered a little. 'I . . . I tried to get the window open but it wouldn't budge. There's a grille across it and that was locked and I couldn't remember where I'd put the key. Then I tried to break the glass with a chair leg but it wouldn't break and by then the smoke was pouring into the bedroom.' She ran her fingers through her hair and groaned. 'I still don't understand why the window wouldn't open. *That* wasn't locked. I thought I could at least yell for help, try and raise the alarm, but . . .'

'Try not to think about it too much.'

Jess shuddered, huddling into the corner of her seat. She was silent again for a while, then she said, very softly, 'Do you think it could have been deliberate?'

Until this moment the thought hadn't even crossed Harry's mind. 'What makes you say that? It could have been anything, faulty electrics, something that was left on. You can't even be sure that it started in your flat.'

Her eyebrows shifted up a disbelieving fraction. 'I suppose.'

He suddenly knew what she was thinking: that Lynda Choi was dead, that David Choi and Sam Kendall had both been threatened – and that she had been next on the list. 'There'll be an investigation. Let's wait until we see the results before we go jumping to any conclusions.'

It was raining hard by the time Harry got back to Station Road. He pulled in by the newsagent's, turned off the engine and gazed out through the windscreen. Dawn had properly broken by now, but the sky remained dark and

215

gloomy, laden with thick plum-coloured clouds. Although it was still early, there were more people around than when he'd left. Most of them were walking quickly with their shoulders hunched and their umbrellas raised above their heads.

'So much for spring.' Harry glanced down at Jess's feet. 'Will you be okay without any shoes? I've got some trainers in the boot. They'll be kind of big for you, but at least they'll keep you dry.'

She unclipped her seat belt and shook her head. 'It's okay. I'll be fine.'

He could hear the tiredness in her voice and knew that she just wanted to get inside, to be somewhere safe and secure where she could order her thoughts and work out what to do next. He wished that he could think of something reassuring to say, something that might help, but nothing came to mind.

They got out of the car and ran for it, splashing through the puddles that had gathered on the uneven pavement. Harry slipped the key into the lock, opened the door and stood aside to let Jess in. As they climbed the stairs he said, 'The place is a bit of a mess, I'm afraid. I'm in the middle of decorating.'

'I wouldn't worry,' she replied drily. 'It can't look any worse than mine.'

A couple of minutes later they were inside the flat. The furniture was still covered with dust sheets and the distinctive smell of paint lingered in the air. He dragged the sheet off the leather sofa and flung it into a corner. 'Grab a seat,' he said. 'I'll put the kettle on.' As he went through to the kitchen, he pondered on why the typically British response to any crisis was to make a cup of tea. Was it a subconscious desire to maintain an air of normality, or simply the need to be *doing* something?

While the water was boiling he nipped into the bedroom and took his dark blue towelling dressing gown off the peg.

'This isn't a bad space,' Jess said as he came back into the living room. She'd forgone the offer of the sofa and was sitting by the window with her elbows on the table and her chin cupped in her hands. 'It'll look good when it's finished.'

Harry glanced around, wondering how he'd ever find the time. '*When* being the operative word.' He gave her the dressing gown. 'Here, put this on. It'll keep you warm.'

'Thanks,' she said. 'And for the loan of this,' she added, taking off his jacket and handing it back to him.

'You'd better take off those socks too. They must be soaked.'

Jess peeled off the wet socks, holding them up with the tips of her fingers. 'I'll give them a wash later.'

'That's okay. I'll sling them in the machine.' He took the socks through to the kitchen, dropped them in the wash basket and then made the tea. He carried the two mugs back into the living room and sat down opposite her. 'Are you hungry? I could make some breakfast, eggs, toast?'

'No thanks. I'm not hungry.'

'Well, help yourself when you get up. There's plenty of food in the fridge.'

'Okay,' she said. She took a quick sip of tea, her grey eyes gazing solemnly at him over the rim of the mug. 'And don't worry, I won't be in your hair for long. I'm sure the last thing you need is an unexpected house guest. I'll get something else sorted by the end of the day. I'm sure I can find a sofa to kip on, or I can always book into a hotel until Neil gets back.'

'Don't be crazy,' he said. 'You're more than welcome to stay as long as you need. I've got a spare room going begging. Why waste money on hotels?' He was about to add that she would need every penny she had at the moment, but wisely held his tongue. That fact, he was sure, was something she didn't need reminding of. Instead he said, 'That's if you can stand the colour scheme. It's not what you'd call restful.'

Jess hesitated, her hands clamped tightly around the mug. 'I don't want to impose.'

'You won't be,' he insisted. 'I'm hardly here anyway. I spend most of my time either downstairs in the office or out on the road. And I'm on surveillance all this week, the late shift over at the Locke place, so you'll even have the place to yourself in the evenings.'

'How's that going?' she asked. 'Have you observed any frolicking yet?'

Harry smiled. 'No frolicking to date, but it's early days. I'm going to Selene's tomorrow. Why don't you come with me?' He thought it might be a distraction for her, a temporary escape from all her troubles.

'Maybe. I'll see how things go.'

'Well, the offer's open if you fancy a night out. I might even throw in some chips. That's the casino rather than the potato kind.'

Jess put her mug to one side, most of the tea still remaining. 'And is that offer of a shower still open too?'

'Of course it is. There's plenty of hot water and you'll find clean towels in the cupboard. And there's a new toothbrush in the cabinet.' He gestured towards the hallway. 'The bathroom's second on the left and the spare room is next door. Try and get a few hours' sleep after. You've got a lot to do, and you'll do it better if you're not dog tired.'

Jess rose slowly to her feet as if every movement was an effort. Her eyelids looked droopingly heavy. 'Thanks again,' she said. 'You're a mate.'

While Jess was in the shower, Harry went through to the spare room and made up the bed. He put a fresh sheet over the bare mattress and threw on a duvet and a couple of pillows. The room was small but clean, and sparsely furnished with a single bed, a chest of drawers and a bedside table. The sunshine-yellow walls – reminiscent of the plastic shoes from the hospital – were overly bright, but didn't seem quite as startling once the curtains were pulled across and the lamp was turned on. Finally, realising that she would need something to sleep in, he dug out one of his T-shirts and left it on the bed.

Returning to the living room, Harry picked up a notepad and pen and pulled out a chair at the table. If he was going to keep his word about helping her, there were things to be done and lists to be made. He scribbled *car, phone, laptop, clothes, cash* before pausing to look out of the window. The rain was still bucketing down, the water streaming along the gutters of Station Road. He thought of Jess trying to smash the window in her own flat, of the fear she must have felt, the gut-wrenching panic. And he remembered the question she had asked about whether the fire could have been arson. He had been cautious in his response, not wanting to add to her anxiety. But what if her suspicions were spot on?

He tapped the end of the pen lightly against his teeth. It was already clear that her intended article about the Minnie Bright case had ruffled some feathers. People weren't happy, they weren't happy at all. Threats had been made, anonymous messages sent, damage inflicted. Maybe someone had decided to sort out the problem once and for all, to go straight for the roots instead of the branches. He didn't want to believe it, and yet he couldn't dismiss it. His forehead crunched into a frown. It was not beyond the bounds of possibility that someone *had* tried to shut her up for ever.

25

Connolly's is warm and steamy, smelling of fried bacon, coffee and damp coats. He's certain now that he has no tail, but while he waits at the counter, he remains alert to everyone who walks in through the door. There is no such thing as being too careful. He asks for a mug of tea and chooses a table near the wall. All the window seats are taken, but there is nothing to see anyway. The rain is falling hard, thrashing against the panes, and the view of the street is obscured.

He blows on the surface of his tea before he takes a sip. He's glad of the change in the weather, of the grey skies and chilly morning air. It suits his mood better. The sunshine belongs to Cadiz, to the towering castles of San Sebastian and Santa Catalina, to La Caleta beach and the boulevard. There is no place for it here.

It is seven o'clock in the morning and the café is busy. It is mainly men who are sitting at the tables, leafing through their tabloids, stocking up on calories before the day's work begins. There is a low hum of conversation, the tinny sound of a radio and the steady scraping of knives and forks against plates. His eyes quickly scan the room, looking for features that might ring a bell with him. Although there is no one here he remembers, *there is a familiarity about these men, about their tough East End faces, their stocky bodies and confident demeanour. They are comfortable in their own skin, devoid of self-doubt. Their lives are solid in a way his has rarely been, defined by the knowledge of who they are, of where they belong. Had things been different, he could have been one of them.*

He feels the cold finger of the past trailing up his spine. He tries to shake it off, but it's too late. He's a young boy again. How old? Six or seven, he thinks. He's sitting here with his mother, the long sleeves of her blue cardigan pulled down to hide the bruises on her arms. She is silent. Her eyes are empty, devoid of all emotion. Does she know how things are going to turn out? Perhaps she doesn't care. His father has already squeezed her dry of all hope and trust and love. She has nothing left to give, nothing left to say.

No, he doesn't wish to dwell on these things. He blinks hard, trying to erase the images from his mind. He doesn't need old ghosts whispering in his ear. How he became the man he is today is irrelevant. Only the present matters now. He glances around the room again, searching for distraction. He watches the guy behind the counter frying eggs. He listens to the shrill hiss of the coffee machine.

The door opens and a bull-necked man walks in with an attractive willowy blonde. Cops. He knows it instantly. Even out of uniform they have a look about them, an aura. He feels a frisson of alarm, a tightening in his chest, but quickly breathes again. There is nothing to be concerned about. They're not interested in him. Cowan Road station isn't far away; they've only come here to grab a coffee on their way to work.

Work. That is what he should be thinking about.

Everything has gone smoothly to date. The first part of his task has been completed, but he can't afford to relax. Every potential problem has to be examined, every obstruction removed. There is a thin line between success and failure, one wrong step and he could still . . .

A dull throbbing has started up in his temples. He rubs at his forehead. He never gets headaches in Cadiz. It is only when he's away that the old affliction returns to haunt him. In Spain, anchored by Anna, by his daily routine, he is always calm and contented. He stirs his tea, just for something to do. Soon, he'll be home soon. In the meantime he has to focus, to concentrate on the job in hand. His freedom came at a price and the bill still has to be paid.

26

Harry took a shower, ate some breakfast and then went downstairs and opened up the office. The first thing he did was to call Snakey Harris, a guy with a garage in Dalston, and persuade him – or rather bribe him – to get out of bed, go round to the flat in Hackney, pick up the Mini Cooper and bring it over to Kellston. Snakey was the kind of mechanic who always had spare keys for any make of car.

'I'll see you in an hour then,' Harry said.

'Two,' Snakey said. 'And that's stretching it. What's the registration?'

Harry didn't have a clue. He racked his brains, thinking back to the Fox, when he'd been standing beside the car with Jess, but still couldn't remember the number plate. 'Sorry, but there can't be that many bright red Mini Coopers parked in the street.'

Snakey made a snorting sound. 'You'd better be right, man, or you'll be paying for a fancy lawyer on top of everything else.'

'Just give me a call if you have any problems.'

'You can bet on it.'

After ensuring that Jess would have transport, Harry

raided the computer room and requisitioned a laptop that she could use until she got herself a new one. He also dug out an old mobile phone and started charging it up. He might not be top of anyone's list when it came to emotional support, but at least he could help with the practicalities.

Lorna and Mac arrived at eight thirty. Mac, predictably, raised his eyes to the ceiling on hearing the news, as if Jess had put a match to the building herself.

'Didn't I tell you? Wherever that girl goes, trouble's never far behind.'

'Have a heart,' Harry said. 'She's lost everything, her home, her clothes, all her worldly possessions.'

'Poor girl,' Lorna said sympathetically, peeling off her jacket and draping it neatly over the back of the chair. She gave Mac a glare. 'And I don't know why you're so down on her. You're hardly a stranger to trouble yourself.'

Mac, sensing a lecture coming on, gave a shrug of his burly shoulders and headed for his office. 'Some of us have got work to do.'

'Don't mind him,' Lorna said to Harry. 'I think it's great that you're helping her out. People need friends at a time like this. Let's make a list of what she might need and I can nip down the high street when we're done.'

'Thanks,' Harry replied. 'You're a star.'

Within twenty minutes, Lorna had compiled a comprehensive list of what she considered to be essentials. This included underwear, clothing, tights, socks, shoes, make-up, an array of toiletries – shampoo, conditioner, cleanser, toner, moisturiser and cotton wool – and a toothbrush and comb.

'Right,' she said, surveying the page. 'I think that's it. Anything else spring to mind?'

Harry gazed down at the list of items. 'You women take a lot of maintenance.'

Lorna laughed. 'These are just the basics, sweetie. But I guess she can pick up the rest as she goes along. Now, what about size for the clothes? I'll just get a few T-shirts and a pair of joggers. Oh, and perhaps a sweater. It's turned a bit cold today. What is she – a ten, a twelve?'

He stared blankly back at her. 'You've met her, haven't you?'

'That was years ago, Harry. And it was only the once.'

'Ah,' he said. 'Well, she's about five foot five, slim and er . . .'

Lorna gave a sigh. 'Try and think of someone who's about the same size. Debbie, Elaine, the girl who works in the newsagent's, an actress off *EastEnders*?'

Harry, who never watched *EastEnders*, had to peruse his brain bank for women closer to home. 'Yeah,' he said. 'I suppose she's about the same size as Debbie. Only Jess has a bit more, you know, on top.'

'How much more?'

Harry frowned, not entirely comfortable with discussing breast size with Lorna. 'A few inches,' he said vaguely.

Lorna shook her head. 'Oh, don't worry about it. I'll just buy stretchy stuff. Can you take care of reception while I'm gone?'

'Sure,' Harry said, rising to his feet. 'And take the money out of petty cash. I'll square up with you later.'

As soon as Lorna had gone, Harry returned to his own

office, leaving the door open so he could hear if anyone came in off the street. He had another call to make, this time to the Fire Service. He didn't know anyone at the Hackney station, but he did have a contact in Shoreditch.

Jeff Bryant finally came on the line after he had been on hold for five minutes. 'Hey, Harry mate. Sorry to keep you waiting. Long time no see. How are you doing?'

They had a quick catch-up, exchanging the usual banter and agreeing that a drink was well overdue. Once the preliminaries had been completed, Harry explained about the fire at Jess's flat. 'I was wondering if you could check as to whether it was accidental or not.'

'I'll make a few calls, see what I can find out. If it's suspicious it will have gone to the Fire Investigation Unit. I'll ring you back later.'

'Thanks. I owe you one.'

'You can buy me that pint sometime.'

Harry put the phone down. There was nothing he could do now but sit and wait. He glanced out of the window. The rain had eased off a little, but the sky remained dark and gloomy. There was no sign of Snakey Harris, but that was hardly surprising. The traffic was bad, the cars and buses crawling slowly along Station Road.

Mac walked out of his office, put his hands on his hips and stared at the empty reception desk. Frowning, he looked over his shoulder at Harry. 'Is anyone planning on doing any work round here today?'

'I'm sure she won't be long.'

'Jesus,' he muttered. 'Why does that woman feel the need to mother every waif and stray she comes across?'

227

Harry grinned, silently thanking God for Lorna's maternal instincts. Left to his own devices he wouldn't have had much of a clue as to what to buy. At least Jess would have something to wear when she woke up.

Before Mac could get the hump about two members of Mackenzie, Lind being overly preoccupied with something other than the business, Harry reached across his desk, picked up the file on Aimee Locke and flipped it open. It made for slim reading. Apart from the cleaner, and the one visit from her crimper – the jury was still out on whether that was personal or professional – there had been no other activity. Still, it was early days. The surveillance had only just begun.

Harry rubbed at his eyes and suppressed a yawn. Although the lights in the Locke house had gone out at midnight, he had stayed in Walpole Close until one o'clock. He'd only been home for a few hours when the call had come from the hospital. He was due to take over the watch again at five. If he was going to stay awake tonight, he'd have to dose himself up with black coffee.

He put the Locke file to one side and reached into his in-tray, retrieving Jess's file on the Minnie Bright case. Last night he had gone through it from cover to cover and found not one jot of evidence that might point to Donald Peck's conviction being unsafe. Yet something was still niggling in the back of his mind. Slowly, he started leafing through the pages again.

27

DI Valerie Middleton strode out through the doors on to the wet steps of the courthouse. Here she stopped for a moment, ran the palm of her hand over the top of her head to wipe away the rain and took a few deep satisfied breaths. That was one more predator off the streets, although she was realistic enough to know that the space wouldn't remain vacant for long. Still, at least the women of Kellston could sleep a little more soundly tonight knowing that Colin Faulkner was safely behind bars. Twelve rapes that they knew about, but there were probably more. Her only regret was that they hadn't caught him sooner.

As she put up her umbrella, she was joined on the steps by DI Simon Wetherby. He was based in King's Cross – another of Faulkner's hunting grounds – and the two of them had worked together on the case for the past three months.

'Good result,' he said, smiling widely.

'Not too shabby,' she agreed. The jury, having slept on it overnight, had come straight back into court with a verdict of guilty.

'Fancy a drink?'

'What, now?' Valerie glanced at her watch and saw that it was ten past ten. 'Tempting, but it's a bit early for me.'

'Tonight then,' he said. 'Come on, I can't celebrate on my own. And we deserve a reward after all the hours we've put in.'

Valerie couldn't argue with that, but still she hesitated. Unless her female intuition was failing her, she suspected that Simon was after more than just a pint of bitter. Although she had grown to both respect and like him in the months they'd been working together, she couldn't see it going any further. She was still involved with Harry Lind, albeit in an ill-defined, confusing kind of way, and didn't need any more complications in her life.

'Sorry,' she said. 'I'm not really sure what I'm doing. Maybe some other time.'

'Well, the offer's open. Give me a call if you ever find yourself at a loose end.'

She nodded. 'Thanks, I will.'

'Well, it's been a blast. We should do it again.' He touched her briefly on the shoulder. 'Take care of yourself, Valerie.'

She watched as he jogged down the steps, a small twinge of regret tugging at her insides. It was odd to think of not seeing him every day; they'd spent so much time in each other's company that she'd grown used to having him around. Wetherby was a tall, broad-shouldered guy, confident and amusing, although perhaps a touch too handsome for his own good. He also had a reputation for being a ladies' man. Not that you could always trust station gossip. She wondered if she'd made a mistake in turning him down, but instantly pushed the thought away.

Switching her attention to her phone, Valerie discovered that she'd missed a couple of calls from her sergeant, Kieran Swann. Now *there* was a man who could irritate the hell out of her without even trying. He'd left a message, but she didn't bother listening to it. Instead she rang him straight back.

'It's me. What's happening?'

'We've got the body of a young woman, guv, on the Mansfield. Strangled by the looks of it.'

Valerie felt the familiar sinking sensation she always got when hearing that a life had been prematurely snuffed out. 'Okay,' she said with a sigh. 'I'm on my way. Tell me where you are.'

She walked quickly to the car park, got into her black BMW and twenty-five minutes later was driving down the main thoroughfare of the Mansfield Estate. She needn't have bothered asking Swann for the exact location, as a large crowd had already gathered around the entrance to Haslow House. 'Ghouls,' she murmured. What was it that drew people to murder scenes? Part of it was just natural curiosity, but there was something more. It was a kind of morbid fascination, she thought, a desire to share vicariously in the horror of it all.

Valerie pulled the BMW up next to a couple of squad cars and switched off the engine. She paused a moment to prepare herself, taking a few deep breaths. Every time she came back to this place she was reminded of the Whisperer. It was here that he'd left one of his sinister notes, tucked beneath her windscreen wipers, the last message before . . .

No, she wasn't going there again. If she allowed him to crawl back inside her head, then she'd never be rid of him. She had to get on with the job and leave the past where it belonged.

Adjusting the rear-view mirror, she glanced at her reflection. A pair of hazel eyes gazed solemnly back at her. In a few years' time she'd be forty, and already some fine lines were beginning to show. She frowned. That was something else that she didn't want to dwell on. Her long fair hair, sleek and shiny, was neatly tied back, but still she lifted her hand to make an unnecessary adjustment. Then, with a final sigh, she got out of the car and began to walk in the direction of the crowd.

The Mansfield Estate was depressing at the best of times. She reckoned that at least ninety per cent of the local crime emanated from the three tall towers. Too many struggling, blank-eyed people crammed together in an environment that was drenched in hopelessness. Her gaze took in the crumbling concrete, the litter and graffiti. She hated the goddamn place but at least she didn't have to live in it.

DS Swann was the first to notice her. He lifted the tape as she approached and gave her a nod.

'Guv.'

Kieran Swann was a bull-necked, stocky guy, a few years older and a couple of inches shorter than herself. Today he did what he always did when she was wearing heels, tilting his head and peering up at her in that false exaggerated way, as if her greater height was some kind of slight on his masculinity. There had been a time when she had thought they would never work effectively together, but things had mellowed since then. Swann was still annoying, but you couldn't hate a man who had once saved your life.

'So, what have we got?' she asked.

He started walking with her towards the door. 'Her name's Becky Hibbert, twenty-four years old. She lives ... lived ... here in Haslow House, tenth floor. The ME's been and gone. He reckons she was killed sometime late last night, early this morning. Can't say more accurately than that at the moment. She was strangled with the scarf she was wearing.'

'Who found her?'

'A couple of fourteen-year-olds,' Swann said. He flipped open his notebook. 'Josh White and Adam Pearse. It was Pearse who recognised her. He lives on the same landing. They're down at the station now, but I don't reckon they had anything to do with it. This was just somewhere they liked to hang out.'

Valerie wrinkled her nose. 'Nice taste in locations.'

'Yeah, but a good place to go and smoke dope, especially if you don't want anyone seeing you.'

'What about the victim's family?' she asked.

'The mother's called Carol Hibbert. She's been informed. Becky had two kids and Carol was taking care of them overnight. She lives here too, a couple of floors down. No current boyfriend that the mother is aware of.'

'What about the father of the kids?'

'Dan Livesey. They split up about six months ago. He's a doorman apparently, but we've got no current address. We're trying to track him down at the moment.'

'So, do we know where Becky went last night?'

'She said she was meeting up at the Fox with the girls from work – that's the Asda on the high street – but we haven't been able to confirm anything yet. I've sent Lister and Franks to see what they can find out.'

Valerie couldn't fault Swann's efficiency. In the time it had taken for her to get here from the court, he had set all the necessary wheels in motion. They stopped at the entrance to the building and she took off her shoes and slipped one of the protective jumpsuits over her clothes. She could see the scene-of-crime officers swarming around inside, hoping to pick up some essential DNA evidence. She tried to prepare herself mentally, to cut herself off from all emotional responses. The only thing she could do for Becky Hibbert now was to try to find her killer.

'Okay, let's go,' she said, nodding at Swann.

Inside, to the left, were the graffiti-covered lifts. To the right lay a flight of grey stone steps and beneath the steps was a space – usually dark and dank, she imagined, but now illuminated by the harsh police lights – that was set back and invisible from the foyer. It was here that the body was lying. A couple of members of the SOCO team stood up and drew back to give her a clearer view.

Becky Hibbert was lying sprawled on her side, her bulging eyes still open, her face tinged with blue. She was an overweight girl dressed in a short black miniskirt and a low-cut glittery top. The long pink scarf she'd been strangled with was still wrapped tightly around her neck.

'Any sign of a handbag?' Valerie asked Swann.

He shook his head. 'Still missing, along with her phone. We got a description of the bag from the mother. She reckons she had about thirty quid on her when she went out.'

'So probably a lot less by the time she got back. Mind, there are some lowlifes around here who'd kill their grannies for a fiver.'

'True enough.'

Valerie continued to gaze down at the body, at the large fleshy legs and freckled arms. 'Do we know if there was any kind of sexual assault?'

'Nothing obvious, her underwear's still on, but we'll find out for sure later. And no signs of a struggle. It looks like she was taken by surprise.'

'If it was a robbery, why kill her, though? Why not just threaten her with a knife or hit her over the head? It takes a lot of effort to strangle someone.'

'Well, there are some right shitbags on this estate. But like you said, there are easier ways to relieve a girl of her cash.'

Valerie left orders for the body to be removed and then headed out of the door with Swann. 'She could have met her attacker at the pub and brought him back here.'

'A bit risky for him. The girls she was with would be able to give a description.'

'He might not have been intending to kill her at that point.' She glanced back at the flats. 'They could have come back here and had some kind of argument. It gets out of hand and before you know it . . .' She stripped off the jumpsuit and squeezed her feet back into her shoes. 'Have we run a check on her?'

'Two charges of shoplifting. That was a couple of years back. She's been clean since then.'

'Nothing else? No soliciting?'

Swann clicked his tongue. 'You think she might have been on the game?'

Valerie gave a light shrug. There had been a lot of cleavage on show, but that was hardly unusual these days. She wasn't making presumptions – just because you wore a miniskirt, were short of a few bob and lived on a lousy estate didn't mean that you'd resort to selling your body – but she had to keep an open mind and consider every possibility. 'Well, she wouldn't be the first woman to try and raise some extra cash. She had two kids to support and I doubt she earned much at the supermarket.'

Glancing over his shoulder, Swann gave an indelicate snigger. 'Wouldn't exactly have been queuing up, would they?'

Valerie threw him a look but didn't pull him up about it. Coppers dealt with violent death in different ways, not all of them tasteful or politically correct. She thought of the Whisperer, a man with a pathological hatred of prostitutes, and felt a clammy shiver run the length of her spine. As if he was still out there, still waiting to pounce, an irrational fear rose up from her gut. Before it could take hold, she quickly swallowed it back down.

'Right,' she said briskly. 'Let's go and check out the flat, and then we'll talk to the mother.'

Becky Hibbert's flat wasn't the cleanest Valerie had ever come across. It smelled bad too, almost as bad as the lift they'd come up in. She left Swann to search the kitchen, strewn with used plates, dirty nappies and takeaway boxes, and made a start on the living room. It wasn't much better in there. With kids' toys littered all over the floor, she had to be careful not to trip and turn an ankle. There was grime on every surface, a stickiness that was a combination of spilled drinks, dust and God alone knew what else. She puckered her lips, not wanting to think about it.

After pulling on a pair of gloves, she started with the coffee table, sifting through magazines, old copies of the *Sun* and a few unpaid bills. Nothing of any interest. She moved on to a mock-mahogany cupboard in the corner. The bottom part was stuffed with even more toys – teddy bears, cars and brightly coloured trains – along with three packs of unopened nappies, a heap of baby clothes and a pile of DVDs. She had a quick flick through the latter. They were romantic comedies mainly, with a few action movies thrown in.

There were two drawers at the top of the cupboard. She opened the left one first and found it jammed full of paperwork. Old bills, receipts and payslips by the looks of it, but there could be something useful hidden there. Not wanting to go through them one by one, she bagged the lot to be perused more carefully back at the station. The right-hand drawer yielded a similar amount of chaos, this of a more general variety – buttons and elastic bands, bits of ribbon and string, a pair of scissors, four half-empty bottles of congealed nail polish and a couple of combs.

Within fifteen minutes she'd finished the search and had moved on to Becky Hibbert's bedroom. It was at this point that Swann appeared at the door, waving a bagged wad of cash in her direction.

'Under the tea bags,' he said. 'Not very original, but there you go.'

'How much?'

'Five hundred and twenty. So either our victim was a very careful saver, or she's been making a bundle on the side. Maybe your hunch was spot-on. Maybe she was a tom.'

'It wasn't a hunch exactly. I was simply covering all the possibilities.'

'Yeah, guv,' Swann said, grinning slyly, as if amused by the correction. 'Still, you could be right.'

Valerie stared at the money for a moment before shaking her head. If Becky had picked up a punter, she could have brought him back to the flats. Perhaps she had changed her mind at the last moment, or perhaps she had just chosen the wrong guy. 'Okay, let's finish off here and we'll see if the mother can shed any light on it.'

It was only five minutes before Swann appeared again. 'Something else,' he said, holding out another clear bag. 'It was under all that mess on the table.'

Valerie reached out and took the bag from him. Inside was a small white business card. She frowned. *Jessica Vaughan.* It was a name that was familiar to her. 'A reporter,' she said. 'What the hell would she want with Becky Hibbert?'

'There's more, guv. Look on the other side.'

Valerie flipped the card over and her heart instantly sank. There, scrawled in blue biro, was Harry Lind's name and phone number. Oh great, this was all she needed. She now had not only a murder victim on her hands, but also a boyfriend – if she could still call him that – who might be involved in some way. Today was just getting better and better.

28

By the time they got back to the station, Valerie was feeling drained. It was always the worst part of the job, dealing with bereaved relatives, and this occasion had been no different. Carol Hibbert had been in a state of shock, her mouth opening and closing, her hands constantly wrestling in her lap. 'I don't understand,' she had kept on repeating, over and over again.

They had not been able to learn anything new. Carol, an overweight woman in her late forties, had been taking care of the kids in her own flat and hadn't expected Becky to pick them up until the morning. She hadn't reported her missing because she hadn't known that she was. So far as she was concerned, her daughter had gone out to meet some friends the night before and was probably still sleeping off the effects of too many drinks.

Valerie had enquired about Dan Livesey, but Carol had no address or phone number for him. 'She ain't seen him in weeks. He's a bloody waste of space.'

Carol Hibbert hadn't been able to enlighten them as to where the money had come from either. There was no good way of asking a mother whether her daughter might have been on the game, but Valerie had tried to do it as subtly as she could. 'Do you have any idea where she might have got this amount of cash? I mean, could she have won it, or borrowed it off someone? A loan perhaps?'

'She didn't have no cash,' Carol had said insistently. 'Who's gonna loan my Becky a sum like that?' And then, as if the knowledge that her daughter was gone for ever had finally sunk in, her face had crumpled and the tears had started to flow down her cheeks.

Valerie had tried hard not to look at the children, at the baby in the cot and the toddler playing on the floor. Two kids who no longer had a mother. Leaning forward, she had laid her hand gently on the other woman's arm. 'I'm so sorry. We'll do everything we can to find out who did this.'

She and Swann had left shortly after and returned to Cowan Road. Now Valerie was sitting at her desk, reviewing the information to date. The news on the forensic front wasn't promising. The ground surrounding the body had been littered with used needles, dead reefers, cigarette stubs, burnt foil, empty cans and the accumulated debris of what could have been years. Finding a trace of their killer was going to be hard. The post-mortem, however, might yield more useful results. It would, with luck, be carried out this afternoon.

Door-to-door enquiries were currently taking place at Haslow House, but Valerie didn't hold out much hope on that front. The residents of the estate were always tight-lipped when it came to talking to the police. Even the murder of a young woman wouldn't be enough to shake them out of their reticence. It was common knowledge on the Mansfield that the only way to survive was to keep your head down and your mouth shut.

DC Joanne Lister and DC David Franks knocked on the door to her tiny office and came in with their notebooks at the ready. Lister was a small, pale-faced girl in her mid-twenties with a mop of curly red hair. David Franks, who played in the Police Rugby League, was a couple of years older and at least a foot taller. The two of them were often partnered up together – they made a good team – and the difference in their physical appearance usually made Valerie smile. Today, however, her lips didn't even twitch.

'So, what have we got?' she asked.

It was Lister who answered. 'We talked to the other girls at the supermarket. There were five of them who met up at the Fox at seven thirty. It was one of the girls' birthdays, Kara Dean, and it was a fairly boozy evening from the sound of it. However, none of them remember Becky Hibbert talking to a bloke – or to anyone other than themselves. They don't remember her making or receiving any calls either. She left at the same time as the others, at around twenty past eleven, and walked up the high street with Kara Dean and ...' Lister glanced down at her notebook. 'Yes, Kara Dean and Chelsea Williams. They both live on the Mansfield, but not in the same block. Dean and Williams live in Carlton House. They separated from Becky at the fork in the path and that was the last time they saw her. That would have been at about a quarter to twelve.'

'And they didn't hear anything? Didn't see anyone hanging about?'

'Only a few of the local youths. Four or five, they think. But they didn't speak to them.'

'Do we have any names, addresses?' Valerie asked.

Lister shook her head. 'They claim they've seen the lads around but don't know who they are or where they live.'

Valerie wondered if the two girls were telling the truth. Even with their friend murdered, they could still be reluctant to cause any trouble for the locals – trouble that could well come back to haunt them. 'Anything else?'

DC Franks said, 'The landlady of the Fox, Maggie McConnell, remembers the group but nothing about Becky in particular. They're regulars apparently, always lively but never any trouble. She backs up their story as regards the time they left.'

Valerie gave a nod. 'Did any of the girls know if Becky Hibbert had a boyfriend?'

Franks shook his head. 'She hadn't mentioned anyone new. But the relationship with the ex sounds like it was pretty stormy. Constant rows over child support, or rather the lack of it.'

'Okay, thanks,' Valerie said. 'Look, I brought back a load of paperwork from Becky Hibbert's flat. One of you start going through it, will you? There may be an address or a phone number for Livesey in there somewhere.'

She saw the look on their faces and felt their disappointment. A murder inquiry and they were stuck with the boring task of searching through a heap of utility bills. 'Problem?' Valerie asked.

'No, guv,' Franks said with an air of resignation. 'No problem at all. I'll get straight on to it.'

Valerie nodded at Lister. 'And you can chase up any CCTV coverage there may be of the area.'

The two officers left the room and Valerie sat back in her chair. Could this have been a domestic? The first direction the police usually looked in a murder inquiry was towards the nearest and dearest. Perhaps Dan Livesey had grown tired of his parental obligations or of Becky's complaints and decided to have it out with her once and for all. Rows could easily escalate into something more violent. They would need to find him quickly, if for no other reason than to rule him out as a suspect.

Becky might have received or made a call before she'd gone out, perhaps arranging to meet someone after the evening with her friends was over. Swann was currently chasing up the phone records, but she knew from past experience that it could take a while for the results to come through. And where had that money come from? Not from Livesey, if his past record was anything to go by.

Of course, the killer wasn't necessarily male. She couldn't rule out the possibility of a woman being responsible. But on balance she was more inclined towards it being a man. Strangulation was a relatively slow and brutal way to kill, involving a particular kind of strength and perseverance. The perpetrator had to hold their nerve – and their grip – while the life of the victim gradually ebbed away.

Valerie leaned forward and picked up the small plastic bag with Jessica Vaughan's card inside. Her mouth slid into a thin, tight line. This was the second murder victim that Vaughan had been connected to. The first had been several years back at Ray Stagg's old club in Shoreditch, when she'd discovered the body of a barman in the car park. Harry had been working with Vaughan on that occasion and it looked like he had got himself involved with her again. So how come he hadn't mentioned it when they'd had a drink together on Sunday night? Or when she'd talked to him on the phone only *last* night? His silence on the subject resurrected old suspicions.

Valerie had been convinced that something was going on between the two of them back then, although she'd never been able to prove it. It had been at the time when she and Harry were on the verge of splitting up, when their relationship was gradually disintegrating, every day a trial, every conversation rapidly descending into an argument. Had he cheated on her, slept with another woman? It might be old history, but somehow it still mattered.

She stared down at the card. Who should she call first – Vaughan or Harry? She decided on the latter. Reporters were hardly renowned for their openness or cooperation. And Vaughan especially was adept at the art of evasion. At least *he*, as an ex-cop, might give her some straight answers. Yes, she would start with Harry and see what he had to say for himself. But first she was going to get herself a strong cup of coffee. She was probably going to need it.

29

It was almost midday before Snakey Harris finally turned up with the Mini. Harry, who'd been keeping an eye on the street, saw him arrive and went down to meet him. Snakey was a tall, lean-faced man in his early fifties with sad brown eyes and closely cropped salt-and-pepper hair. The lower part of his face had a permanent purplish tinge, as if he was in constant need of a shave.

Harry passed the cash over and thanked Snakey for his trouble. As they shook hands, he couldn't help but notice the tattoo of the slim blue-green asp coiled around the mechanic's wrist, its head resting neatly between his thumb and forefinger.

'I appreciate your help,' he said. 'Even if you have taken several hours longer than you said you would.'

'Sorry about that, Mr Lind. I had an urgent call-out or I'd have been here sooner.'

Despite being told to call him Harry on numerous occasions, the invitation had never been taken up. Harry wasn't sure if that was because he'd still been a cop when they'd first met, or because Snakey preferred to keep things on a purely professional footing.

'Better check it's the right car before I go,' Snakey said.

Harry bent down and peered through the passenger window. The Mini was clean and tidy inside, with nothing to indicate whether it was Jess's or not. He glanced back over his shoulder. 'It was the only red Mini Cooper there, right?'

'The only one that I could see, Mr Lind.'

'Okay.' Harry straightened up and nodded. If it was the wrong one, he'd have a lot of explaining to do to the local constabulary. 'Thanks. I'm sure this must be it.'

'I'll be off then.'

'Do you need a lift back to Dalston?'

Snakey shook his head and gestured towards a red Mazda MX-5 parked a little way down the road. 'I'm sorted, ta.'

Inside the sports car, a glamorous brunette was busy reapplying her lipstick in the rear-view mirror. Snakey Harris, for some reason Harry had yet to fathom, acquired one beautiful girlfriend after another. How did he do it? The man had a certain laconic charm, but he was hardly George Clooney.

Harry was still pondering this mystery as he made his way back up the stairs. He had almost reached the landing when his mobile started ringing. He took it out of his pocket and checked the screen. It was Valerie.

'Hey, Val. How's things?'

'I've got a question for you.'

He could tell from her abruptness and the coolness of her voice that this wasn't a social call. 'Okay. Fire away.'

'Would you like to explain to me what your connection is to Becky Hibbert?'

He frowned. 'What?'

'Becky Hibbert,' she repeated. 'One of Jessica Vaughan's business cards was found at her flat with your name and number written on the back.'

Harry stopped, his hand tightening around the phone. It only took him a second to realise that something bad had occurred. If the police had been searching Becky's flat, if Valerie was dealing personally with it, then it could only mean one thing. 'What's happened to her?'

There was a short pause on the other end of the line. 'You haven't answered my question.'

'And you haven't answered mine. For God's sake, Val, just tell me what this is all about.'

He heard a small intake of breath before she answered. 'Becky Hibbert was found murdered this morning at the Mansfield. She'd been strangled.'

Harry felt a constriction in his own throat. 'Christ,' he murmured. 'You're kidding.'

'Hardly. So, if you wouldn't mind explaining what she was doing with your number.'

'It's a long story.'

'Then the sooner you start telling it, the sooner I can get on with this murder inquiry.'

'I'll come down the station,' he said, preferring to speak to her face to face. 'Fifteen minutes, yeah? I'll see you then.' He hung up before she had the chance to say anything else. A chill ran through him as he thought first about Becky Hibbert's untimely death and then the fire at Jess's place. Surely it couldn't be a coincidence that those two things had happened on the same night? He raised his eyes towards the flat, where Jess was still sleeping. She, at least, had had a lucky escape.

Harry stood for a while at the top of the stairs, going over the facts in his head. He thought about Becky Hibbert's phone call and her fear that someone would find out that she'd spoken to him. Had that someone decided that she was a loose cannon, that she couldn't be trusted to keep her mouth shut? Or had they found out that she *had* talked? Maybe she'd known more than she'd said. Or maybe, hidden in her words, was a clue to what had really happened on the day Minnie Bright died. Well, whatever the truth, she would never be the one to speak it now.

Harry let Lorna know that he'd be out for a while, grabbed his jacket from his office and headed back down the stairs to his car. As he drove, he considered the possibility that Becky's death was unrelated to the murder of Minnie Bright. After all, he knew nothing about her life or what she might have been involved in. She could even have been a random victim. But then his thoughts returned to the fire at Jess's flat. Although he was still waiting on the call from Jeff Bryant, there was now little doubt in his mind as to what the news would be.

He parked the car as close as he could to the building and walked the rest of the way. As he stepped through the sliding doors and into the warmth of the foyer, he was met by the usual hustle and bustle of a police station. Thankfully, there was only a short queue at the desk. After a brief wait he approached the middle-aged PC at the counter, gave the man a nod and said, 'Harry Lind. I'm here to see DI Middleton. She's expecting me.'

'Take a seat,' the PC said, gesturing towards a row of plastic chairs. 'I'll let her know you're here.'

Harry sat down, leaned back and looked around. It was a long time since he'd last been here, but the territory was completely familiar to him, from the magnolia walls, through the midday drunks and nervous witnesses, to the strong, persistent smell of disinfectant. He was suddenly assailed by two contradictory feelings, one of belonging and the other of utter estrangement. It was as if his past and present had come together and temporarily knocked him out of kilter. But he had plenty of time to regain his equilibrium. It was another twenty minutes before Valerie finally graced him with her presence.

She gave him a thin smile as she came through the locked glass door into the foyer, but that was the sum total of her greeting. There was no apology for keeping him waiting. 'This way,' she said brusquely, opening another door that led off to the right.

Harry rose to his feet and followed her. He noticed that she was wearing one of her smarter suits, a grey pinstripe with a white blouse underneath. She'd either been in court or had an important meeting to attend. As she strode along the corridor, her high heels made a sharp tapping sound against the lino.

The room was the same as every other interview room Harry had ever been in, small and soulless, with a single high window, a table with four chairs and a scuffed and stained floor. There was another, smaller table set off to the side holding a bank of recording equipment.

Valerie sat down and laid her notepad and pen on the

table. 'So,' she said. 'What have you got to tell me?' Her voice was as chilly as it had been on the phone.

He sat down opposite her. Under different circumstances he might have been put out by her manner, but he understood that she was under pressure and that his involvement in the case, however peripheral, was a complication that she really didn't need. 'How's the investigation going?'

She frowned, ignoring the question. 'Harry, as I'm sure you appreciate, I'm pretty busy at the moment. Can you please just tell me what Becky Hibbert was doing with your phone number?'

He would usually have been cautious about what he told the police regarding a client – no one wanted a private detective who blabbed about their business as soon as the law started asking questions – but this was a murder inquiry. Anyway, Sam Kendall had already reported events to her local station, so he wouldn't be betraying a confidence. Accordingly, he gave a concise summary of the situation, of the damage to Sam's car, the malicious notes and her connection to the killing of a child. He saw Valerie's face go blank when he mentioned Minnie Bright and realised that she probably didn't remember the case. At the time in question she hadn't even been working in London.

'She was a ten-year-old girl who was murdered in Kellston in 1998,' he explained. 'A man called Donald Peck, a known sex offender, was convicted and sent down for life. He hanged himself in prison. Sam was one of the girls who was with Minnie on the day she was killed. As was Becky Hibbert.'

Valerie's frown deepened. 'So what are you saying – that

Becky Hibbert's murder is connected to this other one?'

'I'm not saying anything of the sort. I'm just telling you the facts. It's up to you what you do with them.'

There was a brief silence before Valerie waved her hand impatiently and said, 'Go on. I'm presuming there's more.'

'Well, it was Jess Vaughan who introduced Sam to me. Jess was writing an article about Minnie Bright's murder, and—'

At the mention of Jess's name, Valerie's mouth turned down at the corners. 'Very tasteful,' she murmured.

Although it was obviously a mistake to attempt to mount any kind of defence of Jess's motives – Valerie had always disliked her – the words slipped out before he'd really thought them through. 'Actually, the piece was going to be about the ongoing effect that murder has on other people, how some learn how to cope with the trauma and others don't.'

'Yes,' Valerie replied drily. 'I'm sure there was nothing salacious about it at all. But can we get to the point, do you think? You still haven't explained why Becky Hibbert had your number.'

Harry told her about how Paige Fielding and Becky had agreed to be interviewed but had then changed their minds. 'Jess thought there was something odd about it, especially because they'd seemed so keen when she'd first approached them. She went to see Becky again to try and find out what was going on, and by this point Sam Kendall was my client so she left my number too in case Becky felt more comfortable talking to me.'

'Why should she?' Valerie asked. 'I mean, why should Becky feel more comfortable?'

He gave a shrug, deciding that it was probably best not to mention Jess's threat to ring Social Services. 'Because I'm not a journalist?'

Valerie narrowed her eyes as if this explanation was far from adequate. 'And did she call?'

Harry nodded. 'Yesterday morning. She sounded nervous, agitated.' He paused, and then added, 'No, more than that. She was scared. She seemed scared that someone would find out that she'd talked.'

Valerie leaned forward, putting her elbows on the table. 'What did she say to you?'

He explained what Becky had told him about Lynda Choi and the phone calls she'd made on the night she'd drowned. 'Look, Val, I don't know if any of this is relevant. It may have nothing to do with Becky Hibbert's murder. Have you talked to Paige Fielding yet? She was a friend of Becky's. She may be able to tell you more.'

'Have you got a number for her, an address?'

'Not on me, but I can text it through to you. It's in the office. You may want to talk to Fielding's boyfriend too. He's a nasty bit of work called Micky Higgs.'

'Okay. Thanks.' Valerie wrote down the names before glancing up at him again. 'So, is that everything? There's nothing else I should know?'

'Well, there is other one other thing. Last night someone set fire to the block of flats Jess lives in over in Hackney. We don't know if it was deliberate yet. I'm still waiting to hear back from Jeff Bryant.'

Valerie assumed the same expression he had seen on Mac's face earlier in the day, a kind of resigned acceptance

253

that trouble and Jessica Vaughan were rarely apart for long. 'No one hurt, I hope.'

'No, nothing too serious. Shall I ask Jess to give you a call?'

'No need,' she said. 'I can do it myself.'

'Not on the number you've got,' he said. 'Her phone was destroyed in the fire along with all her other stuff. I'll ask her to ring you when I get back to the flat, that's if she's awake yet.'

As if he'd just confessed to some sordid affair, Valerie's whole body stiffened. 'She's at your flat?'

'She needed somewhere to go.'

'A hotel?' Val suggested tightly. 'Friends?'

'I am a friend,' he said, irked by her attitude. He sat back, folding his arms across his chest. 'And it was five o'clock in the morning. God, Val, it's only for a few days, just until her boyfriend gets back.'

As if realising that the interview, informal as it was, had strayed out of the professional and into the personal, Valerie sat up straight and pushed back her shoulders. Nothing, however, could disguise the look in her eyes. 'Perhaps you could get her to give me a call then. Today, if it isn't too much trouble.'

'Sure,' he said. 'I'll do that.'

Valerie snapped shut her notepad and rose smartly to her feet. 'Right, if you've nothing else to add, I think we're done. I'll see you out.'

They walked in silence back to the foyer. Harry, although his conscience was clear, searched for something to say that might heal this new breach between them. It was not as

x

x

though he had deliberately withheld the information about Jess staying at his flat – she'd only been there since the early hours of the morning – but perhaps he should have told her straight away.

At the door, he stopped and looked at her. 'Hey, I'm sorry if—'

But Valerie clearly wasn't interested in his explanations. She gave a quick shake of her head. 'I've got to get on,' she said. 'I haven't got time for this.' And with that she turned on her heel and left him standing there.

Valerie punched in the code, went through the glass door and headed back up the stairs. Was she behaving irrationally? She didn't think so. Jessica Vaughan, boyfriend or not, wasn't to be trusted. And now the two of them were living under the same roof. How long before this new-found friendship turned into something more?

On the first floor she stopped at the landing and gazed out of the window. She watched as Harry strolled down the road towards his car. His damaged left leg gave him a slightly swaying gait, but the limp was barely noticeable now. It would be easier, she thought, to just let him go, to sever the ties between them for ever. So why couldn't she? Her head told her that was the smart thing to do, but her heart wasn't ready for anything so final.

With a sigh, she carried on climbing the stairs. It was time to get focused again, to concentrate on the job rather than her personal life. Becky Hibbert deserved her full attention. She could think about everything else later.

The incident room was buzzing with talk, with the

tapping of fingertips on keyboards, with the sound of phones constantly ringing. Valerie went over to Swann and perched on the edge of his desk.

'Any news on Dan Livesey yet?'

'Yeah, we've been calling round the local clubs and eventually managed to find his employer. He's been working for Chris Street, sometimes at Belles, sometimes at the Lincoln.'

'So we've got a home address?'

'Not yet. Chris Street refused to give out any information over the phone, so I've sent Daley over to see him.'

'Typical,' she muttered. Chris Street, like his father Terry, was gangster through and through. The family owned a few clubs and bars, but made most of their money from drugs and prostitution. She wasn't surprised that he was being obstructive. Chris Street would rather pull out his own teeth with pliers than voluntarily help the law.

'I've run a check on Livesey,' Swann said. 'A couple of arrests for drunk and disorderly and a six-month stretch for assault ten years ago. So we've got his prints and his DNA, but unless we find something to match them with . . .'

'Exactly. Mind, you have to get pretty up-close and personal if you're strangling someone. Maybe the lab will come up with the goods.' She shifted slightly on the desk, glanced around the room and then looked back down at Swann. Lowering her voice, she said, 'What do you know about the Minnie Bright murder?'

It took a moment for the name to register with him, and then his brows shot up. 'Hannah Bright's kid, right?'

'You knew the mother?'

'Everyone knew Hannah. When she wasn't being done for soliciting, she was raising hell in some pub or other. She spent more time in the cells than she did at home. I'm surprised that poor kid wasn't taken into care.' He gave a slow shake of his head. 'Come to think of it, she'd have been a damn sight better off if she had been.'

'What happened to her, to Hannah?'

'Not a clue. She hasn't been around for a while, though. I reckon she took off after the trial. I don't imagine the locals were entirely sympathetic; she probably got out before they drove her out.' He paused before adding, 'What makes you ask?'

Valerie gave him a quick rundown of what Harry had told her.

Swann listened carefully. 'Odd. You think there's anything in it, guv?'

'I don't know, but I guess we'll have to check it out.'

'Nasty business, that. Still, Harry knows what he's talking about. I mean, he was one of the poor sods who went into the house and found the body.'

Valerie tried to mask a jolt of surprise. She hadn't been aware of that. In all the years they'd been together, Harry had never once mentioned it. A ripple of frustration ran through her. She wondered sometimes if she knew him at all. 'Yes, of course.'

Swann gave her a sly look. 'And you'll be keeping the super informed?'

'Redding?' she said. 'I don't see much point in telling him at this stage.' She got up to leave, but Swann hadn't finished yet.

'Are you sure about that?'

She stared at him, her eyes growing cautious. 'What are you trying to say exactly?'

'That was his case, guv. If you start reviewing the original investigation, he'll want to know. I don't suppose he'll be that happy about it either.'

'Damn it!' she muttered. 'That's all we need.' And damn Harry too, she thought. Something else he hadn't bothered to tell her.

30

Jess opened her eyes and blinked, confused for a moment as to where she was and what she was doing there. And then, all in a rush, it came flooding back. She remembered the fire, the smoke pouring into the bedroom, those last few panic-filled seconds before she'd been rescued. She recalled, with a sinking heart, how everything she'd owned was now ashes. A low groan escaped from her lips. Before self-pity could get the better of her and send her diving back under the duvet, she forced herself out of bed and padded across the room. She put her head round the door and peered along the hall. 'Hello?'

There was no response.

Pulling on Harry's dressing gown, she went through to the living room. It was empty, but sitting in the middle of the table were a heap of carrier bags, a laptop, a mobile phone and two sets of keys. There was a white envelope with a scrawled note from Harry on the front: *Just some things to tide you over. Your car's outside. If you need me, I'll be downstairs. H.* Inside the envelope was a hundred quid in twenty-pound notes.

Jess walked over to the window and looked down on the

street. Her red Mini Cooper was parked behind Harry's silver Vauxhall. She shook her head in astonishment – how on earth had he managed that? Returning to the table, she examined the contents of the bags and found clothes, underwear, toiletries and even some make-up. As she stared down at everything, a lump formed in her throat. She had woken a few minutes ago imagining she had nothing, and now she had all this. In a crisis, she thought, it was the kindness of others that made the difference between staying afloat and drowning.

She was still gazing down at the table, her emotions in tumult, when she heard the front door quietly open and close. A few seconds later, Harry walked into the room.

'Hey, you're up. Did you manage to get some sleep? How are you doing?'

'I can't believe you did all this,' she said, raising her grey eyes to him. Her voice was shaky, her lower lip trembling.

Harry pulled a face. 'You're not going to cry, are you? I hate it when women do that. It's only a few bits and pieces. And I'm not responsible in any way for the shopping – that was down to Lorna.'

'And the car?'

'That was Snakey Harris. Granted, I made the phone call, but he was the one who did all the hard work.' He grinned. 'It *is* your Mini, isn't it? I couldn't remember the registration.'

'Yeah, it's mine.'

'Thank God for that. I didn't fancy a visit from the law.'

Jess managed a faltering smile. 'Thanks, Harry. For

everything you've done. I really appreciate it. I don't know what to say. I—'

'You don't need to say anything. That's what friends are for. Look, why don't you get dressed – hopefully you'll find something that fits – and I'll make us some coffee.'

Jess gave a nod, picked up the bags and retreated to the bedroom. She sat on the edge of the bed for a minute, trying to fight back the tears. She had a horrible feeling that if she started crying now it would be a good few days before she stopped. 'Pull yourself together, Vaughan,' she murmured. 'Don't be such a wimp.' Then she took three deep breaths, rose to her feet and dived into the bags.

Lorna's choices had been conservative, for which she was grateful: plain black joggers, one loose black T-shirt and one white, a light grey sweater, socks and a pair of black pumps. There was also a three-pack of white cotton pants and a white bra. The bra was a size too small, but by loosening the straps she could just about manage to squeeze into it.

After getting dressed, Jess looked in the mirror. She was all in black and it suited her mood. She was still in mourning for everything she'd lost. The clothes were fine, but the same couldn't be said for the face that returned her gaze. It was ghostly pale, with dark rings under the eyes. She wrinkled her nose, unimpressed with what she saw.

Turning back to the bed, she found the bag with the cosmetics and rooted through the contents. Five minutes later, after the application of tinted moisturiser, eyeshadow, mascara and a lick of lipstick, she was beginning to look almost human again. She ran a comb through her hair, stood back and nodded. Well, hardly perfection, but at least she wouldn't be mistaken for an escapee from the morgue.

As Jess walked back into the living room, she was greeted with the smell of real coffee. Good, just what she needed to give her a kick-start and get her moving again. She had a lot to do this afternoon. Already she was going over the list in her head, prioritising a visit to the bank and a call to the insurance company. Automatically she glanced down at her left wrist, but of course her watch wasn't there. That was something else she'd have to buy.

Harry came out of the kitchen brandishing a plate of scrambled eggs on toast. 'Grab a seat,' he said. 'I made you some breakfast, or brunch or whatever you want to call it. I know you might not feel that hungry, but you should try and eat something.'

Jess pulled out a chair and sat down. She went for the mug of coffee first, adding a splash of milk and then blowing on the surface before she took a couple of fast gulps. 'Thanks,' she said. 'That hit the spot. And actually I am quite hungry.' She picked up the knife and fork and dug into the eggs.

While she ate, Harry went to stand by the window. He stared out at the street for a while with his hands in his pockets.

She glanced over at him. 'Is everything okay?'

He didn't answer straight away.

'Harry?'

'I've got some news,' he said, coming back over and sitting down opposite her. His face was solemn, his eyes full of concern.

'I can guess,' she said. 'The fire was deliberate, right? Don't worry. I'd pretty much figured that out already.'

'Yeah, someone poured petrol through the main letter box and then set it alight. Course, it could have just been your friendly passing arsonist, but—'

'But it's unlikely. Especially with everything else that's been going on recently. And anyway, I'm sure someone was watching me when I went to the shops last night. I had this really creepy feeling. I looked around and couldn't see anyone, but I'd swear I wasn't imagining it.'

'No,' Harry said. 'I don't think you were.'

Jess put down her knife and fork and pushed the plate to one side. 'So someone's probably trying to kill me. That's a cheery thought. Not that I can prove it. I mean, there are six flats in that block. Theoretically, any one of us could have been the target.'

Harry put his elbows on the table and sighed. 'There's something else,' he said. 'I've just come back from Cowan Road.'

She only had to hear the tension in his voice to know there was more bad news on its way. 'Tell me,' she said softly.

He hesitated, unwilling or perhaps just unable to find the right words.

She stirred uneasily in her chair, alarm starting to grow inside her. 'Harry?' she prompted.

'It's Becky Hibbert,' he said finally. 'She's dead.'

The shock of the announcement was like a thump to her stomach. The breath caught in her throat. 'What? How? I don't understand.'

'They found her this morning on the Mansfield. She'd been strangled.'

'She was *murdered*? Oh my God! Do they ... do they know who did it?'

Harry shook his head. 'I don't think so. Not yet. The police found your card in her flat and it had my number written on the back. Val called me this morning. I went down to the station and told her what I could.'

Jess was still desperately trying to absorb the information. 'Right,' she murmured.

'But she's going to want to talk to you too,' he added gently. 'I can come with you if you like.'

Jess raised a hand to her mouth and chewed on a fingernail. She could feel her heart beating faster, thumping in her chest. For a while, unfocused, her eyes gazed off into the middle distance. Then suddenly, as if all her bones had turned to jelly, she slumped forward and covered her face with her hands. 'Jesus,' she groaned. 'What have I done? This is all my fault.'

'How the hell is it your fault?'

But Jess could only think of the pressure she'd put on Becky Hibbert, of how she'd deliberately targeted the girl she believed to be the weakest link in the chain. And Becky *had* talked and now she was dead. Had someone guessed that she wasn't going to keep her mouth shut, that she couldn't be trusted? Was that why she'd been murdered?

Harry leaned forward and laid the tips of his fingers on her arm. 'Jess, you're not to blame for this.'

She dropped her hands and stared at him. 'And how do

you figure that out? If I hadn't gone round there, if I hadn't—'

'You can't go down that road. We don't know why she was murdered.'

'What does Valerie think? You told her about Minnie Bright? About Sam? About everything that's been happening?' She could hear the hysteria in her voice and tried to swallow down the panic. A combination of fear and guilt and remorse was running through her head, a dizzying rush that made her feel sick.

'Of course I did. But she has to keep an open mind. They're still waiting on forensics.'

Jess rubbed hard at her temples, fighting a fruitless battle to get her thoughts in order. 'But it must be connected to Minnie. It has to be.'

'We don't know anything yet – not for sure.'

Jess stood up quickly, but her legs felt so weak she had to grab hold of the edge of the table. 'I have to go to the station. I have to see Valerie.'

'There's no rush,' Harry said.

And of course there was no rush. Not really. Becky Hibbert was dead, and nothing Jess could say would ever bring her back. But she still felt the need to be doing something, to be moving, to be contributing in any way she could. Her legs, however, refused to cooperate. As her knees buckled, she dropped back into the chair.

'You'd better give her a call first,' Harry continued. 'Or I can ring for you and arrange an appointment. She may not be able to see you today.'

Jess was only half listening, the words washing over her.

She was remembering Becky Hibbert standing on the walk-way at Haslow House, her hands gripping the handles of the pram, her face sullen and wary. She was remembering how she had tried to manipulate her into revealing the truth about the past. 'I pushed her too hard. I forced her into making that call to you.'

'You didn't force her into anything,' Harry insisted. 'And you didn't kill her. You're an investigative journalist. It's your job to put pressure on people. If you recognised that she was the one most likely to break, then someone else could have realised it too. Maybe Becky panicked, maybe she called someone else and ... I don't know. But that's the thing. Neither of us knows at the moment, so let's not start jumping to any conclusions.'

Jess rubbed at her forehead again. She wanted to believe him, wanted to find a way out from the tugging quicksand of guilt, but nothing he said could free her from her conscience. And then another shocking thought suddenly occurred. Her eyes widened with alarm. 'Oh God, what about Sam? What if—'

'She's fine. I called her a couple of hours ago and told her about Becky. I don't think she's in any danger. Whatever's being covered up has nothing to do with her. At the beginning someone clearly wanted to warn her off, to stop her getting involved with you, but I think that's as far as it goes. She obviously doesn't know enough to be a direct threat to anyone.'

'I hope you're right.'

There was a short silence, broken only by the sound of the rain falling gently against the window pane. The room was warm, the pungent smell of paint still lingering. Jess felt a desperate need to get outside and breathe some fresh air. Heaving herself to her feet again, she swept up the keys, the cash and the phone from the table.

'I have to go,' she said. 'I've got things to do.'

Harry stood up too. 'I'll come with you.'

'I don't need a bodyguard,' she snapped, but then immediately felt bad about it. 'Sorry, I'm sounding like an ungrateful bitch. I don't mean it like that. I just want to be on my own for a while.'

Slowly, he sat back down again. 'It's okay, I understand. But watch yourself, yeah? Come straight back when you've finished.'

'Sure. I'll see you later. And thanks again – for everything.'

'No problem.'

Jess was aware of his eyes on her as she walked across the room. Her legs still felt unsteady, but sheer determination got her into the hall and out through the door. She gripped the banister as she descended the stairs. Pausing on the first-floor landing, she could hear the rhythmic tapping of fingers on a keyboard coming from the office of Mackenzie, Lind. Should she go and thank Lorna now, or leave it until later? Later, she decided. She wasn't yet strong enough to face all the inevitable questions about how she was and how she felt and what she was going to do next. She was already standing on a precipice. Lorna's maternal instincts might just be enough to tip her over the edge.

Jess went quietly down the last flight of stairs and out into the street. She raised her eyes to the cooling rain and let it trickle down her face. It seemed like a long time since she had tried to open that window in her flat, since she had lain down on the floor and curled up into a ball, since she had felt the hot grey smoke creeping into her throat and lungs. She had been lucky. Becky Hibbert had not.

Shaking the rain from her hair, she opened the door of the Mini and climbed in. She dropped the keys, the phone and the money on to the passenger seat. Then, as if it might anchor her, she grabbed the wheel tightly with both hands, leaned forward and breathed deeply, in and out, in and out. What now? She didn't know where to start. What she wanted was to make things right, but it was way too late for that.

31

Detective Inspector Valerie Middleton leaned over the shoulder of DC Lister and viewed the grainy images from the CCTV. There was no coverage from inside the estate – cameras had been installed a few years ago, but they'd been vandalised with such frequency that the council had long since given up repairing them – but there was one surviving camera on the Mansfield Road, set up high and covering the main entrance.

'That's him,' DC Lister said, staring at the image that was frozen on the screen. 'That's Dan Livesey. I'm sure of it. We pulled him in when I was still in uniform – it must have been about ten months ago. A fight broke out at the pool hall, the usual carnage, and he was interviewed along with several others.'

Valerie wasn't surprised to hear about the trouble at the Lincoln. It was one of the Streets' businesses, a place where the Kellston lowlifes gathered to get hammered, do their dodgy deals and make contact with other local criminals. The building had burned down a few years back but had since been rebuilt.

She peered down at the screen. Livesey was in his mid-thirties, an ugly, thickset man with a square face and a shaven head. Dressed in a long dark overcoat, he had his hands deep in his pockets, thus making it impossible to tell if he was wearing gloves or not. She checked the time on the screen: 00:03, about twenty minutes after Becky and her two friends had arrived back from the Fox.

'Have we got him leaving?'

'Yes,' Lister said, pressing a button and fast-forwarding the tape. 'Here it is. A quarter past twelve.'

Valerie stared hard at the screen. Did he look like a man who had just strangled his ex? Livesey was walking quickly, his shoulders hunched, his collar up, head down. Was he hurrying to escape the scene of a crime? Was he trying to hide his face or simply protect it against the chill of the night air?

'Play it again,' she said.

The second and third viewing didn't help her come to a decision. The camera picked up Livesey as he approached the gateway, exited the estate and turned left along Mansfield Road. He disappeared from view within a few yards.

'I take it we've got the victim on tape too?'

'Yes, guv,' DC Lister said. She pressed the button again, rewinding until the time read 23:40. Valerie saw a few seconds tick by, and then suddenly the living breathing version of Becky Hibbert appeared, her elbows linked into those of her mates, the three of them walking through the gates in a line. They were laughing and joking, clearly drunk but not completely inebriated. Valerie felt a lurch in her stomach. She was watching a smiling woman who was heading towards her death.

'And then a few minutes later we get the lads they passed,' Lister said. She forwarded the tape again, and four boys came in to shot. They were all wearing the familiar garb of the young, low-slung jeans, trainers and hoodies. Their faces, framed by the pulled-up hoods, were no more than a blur. How old were they? Valerie reckoned mid- to late teens. Beyond their age – and she couldn't even be sure of that – there was nothing to identify them. They could have been any four lads from anywhere in the country.

'Let's run off some prints and show them around the estate. Someone might come up with a name.' It was a shot in the dark, bearing in mind the residents' general reluctance to talk to the law, but it had to be done. The lads could be potential witnesses. They might have seen or heard something vital.

'So,' Valerie continued, 'Livesey's on the estate for about twelve minutes. Not long, but long enough. We haven't got an exact time of death for the victim, but it seems to fit in with the ME's estimate. He could have gone looking for Becky Hibbert, got into an argument with her and . . .' She stopped and frowned. 'But if Becky had arrived back twenty minutes earlier, why wasn't she in her flat?'

'Maybe she got talking to someone,' Lister suggested. 'Or maybe she was in the flat but didn't want him there. Especially as she was on her own. If the relationship was as stormy as her mates claim, she may have felt safer talking to him in a more public place. Even at midnight, there are always people milling around on the Mansfield.'

'Or maybe *he* didn't want to go up to the flat in case he was spotted by one of the neighbours. He might have given

271

her a call and asked her to meet him in the foyer. He could have suggested going for a drink at some club while they talked things over.' Valerie gave a light shrug. There were a lot of maybes. 'Have we got an address for him yet?'

'Yeah,' Swann said from behind. 'Daley just called it in. 61b, Rayton Road. And we've got a motor registered to him too, a dark blue Audi A3.'

Valerie turned and nodded. 'Okay, let's get over there and see what Mr Livesey has to say for himself. That's if he hasn't already done a runner.'

Rayton Road was a long terrace of three-storey Victorian houses, a few of them lovingly restored into family homes but most of them shabby and dilapidated, converted long ago into multiple flats or bedsits. Livesey's abode fell into the latter category, a building that had been subject to years of neglect, with mortar crumbling from the walls, flaking paint, rotting sills and cracked window panes.

'There's the Audi,' Swann said, as he parked up beside the house. 'We could be in luck.'

Valerie wasn't so optimistic. She peered through the rain-spattered windscreen as the second squad car, containing a couple of uniforms, pulled in behind them. 'Or he could have decided that it was too risky to take. If he is guilty, he wouldn't have known when the body was going to be discovered. Taking the car would have upped the chances of him being picked up.'

Valerie's mobile bleeped and she took it out of her pocket. A message from Harry. She opened it. It was Paige Fielding's address and phone number. She didn't bother replying, but instead put in a call to DC Lister back at the station. After reeling off the contact details, she said, 'Check her out, will you? Take Franks with you and find out what she knows about Livesey, and the money Becky Hibbert had in her flat.'

'Ready?' Swann said when she was finished.

Valerie nodded. 'Let's go.'

As she got out of the car, she gazed up at the grimy windows. From Livesey's second-floor flat there would be no access to the rear of the house unless he wanted to take his chances and jump. She walked up the short drive, followed by Swann and the two other officers. In the front yard there were a couple of overflowing wheelie bins with a heap of carrier bags at their base. Some of these had burst open, littering the concrete with empty lager cans, fag ends and sodden rotting food. Valerie stepped carefully around the mess, trying not to breathe too deeply.

There were three bells on the porch wall, containing only the numbers of the flats rather than any names. She rang the one for 61b and waited. Nothing happened. She rang again, put her ear to the door and listened. Silence. She tried the other bells, a series of long rings on each of them. There was no response. She was about to order the door to be broken down when there was a clattering noise from within. It was the sound of footsteps moving heavily down uncarpeted stairs.

A few seconds later the front door was opened by a skinny guy in his early twenties with a skull tattoo on his neck. His face, thin and gaunt, with dark purplish circles under the eyes, was adorned with a hand-rolled cigarette hanging limply out of the corner of his mouth. He had the distinctive look of the junkie. 'Yeah?' he said. 'What d'ya want?'

'Police,' Valerie said, holding up her identification. 'DI Valerie Middleton.'

'I ain't done nothin',' the man said defensively. His eyes flickered warily from Valerie to Swann and then to the two officers behind.

'Good,' she said, moving forward. 'You won't mind us coming in, then.'

The guy stood his ground for a moment, one hand still holding on to the edge of the door, his body blocking the entrance, but then thought better of it. He stepped back into the hall and let the four of them pass.

'Which flat is yours?' Valerie asked.

The man hesitated again before jerking his head in the direction of the stairs. The cigarette remained firmly attached to his lip. 'First floor.'

'You know the guy who lives above? 61b?'

'Seen him around,' he said cautiously.

'Know if he's in?' Swann asked.

'No idea, man.'

'Wait here,' Swann said.

Valerie skirted around a table overflowing with old junk mail and fliers and headed up the stairs. Her heels clicked against the bare wood as she ascended. The peeling walls were a dreary shade of grey and the air smelled of dry rot, stale food, cigarettes and sweat. As she approached the first floor, she put out her hand to take hold of the banister, saw how filthy it was and quickly withdrew her fingers.

On the second floor, Valerie waited by Livesey's flat until all four of them were gathered outside. Then she knocked sharply on the door. No one answered, and there was no movement from within. She tried again.

'Best break it down,' Swann said.

Before one of the uniforms could commit GBH on the door, Valerie tried the handle. It turned smoothly in her hand and the door swung open. She knew then that Livesey was gone. No one would leave their flat unlocked with a junkie living downstairs.

She stepped inside and looked around. The living room was sparsely furnished with just a battered sofa, a small table, a lamp and an old TV. The patterned carpet was threadbare and pocked with cigarette burns. Yellowing nets, stained with nicotine, hung at the windows, but there were no actual curtains. A copy of the *Sun* was lying on the sofa. She reached down and picked it up. Yesterday's date.

'Swell place,' Swann murmured.

There was a tiny kitchen off to the left and a bathroom to the right. Leaving the two PCs to have a look round these rooms, she went into the bedroom with Swann. The double bed was unmade, the duvet hanging over the edge. There was nothing inside the wardrobe but a few metal hangers and a layer of dust. A chest of drawers beside the bed had its top drawer open. That was empty too.

'Reckon Danny boy's done a flit,' Swann said, stating the obvious.

Valerie closed the top drawer and opened the two underneath. She found a couple of old T-shirts and a grubby-looking towel. 'But not in his Audi. We'd better check the local cab companies, see if any of their drivers picked him up in the early hours. Or maybe a mate helped him out, gave him a lift somewhere or the loan of a car.'

PC Bennett came in, brandishing a mobile in his right hand. 'I found this in the kitchen, guv.'

'Okay, bag it and bring it back to the station.' She turned to Swann. 'So Livesey either left in a hurry and forgot all about his phone, or he's smart enough to know that we can trace him through it.'

'Easy enough to pick up another one. Or maybe he already had two.'

Once they'd finished the search of the bedroom, which took them all of five minutes, Valerie and Swann went back through to the living room. 'You know what's odd?' she said. 'There's no paperwork in this flat, no bills, no bank statements, no tenancy agreement, nothing.'

Swann gave a shrug. 'It's the paperless society. Everything's done by computer these days.'

'Really? Try telling that to the powers that be. I spend half my damn life filling out forms and reports.' She smiled at PC Bennett. 'You're going to hate me for this, but I think you'd better do a search of the bins outside. I reckon Livesey cleaned this place out before he left. He must have been in a hurry, so he may have dumped something that could be useful.'

PC Bennett gazed gloomily back at her. It was a couple of weeks since the last refuse collection and he was, understandably, less than happy at the prospect of rooting through a fortnight's worth of stinking trash 'Okay, guv. We'll get on to it.'

'And we'll get back to the station,' Valerie said to Swann. 'It looks like Livesey's in the frame. We'll put out an alert to the airports and ferries.'

'If he did take off in the early hours, he could be in Spain by now.'

'I know.' She sighed. 'He could be bloody anywhere.' It wasn't good news that he'd managed to slip through their fingers, but at least they now had a viable suspect. Livesey had gone to the estate after Becky Hibbert returned home last night. Right place and probably right time. And now he was missing. Yes, he had to be their main suspect. No man did a runner unless he had something serious to run from.

32

Paige Fielding opened her second can of lager and lit another fag. She took a drag, went over to the window and gazed down on the estate. Becky's body had been taken away hours ago, but a large crowd still remained by the entrance to Haslow House. Murder was hardly unknown on the Mansfield, but it was usually the dealers or skagheads who ended up dead, shot in the chest or knifed in the guts. A young mum who'd been strangled was something different. A young mum had novelty value.

Although she was too far away to be able to hear anything, she could imagine the buzz running through the crowd. She could see it in their body language, in the way they huddled together, gawping and whispering. Old Bill was still in evidence too, searching the surrounding area and bagging all the crap that was lying around. The place had never looked so tidy.

The key turned in the front door, and seconds later Micky came into the flat. He dropped the holdall he was carrying and stood by the entrance to the kitchen with his hands on his hips. 'Have they gone, then?'

Paige raised her eyes to the ceiling. 'No, hun, they're the

bloody invisible cops. What do *you* think?'

'Okay, no need to go off on one. What are you doing?'

'What does it look like?'

'Like you're staring out of the window.'

'Ain't you a bleedin' genius.' She took a swig of lager and ran the tip of her tongue along her upper lip. 'Have you seen that lot? They can't get enough of it. None of them gave a toss about her when she was alive, but now ... now she's ... they're all acting like it's the worst fuckin' thing that's ever happened to them.'

'So what's your problem? You couldn't stand the stupid cow. She's out of the picture now, so you can stop stressing about it.'

Paige turned her head and glared at him. 'She may have been a pain in the arse, but I didn't want her dead.'

'Well, it don't really matter what you wanted, babe. She's brown bread and that's the end of it. So what did the filth say?'

She gave a shrug. Micky had cleared off, taking his dodgy gear with him, as soon as he'd heard the law were coming round. The only people he hated more than Old Bill were Arsenal supporters. 'They asked me about Dan, and about the cash Becky had at the flat.'

'And?'

'And I told 'em what I said I would – that Dan was the nasty type and used to knock her about and that I hadn't got a clue where the notes had come from.' She walked over to the table, ground out the cigarette in the ashtray and immediately lit another one. 'They reckon she may have been on the game. I didn't say yes or no. I claimed there'd been some rumours but I didn't know for sure. And I told them that if Dan had heard about it he'd have done his fuckin' nut. He may have done sod all for his kids, but he wouldn't stand for their mother being a brass.'

'Well done, babe,' Micky said, advancing into the kitchen and wrapping his arms round her. 'You did good.'

'No thanks to you.' As his hands strayed on to her breasts, she pushed him away roughly. 'Get yer fuckin' mitts off me!'

'What's the problem?'

'I'm not in the mood, okay? I've got things to do.'

'Like?'

'Like meeting Kirsten five minutes ago.' She picked up her coat from the back of the chair. 'I've got to split. She's shitting herself about all this.'

'Well, make sure you get something decent this time. Don't let the bitch screw you over.'

Paige gave him a hard look. 'No one ever screws me over, hun.'

'All I mean is that you have to take advantage of the situation. She's loaded and she ain't in a position to argue. You've gotta grab your chances when you can.'

'Tell me something I don't know.'

His face took on a sulky expression. 'Yeah, well, I was just saying.'

Paige raised her eyes to the ceiling and headed for the door. Micky had his uses, but brain power wasn't one of them. If they gave out prizes for stating the obvious, he'd be a gold medal winner every time. 'See you later. And don't turn this place into a pigsty while I'm gone.'

Outside, she strode along the walkway to the corner, where she took the steps instead of waiting for the lift. There was a thin drizzle falling, and as she jogged down the four flights, she pulled up the hood of her parka. She glared briefly at the crowd over at Haslow House before making her way to the main path and out of the gates.

Striding briskly along the high street, Paige went over what she was going to say in her head. She had Kirsten over a barrel and she knew it. She grinned. Kirsten Roberts – she could never think of her as Cope – was a stuck-up cow who reckoned she was better than everyone else because she was on TV. Jesus, it wasn't as if she could even act. The only reason she was in that lousy soap was because she had long blonde hair and a half-decent pair of tits. And even the tits weren't her own.

Paige weaved her way through the shoppers, occasionally pausing to gaze into a window. At Ruby's, the jeweller's, she let her gaze linger for a while on the gold chains, the rings and the watches. If she played her cards right, she could have anything she wanted. It was just a matter of applying the right amount of pressure at the right time. And Kirsten, especially at the moment, wasn't in a position to refuse.

Paige saw her as soon as she pushed open the door. The café was busy, but her old school friend had found a free table to the right of the counter. Kirsten looked pale and strained and was stirring a cup of coffee distractedly. She was dressed head to foot in black, which might have been a nod to their recent bereavement but was more likely just a fashion statement.

As Paige approached, Kirsten raised her eyes and

frowned. 'God, what have you been doing? I've been here for ages.'

'You know what I've been doing. Had to go down the cop shop, didn't I? I told you that when I called.' Paige sat down and put her elbows on the table. She'd decided that this version of events sounded more serious than a couple of plods calling round to the flat for a ten-minute chat. 'Bastards kept me waiting for ages and then gave me the real third degree. I thought they were never gonna let me go.' She was laying it on thick, making sure that Kirsten understood the enormity of the favour she'd just done her. 'Kept going on and on about that bloody cash they found. They reckon it's connected to the murder.'

Kirsten face, already pale, went ashen. She dropped the spoon into the saucer with a clatter. 'What did you tell them?'

'Don't worry, love. I didn't say it was you that gave it to her. The last thing you need is the filth knocking on your door. It'd be all over the tabloids the next day. Not the kind of publicity you want, huh?'

Kirsten worried on her lower lip. She picked up her cup and then put it down again. Her right hand fluttered up to her face. 'Where did you say it came from?'

'I didn't, did I? Said I didn't know nothin' about it. They seem to have the idea she might have been on the game, so if no one tells them any different ... Course, I'll be in the bloody shit if they ever find out I lied to them. Perverting the course of justice, that is. They'll probably put me in the slammer.'

Kirsten's voice went up a pitch. 'They won't find out.

Why should they?' She looked anxiously round the surrounding tables in case anyone was listening. 'Why should they?' she asked again.

Paige gave a shrug. 'No reason,' she said slyly. 'But I've put my neck on the line for you. I reckon I deserve something in return.'

'Like what?'

She smiled back smugly. 'Five grand should do it. I reckon that's fair. Yeah, five grand and we'll call it quits.'

'For God's sake,' Kirsten hissed. 'Where am I supposed to find that kind of money? You and that fat cow have already had two K off me. Why should I give you any more?'

'That *dead* fat cow,' Paige reminded her. She stared at Kirsten's designer clothes, at the Gucci bag lying on the table, and made a quick mental assessment of what they must be worth. Jesus, a few grand was nothing to Kirsten. 'You owe me big time and you know it. I've covered your lying little arse for you. And if my memory suddenly comes back, I might just recall why you really gave her that cash.'

Kirsten glared at her, her teeth bared. 'So I'll tell them I lent it to her, that she was in debt, that I was doing her a favour.'

Paige leaned forward so that her face was only inches away. 'Yeah, right. You just bunged a grand to some woman you haven't seen for fuck knows how long. They're really gonna believe that. Especially when I tell them a much more interesting story.'

'You can't do that,' Kirsten said defiantly. 'If you do, you'll have to admit that you lied to them in the first place.'

'So? Maybe I'm willing to take that chance.' Paige smirked. 'Or maybe I could get in touch with that reporter and tell her what she really wants to know.'

Kirsten pulled in a breath and her eyes blazed momentarily. Then, as if she knew she was defeated, the light suddenly went out of them.

'Think about it,' Paige said, rising to her feet. 'But don't take too long. I'm not the patient sort.'

33

It was five thirty by the time Jess got back to Station Road. First she called in at Mackenzie, Lind to present Lorna with a large bouquet of flowers and thank her profusely for what she'd done. 'You're an angel. I don't know how I'd have managed without your help. All those clothes and everything. It was so kind.' She rooted in her pockets and took out some of the money she'd withdrawn from the bank. 'How much do I owe you?'

Lorna flapped a hand. 'Oh, don't worry about that now. It came out of petty cash and Harry has all the receipts, but there's no rush. The main thing is that you're still in one piece.'

'Just about.'

'And you didn't need to do this,' Lorna said, sniffing appreciatively at the roses. 'You've got enough on your plate. They're lovely. I can't remember the last time anyone bought me flowers. I think Mac's forgotten what a florist is.'

As if on cue, Mac came out of his office. When he saw Jess, he gave her a brusque nod and retreated back inside.

'Don't mind him,' Lorna said. 'He's got a lot on his mind at the moment.'

Jess, who had seen the expression on Mac's face, suspected that his coolness was down to something more personal. Still, that was hardly surprising. On the trouble front, her record left a lot to be desired. She wondered if Harry had told him about her investigation into the Minnie Bright case. As an ex-cop, Mac would probably be none too pleased about that either.

Jess repeated her thanks to Lorna and then, laden with shopping, trudged up the stairs to the flat. Inside, she dumped the carrier bags on the table and sat down wearily in a chair. It had been a long day, but at least she'd begun the process of sorting things out. Having to deal with the practical stuff, with the bank, the insurance company and the replenishing of her wardrobe, had been a temporary distraction, but when she'd gone down to Cowan Road police station, she'd had plenty of time to think about Becky Hibbert again.

Despite having arranged an appointment for four o'clock, Jess had been made to wait for over fifty minutes before Valerie Middleton had deigned to put in an appearance. And even then she'd been about as welcoming as Mac. She had looked Jess up and down, pursing her lips as if Jess had been found wanting in some fundamental way. Granted, the woman was up to her ears in a murder inquiry, but a little politeness wasn't too much to ask. Instead, the DI had been decidedly offhand, as if Jess was one of those familiar time-wasters who had to be listened to but who no one took particularly seriously.

Jess shook her head, not wanting to think about it any more. She'd done her duty and told the inspector about her article and her association with Becky Hibbert. What Valerie chose to do next was up to her. After waiting all that time, Jess had been in and out of the interview room in less than fifteen minutes.

Rising to her feet, she picked up one of the bags and took it through to the kitchen. She emptied the contents – milk, pizza, salad and wine – into the fridge. Then she returned to the living room and took the rest of the bags through to the bedroom. Her clothes shopping had been fast and furious. Normally she'd have spent hours choosing new jeans, but today she'd bought the first pair that had more or less fitted. She had new trainers too, as well as a smarter pair of black shoes, underwear, shirts, T-shirts, trousers, a simple black dress and a black jacket. She hung some of the garments in the wardrobe and put the rest, apart from the trainers, in the chest of drawers.

The final carrier bag contained a wallet, cosmetics, a cheap watch, a handbag, phone, notepads and pens. She sat on the edge of the bed, took the phone out of its packaging, inserted the battery and plugged it in to charge. Earlier, she had called Neil from the mobile that Harry had lent her, telling him that her phone had broken down. She hadn't mentioned the fire or the murder of Becky Hibbert or the fact that she was currently staying at Harry's place. He would only feel obliged to rush back, and she didn't want that. There was no point in disrupting both their lives. He'd be home at the weekend and she'd explain everything properly to him then.

Jess gathered up the receipts from the bottom of the bags, wincing as she thought about the hit her credit card had taken. Hopefully the insurance wouldn't take too long to come through, or she'd be living off bread and water for the foreseeable future. She went back into the living room and stood by the window. She was glad to be alone, needing the time to get her thoughts together. Harry had called her in the afternoon, saying he could get someone to cover his surveillance if she'd like some company tonight, but she'd told him she'd be fine. Was she fine? Well, she was at the moment, knowing that Lorna and Mac were still downstairs, but she wasn't sure how she'd feel when they left and it got dark.

Not wanting to dwell on that too much, she turned and walked into the kitchen. What she needed was food and alcohol. Food for energy and a few glasses of wine to take the edge off her fear. She still hadn't really faced up to the fact that someone had tried to kill her last night – the same someone who in all likelihood had murdered Becky Hibbert. And she couldn't shake off the thought that she had been in some way responsible for Becky's fate, her constant pushing and probing a catalyst for what had come next.

She reached into the fridge, took out the pizza, unwrapped it and put in it in the microwave. While it was heating up, she opened the bottle of wine and poured herself a glass. Returning to the living room, she switched on the TV and found the local news. There were pictures of the Mansfield Estate and a report about the murder. Detective Inspector Valerie Middleton, with professional ease, gave a brief statement saying that they were searching for a man called Dan Livesey – Becky Hibbert's ex-boyfriend and the father of her children — to help with their enquiries.

Jess took a sip of her wine as she stared at the mugshot on the screen. She frowned. If this Livesey guy *had* killed Becky, then there was no obvious link to the Minnie Bright case. She understood now why the inspector had been so offhand with her; if the police already had a suspect, they wouldn't be interested in pursuing what probably seemed like an unlikely connection to events from the past.

But Jess didn't like coincidences. Becky had been murdered on the same night as someone had set fire to her flat. That couldn't just be chance. She refused to believe it. And if the cops weren't going to investigate, then she would damn well do it herself. The thought of what this might mean — there was clearly someone out there who would stop at nothing to preserve the secrets of the past — sent a small shiver through her. But fear was no excuse for cowardice. She was the one who had lit the fuse and it was down to her to deal with the explosive consequences.

The microwave pinged and Jess switched off the TV. She retrieved the pizza and took it back to the table. She'd intended to have a salad with it, something healthy to balance out the fat and calories, but lethargy got the better of her. She couldn't even be bothered to open the packet.

While she ate, she booted up the laptop and connected to the internet. The one sensible thing she had done was to save most of her notes and research to an external vault. She also had Harry's hard copy of all the press cuttings connected to the Minnie Bright case. It was time to get back to work.

Two hours later, Jess was looking again at the timeline for

the day Minnie had died. Her head was starting to ache, a combination of too much screen-staring and too much wine. She sighed and sat back. The remains of the pizza lay congealing on a plate. Wrinkling her nose, she leaned forward again and pushed it away. The trouble with comfort food was that it came with a mighty dollop of guilt – and her guilt levels were already in overdrive.

Fatigue was tugging at her bones. The day, despite a few hours' kip in the morning, had been a long and stressful one. She blinked twice and yawned, thinking how nice it would be to have a hot bath, curl up in bed and go to sleep. But she refused to give in to the temptation. Placing her elbows firmly on the table, she shook her head and tried to focus on the job in hand. What about Hannah Bright, Minnie's mother? No one seemed to know where she'd gone to, or when. Surely that was worth following up.

She did a search on the internet, checking out the social network sites. She came up with a few hits, a few other Hannah Brights, but not the one she wanted. Next she tried the electoral register, but she got no joy there either. It was what she'd been expecting. If Hannah was still living the same kind of life as she had been, she'd be one of those people who slipped under the radar, not paying tax or insurance, probably not even in possession of a computer.

The next person she thought about was Clare Towney, Donald Peck's niece. As a teenager, her life had been turned upside down. Her uncle had murdered a child and her mother had borne the brunt of local protest. Clare had moved away but had been forced to come back. Yes, that woman had every reason to be angry.

Jess jotted down Clare's name in her new notebook and then moved on. It was Lynda Choi's phone calls that were still really bugging her. Why were they important? So important that nobody wanted to talk about them. Except David Choi. And he'd had his card marked, been threatened, told to stop. But why? None of it added up. So Lynda had gone back to the house, seen a light go on and off, banged on the door, got no response and left. There was something wrong about it all, but she couldn't work out what.

Staring down at her timeline, Jess read through the details again. When she'd reached the end she went back to the beginning and started to wonder about Donald Peck's testimony. What if he hadn't been lying? What if he hadn't killed Minnie Bright? She needed to talk to someone who had known Peck, someone impartial who had nothing to gain or lose by telling her the truth. Her eyes alighted on the name of his ex-probation officer, Ralph Masterson, who had given evidence at the trial. Of course there was no saying that he was still alive. He'd already been retired at the time of the trial, and that had been fourteen years ago. That would make him in his late seventies or early eighties now. And even if he was still around, would he be living locally? Well, there was only one way to find out.

Jess checked out the electoral register for Bethnal Green. Bingo! There was a Ralph Masterson of the right age living in Banner Road. She cross-referenced the information with a phone directory and came up with a number. Taking a quick breath, she dialled and waited. It was answered after a couple of rings.

'Hello?'

'Is that Mr Ralph Masterson?'

'It is.'

The voice, although she'd only heard a few words, sounded elderly but strong. 'I'm sorry, this is going to seem a little strange, but are you the Ralph Masterson who used to be a probation officer?'

'I am. And who are you, may I ask?'

'I'm really sorry to bother you. My name's Jessica Vaughan. I'm a freelance reporter. I've been looking into the Minnie Bright case and I was wondering if—' She didn't have a chance to finish before he interrupted her.

'I've got nothing to say. For God's sake, why are you bringing all this up again? It's ancient history. Haven't you got anything else to write about? I had enough of you lot back then. It's over and done with.' A sigh rolled down the line. 'Why can't you leave it alone?'

Jess felt her eyebrows shifting north. For a man who claimed to have nothing to say, he didn't seem to be doing too badly. She wasn't sure if it was anger she was hearing or simply exasperation. 'It's not what you think,' she said quickly, hoping that he wouldn't hang up on her. 'There have been some developments. I understand you knew Donald Peck, and I was wondering if I could come and talk to you.'

'What sort of developments?'

But Jess didn't want to say too much. 'I think a face-to-face meeting would be more useful than discussing it over the phone.'

'I'm sure you do, Ms Vaughan, but I've got better things

to do with whatever limited time I have left on this earth than to waste it in pointless resurrections of the past.'

'I wouldn't dream of wasting your time, sir.'

'It would appear you are already doing so.'

'Okay, just let me ask you one question and then I'll leave you in peace.' She left a short pause, then said, 'Are you absolutely convinced that Donald Peck was guilty of murdering Minnie Bright?'

There was a distinct hesitation on the other end of the line. 'The jury believed him to be so.'

'With all respect, sir, that wasn't what I asked. What was *your* opinion?'

'My opinion is irrelevant.'

'I don't think so,' Jess said. 'Please could we meet up? I assure you I'm not some scandal-mongering hack. But I do have important new information and I'd really value your take on it. I mean, your professional and your personal take.' Jess pulled a face. Was she being too obsequious? 'You're one of the few people who actually knew Donald, so I'd like to hear your thoughts.'

Masterson thought about it for a moment. He might have been flattered by her comments, but more likely he was just curious. 'Very well,' he said at last. 'I suppose I can spare half an hour. Why don't we say ten o'clock tomorrow morning? Would that suit?'

'That would suit me just fine,' she said. 'Thank you. Should I come to your place or would you rather meet somewhere else?'

'I think we'd better meet here. It's hardly the kind of subject to be discussed in public. I take it you have my address?'

Jess glanced at the computer screen, where his details where still on display. 'Twenty-four, Banner Road? Is that right?'

'It is indeed. I won't ask how you got it. I'm sure you journalists have your methods. And you'd better give me your phone number in case I need to contact you.'

Jess recited the number of her new mobile and said, 'Tomorrow morning then. Thank you again.'

'Please don't be late. I may be old, but my time is as precious as anyone else's.'

'I won't. I promise.' Before he could change his mind, she quickly said goodbye and ended the call, then laid the phone down on the table, feeling pleased and relieved that he'd agreed to see her. Perhaps she was finally making some progress. The positive feelings didn't last for long. She suddenly found herself thinking about Becky Hibbert's kids, two children who would grow up without a mother. Maybe Dan Livesey had murdered Becky, or maybe he hadn't. She was more inclined towards the latter. The cops, she suspected, had got it wrong.

34

Valerie Middleton looked up at the clock on the wall. It was getting on for nine o'clock, time to call it a day. The evening shift was already in full swing, dealing with calls and chasing up any leads that came in. The news appeal had produced hundreds of so-called sightings of Dan Livesey, from Glasgow to Plymouth and plenty of places in between. Some of those claims were being investigated, but she wasn't holding her breath.

She had, however, been holding it in a more literal sense when she'd attended Becky Hibbert's autopsy late that afternoon. The smell still lingered in her nostrils, harsh and distinctive. No amount of disinfectant could completely erase the stench of death. And the results had only confirmed what they'd already suspected – that Becky had been strangled by the scarf she was wearing. There wasn't any useful material under the fingernails, no blood or tissue, but there were some cotton fibres. She must have clawed at the scarf in her last few seconds of life. Valerie thought about the panic she must have felt, the sick and horrifying fear as she helplessly succumbed to her assailant.

She was sitting at a desk opposite Kieran Swann, who

was humming something tuneless while he tapped the end of a pen against his jaw and stared at a computer screen.

Neither of them had spoken for the last fifteen minutes, but she knew that he was trying to put the pieces together just as she was.

'Livesey used her scarf,' she said, 'so maybe it wasn't premeditated. He couldn't have known that she'd be wearing it. Maybe he went to the estate to confront her, they got into a row and he lost his temper.'

Swann glanced over at her. 'Confront her about what?'

'The fact that she was moonlighting as a tom. According to Lister, Paige Fielding reckoned there were rumours going around. If they were true it would account for all that cash Becky had stashed away.'

'Or maybe he wanted a share of the proceeds and she wouldn't play ball.' He smirked. 'So to speak.'

Valerie frowned at the pun. 'But if it was a spur-of-the-moment thing, then I don't get why he went home and cleared out his flat. I mean, yes, you'd go back and pick up some stuff, the bare essentials you'd need if you were going to make a run for it – but you wouldn't hang around any longer than you had to. You'd be out of there as quickly as you could in case someone discovered the body. But PC Bennett found lots of things – bills, food, old payslips and the like – in the outside bins.'

'Which suggests that he *did* plan the murder and had a good clear-out before he went to meet her.' Swann smirked again. 'He wouldn't have wanted to leave anything lying around with that junkie living downstairs. Even murderers don't want their identities being nicked.'

'But if he did plan it, then he must have been aware of the camera out on the street, so why didn't he wear something that would obscure his face?'

'He could have forgotten about it. Or he could just be bloody stupid. Maybe he didn't think anyone would recognise him.'

Valerie could just about go along with that. If it hadn't been for DC Lister's eagle eyes, they could still be trying to work out the identity of the man on the CCTV footage. 'And then he doesn't take his car. Or get a cab so far as we know. So how did he get away? Either somebody helped him, or he hasn't gone far.'

'Yeah, he could still be on the manor, lying low until the heat dies down.'

'We need to check out all his known friends and work associates. I'm sure Chris Street and his daddy will be none too pleased, but the quicker they cooperate the sooner they'll have us off their backs. I don't suppose they'll want a police presence in their clubs and bars. It won't do much for trade.'

'Sounds like a plan,' Swann said. He leaned back and put his hands behind his head, exposing two damp patches in the armpits of his white shirt. 'But for now I'm going to hit the Fox and have a pint. Fancy one, guv?'

Valerie shook her head. She could have done with a drink, but in the crowded confines of the pub there would be no escape from Swann's perspiration or his interminable musings on the state of the world. 'No thanks. I've got a couple of things to finish up and then I'm off home. I'll see you in the morning.'

Swann yawned and stretched and then stood up. He took his jacket off the back of the chair and flung it over his shoulder. 'Okay, see you tomorrow. Night, guv.'

'Night.'

After he'd gone, Valerie sat for a while, her mind still focused on Dan Livesey. She tried to construct in her head a scenario for what had occurred last night. Had Livesey arranged to meet Becky at the entrance to Haslow House, or had he simply turned up unannounced? More likely the latter if he had intended to kill her. He wouldn't have wanted to take the risk of her telling someone else about the meet.

'And then what?' she murmured to herself. If no one else was around, it would have been easy for him to grab Becky and push her away from the light and into the shadowy gloom beneath the stairs. Under the influence of alcohol her reactions would have been slow. Before she'd barely realised it, he could have pulled the long scarf tight around her neck and . . .

Valerie rubbed hard at her temples. It was all conjecture, when what they needed was good hard proof. Livesey's presence on the estate, although highly suspicious, was circumstantial and wouldn't be enough to convict him. They were still waiting on forensics. Becky Hibbert's clothes had been sent for testing – it was even possible to lift prints and DNA traces from fabric these days – but it all took time. And of course, if Livesey had planned it, he would have been wearing gloves.

She had no doubt that they would eventually catch up with him. It wasn't easy to stay on the run unless you had large sums of money, a smart brain or excellent contacts. Any withdrawals from an ATM would give away his location. If he'd gone abroad it would make him more difficult to find, but something in her gut told her that this was unlikely. He was a local boy, born and bred in Kellston, and in all likelihood wouldn't stray far from his roots.

Valerie lifted her preliminary report out of the tray and leafed through it again. At least with Livesey in the frame she no longer had to worry about that complicating Minnie Bright connection. However, Harry Lind had been a great cop with excellent instincts, and she couldn't afford to dismiss the information out of hand. Even though it didn't seem to have any bearing on the case, she had logged his comments and sent a copy to Superintendent Redding.

Thinking of Harry immediately reminded her of Jessica Vaughan and their meeting a few hours earlier. It had been a short if not entirely sweet interview. Valerie, even though she'd been aware of behaving unprofessionally, hadn't made much of an effort to hide her antagonism. She'd been stressed, under pressure and not especially interested in what Vaughan had got to say. Maybe the girl had been the target of an arson attack last night, but so what? That didn't mean there was any link to the death of Becky Hibbert. Reporters, like police officers, must make lots of enemies.

Valerie could have, maybe *should* have, got someone else to talk to Vaughan, but a rather perverse curiosity had prevented her from doing so. It was a few years since they'd last had any contact and she'd wanted to take another look. The bottom line, and she wasn't especially proud of it, was that she'd been checking out the competition. Although neither of them had mentioned Vaughan's new status as Harry's temporary flatmate, it had been forever present like a big fat elephant in the room.

Jessica Vaughan, she thought, wasn't Harry's usual type – that tended more towards the classic leggy blonde – but perhaps she had qualities that Valerie had yet to grasp. The girl was moderately pretty, intelligent enough and certainly possessed a streak of determination, but what did she have that Valerie didn't? She knew it was pathetic making comparisons like these, but somehow she couldn't help herself.

Valerie released a long and weary sigh. Perhaps what irked her most was that Harry hadn't told her about his new guest. One simple phone call was all it would have taken. And yes, okay, so it had only happened last night, but he could have given her a ring in the morning to let her know what was happening. Instead, she had had to find out by default. How long would it have taken him to tell her if they hadn't discovered that business card in Becky Hibbert's flat? And he hadn't exactly volunteered the information even when he'd come to see her. He'd only mentioned it when she'd said that she'd call Jessica herself.

Snapping the file closed, Valerie leaned forward and dropped it back into the tray. It was time to go home, to head back to Silverstone Heights, make herself something to eat and recharge her batteries. Trying to second-guess Harry Lind was utterly pointless. She had lived with him for years and still wasn't sure what make him tick.

She rose to her feet and put on her coat. It would help, she thought, if she could come to a decision about what she really wanted. The professional side of her life was sorted but the personal side was a mess. If she wasn't careful, their on-off relationship could drift on for years. Before she knew it, she'd be drawing her pension, unmarried and childless and still waiting for Harry to make a commitment.

On impulse, she sat down again and picked up the phone. She dialled the number before she had too much time to think about it. It was picked up after three rings.

'Wetherby.'

Valerie could hear music and voices in the background. She had a moment's hesitation – should she? Shouldn't she? – and almost hung up.

'Hello?'

'Hi,' she said brightly. 'It's me. It's Valerie.'

He sounded pleased to hear from her. 'Ah, my favourite inspector. How's things? Everything okay? Oddly enough, I was just thinking about you.'

'Oh yes? Thinking what? Or shouldn't I ask?'

'I couldn't possibly comment.' He gave a light laugh. 'Hang on a sec, I'm just going to go outside. I can't hear myself think in here.'

As she waited, Valerie wondered if he was with a woman, someone he didn't want eavesdropping on the conversation. She heard the sound of a door opening and closing, the noise of the music replaced by a dull drone of traffic before he came back on the line.

'Sorry about that. It's mayhem in there. One of the lads just got promoted, so we're having a few pints. It's always good to have something to regret in the morning. But enough of that. What can I do for you?'

Valerie hesitated again. She could still change her mind.

It wasn't too late. She could pretend she'd called about some work-related problem. But then she thought about Harry playing happy flatmates with Jessica Vaughan. Well, if he was moving on, so could she. 'Actually, I was wondering if you were still up for that drink. Tomorrow evening, maybe? You were right, we should celebrate. We had a good result.'

'Yeah, that sounds great. Where do you fancy?'

'How about the Fox, if you don't mind coming over to Kellston? Somewhere local would be better for me.' And even better, she thought, if she happened to run into Harry. If he was going to play fast and loose with whatever remained of their relationship, then so could she. Having a good-looking man on her arm might help him to realise that she wasn't going to wait around for ever.

'The Fox is fine. What shall we say – seven o'clock? You can always give me a bell if you get held up.'

'Good. I'll see you then,' she said.

'And hey, Valerie?'

'Yes?'

He paused. 'I'm glad you called.'

'I'll see you tomorrow.' She smiled and put the phone down. Immediately she thought of Harry again and felt a twinge of guilt. What was she doing? But she quickly pushed the question aside. It was only a drink, nothing serious. She wasn't planning on eloping with the guy.

35

Jess rolled over in bed, stretched out her hand and turned off the thin, annoying beep of the alarm clock. She rubbed at her eyes, still scratchy with fatigue. She had slept only fitfully, a part of her constantly alert to the night-time noises of a flat that was not her own. Every creak, every bump, even the patter of the rain against the window had lifted her out of her dreams and back into a nervous consciousness.

The scariest time had been just after one o'clock, when she had woken to the sound of footsteps. Her stomach had clenched, her heart starting to hammer out a thunderous beat. She had thought of the man who had strangled Becky Hibbert. She had thought of the man who had tried to kill *her*, here now perhaps to finish the job. Her whole body had gone rigid, sweat forming on her forehead, her pulse racing.

It had taken a long and terrifying thirty seconds for her to realise that it was only Harry coming in from his surveillance. His kind and thoughtful attempt at not disturbing her had backfired spectacularly. Mistaking his careful tread for that of an intruder, she had only realised her mistake when she'd heard him cough softly as he went into his room.

Jess shook her head, trying to clear her mind of the last eight hours. She got out of bed and padded out to the bathroom. There she stood for a long while under the shower, letting the hot water slough away the night terrors. Then she brushed her teeth and examined her face in the mirror. Frowning at the dark shadows under her eyes, she hoped that a layer of concealer might disguise the worst of the damage.

Back in the bedroom, she wondered what to wear for her meeting with Ralph Masterson. Not that she had a whole lot of choice. Her wardrobe still only consisted of a few essential items. Jeans, she decided, were out of the question, and she eventually settled on the black trousers, white shirt and black jacket. Although she had only talked to him on the phone, she had the impression that Masterson would respond better to someone who was smartly dressed.

She checked her watch as she put on her clothes. It was only eight o'clock, another two hours before the appointment. She would spend them going over her notes so that she was fully prepared when she arrived at his house. A faint flutter of excitement tugged at her insides. Masterson, she was sure, was not convinced of Donald Peck's guilt. Why else would he have agreed to see her? And if he was right, then the Minnie Bright murder case would be blown wide open. It would be a scoop, there was no doubt about that, but her motives in pursuing the truth had shifted from the professional to the personal. She could not shake off the nagging guilt that she was responsible for Becky Hibbert's death. If it was the last thing she did, Jess was determined to uncover the truth.

In the kitchen, she made coffee and toast and carried them through to the living room table. She sat by the window and gazed down on Station Road. It was another grey day, the rain falling steadily. The sunny weather of a few days ago already seemed like a distant memory. Still, the greyness suited her mood. After reaching for her notes, she bent her head and started to read.

Fifteen minutes later, she heard the door to Harry's bedroom open, and he wandered into the living room wearing his dressing gown. 'Morning,' he said. 'You sleep okay?'

'Like a baby,' she lied.

'Good. You want a coffee?'

'I'm sorted, thanks.'

As he went through to the kitchen, Jess noticed the deep scars on his left leg. They were the result, she knew, of a blast at a crack factory, a blast that had destroyed his police career. She thought how hard it must have been for him to have his life shattered in such a way. The scars, she suspected, were more than just physical.

Harry came back a few minutes later and sat down on the opposite side of the table. 'So,' he said, 'what are your plans for today?'

'I managed to track down Ralph Masterson, Peck's probation officer. I'm seeing him at ten o'clock.'

Harry paused for a moment, then said, 'So you're carrying on?'

Jess looked at him. 'Of course I am. Whoever torched my flat is still out there somewhere. What else can I do?'

'Leave it to the cops?' he suggested.

'They're too busy searching for this Livesey guy. They don't think there's any connection to the fire.' She remembered Valerie Middleton's curt conversation with her yesterday. 'And they certainly don't think that Becky's death has any link to the Minnie Bright case.'

'Maybe it hasn't.'

'Or maybe they've got the wrong guy. Or maybe someone paid Livesey to kill her.'

Harry's eyebrows shifted up.

She saw his expression and said, 'Yes, I know. It sounds kind of far-fetched. But doesn't it strike you as mighty convenient that Becky gets murdered the minute she opens her mouth and starts talking? And that someone tries to cook my arse on the very same night? That's just too weird to be a coincidence.'

'Perhaps.'

'There's no perhaps about it.'

Harry opened his mouth but then closed it again, probably realising that once Jess's mind was made up, no one was likely to change it in a hurry. He drank some of his coffee, glanced out of the window then looked back at her. 'So have you thought any more about tonight?'

'Tonight?'

'The casino,' he said. 'An opportunity to mingle with the big spenders and see how the other half live.'

Jess had forgotten all about his invitation. She was about to turn him down when she had a flashback to the evening before, of how jumpy and nervous she had felt. Harry probably wouldn't get back until the early hours, and as a result she was likely to have another anxious night. At some point she would have to get used to living alone again, but right now – at least while there was a killer on the loose – she preferred to be in company.

'Okay,' she said. 'Why not? What's the dress code, though? I'm a bit short on tiaras at the moment.'

Harry smiled. 'Just something smart, I guess. Are you okay for cash, only I could—'

'No, I'm fine. I sorted things with the bank yesterday and I've got my credit cards.' The other advantage of going to the casino, she thought, was that it would give the two of them the chance to have a proper conversation after she'd seen Masterson. It helped to have someone to bounce ideas off, especially in a situation as complicated as this one.

'Right,' he said, rising to his feet. 'I'm off for a shower. I'll be leaving about seven, so I'll meet you back here then.'

'Seven it is. I'll be ready.'

Jess finished her toast, thinking idly about the lovely Aimee Locke. She wondered what it was like to be married to a man who had so little trust he employed a private detective to spy on you. What kind of a relationship was that? But then when it came to honesty, she was hardly in the Premier League herself. She hadn't exactly lied to Neil, but she hadn't told him the whole truth either. She knew that when he heard about what had happened he'd be afraid for her safety and would try to persuade her to back off from the investigation. But she'd come too far to pull out now. Whatever the cost, however long it took, she was committed to seeing things through to the end.

36

Banner Road was only a short distance from Bethnal Green tube. Knowing that Ralph Masterson was the kind of man who would not appreciate tardiness – he'd made that perfectly clear on the phone – Jess had left herself plenty of time. Once she'd worked out where the road was, she went around the block, parked and waited there until it was almost time for their appointment. She used the ten minutes to take another look at her notes and to consider the questions she would ask.

As she drove slowly down the cul-de-sac, Jess saw a series of neat two-storey red-brick houses and realised from a For Sale sign that these were retirement homes. The buildings looked fairly new, and the front gardens, although small, were all carefully tended. Number 24 was at the end of the road. She pulled in to the kerb and turned off the engine.

As she got out of the Mini, she was instantly aware of being observed. At least three pairs of curtains twitched as she headed for Masterson's house. The Neighbourhood Watch scheme was in full swing here, the residents zealously guarding themselves and their properties. And who could blame them? London had plenty of junkie scumbags who wouldn't think twice about robbing or attacking the elderly.

Jess walked up the short driveway, pressed the bell and heard it ring inside. The door was answered almost immediately by a small, wiry man with more wrinkles than a walnut. A few thin grey hairs had been brushed back from his forehead in a vain attempt to cover the pink scalp underneath. His face, however, was full of character, and despite his age, the brown eyes were bright and alert.

'Hello,' she said, smiling and extending her hand. 'Mr Masterson? I'm Jessica Vaughan. Thank you for seeing me.'

He took her hand and shook it, his palm dry and papery but the grip still firm. 'Ms Vaughan,' he said, simultaneously giving her a nod. 'You'd better step inside before my overly vigilant neighbours raise the alarm.'

'Oh,' she said. 'Do I look that suspicious?'

He stood aside to let her in. 'Banner Road, I'm afraid, abounds with Miss Marples, all ready and eager to fear the worst. Already their tongues will be wagging ten to the dozen.' He expelled a thin sigh. 'In a community like this, every unknown visitor provides an opportunity for endless conjecture.'

Jess smiled again. 'Still, it must be nice to know that someone's watching out for you.'

'If you don't mind being under surveillance twenty-four hours a day.' He closed the door and led her into a room off the hallway. 'Please take a seat,' he said, gesturing towards a dark blue sofa. 'I took the liberty of making tea. I hope you drink tea. Or would you prefer coffee?'

'Tea would be lovely. Thank you. That's very kind.' She

sat down in the corner of the sofa closest to the matching easy chair and had a quick look around the room. It was hardly generous in its proportions, but it was light and clean, the walls painted cream, a beige carpet adorned with a rectangular rug patterned with deep blues and greens. There was a small mahogany table by the window. Uncluttered by too much furniture, it was a very male room, purely practical and without any of the softer feminine touches. An alcove to the right had been lined with shelves, and these were full of books, the spines revealing volumes of criminal law, biography and serious fiction.

Masterson lowered himself into the easy chair and leaned forward towards the tray on the coffee table. On it stood a white ceramic pot along with two china cups, a sugar bowl and a milk jug. Jess couldn't recall the last time she'd had tea made in a pot. She never got beyond dunking a bag in a mug of boiling water.

'So,' he said as he poured. 'You want to know about Donald Peck.'

'That's right,' Jess said. 'Although when I first started writing the article I wasn't interested in the original case. I was planning a piece about the long-term psychological effects on people who knew someone who had been murdered. I got friendly with a woman called Sam Kendall. Does the name mean anything to you?'

Masterson put down the pot and shook his head. 'I'm afraid not.'

Jess wasn't surprised. Sam hadn't given evidence at the trial, and although her name must have been known locally at the time of the killing, there was no reason for him to recall it fourteen years later. 'She was one of the girls who were hanging out with Minnie Bright that day.'

'I see.' His right hand trembled as he passed her the cup, but she had no way of knowing whether this was down to the emotive nature of the subject matter or simply the ravages of old age. 'Help yourself to milk and sugar.'

'Thank you.' Jess added some milk to her tea and stirred it. Then she took a quick breath and gave him a rundown on the threatening notes, the damage to Sam's car and the sudden decision of the two other girls not to talk. She didn't mention the fire, or Becky Hibbert's death. He may have heard about the murder on the news, but if he hadn't recognised Sam's name, then he probably wouldn't have recognised Becky's either. The one thing she didn't want to do was spook him. If he thought there was a chance of getting caught up in a murder inquiry, he might decide to keep quiet.

When she came to the end of her story, she took a sip of tea and put the cup down again. 'So that's how I started to wonder if there was more to the case than had come out at the trial. I could be completely wrong, but I'd like to hear your take on things. You were Peck's probation officer, so I imagine you knew him pretty well.'

Masterson paused for a moment, as if gathering his thoughts together. 'I'm not sure if anyone can really claim to understand a man like Donald Peck. He was . . . how shall I put it? . . . a highly complex and damaged man. I imagine you're aware of his history. Do you know much about exhibitionism?'

'No, not really,' Jess admitted. 'When I hear the word I

311

tend to think of furtive men in shabby raincoats jumping out from behind bushes and flashing their bits, but I'm sure there must be more to it than that. I presume it's a psychological disorder and that they get some kind of sexual thrill from exposing themselves.'

Masterson paused again before answering. 'That sums it up to a degree. I'm no expert, you understand, but I did look into the subject. It's helpful to know what you're dealing with when you have clients like Donald.' He put a level spoonful of sugar into his cup and stirred it carefully before looking up at her again. 'Research suggests that the main perpetrators of such acts generally fall into two groups: in the first are those who are shy and inhibited, unable to relate well to others and often suffering from feelings of guilt and sexual inadequacy; in the second are the more dangerous, possibly psychopathic offenders who may go on to commit much more serious and violent acts.'

'And which group did Donald fall into?'

Masterson's thin lips crawled into an uneasy smile. 'For the fifteen years or so that I worked with him, I always believed it to be the first. As indeed did the many doctors and psychiatrists. He was not a man who related well to other people, especially women, but he never displayed any tendencies towards violence.'

Jess frowned. 'But isn't flashing an act of aggression? I mean, surely the perpetrator must be aware that he's going to scare the hell out of the women and children he exposes himself to?'

'Well, that's the complicated part. In some respects you're

right, but the reasons behind it aren't always straightforward. He wants to provoke a response as the only way of proving his virility, his power, in a world where he possesses neither. The response may be a negative one – one of fear and hostility rather than love – but it's still a reaction. It proves that he's powerful enough to make an impact.'

'And that's enough? That's what he's after – just a quick thrill from scaring some unsuspecting girl?'

Masterson's shoulders shifted up. 'For men like Donald, who are incapable of forming normal human relationships, any connection is a gratifying one. In all the time I knew him, he never displayed any desire to touch or even talk to his victims. The very idea filled him with horror. He was incapable of having a normal sexual relationship but still craved some kind of contact. That's why ... why I found it so hard to come to terms with what happened.'

'You think it was out of character?'

'From what I knew of him, yes. His background, of course, was a troubled one. These things usually start in childhood, and his was particularly traumatic. I won't go into details, but suffice to say that by the time he was taken into care, the damage had already been done. He'd seen psychiatrists, had years of counselling, but some disorders are so entrenched that they can never be eliminated. Controlled perhaps, but never cured.' He raised a hand briefly to his chest, a thin, wheezy breath escaping from his lungs. 'Was he capable of murder? The truth is that I just don't know.'

'But you had doubts about his guilt?'

'Donald was always very honest with me. He freely

admitted to his crimes, never tried to deny them. This time he swore that he was innocent, but ...' Masterson spread out his hands, palms up. 'It's possible that finding the girl in his house made him angry, in much the same way anyone would be angered to find an intruder in their home. His reaction, however, could have been more extreme. He may have felt threatened, out of his comfort zone. Perhaps he lost his temper and lashed out.'

'And staring at a life sentence, he might not have been quite so inclined to tell the truth this time.'

'Possibly,' he agreed.

Jess was listening intently, making sure that she remembered everything. She had lost her tape recorder in the fire, and although she had a notepad in her bag, she'd decided not to use it. She wanted Masterson to speak freely, without worrying about his words coming back to haunt him. 'I hope you don't mind me asking, but why were you still seeing Donald Peck at that time? I mean, you'd already retired as a probation officer, hadn't you?'

'That's correct. I wasn't seeing him officially. It was more of an informal arrangement. As I mentioned earlier, Donald struggled to make connections with people, but over the years, he'd come to trust me. I was someone he could talk to. He viewed me as a friend, and to suddenly withdraw that support ... well, I'm not sure how he'd have coped with it.' He glanced briefly down at the floor before lifting his gaze to meet her eyes again. 'When Donald was anxious, his impulses took over. And when he felt insecure, he was more likely to offend. By talking to me, sharing his thoughts, he was able to find an outlet for his frustrations.'

Jess asked her next questions as casually as possible. 'There were relatives, weren't there? Didn't he have a sister?'

'That's right,' he said. 'Her name's Stella Towney.'

'But they weren't close?'

Masterson frowned a little. 'I wouldn't say that. But he didn't want to burden her. There were things he couldn't talk to her about, didn't *want* to talk to her about. I'm sure you can understand the reasons why.'

Jess gave a nod. 'It must have been tough on her, the trial and everything.'

'Indeed,' he replied shortly.

Jess sensed a discomfort in him, a sudden wariness. She saw his body stiffen as his eyes flitted down towards the floor once more. His hands, resting in his lap, began to tremble again. 'Does she still live locally?'

Masterson lifted his shoulders again in an exaggerated shrug. 'I've no idea. I'm sorry. We lost touch after the trial.'

Jess was sure he was lying. She'd have liked to press him further, but suspected that he might clam up completely. She decided to drop the subject and move on. 'Would you mind if we went over the day that it happened? It was a Wednesday, wasn't it?'

Masterson, back on safer ground, visibly relaxed. 'That's right. I saw him once a week, always on a Wednesday. I wasn't living here then. I only moved a couple of years ago, after my—' He stopped, and gave a thin smile. 'But that's of no relevance. The house that Donald came to was off Cambridge Heath Road. The bus stop was only a thirty-second walk away. He arrived at his usual time, about half twelve.'

Jess wondered if Masterson had been going to say *after my wife died*. Was he a widower? There was no ring on his finger, but then lots of men didn't wear rings. She gave the room another quick glance, but found no photographs on display, no evidence at all that he had ever been married. 'And he stayed for how long?'

'About twenty minutes. Usually it was longer, but on that particular day I was feeling under the weather. I'd had a dose of flu that had knocked me for six and wasn't really in the mood for company. Donald was kind enough to pick up some shopping for me and bring it over. He was very good like that. I made us both a cup of tea, we had a chat and he left at around ten to one. Perhaps a little after.'

Jess remembered what Sam had told her about the black holdall that Donald had been carrying when the girls had spotted him on Kellston High Street. So not, of course, full of tiny hands and arms and legs, but only containing some mundane groceries for Ralph Masterson. 'And if he managed to catch a bus fairly quickly, he could have been back at Morton Grove by about one thirty.'

Masterson gave a slight tilt of his head. '*If* he got a bus. He always maintained the story that he walked around for most of the afternoon and didn't return to his house for several hours.'

'By which time there'd be no reason for Minnie Bright to still be there. The key was in the back door and she could easily have let herself out.'

'Exactly,' he murmured.

There was a short silence while they both thought about this. It was Jess who was the first to speak again. 'Even if he

316

did go straight home, that would still mean that Minnie Bright had been there for over an hour. What on earth was she doing for all that time?'

Masterson leaned forward a little, placing his hands on the tops of his thighs. 'Well, the prosecution had two theories about that. One was that she was still searching for the treasure that she believed to be hidden there. The other was that, having failed to open the door when she was told to, she was scared of facing the other girls and wanted to be sure that they had gone.'

Jess could see how a jury would have accepted either of the options. 'It would have helped if Donald had been less vague about what he had been doing during the rest of the afternoon.'

'He'd often tramp the streets, sometimes for miles. I doubt if he recalled where he'd been or what route he'd taken. He may have ... Well, he may have given in to his impulses at some point and not wanted to admit to it.'

'Better than going down for murder.'

Masterson, as if the memory of it all was almost too much to take, slowly shook his head. His voice was tinged with resignation. 'Except he may have believed that admitting to such an act would make the jury more inclined to convict him. It would hardly make them more sympathetic, would it? And anyway, there was no exact time of death for Minnie Bright, and so even if Donald hadn't got back until much later in the afternoon, it could still have been argued that the girl had, for whatever reason, remained in the house.'

'But it would have cast some doubt. A decent lawyer

317

could have claimed that Minnie staying for an hour was just about possible, but not for two or three.'

'Perhaps you're right. Unfortunately there were no witnesses either to Donald's walkabout or to what time he returned home.'

'Okay,' Jess said. 'What if, for argument's sake, he didn't do it? What I still don't get is why he didn't realise that the body was there. There must have been . . .' She wrinkled her nose. 'Er, some kind of smell.'

'There probably was, but that would have been nothing unusual. The building was falling down and riddled with damp. And Donald wasn't the best of housekeepers. I imagine he was used to his surroundings smelling less than aromatic.' Masterson lifted his chin, and a flash of anger blazed into his eyes. 'If it hadn't been for those damn girls . . .'

'For those girls?' Jess urged softly.

'They should never have made Minnie Bright go into his house,' he hissed. 'Why did they do that? What kind of ten-year-old doesn't know the difference between right and wrong? And they're still out there now, living their lives as if nothing—' He stopped suddenly, as though he knew he'd said too much. His hands, which had been raised, dropped like stones to his knees.

Jess could have replied that not *all* of them were still living their lives. Lynda Choi was dead, and so was Becky Hibbert. As she looked at his face, she felt a wave of suspicion roll over her. Could Masterson be nursing a grudge? He was certainly full of anger about what had happened, and earlier he'd been evasive about Stella. No, more than evasive. She was certain he'd been lying. But could she really envisage him running around slashing tyres, pouring petrol through letter boxes and strangling a woman more than half his age? The idea was beyond ludicrous, and yet she couldn't entirely dismiss the idea that he could have been involved in some way.

Masterson gave a sigh. 'I must apologise,' he said. 'I spoke out of turn. I didn't intend to . . .'

'That's all right,' Jess said. 'No problem.' As if something toxic has been released into the atmosphere, she was feeling a sick sensation in the pit of her stomach. Suddenly she was eager to be away from this room, out of the house and back in the fresh air. Quickly she rose to her feet. 'Look, I've taken up enough of your time. Thank you so much for talking to me. You've been very helpful. And thank you for the tea.'

Masterson stood up too. 'You'll stay in touch? You'll let me know if there are any developments?'

'I will,' she said, heading towards the front door. Knowing that he was close behind her, she glanced back anxiously over her shoulder, as if he might be about to hit her over the head with a heavy blunt instrument. She gave herself a mental shake. Her imagination was running away with her. Masterson might not be all that he seemed, but he was hardly likely to bludgeon her to death in his own home. Despite these private assurances, she still had to force herself to pause on the doorstep, to shake his hand again, to smile and say goodbye.

As she hurried along the drive, Jess could feel his eyes boring into her. The hairs on the back of her neck stood on end. Hastily she got into her car and locked it. By the time she looked across again, his front door was closed. She pulled the seat belt across, her heart pounding. Something was wrong, very wrong. Perhaps the local Miss Marples had something to worry about after all.

37

It was almost midday when DI Valerie Middleton drove into the car park of Belles and pulled up beside a sleek green Mercedes. 'Good, he's here,' she said to Swann. 'That's Chris Street's car.'

'Jesus,' he murmured. 'And they say crime doesn't pay. We're in the wrong job, guv. How much do you reckon a motor like that costs?'

'More than we'll ever be able to afford.' She turned off the engine, sat back and gazed for a while at the entrance to the building. Despite the endless talk of an economic crisis, the club was doing a brisk trade even at this hour. The City boys, all suited and booted and flashing their gold Rolex watches, were pouring out of black cabs. 'Look at them,' she said. 'You'd think naked girls were going out of fashion.'

'It won't just be the girls they're here for. They'll be after a bit of the white stuff too, something to give them a lift before going back to work.'

Valerie gave a nod. 'And the delightful Street family will be happy to oblige.'

'Always the perfect hosts.'

'One day we'll catch the bastards at it.' She frowned as

she thought about the Streets. There had been a rumour a couple of years ago that the family was finally losing its grip, that their time as a major criminal force was drawing to an end. Unfortunately, a rumour was all it had turned out to be. Since then, Belles had been completely refurbished, redecorated inside and out, and become more popular than ever. Quite where all the cash had come from for such a major overhaul was anyone's guess, but drugs, prostitution, extortion and theft probably figured somewhere on the list.

Swann slipped off his seat belt. 'I wouldn't hold your breath. Terry's had a hold on this manor since before you were born.'

'All the more reason to go after him. In fact that whole damn family needs locking up.'

'And then what? The minute they're gone, they'll be replaced by some other piece of shit. Nature, as they say, abhors a vacuum.'

Valerie gave a snort. 'So what do you suggest? We just sit back and let them get on with it?'

'I didn't mean that, guv. All I'm saying is that sometimes it's better the devil you know. At least Terry doesn't let things get out of hand. He knows how far he can go without crossing the line.'

'He's always crossing the line.' She understood what Swann meant, though. A gap in the market simply created an opportunity for other firms to move in and try to take over. And if the crime level was bad now, it would be ten times worse with several warring factions battling for power.

'Shall we go?'

'Just a minute.' She reached up, twisted the rear-view

mirror and checked her hair and face. Feeling Swann's eyes on her, she turned her head to look at him. 'What?'

He smirked. 'You thinking of applying for a job while you're in there?'

'Why, do you think I'm not up to it?' As soon as she'd asked the question, she wished she hadn't. A blush rose to her cheeks as she remembered that Kieran Swann was in a better position than most to evaluate her assets. When he'd saved her from the Whisperer, he'd also seen her in all her glory, naked as the day she'd been born. And that was a memory she had no desire to dwell on. Before he could even begin to think of one of his smart-arse replies, she quickly changed the subject. Turning the mirror back into position, she flapped a hand towards a massive black guy standing just outside the door to Belles. He was staring hard at them whilst speaking rapidly into a walkie-talkie. 'I think we've been spotted.'

'Solomon Vale,' Swann said. 'He'll be passing on the good news to Street.'

'And giving him time to clear the place of anything incriminating.'

They got out of the car and strode over to the door. Solomon shifted back a few steps, his massive bulk effectively blocking the entrance. Valerie looked up at him. The guy must be six foot five, maybe even taller. And solid with it. The muscles in his upper arms strained against the fabric of his dark suit. She took her ID from her pocket and flashed it at him. 'DI Middleton and DS Swann. We're here to see Chris Street.'

Solomon made a show of carefully examining her ID,

even though he'd already sussed them as cops. 'If you'd like to wait a moment, I'll let him know that you're here.'

'No point in telling him what he already knows,' Valerie said. She moved forward until they were only inches apart, all the time keeping her eyes locked on his. 'So if you wouldn't mind ...'

Solomon hesitated, but not for long. Winding up the law was a pleasure, but it wasn't as important as business. Another black cab had pulled in, and the occupants, four middle-aged businessmen, were already in the process of climbing out. It was never good for trade to have cops hanging around, and so with a shrug of his huge shoulders he stood aside and waved the two of them in.

It was a while since Valerie had last been in the club, and it had certainly smartened up a lot since then. The foyer was all gleaming chrome, potted palms and arty black-and-white photographs. But she knew it was entirely cosmetic. Underneath the slick exterior lay the same sleazy lap-dancing joint with the same sleazy lowlife owners.

The girl on reception was a bored-looking blonde wearing a tight silver dress with a lot of cleavage on view. Her breasts, almost ludicrously large, must have depleted the UK stocks of silicone. Valerie flashed her ID again. 'Chris Street,' she said. 'Where's his office, please?'

The girl looked past her towards the main door they'd just come in by. Valerie turned to see Solomon Vale standing there. He gave the receptionist a brief nod before heading back outside again.

'Take a right, end of the corridor,' the blonde drawled lazily.

'Thank you.' As Valerie turned to go, she noticed Swann's gaze fixed firmly on the girl's breasts. 'If you've quite finished,' she said to him.

'I was just making sure that—'

'Yes, I know exactly what you were making sure of.'

Swann gave another of his annoying smirks as they walked towards the rear of the foyer. Valerie took a deep breath, trying to suppress her irritation. Even after all the years they'd worked together, she was never sure how much of Swann's behaviour was natural and how much was deliberately contrived to wind her up.

Straight ahead was a pair of heavy double doors, from beyond which came the sound of music, the chink of glasses and applause. Veering to the right, Valerie pushed open the door marked *Staff Only* and stepped into the corridor. 'Ever get the feeling you're being watched?' she said as she glanced up at the cameras set high on the walls and close to the ceiling.

'Our Mr Street doesn't like any unhappy surprises.'

'Clearly. He's got more security here than we've got down the nick.'

'Yeah, well, he's probably got a lot he needs to keep secure.'

They kept going until they came to the end of the corridor and a door marked MANAGER. Valerie gave a cursory knock and walked straight in without waiting for a response. The office was light and spacious, with royal blue walls, gold woodwork and a cream-coloured carpet with a pile so deep she could feel her heels sinking into it. The paintings on display, all of them of naked women, were bordering on the pornographic. The room was about as tasteful as a tart's boudoir.

There were three desks, but only one of them was occupied, a pale wood affair curved around the left-hand corner. Behind it sat Chris Street, dressed in a smart grey suit and staring at a computer screen. He didn't bother getting up. He simply raised his eyes and smiled.

'Inspector. It's been a while. And Sergeant Swann too. To what do I owe the pleasure?'

Valerie approached his desk and looked down on him. Street was about forty, dark-haired and dark-eyed, with a pair of cheekbones sharp enough to cut your fingers on. She supposed that some women, especially those who didn't mind their men a little rough around the edges, found him tolerably good-looking. 'We're here about Dan Livesey.'

He frowned. 'Who?'

'I'm sure your time, Mr Street, is as precious as mine. So let's not waste it, huh? Dan Livesey, your employee, the man whose wages you pay every week.'

Street pushed the keyboard away from him, placed his elbows on the desk and steepled his fingers. 'Ah, *that* Dan Livesey. I believe I furnished one of your officers with the information you required yesterday.'

Valerie tilted her head to one side. 'That was yesterday. Things have moved on since then.'

'Yes, things have a habit of doing that, don't you find? But I don't see how I can be of any further assistance.'

'I'd like a list of all his known friends and associates.'

'Well then you've come to the wrong place. I hardly know the man. I may pay his wages but I don't organise his social life. I'm not his keeper, Inspector.'

Valerie leaned down, put her hands on the desk and lowered her voice. 'But I'm sure, if you put your mind to it, you could come up with some names. Like who he regularly worked with both here and at the Lincoln.'

Street's thin lips gradually widened into a mocking smile. 'And why should I do that?'

Valerie stood up straight again and looked over at Swann. 'Why don't you tell him, Sergeant.'

Kieran Swann sauntered over to the desk, folded his arms across his chest and stared down at Street. 'Because we're dealing with the murder of a young woman and we have reason to believe that the suspect may still be in the area.'

Street gave a shrug. 'I still don't see what that has to do with me.'

'He could be hiding out at a friend's, or in a building he's familiar with. A building like this one, for example. It must have lots of nooks and crannies. A basement too, I should think. We may have to make a thorough search.'

Street's smile slowly faded. 'Not without a warrant,' he snapped.

'Oh, that can be arranged,' Valerie said. 'But it will mean the cops crawling all over the place. I hope it won't inconvenience you too much.' She glanced at Swann. 'How long do you think a search like that might take?'

Swann drew in an exaggerated breath and shook his head ruefully. 'A place this size? Could take half the night, guv. And that kind of thing – well, it tends to scare the punters off. It would be a shame if that happened to a good upright business like this.'

Street looked from one to the other as he considered his options. His dark eyes had turned to stone. 'Well,' he said after a while. 'It would be a shame to waste the taxpayers' money on a futile search. I can assure you that Livesey isn't on the premises. However, as I always like to help the local constabulary, I can maybe sort that other little matter.'

'Ah,' Valerie said. 'I knew we could rely on that public-spirited nature of yours.'

Chris Street stood up and strode over to a blue-and-gold metal filing cabinet on the other side of the room. He opened the top drawer, flicked through the files inside and drew out a sheaf of papers. Then he walked back to Valerie and held them out. 'This is the best I can offer. It's a list of the rotas for the past three months, showing where Livesey was working and who he was working with.'

'Thank you,' Valerie said, taking the papers. 'It'll do. For now.' She gave him a nod. 'Goodbye, Mr Street. We appreciate your cooperation.'

Street sat back down behind his desk. 'Yeah,' he said. 'I'm sure you do.'

Valerie smiled as she and Swann left the office. It was nice to win the occasional battle in what was always going to be an ongoing war. Her good mood didn't last for long, however. The foyer was much busier than when they'd arrived, and they had to force their way through a crowd of rowdy male customers. The normal social niceties had apparently been left at the door, and she was aware of eyes blatantly looking her up and down as if she was a piece of meat. If leering had been classed as an illegal activity, she could have arrested the whole damn lot of them.

Once they were outside, she tossed the car keys to Swann. 'You drive. I want to look through these rotas.'

'You okay, guv?' he asked, seeing the expression on her face.

'Why shouldn't I be? It's the twenty-first century, supposedly an age of equality, and yet women are still peeling off their clothes to give mindless overpaid wankers a lunchtime thrill.'

Swann grinned. 'No change there, then.'

'More's the pity.'

They got into the car and Swann started the engine. 'That Chris Street's a piece of work.'

'Like father, like son. Still, he's an angel compared to his brother.' Valerie was relieved that Danny hadn't been around. The guy made her flesh creep. Chris's psychotic younger brother was every woman's nightmare – cruel and vicious and predatory. And if everything else they said about him was true . . . She shuddered at the thought.

'Back to the nick?' Swann said.

'Back to the nick.'

As Swann drove along Shoreditch High Street, Valerie bent her head and flicked through the sheets Chris Street had reluctantly given her. Livesey had been working the door at the Lincoln on the night that Becky Hibbert had been murdered – and the Lincoln was right beside the Mansfield Estate. He must have gone there right after the pool hall closed for the night.

Working backwards through the rotas, she studied the list of people who had worked with Livesey over the past three months. There was obviously a fast turnover of staff, and some employees came and went within a matter of weeks. Being employed by the Streets probably wasn't to everyone's taste. There were three or four guys, however, who'd regularly done shifts with Livesey. Only one of the names was familiar, but she couldn't quite place it.

'Michael Higgs?' she said, glancing over at Swann. 'Mean anything to you?'

'Yeah, I've heard that name somewhere.' He thought about it for a while, his forehead creased in concentration. The seconds ticked by, and suddenly his brow cleared. With the tips of his fingers he did a mini drum roll on the steering wheel. 'I've got it. That girl Harry told you about, the one Lister went to see yesterday. Paige something? The friend of Becky's.'

'Fielding,' Valerie said. And then it came to her too. 'Ah, *Micky* Higgs. That's it. He's the boyfriend, right? She flapped the sheets of paper against her right thigh. 'Which means he's not likely to be offering a helping hand to Livesey, not when the guy's a prime suspect for murdering his girlfriend's mate.'

Swann made a grunting sound in the back of his throat. 'Can't rule him out, though. Depends on how pally the two of them were. And what the girlfriend doesn't know, the girlfriend isn't going to grieve over.'

'Is that the voice of experience speaking?'

'Not me. I'm the honest, loyal type.'

In truth, Valerie hadn't got a clue about Swann's private life. She didn't even know if he was in a relationship. Her own desire for privacy prevented her from enquiring too closely into the personal lives of her workmates. She did, however, recall the way he'd ogled the receptionist at Belles. 'Yes, that's you all right. Never one to lech over a woman's cleavage without a perfectly valid reason.'

Swann grinned. 'Not leching, guv, *examining*. She could have been carrying a concealed weapon. I was just covering your back.'

'Concealed?' Valerie said. 'She couldn't have concealed a bee's kneecap in that dress.' She looked back down at the rotas and sighed. 'I suppose we'd better talk to this Micky Higgs. And there are a few others it could be worth having a chat with too.'

Swann gave her a sideways glance. 'You thought any more about what Harry said?'

Valerie bristled. Partly this was down to a deep-seated insecurity about being compared to Harry Lind in a professional capacity, but mainly it was because she was still annoyed by the presence of Jessica Vaughan in his flat. 'Harry?'

'About a possible connection to Minnie Bright.'

'Do *you* see a connection?' she asked, a little more sharply than she'd intended.

Swann considered the question before giving his answer. 'Well, from where I'm sitting it still looks like a straightforward domestic, but . . .'

'But?'

He shrugged and heaved out a breath. 'It could be that we're missing something.'

Valerie turned her face away and gazed out of the side window. They were words she hadn't wanted to hear. She was still convinced that Livesey was their man – why else would he have run? – but his reasons for killing Becky Hibbert might have their roots more in the past than the present. She couldn't dismiss the possibility that there was more to this murder than they'd originally thought.

38

Jess had driven straight back from Bethnal Green. Now she was sitting at the table in Harry's flat, her fingers flying over the keys of the laptop as she typed up her interview with Ralph Masterson. She wanted to get it all down while it was still fresh in her mind. He had provided some excellent background information, revealing to her a man who was perhaps more pathetic than demonic, and yet she was still no closer to knowing whether Donald Peck had been innocent or guilty.

As she worked, her gaze frequently darted out of the window and on to the street beneath. Since the fire, she'd been constantly alert, on the lookout for strangers hanging around or for anyone who might be acting suspiciously. She'd had one near-death experience and didn't relish the prospect of another. Suspicious strangers, however, were pretty much the norm in London, and she knew that if she wasn't careful, she'd develop a seething paranoia about every guy who had a shifty expression, who walked a little slower than he should or who stopped to light a cigarette.

The factual part of her summary flowed quickly and easily, but she hesitated when she came to the more subjective side. What did she actually feel? What did her instincts tell her? Well, for one thing she was sure that Ralph Masterson was hiding something – but then that was nothing new. The whole Minnie Bright case was under-pinned by secrets. And for another, she hadn't imagined Masterson's anger. His words echoed in her ears: *What kind of ten-year-old doesn't know the difference between right and wrong?* Now there was a man with an axe to grind. He'd also been evasive about Stella Towney.

Jess stopped typing, picked up her mug and drank the dregs of her coffee. It was cold but she barely noticed. Outside, the grey clouds had parted and a few thin rays of sunshine were slipping through. She got up from the chair and stretched her arms up over her head. What she needed was a walk, some exercise to get the blood pumping to her brain again.

She put on her jacket, grabbed her bag and headed for the door. As she passed the first-floor landing, she could see the open door to Mackenzie, Lind and considered going in to get Harry's take on what Masterson had told her. She stood for a moment, her hand on the curve of the banister, but then decided to leave it. Her news could wait until tonight.

Despite the sun, the air still had a chill to it. A cool breeze flapped at the thin fabric of her white shirt and made her shiver. She zipped up her jacket and bent her head as she walked to the end of Station Road and turned right on to the high street. What she had in mind was an afternoon of therapeutic shopping. If she was going to the casino with Harry tonight, she'd need a pair of killer heels to go with the little black dress that was hanging in the wardrobe. She could do with some jewellery too. Nothing fancy, just a few accessories to finish off the outfit.

She spent the next hour flitting from shop to shop, trying to balance her desire against her limited budget. She couldn't afford to go mad; her choices had to be sensible ones. When she found the shoes, however, all thoughts of economy went straight out of the window. The black stilettos with the tiny cream bows on the front were irresistible. She tried them on and they fitted perfectly. She glanced at the price, ninety-five pounds, and winced. Still, she decided, it would be pointless to buy a cheaper pair that she might never wear again. At least she would get some use out of these. And every girl, even those who spent most of their lives in jeans and trainers, needed to be prepared for those occasional visits to the casino.

Having spent more than she'd intended, Jess put herself in budget mode as she entered Ruby's. The jewellery store had plenty to tempt her, and she spent the next twenty minutes browsing the display cabinets. A gold chain? A silver one? Eventually she settled on a simple string of pearls with matching pearl earrings. They were fake, but would easily pass for real, especially in a dim light.

With her shopping finished, Jess stood on the pavement and wondered what to do next. She didn't want to go back to the flat just yet. She felt too restless, her mind running once more through all the thorny complications of the Minnie Bright case. She was waiting for things to drop into place, for the fog to clear and the truth to be revealed. She had the feeling she could be waiting for a very long time.

Looking across the street, she saw the supermarket and had an idea. Perhaps Clare Towney was working there today. It was about time, she thought, that she put a face to the name. She had no intention of talking to her – she had promised Harry that they'd see her together – but a sneaky glimpse was hardly breaking her word.

Jess crossed over, jaywalking through the slow-moving traffic. Inside the shop, she picked up a basket and joined the throng. This high-street store was one of the smaller supermarket outlets, but it was still busy. As she wandered along the aisles, gathering a few random items – apples, bread, pasta, toothpaste – she glanced surreptitiously at the name badges of all the girls of a certain age who were stocking the shelves. By the time she'd completed three circuits, it was clear that Clare wasn't around. Disappointed, she headed for the checkout, where two middle-aged women and a young, lanky bloke were manning the tills.

Jess had moved up to third place in the queue when her mobile started ringing. She put her basket on the ground, pulled the phone out of her pocket and checked the caller. It was an unidentified number.

'Hello?'

'Jessica?'

'Yes,' she said, pressing the phone closer to her ear and trying to identify the voice. It was male, but it sounded muffled, as if it was coming from a very long way away. Not Neil, though, and not Harry either.

'How are you?'

'I'm good,' she said, playing along while she tried to figure out who it was. An old colleague? Someone she'd been talking to recently? 'Sorry, I can't hear you very clearly. It's a really bad line.'

There was a rustling from the other end. Then silence.

'Hello?' Jess said. The queue shifted and she shuffled forward, using her right foot to move the basket. 'Hello?'

'Not much shopping,' the voice said. 'What's the matter, babe, lost your appetite?'

She felt a jolt run through her. 'What?'

'Nice shoes, by the way. Black. That's always a good choice.'

Jess whirled around, panic rising in her throat. Her gaze quickly raked the aisles for a man using a phone. She couldn't see one. 'Who is this? What do you want?'

There was a low, sinister laugh. 'I want you to mind your own fuckin' business, love. Do you think you can manage that?'

She could feel a cold sweat forming on her forehead. A sliver of ice slid down her spine. The man was here, close by, the man who had set fire to her flat and tried to kill her. Her first instinct was to run, but then her gaze darted to the wide glass windows. Maybe he was outside rather than in. Maybe he was waiting for her out on the street. Her fingers tightened around the phone. She said nothing. She couldn't. Her throat had closed up and her lips were dry as parchment.

After a few seconds the voice came again, soft and menacing. 'Be careful when you close your eyes at night, Jessica. You never know who'll be there when you open them again.'

And then the line went dead.

For a moment she stood rooted to the spot. Her breath was coming in short, fast pants, her heart racing. And then the adrenalin kicked in. She couldn't stay where she was. Abandoning the basket, she rushed out of the store and into the street. She looked left and right, scanning faces and examining the cars parked along the kerb. Where the hell was he? Still watching her, or already gone? Well, she wasn't going to hang around to find out.

As she fled back towards Station Road, glancing constantly over her shoulder, another grim thought entered her head. What if he was waiting for her there? The front door would be open. He could walk straight in. She paused on the corner, racked by indecision. But where else could she go? Then her brain kicked into gear. No, he couldn't get in without Lorna hearing him. It was impossible. The buzzer sounded as soon as the door was opened.

Jess set off again, jogging the last few yards to the entrance to Mackenzie, Lind. The carrier bag with the new shoes bounced hard against her thigh. She hesitated when she reached the door, fear scratching at her nerves. Then she swallowed hard and quickly pushed it open. She gazed up the staircase. It was empty. She listened, but couldn't hear anything. She took a deep breath, went inside, closed the door firmly behind her and ran up the stairs.

Lorna was sitting at her desk, hunched over a pile of paperwork. She lifted her head as Jess came into the office, and smiled.

'Hi, how are you?'

Jess's heart was still thumping in her chest. 'Good, thanks. Is Harry here?'

'Sorry, love. He's out for the afternoon. You can get him on the phone, though.'

Jess was tempted to blurt it all out, to tell Lorna what had happened, but she bit her tongue. She'd inflicted enough of her problems on the woman already. 'Oh, okay. I'll do that.' She turned to go, then stopped. Before she went up to the next floor, she had to ask the question. 'Er . . . no one's come in here, have they? I mean in the last five minutes or so.'

'No. Were you expecting someone?'

Jess shook her head, relieved. 'Not exactly. I just thought . . . it doesn't matter.'

'Well, only Mac, but you didn't mean him, did you?'

'Mac?' Jess repeated unsteadily. It came out as more of a croak than a query.

'Yes, he just nipped out for a sandwich.' Lorna frowned. 'Are you sure you're all right? You look like you've seen a ghost.'

'Do I?' Jess said, feebly attempting a laugh while her thoughts began to spin. So Mac had been out at the same time as the call had been made. How long had he been gone? It was hardly a question she could ask. And surely it couldn't have been him. Why would he be threatening her? Except the voice had been so muffled, she couldn't swear that it *hadn't* been his.

Lorna gazed up at her, a quizzical expression on her face.

Jess backed away. 'Sorry, my head's all over the place at the moment. I'd better go. I'll see you later.'

She dashed up the stairs, unlocked the door to Harry's flat and then locked it behind her. For a while she stood very still, leaning back against the wood. Her legs felt shaky and her stomach was churning. Not Mac, it couldn't be Mac. He might not like her – he'd made that pretty clear – but what reason could he have for warning her off? Except he was an ex-cop, and ex-cops had cop friends they might still be loyal to. If there had been some kind of a cover-up on the Minnie Bright case . . .

Jess waited until her legs had steadied before pushing off the door, dropping the carrier bag and her handbag on the table and going over to the window. She stood to one side, hidden by the curtain, and peered out, looking down the road towards the station and the Fox. Was paranoia starting to eat away at her reason? If Mac had only nipped out for a sandwich, he wouldn't have had time to see her buy the shoes. It must have been at least an hour after that that she went on to the supermarket. Jesus, she had to stop jumping to crazy conclusions. If she wasn't careful, she'd start suspecting anyone and everyone. And that, she knew, was the road to madness.

39

At six thirty, Harry took a shower, had a shave and then got dressed. He put on his grey Armani suit with a crisp white shirt and a red tie, ran a comb through his damp hair and gazed at his reflection in the mirror. He frowned. Perhaps he didn't need the tie. He took it off and opened the top button of his shirt. Then he wondered if the casino had a dress code. Deciding that it was probably better to be safe than sorry, he refastened the button and put the tie back on again.

On the off chance that Aimee Locke wasn't going to work tonight, Warren James would stay in Walpole Close and follow her if and when she left. That way they could be sure of not losing her. Harry could go straight to the West End, find somewhere to park and – so long as she was going to Selene's – be there by the time Aimee arrived.

Not counting the Friday, it was three days since the surveillance had started, and to date there was not a shred of evidence that Aimee Locke was playing away. In fact she rarely left the house. Apart from her dinner with Vita Howard, she had gone out only once, and that was to do some window-shopping on the high street. There had been the visit from the crimper, of course, but Harry tended towards the opinion that if she *was* having an affair, she was unlikely to invite her lover to Kellston. Less risky, surely, to take the car and meet him somewhere away from the prying eyes of neighbours.

He was surprised that Martin Locke hadn't called to find out what had happened on Friday. For a man who was convinced of his wife's infidelity, and willing to pay good money to have her investigated, he seemed curiously uninterested in the outcome. But then again, he could simply be putting off the news – be it good or bad – until he returned from his business trip. There was nothing Locke could do while he was away, so perhaps he preferred to remain in ignorance.

Harry took one last look in the mirror, made a final adjustment to his tie and went through to the living room. Jess was already there, sitting on the sofa and flicking through a magazine. She stood up as he came in and his eyes widened in appreciation. She was wearing a simple but classy sleeveless black dress that showed off all her curves. His gaze ran the length of her body and lingered for a second on her feet and ankles. What was it about high heels that always set his pulse racing? He gave a low whistle of appreciation.

'Very foxy, Ms Vaughan.'

'Thank you. You don't look so bad yourself.'

'So, ready for a night on the town?'

She picked up her bag and slipped it over her shoulder. 'Don't you mean a night spying on some poor unsuspecting woman who has seriously bad taste in husbands?'

Harry grinned. 'Well, that might be what I'll be doing, but you'll be free to squander all my money on the roulette table.'

'And if I win?'

'Then we split the proceeds,' he said. 'Fifty-fifty.'

'It's a deal.'

Harry locked up the flat and they went downstairs. Outside he beeped open the doors to the silver Vauxhall and walked around to the driver's side. He got in straight away, but Jess stood for a while gazing along the street in the direction of the Fox. He glanced behind to see what she was looking at but couldn't figure out what or who had caught her attention. It was just after seven, and the rush hour was over. Apart from a short queue at the bus stop, there was nothing much to see. A few seconds later she climbed in beside him.

'Everything okay?' he asked.

She hesitated, then gave a shrug. 'It's nothing. I just thought . . . It doesn't matter.'

'You still worried about that phone call?' Jess had told him about what had happened in the supermarket. It was enough to freak anyone out, especially after what she'd already been through.

'I suppose if nothing else it shows that I must be on the right track. Someone's certainly worried about what I'm doing.' She pulled her seat belt across and clicked it into place. 'But I still can't figure out how they even got hold of the number. I only bought the phone yesterday.'

Harry started the engine, checked his mirror and moved off. 'Who have you given it to?'

'You, Neil, Lorna, Sam.' She furrowed her brow, trying to remember. 'Oh, and Ralph Masterson has it too.'

'You think he could be involved?'

'Well I don't think it was him on the phone, and I can't really see him following me around Kellston. But I suppose he could have passed it on to someone else.'

'Anything distinctive about the voice?'

Jess shook her head. 'It wasn't that clear, but I think it was a London accent. Not especially old or young.' She gave a light laugh. 'Which really narrows it down. A man somewhere between twenty-five and fifty-five who owns a mobile phone. Shouldn't be too difficult to find, huh?'

Harry gave her a sideways glance. Despite all the bravado, he knew that she was shaken up. First the fire, and now this. 'Maybe you should let the police know.'

'What's the point? There's nothing they can do about it. I'd only be wasting my time.'

Harry shrugged. Although Jess hadn't given any details, he suspected that her interview with Val hadn't gone well. Which wasn't that surprising bearing in mind his own frosty reception. Anyway, most of the police effort was currently concentrated on finding Becky Hibbert's ex, Dan Livesey, and they simply weren't interested in an unlikely link to the past. 'So what about Masterson? Did he have anything interesting to say?'

As Jess was repeating her conversation with the old probation officer, Harry noticed how she kept glancing over her shoulder.

'Don't worry,' he said. 'We're not being followed.'

'How can you be sure? I mean, with all this traffic . . .'

'Because I've been keeping an eye out. Unless we're dealing with professionals using two or three vehicles, there's definitely no one on our tail.' He heard her expel a light sigh of relief. 'And don't worry about the flat, either. We've got cameras being installed on the stairs soon. That way we can see everyone who comes in off the street.'

Jess frowned at him. 'Not on my account, I hope. I'm okay. That call just ... it just shook me up a bit.'

'I know. But it makes sense to have more security about the place. Lorna's often in the office on her own. She'll feel safer with the cameras there.' They hit a red light and Harry pulled up. While they were waiting, he returned to their earlier subject. 'So,' he said, 'what's your gut feeling about Ralph Masterson?'

Jess pulled a face. 'Good question. He's certainly angry and resentful, but whether he'd go as far as murder ... I'm not sure if he's capable of that. He didn't want to talk about Stella Towney, though. He claimed they hadn't been in touch since the trial.'

'You think he was lying?'

Jess gave a nod. 'For sure. But I don't understand why.'

'Maybe he's trying to protect her. Maybe he thought that if he agreed to talk to you, if he gave you as much information as he could, then you wouldn't go sniffing round Stella.'

'Er, excuse me,' she said. 'I don't *sniff*. I investigate and I report.'

Harry grinned. 'My mistake.' The lights changed and he shifted the car forward. 'Well, maybe he just didn't want

Stella bothered, especially if what Maggie McConnell said is true.'

'I'm hardly likely to go hassling a woman with Alzheimer's. Give me some credit.'

'I suppose he doesn't know what you're capable of. Some journalists – present company excepted – don't have too many moral boundaries when it comes to rooting out a story.'

Jess glanced over her shoulder again, as if she simply couldn't help herself. She saw him looking at her and smiled. 'Sorry. It's developing into a nervous twitch.' She chewed on her lower lip for a moment and then said, 'I thought I might try and see Clare Towney tomorrow. Do you want to come along?'

'Do you really think that's a good idea?'

'What, you coming along or my going to see Clare?'

'The latter,' he said. 'I don't imagine she'll take too kindly to being doorstepped. I know I wouldn't.'

'Well, I'll call her first. I won't just turn up.'

'And if she refuses to talk to you?'

Jess was saved from making a reply by an incoming phone call on the hands-free system. Harry pressed and released the button on the steering wheel. 'Warren,' he said. 'Good news, I hope.'

'Yeah, no problems. She's in a cab and heading towards the West End.'

'Great. Stick with her for a while just in case.'

'Will do,' Warren said. 'I'll give you a call if anything changes.'

'Thanks. See you later.' Harry ended the call, relieved

that they hadn't had a wasted journey. 'Game on,' he said as they joined the line of cars in Park Lane. 'It looks like she's going to work.'

The corners of Jess's mouth twitched before her lips widened into a mischievous smile. 'So you're about to see the lovely Aimee Locke again. Is your heart beating just a little bit faster?'

In truth, Harry *was* looking forward to seeing Aimee again. He hadn't had a glimpse since last Friday night at Adriano's, and she had made quite an impression on him then. On the single other occasion that she had gone out, it had been Warren who'd been on surveillance. 'If I didn't know you better, Vaughan, I might think you were the one with a teensy-weensy little crush.'

'In your dreams, sweetheart. Mind, if I *was* that way inclined . . .'

Harry raised his eyebrows. 'Do you mind? I'm trying to negotiate some tricky traffic here. I don't need images like those running through my head.'

'Admit it,' she said. 'You wouldn't kick the goddess out of bed.'

Harry wasn't about to admit anything. The last time he'd mixed business with pleasure, it hadn't ended well. Bones had been broken and people had died. A sudden image of Ellen Shaw, small and dark and vulnerable, rose into his mind. He felt a tightening in his chest, a squeezing of his heart. He might be a fool when it came to love, but even fools learned from their mistakes. On no account was he ever going *there* again.

40

Valerie had left Cowan Road at six and driven home to get changed. After taking a shower and doing her make-up, she'd spent the next half-hour trying to decide what to wear for her drink with Simon Wetherby. She'd been reluctant to think of it as a date, partly because of her confusing on–off relationship with Harry and partly because she didn't want to ponder too much on what it would mean to embark on a relationship with someone new.

Unsure as to what effect she wanted to create, she had gone through the palaver of dragging endless garments out of the wardrobe, holding them up to her body, gazing into the mirror and then throwing them on the bed. Too smart, too casual, too sexy, too boring. By the time she'd eventually chosen a dark green dress that flattered her figure without being too revealing, it had been time to leave.

The Fox was only five minutes from Silverstone Heights, and so she'd left the car at home and walked. Simon had been waiting for her outside the pub when she'd arrived shortly after seven. She had felt butterflies in her stomach as she saw him standing by the door. He really was very good-looking, with his wide brown eyes and tawny gold hair.

Dressed in a smart grey suit, he'd obviously made an effort, and Valerie was glad that she had worn the dress rather than anything more casual.

Simon had greeted her with a peck on the cheek, told her she looked stunning and held the door open for her as they went inside. So far, so good, she had thought. But she'd still been nervous about how the evening would go. Getting on with someone on a work basis was one thing, but socialising with them could be quite another.

Within a few minutes, however, all her reservations had disappeared. Over a glass of wine the conversation flowed easily, and she quickly relaxed. He was amusing, intelligent and charming. He also listened to what she had to say. After the frustrating day she'd had – still no leads on the where-abouts of Dan Livesey, and a blank on any useful forensics – it was a relief to wind down and relax with someone who understood the trials and tribulations of the job.

Now, almost an hour after they'd arrived, he leaned across the table, smiled and said, 'So, Inspector, if you don't mind me asking, what made you change your mind about coming out for a drink?'

She smiled back at him. 'You want the honest truth? I couldn't bear the tragic disappointment on your face.'

He grimaced in mock dismay. 'Was it that obvious? And here was me thinking I was being Mr Cool.'

'Mr Cool? I think that one needs some work.'

Simon laughed, opened his mouth to say something, then changed his mind.

'What is it?' she asked.

'Oh, I was just . . . No, it doesn't matter.'

'Go on,' she urged. 'If you don't tell me, I'll spend the rest of the night wondering what it was.'

Simon played with his glass for a moment, turning it in circles before slowly raising his eyes to look at her again. 'Well, I like you, you already know that, but I don't want to tread on anybody's toes.'

Valerie stiffened a little. She pushed a strand of hair back from her face. 'And whose toes would those be?'

'Harry Lind's. Someone said that you two were still together, and ...' He let go of the glass and placed his elbows on the table. 'Hey, it's none of my business, right? Just tell me to keep my nose out.'

'You've been listening to office gossip.'

He put his hands up for a second. 'Guilty as charged. Except ... well, no one was actually gossiping about you. I made a few discreet enquiries. Do you mind?'

Valerie gave a light shrug. She wasn't sure whether she minded or not. On one hand, it was flattering that he'd been interested enough to find out if she was single or not; on the other, she was none too happy to discover that her private life apparently wasn't that private. She wondered who'd told him about Harry. Swann perhaps. Simon had spent a fair amount of time over at Cowan Road recently, and Kieran was hardly the discreet sort.

'Forget it,' he said. 'I shouldn't have asked.'

'No, it's okay.' She took a sip of wine and put the glass back on the table. 'I do still see Harry, we've stayed in touch, but we're not ...' She struggled to complete the sentence. Not serious? Not going anywhere? Not committed? Thinking of Jessica Vaughan, she frowned. She doubted if

Harry's conscience was bothering him as much as hers was. 'We're still friends,' she said finally.

Simon gave a nod. 'That's good.'

'And you?' she said.

He wrinkled his brow, as if he didn't understand. 'Me?'

'You know what I mean.'

He smiled at her again. 'Actually, I just met someone. But I'm not sure how much she likes me.'

Valerie felt a light blush rise into her cheeks. She'd been out with other men during her split from Harry, but none of them had made her feel the way she was feeling at the moment. She had a connection with Simon that had been missing with the others. She looked into his eyes and said softly, 'Maybe she's still making up her mind.'

'Well, I'm the patient sort. She can take as long as she likes.'

There was one of those brief silences that seemed to brim over with unspoken words, with possibilities and tingling hopes. Valerie was the first to break it. 'Changing the subject,' she said. 'Have you ever come across a guy called Micky Higgs?'

'Doesn't ring any bells.'

'He's a doorman at the Lincoln Pool Hall. I went to see him today about the Hibbert murder on the Mansfield.'

'Oh yeah,' he said. 'I heard you'd got that case. What's the Higgs connection?'

'He used to work with Dan Livesey, so we figured he might have some idea of Livesey's whereabouts.'

'But he didn't?'

'*Claimed* he didn't.'

'You don't believe him?'

Valerie shook her head. 'I don't know. There's something off about this whole case. Livesey cleared out his flat either before or after the murder. If it was before, then the killing of Becky was probably premeditated, and yet he didn't make any real attempt to hide his face on the way in to the estate. But he knew the Mansfield, so he must have realised that he'd be caught on camera.'

'So maybe he didn't plan it. Could have been a domestic that simply turned nasty.'

'But if you'd just killed someone . . . well, okay, you might head home to pick up some essentials like your passport or money or whatever, but surely you'd be in and out as quickly as you could? I mean, you wouldn't hang about to do a proper clear-out.'

Simon lifted a hand, lightly stroking his chin while he thought about it. 'Unless you were pretty sure the body wouldn't be found for a while.'

She gave a sigh of frustration. 'But even then. And he couldn't have known anything for sure. There are lots of people wandering around that estate at that time of night. Any one of them could have stumbled on her.'

'You've got a point.'

Valerie raised her eyes to the ceiling. 'God, I'm sorry. I shouldn't be talking work with you. You've come out to relax, not listen to all this.'

'We're cops,' he said, smiling. 'We never relax. We don't know how. So tell me about this Micky Higgs. I take it he's not the most trustworthy of citizens.'

And Valerie suddenly realised that this was what she'd

missed – being able to share her problems, her worries and concerns with someone who truly understood. Ever since Harry had been invalided out of the force, she'd felt bad about mentioning anything even remotely connected to the job. She knew how much he missed it, and discussing her cases would have been like rubbing salt in the wound.

'About as trustworthy as your average Kellston lowlife,' she said. 'And he gave us a story that was suspiciously similar to his girlfriend's. Almost word-perfect, in fact. The girlfriend's called Paige Fielding. And Paige was a friend of Becky Hibbert's. And that's where it gets complicated.'

'Complicated?'

'It's a long story, one that goes back over fourteen years.'

'In that case,' Simon said, 'I'll get another round in before you tell me all about it.' He picked up the empty glasses, rose to his feet and gave her a probing look. 'That's if you haven't had enough of me already.'

She smiled up at him. 'Are you fishing for compliments?'

'Yes,' he said. 'I'm highly insecure. Feel like throwing one in my direction?'

She inclined her head, pretending to think about it. 'Well, you do have quite nice eyes.'

'*Quite* nice?'

'Be grateful for small mercies,' she said. 'Are you going to get those drinks, or are you going to stand there all night?'

'Two minutes,' he said. 'Don't go away.'

Valerie watched him as he walked off to the bar, her eyes firmly fixed on the back of his head. He had no worries on that score. She had no intention of going anywhere.

41

It was the first time Jess had ever been inside a casino, and this one was the very picture of opulence, all deep-pile carpet, red walls and crystal chandeliers. The surfaces were immaculately clean and gleaming. Situated down in the basement, below the nightclub, it had no windows and the lighting was mellow. She had heard that casinos were always windowless and often without clocks, so that the punters had no distractions and were less aware of the passing of time. No opportunity to notice the afternoon slip into dusk, or the night into dawn.

Jess glanced at her watch. It was getting on for eight o'clock, and already the place was heaving. There was an electric buzz in the room, as if a big win was just around the corner – one turn of the wheel, one throw of the dice, a single card that could be worth a fortune. She could see how easy it would be to get caught up in the atmosphere, to chance your arm on Lady Luck.

Harry had bought fifty pounds' worth of chips, but they hadn't put a bet on yet. Instead, they had got a couple of drinks and settled down on a plush leather sofa where they had a good view of the activity going on around them.

Warren had called again to say that Aimee Locke had been safely delivered by cab, but as yet she hadn't put in an appearance.

Jess sipped on a Singapore Sling, feeling an instant impact from the alcohol. She wondered if the bar staff deliberately made them extra strong or if she just wasn't used to drinking cocktails. A couple more of these, she thought, and she'd feel happy enough to gamble her life savings away. Well, what little was left of them. Harry was drinking tonic water in a tall glass with lots of ice and a slice of lemon.

'So what happens next?' she asked him. 'You just sit here, wait for her to show up and then watch her?'

'That's about the sum of it.'

'You think she might be seeing someone from the casino?'

'Could be.'

Jess wrinkled her brow. 'But even if she is, I don't see how you'll know about it. They're hardy likely to dance the fandango on the roulette table.'

'Granted, but they probably will talk to each other. And body language changes when people are involved in a relationship.'

A pretty blonde waitress glided past them with a tray of drinks. Jess noticed Harry's appraising glance and gave him a look.

'What?' he said.

'Er, I hate to tell this, but you're about to blow your cover.'

'How do you figure that one out?'

'Because you're supposed to be here with me, and anyone can see that I'm not the sort of girl who appreciates my man giving the glad eye to every passing piece of totty.'

'Sorry,' he said, grinning. 'I didn't think we were that serious.'

Jess put a hand on her chest, her eyes widening. 'How can you say that? You're breaking my heart.'

Harry sat back and laughed. 'Hang on a sec, aren't *you* the one doing the cheating here? Out on the town with your fancy man while your other half's away on business.'

'God, you're right,' she said, sucking in a breath. 'I'm such a hypocrite.'

'How's that going, by the way? Neil, isn't it? Think you might make it permanent?'

Jess felt a familiar knot twist into place in her stomach. She liked things the way they were with Neil and didn't want them to change. 'Marriage, you mean?' she said glumly.

Harry slowly shook his head. 'And you reckon I've got issues with commitment.'

Jess took another swig of her Singapore Sling. 'Hey, I've got nothing against commitment. It's just marriage I've got a problem with. And you would too if your parents were addicted to the institution. They're both on their third, and I doubt these will last any longer than the others.'

'Yeah, I can see how that might colour your view of things.'

'So, what's your excuse? I mean, you've still got this thing going on with Valerie, haven't you?'

'Thing?' Harry said.

'You know what I mean. You don't seem to have made a complete break from each other. Maybe she's the one.'

'And how are you supposed to know when someone *is* the one?'

'God knows,' Jess said, tilting her head back and laughing. She didn't want him to suspect, but her reasons for asking how he felt about his ex had their roots in more than idle curiosity. This evening, as they'd been leaving the flat, she had looked along the road and seen Valerie Middleton with a tall, good-looking man outside the Fox. There had been something about the way the two of them had looked at one another, at the way they'd smiled, at the way the guy had leaned down to kiss her cheek that ... well, it had suggested something more than friendship. 'I mean, how would you feel, for example, if she started seeing someone else?'

'I suppose she will eventually.'

'And that doesn't bother you?'

Harry hesitated before giving a small shrug.

Jess was none the wiser. She had been hoping to discover if he still wanted a future with Valerie, but getting information on his emotional life was like trying to squeeze blood from a stone. It was best, she decided, to keep her mouth shut. She didn't want him to get hurt, she liked him too much for that, but she didn't want to be a stirrer either. No matter how good their intentions, it was usually the messenger who got shot.

42

Harry leaned his spine against the soft leather of the couch and let his gaze slide back across the room to Aimee Locke. It was a couple of hours now since she'd started dealing blackjack, and there hadn't been an empty seat at the table since she'd arrived. Most of the punters were men, and none of them could keep their eyes off her. He had the impression that each and every one would be prepared to squander a fortune just for the pleasure of seeing her smile.

Tonight she was dressed in a long, silky red dress, styled to accentuate every beautiful curve of her body. Her lightly tanned arms were bare and smooth. He watched as she quickly dealt the cards, admiring her dexterity and her slim, elegant fingers. Despite a superficial friendliness – the men engaged her in almost constant conversation – there was something distant about her, a remoteness that made her all the more attractive. With her high cheekbones and grey-green eyes, she reminded him of an exotic cat, graceful and aloof, that gave and received love only on its own terms.

Jess, who had gone off to play on the slot machines, returned and sat down beside him. 'Anything happening?'

'Nothing yet.' Reluctantly he shifted his gaze off Aimee Locke. 'So, have you made me a fortune?'

'Sadly not, but I haven't lost you one either. I won a tenner, so I thought I'd quit while I was ahead. Pretty good self-control, even if I do say so myself.'

'Admirable,' he agreed.

'This place is a maze, though. It took me ages to find the loos, and then another twenty minutes to find my way back here.'

'Yeah, they do that deliberately,' he said. 'It's so they can put constant temptation in your path. All those flashing lights, all those coin-filled machines screaming *Play me, play me!* It's like an obstacle course in temptation.'

'Talking of which,' she said, looking across at Aimee. One of the punters had just had a big win and was in the process of handing over a substantial tip. 'She must make a bundle if everyone's that generous.'

Harry rubbed at his temples and frowned. 'You know, I still can't figure out why she's working here. The hours aren't exactly sociable and she can't need the money. Locke must be rolling in it.'

Jess finished the last inch of her drink and put the glass back on the table. 'Maybe she just needs a twice-weekly fix of lustful admiration.'

'Miaow,' he said. 'Have you got the claws out, Vaughan?'

She grinned at him. 'Sorry, let me rephrase that in language more suitable for a fully paid-up member of the sisterhood. Maybe she's the independent sort who likes to earn her own money and not be beholden to any man.'

'It's a theory.'

'Got a better one?'

It was at that precise moment that a door on the far side of the casino opened and Ray Stagg walked in. He was a sleek, handsome, fair-haired man a few years older and a few inches shorter than Harry. Dressed in a white tuxedo, he started on a leisurely tour of the room, stopping to talk to the regulars, to share a joke and do some convivial back-slapping. Just the sight of him made Harry bristle. Stagg was one of those villains who had used his filthy money – all made from drugs and prostitution – to buy into legiti-macy. Now he was the king of the castle, the beneficent host, and everybody loved him.

Well, almost everybody. It still stuck in Harry's craw that several years ago he'd been forced to make a deal with the bastard. He'd let Stagg keep a large supply of coke in exchange for information that was to put Jimmy Keppell away for life. It was a deal that still caused him sleepless nights. Keppell, of course, had deserved everything he'd got; he was a vicious hardcore gangster who had been responsi-ble for the blast that had killed two of Harry's colleagues. But had making the deal been the right thing, the *moral* thing to do? Sometimes, in those grey pre-dawn hours when his conscience came knocking, Harry still wondered if the end could ever justify the means.

It was another half-hour before Stagg sauntered over to the blackjack table. He waited until the hand that was being played was finished and then bent across to whisper in Aimee Locke's ear. Harry watched them closely. She gave a small nod, the merest hint of a smile, but there was nothing in her face to betray what she was thinking.

Jess followed his gaze and said, 'You spotting any useful body language, hun?'

'Are you taking the mick, Vaughan?'

'Just trying to be helpful.'

Ray Stagg left the table, went to the bar and got himself a drink. He stood there for a while, sipping on a Scotch while he surveyed his empire. Harry knew that with every minute that passed, Stagg's wealth was accumulating. No wonder he looked so smug. For all the jackpots, for all the big wins, it was always the house that came out on top in the end.

Aimee Locke continued to deal. She didn't look in Stagg's direction again, but his gaze returned constantly to her. It was as if he couldn't help himself. But then he wasn't alone in that. A quick glance around the casino confirmed to Harry that half the men in the room were equally enchanted. There was something unique, something mesmerising about Aimee Locke.

Suddenly, without any warning, Stagg put down his glass, moved away from the bar and headed straight towards Harry and Jess. Seconds later he was standing over them, an oily smile on his face.

'Mr Lind,' he said. 'How nice to see you again. It's been a while.'

Not long enough, Harry thought. He gave Stagg a nod but said nothing.

'I hope life's been treating you well.'

Harry maintained his silence.

Stagg's blue eyes hardened. He turned his attention to Jess. 'And Ms Vaughan too. To what do I owe the honour, business or pleasure?'

'Pleasure,' Jess said, smiling back nicely. 'We felt the urge to squander some money.'

'And win a bundle too, I hope.'

'Well,' she said. 'We don't ask for miracles.'

Stagg's smile faltered, but only for a second. The place was busy, the tables around them full, and he knew that the conversation could be easily overheard. Leaning in towards Harry, he said, 'If I could have a word in private.'

'Anything you've got to say, you can say it here.'

'I don't think so. Five minutes, that's all I'm asking.'

Harry decided to go along with it. If nothing else, he wanted to know what was on Stagg's mind. Rising to his feet, he looked at Jess. 'Excuse me,' he said. 'This won't take long.'

She gave a nod. 'Don't mind me. I'll be fine.'

Harry followed Ray Stagg across the casino and out through a staff door. There was a long, empty corridor beyond. Stagg walked briskly to the end of it and then turned right. His footsteps echoed on the wooden floor.

'Where are we going?' Harry asked.

'Somewhere we won't be disturbed.'

'If I was of a nervous disposition, that might worry me a little.'

Stagg ignored the comment. He didn't even look over his shoulder. Instead he kept on walking until he came to the end of the corridor. Pushing against a metal bar, he opened a fire door that led outside. The cool evening air flooded in, along with the sound of the traffic from the street.

'This is where we say goodbye,' Stagg said. He turned towards Harry, his face hard and angry. There was no pretence now, no trace remaining of that veneer of charm. 'Stay out of my club and stay away from her.'

Harry frowned, pretending not to understand. 'Her? I don't—'

'Don't even go there!' Stagg interrupted fiercely. 'You think I don't know what you've been doing? You're been watching her all night. Don't even try to fuckin' deny it.'

Harry didn't. The casino was covered with tiny cameras fixed into the ceiling. Stagg must have been watching him watching her for the best part of the evening. 'Well, she's a beautiful woman. Kind of hard to ignore.'

Stagg leaned forward until his face was only inches from Harry's. His breath smelled of whisky and cigarettes. 'Stay away from her,' he hissed again. 'You go near her one more time and—'

'And what?' Harry asked. He stared defiantly into the other man's eyes.

Stagg held his gaze, his face hard as stone. 'Let's just say I don't like scumbag peepers spying on my employees. Get the message?'

'Loud and clear.'

Stagg stood aside and gestured towards the open door. 'Take a left and you'll come to the front of the building. Your girlfriend's waiting for you there.'

Harry didn't move. He put his hands in his pockets and smiled. 'Are you this protective of all your employees, or just the ones you're sleeping with?'

'Get out of here!' Stagg's features twisted with rage and two thin stripes of red appeared on his cheeks. 'Get the fuck out of here while you can still walk!'

Harry laughed as he strolled out of the door. Seconds later it was slammed shut behind him. Quickly he headed back round to the entrance. Stagg's reaction had already told him what he'd wanted to know – that his interest in Aimee Locke went far beyond the purely professional.

Jess was waiting for him on the corner of the street. 'Ah, still in one piece,' she said as he approached. 'I was starting to worry.'

'Are you okay?'

She grinned. 'Nothing damaged apart from my pride. First time I've been to a casino and I get thrown out. That's a record even for me.'

'Sorry about that.'

'Oh, don't worry. It was all done very discreetly.'

They started walking along the street towards where the car was parked. 'Well, we've learned something tonight,' he said. 'Ray Stagg's certainly looking out for Aimee Locke.'

'Yes, but is it true love?'

Harry breathed in the night air and breathed out a sigh. 'I wonder.'

43

It was Thursday morning, shortly after ten, and Jess was alone in the flat. She was sitting working at the table – or at least trying to work. No matter how many times she went through her Minnie Bright notes, the pieces still wouldn't come together. All she knew for certain was that someone didn't want the truth coming out.

Her mind drifted back to the previous night, to Aimee Locke and Ray Stagg and the buzz of the casino. The legacy of three Singapore Slings, even after a decent night's sleep, was a small dull headache that nagged at her brain and made her thoughts sluggish. She wondered if Aimee's husband was the guy she had seen hanging around outside the office last Friday, the man who had kept walking past, unable to make up his mind about whether to go in or not. Of course, once that step was taken, there was no going back. And once suspicion had rooted itself, it would grow ever deeper. That marriage, she was sure, was already doomed.

With a yawn, she turned her attention back to her notes. Clare Towney was the next person she had to see. She checked the internet for a number but wasn't surprised to find it absent. The household was probably ex-directory. Her only other option, other than turning up unannounced, was to call her at work. But would that get Clare into trouble? Personal calls probably weren't encouraged, and Jess didn't want to alienate the girl before they even got a chance to talk.

She thought about it for a moment and then had another idea. She found the number for the Kellston branch of the supermarket and dialled. It was answered after a couple of rings, and she instantly put on her professional voice. 'Good morning,' she said briskly. 'This is Jane Woods from Human Resources. Could I speak to Clare Towney, please?'

'Oh, okay,' a man said. 'Just one moment. I'll see if I can find her.'

Jess gave a sigh of relief. In her experience, claiming to be from Human Resources was a fairly safe bet when ringing any large organisation. No awkward questions about what the call was about or any nasty comeback on the recipient. It didn't always work, but thankfully on this occasion it had.

A couple of minutes passed before a girl's voice, small and tentative, came on the line. 'Hello?'

'Hi,' Jess said. 'Is that Clare?'

'Yes.'

'I'm sorry to bother you at work,' Jess said. 'I told the man who answered I was from head office but ... well, actually I'm a reporter. My name's Jess Vaughan.'

'Is this about—' Clare stopped abruptly. 'What do you want?'

'It's about your uncle, Donald Peck. I have some new information and I'd like to discuss it with you.' Fearing that she might hang up, Jess quickly added, 'I talked to Ralph Masterson yesterday and he was very helpful.'

'I don't see how I can ...'

Clare's voice trailed off and Jess smartly filled the gap. 'I think you'll be interested in what I've got to say. How about this afternoon, after you've finished your shift? It won't take long. I could come to your house. Palmer Street, isn't it? What time would be good for you?' Jess knew that she was railroading her, but she was also aware that this might be the one and only opportunity she got to secure the interview.

There was a silence, as if Clare Towney was trying to decide what to do or say next. Jess plunged in again, eager to persuade her. 'Look, what I've found out could change everything. And I think you have the right to know about it first.'

'All right,' Clare eventually said, albeit without much enthusiasm. 'Come over at two o'clock.'

'Thank you.' Jess asked for the number of the house and scribbled it down. 'I'll be there.' She said her goodbyes and hung up.

Sitting back, she pondered on what approach she should take when they met. Clare Towney had every reason to be angry and resentful about what had happened in the past. She and her mother had been made to suffer for someone else's crime. Over fourteen years, rage could easily build up and resentments could fester. Donald Peck may or may not have been guilty of murder, but if the girls hadn't encouraged Minnie to go into the house in the first place ...

Jess recalled her conversation with Masterson and his

367

sudden outburst about the ten-year-olds. *His* anger had been clear as day. Did Clare share his bitterness? Did she also believe that the girls had got off lightly? After having made a new life for herself, she had had to return to Kellston, to a community that had once rejected her. And what had she discovered when she'd got back here? That the girls who had abandoned Minnie Bright to her fate were all getting on with their lives, oblivious or maybe just indifferent to the damage they had caused. Well, all apart from Lynda Choi.

Jess was still pursuing this line of thought, wondering how she'd feel in the same situation, when she heard the door to the flat open. She looked up as Harry came into the living room.

'Hi,' she said. 'Are you free at two o'clock? I've just spoken to Clare Towney. She's agreed to a meeting.'

Harry pulled out a chair and sat down on the opposite side of the table. He was wearing his serious face.

Jess tried to deflect any imminent objections. 'Hey, I know you're not happy about it, but I've really got to talk to her. She's got more reason than most to bear a grudge.'

'It's not that,' he said. 'I've just had Jeff Bryant on the phone.'

The name was familiar, but she couldn't quite place it. 'Who?'

'From the Fire Service.'

'Oh,' she said.

'Apparently the guys from the Fire Investigation Unit have had a chance to take a closer look at your flat and ... Well, it seems like you were definitely the target. The bedroom window, the one you couldn't open, had been sealed from the outside.'

'Sealed?' Jess echoed weakly.

'Some kind of industrial-strength adhesive, they think. It still needs to be analysed.'

Jess swallowed hard. Although she thought she'd come to terms with the fact that she was probably the intended victim, the confirmation still rattled her. She had a sudden flashback to the room filling with smoke, to her desperate attempts at escape. Her heart began to pump a little harder. She realised now that it wouldn't have mattered if she had been able to open the grille – the window still wouldn't have shifted.

Harry reached across the table and touched her hand. 'Are you okay?'

'Sure,' she said over-brightly. 'I mean, we'd already guessed that the fire was meant for me, hadn't we?'

'Except there's a difference between someone trying to scare you into silence and a full-blown murder attempt.'

'Thanks for reminding me.' Jess could see now how the killer had figured it would pan out. By starting a blaze in the hallway, a fire that would quickly spread to her flat, he or she would effectively block the exit from her front door and her living room. The only way out would be through the bedroom window, and so that had to be sealed off too. They had, in effect, created a tomb for her.

'The Hackney police will want to talk to you,' Harry said. 'We could go now if you like. Do you feel up to it?'

She lifted and dropped her shoulders. The last thing she wanted was another conversation with the cops, but if it had to be done, she'd rather it was sooner than later. 'I suppose.'

Harry gave her hand a squeeze. 'Don't worry. They'll find out who did this, Jess. I'm sure they will.'

Jess gave a nod, forcing a shaky smile on to her lips. Although she didn't share his level of confidence in the law, she still appreciated his attempts to reassure her. At a time like this, a girl needed friends she could rely on. 'And then you'll come with me to see Clare Towney?'

'If that's what you want.'

Jess sucked in a breath. The sensible, logical, self-preserving thing to do would be to drop all her enquiries into the Minnie Bright case . . . but she couldn't. No matter how scared she was, it wasn't in her nature to back away from trouble. She'd travelled too far down the road to stop the journey now. 'Yes,' she said. 'It is.'

44

Harry drove Jess over to Hackney and stayed in the car while she went into the station to talk to the police. On the journey he had kept an eye on the rear-view mirror, making sure that they weren't being followed. Now, as he waited, he had another good look round. Someone had tried to kill her once – it was probably only a matter of time before they had another go.

He pondered a while on the Minnie Bright murder, trying to figure out the missing piece of the jigsaw. It had all seemed so black-and-white at the time, but now, four-teen years later, shades of grey were starting to creep in. The past was swathed in secrets and lies, and at least one person was prepared to go to any lengths to keep it that way.

Harry got out his phone and made a call to Mac. He out-lined the new evidence about the fire at Jess's place and asked him if he could use his contacts to try and track down Hannah Bright, Minnie's mother. 'And maybe you could check if there are any other relatives around, aunts, uncles, half-siblings and the like.'

Mac heaved out a sigh. 'You sure about this, Harry?'

Harry furrowed his brow in exasperation. 'What, you think I should just drop it?'

'I thought you were supposed to be investigating the damage to Sam Kendall's car. And a few malicious notes. You start digging around in an old murder inquiry and you're going to make enemies.'

'Yeah, I know. You've already mentioned it. But I don't see what other choice there is.'

'There's always a choice.'

'Come on, Mac. Whoever torched Jess's flat isn't going to give up until they've finished the job. I can't just turn my back on her.'

From the snort on the other end of the line, Harry could tell that Mac would be more than happy for him to do exactly that. 'Okay,' Mac said. 'I'll see what I can dig up. But do me a favour, right. The next time she tries to involve you in one of her investigations, tell her you're busy.'

'I'll lock the door and bar the windows.'

'Shame you didn't do that last Friday.'

Harry hung up and put in a quick call to Warren. There was no news from Walpole Close. Aimee Locke hadn't gone out, and only the cleaning woman had gone in. After being unceremoniously ejected from the casino last night, Harry had called it quits and returned to Kellston. The surveillance was probably a waste of time now; Stagg would have tipped off Aimee and she'd know that she was being followed. Would she challenge her husband about it? He thought it unlikely. Better, surely, to keep quiet and let Mackenzie, Lind file a report that put her in the clear.

The sun was shining on the windscreen, making the car

feel uncomfortably warm. He put the phone down, opened the window and rolled up his sleeves. A motorbike roared past, leaving a trail of exhaust fumes, and Harry followed its progress until it reached the end of the road and turned left. With less chance of getting snagged up in traffic, a bike was a good way to tail people in London.

Whoever was out to get Jess obviously knew where she was living now. The threatening call at the supermarket proved that much. But then it wouldn't have taken too much brain power to track her down. Anyone who'd been following her movements over the past six days could have guessed where she would be.

Harry thought about Becky Hibbert, mercilessly strangled on the Mansfield Estate. Murdered because of what she knew, what she might tell, or for reasons completely unrelated to the Minnie Bright case? Valerie was clearly working along the lines of the latter option, but then she wasn't in possession of all the facts.

He picked up the phone again and stared at it. After the coolness of their meeting on Tuesday, he was tempted to keep his distance. But he couldn't let personal problems stand in the way of a murder inquiry. Reviewing the conversation in his head, he was aware that he hadn't told her everything.

Valerie answered her mobile straight away. 'Harry,' she said, her voice edged with irritation. 'What is it? What do you want?'

He was unsure whether the tone of her response was down to him or whether he'd caught her at a bad time. 'I won't keep you. I was just wondering how it was going. Any sign of Dan Livesey yet?'

Valerie hesitated, clearly unwilling to discuss the case with him. 'We're following up a number of leads,' she said briskly, as if she was talking to a probing journalist.

'Right. Only . . . only I think there are a couple of things you should know.'

'Really?' she said coldly.

He knew that bringing up the subject of Jess wouldn't do much to raise the temperature, but there was no way round it. 'Well, we've just found out that the fire at Jessica Vaughan's place *was* deliberate and that she was definitely the intended target. She's had to go and see the police at Hackney, so you may be hearing from them at some point.' He decided not to mention that he was currently sitting outside the station. 'I guess they'll want to liaise with you in case there's a connection to the Becky Hibbert murder.'

Valerie gave a sigh. 'Right,' she murmured.

'And there's something else. Apparently someone looking very like Micky Higgs threatened Lynda Choi's brother with a knife about five months ago. David was trying to get some information on the calls Lynda made to the other girls on the night she died, and Higgs seemed to take exception to it.'

'Did Choi report it?'

'No, and if you ask him he's probably going to deny that it ever happened. He doesn't want to cause any grief for his family.' Harry squinted into the sunlight, screwing up his eyes. 'But I suppose the big question is why Higgs – if it was him – would go to all that trouble if his girlfriend had nothing to hide.'

'And you didn't think this was worth mentioning when

374

we talked on Tuesday?' she said crossly. 'What's the matter with you? Is there anything else you haven't told me?'

He pulled a face, aware that he'd blotted his copybook yet again. 'No, I don't think so.' In his defence he could have said that she hadn't taken seriously the idea that there could be a connection to the Minnie Bright murder, but he was smart enough to keep that suggestion to himself. 'I'm sorry, okay. I just thought that with Livesey in the frame all this stuff was probably irrelevant.'

'Maybe in the future you could let me decide what's relevant and what isn't.'

'Sure,' he said. 'I'll do that.'

'Do you have a number or an address for this David Choi?'

Harry had got David's number off Sam Kendall but decided not to give it out. The least he could do was ring David first and warn him that the law was about to come visiting. 'Not a home address, but he works at a dry-cleaning place on the industrial estate. His family owns it. I don't know exactly where the unit is.'

There was a short pause while Valerie wrote down the information. 'And that's it? You're sure there's nothing else you want to share with me?'

Harry winced at the sarcasm in her voice. 'No, nothing else.'

'Well, in that case, I'd better get on.'

Harry was about to suggest that they get together for a drink sometime, but she'd already hung up. 'Well done, Mr Lind,' he said softly. 'Beautifully handled as usual.' He leaned back and rubbed at his temples. Why did he have the feeling that another large nail had just been hammered into the coffin of their relationship?

It was almost an hour before Jess finally emerged from the police station and climbed into the car beside him. She looked tired and drawn, as if the very last of her energy had been drained away. He waited until she'd fastened her seat belt and had a moment to gather her thoughts.

'So, how did it go, or shouldn't I ask?'

Jess gave a shrug. 'I'm not sure. You know what coppers are like.' She smiled thinly at him. 'No offence, but you're never sure what they're really thinking. They recorded it all, all the stuff about the Minnie Bright article, but then they kept asking what other stories I'd worked on in the past six months and whether someone might bear a grudge. And then after that they wanted to hear all the gory details of my personal life.'

'I guess they've got to cover every angle.'

'They seemed to think it was very convenient that Neil was away in Edinburgh when the flat was burnt down. I mean, what do they imagine: that he tried to have me knocked off while he got himself the perfect alibi?'

Harry started the engine and slid the car out into a line of traffic. 'Well, you can be highly annoying, Vaughan. Perhaps he just couldn't bear the prospect of being your boyfriend any longer.'

Jess put out her tongue and scowled at him. 'Oh, thanks for that. You really know how to cheer a girl up. And Neil's going to be overjoyed to get home and find himself under suspicion for attempted murder.'

'I'm sure it won't come to that.'

'Are you? Because I'm not sure of anything any more.' Jess folded her arms across her chest and gazed dolefully at the road ahead. 'I'm beginning to wish I'd dropped this damn story weeks ago.'

Harry knew that it was only the tiredness talking. Jess had never walked away from trouble in her life and she wasn't about to start now. 'I'll tell you what. Let's get back to Kellston and grab some lunch before we go and see Clare Towney.'

Jess gave him a sidelong glance and smiled. 'In other words, stop your whining, Jessica, and just get the hell on with it.'

'Your words,' he said. 'Not mine.'

Twenty minutes later, Harry and Jess were squashed into a corner at the back of Connolly's. The café was doing a brisk lunchtime trade and all the other tables were full. The noisy hiss of the coffee machine vied with the clatter of cutlery, music from the radio and the general babble of conversation. While Harry tucked into a chicken salad, Jess picked unenthusiastically at an omelette, sawing off tiny pieces and moving them aimlessly around the plate.

'You going to eat that or just play with it?' he asked.

Jess glanced up at him. 'Since when did you turn into my mother?'

'Only looking out for you, hun. I wouldn't like to see you waste away.'

Spearing a morsel of omelette, Jess put it in her mouth, chewed and swallowed. 'There,' she said. 'Happy now?'

Then she put down her fork and heaved out a sigh. 'Sorry, I don't mean to take it out on you. All this stuff, it's just ... I can't get my head around it. I feel like there's something staring me in the face but I'm too blind to see it.'

'You and me both,' he said.

Jess topped up her glass from the jug of water on the table, then lifted it to her lips and took a few quick sips. 'I mean, when you think about it, it all comes down to what *really* happened on the day that Minnie Bright was killed. We know what the girls said to the cops at the time, but what if they were lying?'

'About what part of it?'

Jess's brow furrowed in concentration. 'Well, Paige, Kirsten and Becky claimed they ran off and left Minnie in the house. But what if they didn't? Or what if, like Lynda, they went back? Perhaps Minnie did what she was told and opened the door for them. They all went in and ... I don't know, maybe there was some kind of argument or fight over what was being taken and one of them pushed Minnie and she fell and ...'

Harry pursed his lips. 'That doesn't account for Peck's DNA being on her clothes.'

'But it would account for why the three of them didn't want the case re-examined. And there could be reasons for the DNA. Minnie was lying on the floor, wasn't she? There could have been contamination.' Jess picked up her fork again and tapped it against the edge of her plate. 'If all three girls stuck to the same story, they'd be free and clear. Who was going to suspect them when Minnie's body was lying in the home of a known sex offender?'

Harry could see where she was going but he wasn't convinced. 'They were only ten years old, Jess. They were just kids.'

'Streetwise, though. And if the police already had Peck in the frame, how hard were they going to question them? Those girls had forty-eight hours to get their story straight. So long as they kept it simple and consistent ...'

'But why would Paige and Becky have agreed to talk to you if they had something to hide?'

Jess gave a shrug. 'I don't know. Because fourteen years had gone by and they thought they'd got away with it? Everything revolves around fame today, about having your photo in a magazine or the paper, about being the centre of attention even if it is only for five minutes. Maybe the lure of that outweighed any minor risk of the truth coming out.'

'Not for Kirsten Cope, though.'

'No,' she agreed. 'Not for Kirsten. Which means either that she's smarter than the others or she's got more to be afraid of. She was the one who was on the phone to Lynda Choi for over forty minutes on the night Lynda died. Now correct me if I'm wrong, but Kirsten doesn't strike me as the type who spends vast amounts of time on Friends Reunited, so what was so fascinating about that conversation?'

Harry recalled his last glimpse of Kirsten Cope at the flat in Chigwell, sitting on the sofa and biting down on her knuckles. Yes, she'd certainly been worried.

'Lynda Choi remembered something that the others didn't want coming out,' Jess continued. 'Why else would they lie about her calling them?'

Harry finished his chicken salad and pushed the plate aside. It was a theory but it had a lot of loose ends. 'So where does Clare Towney fit into the scheme of things?'

'I've no idea,' Jess said. 'Why don't we go and find out?'

45

Palmer Street, running in an easterly direction off the high street, was only a short walk from Connolly's. The terrace was much the same as all the others in the area: a row of small red-brick houses with one window on the ground floor and one on the first. Most of the square front yards were concrete or gravel, the limited space filled by council wheelie bins.

'This is it,' Jess said, stopping outside number 36. The exterior of the house was neat and tidy, the paintwork in good condition. A pair of starched white nets obscured her view of the inside, but she thought she sensed a movement behind them. She checked her watch. Five minutes early.

'So, how are you going to handle this?' Harry said.

She glanced up at him, realising that despite a great deal of thought, she hadn't yet come to any firm conclusions. 'With tact and diplomacy?'

'Sounds like a plan.'

They walked up the path and Jess rang the bell. The door was answered almost immediately by a tall, slim girl who looked closer to eighteen than twenty-eight. She had a pretty heart-shaped face, wide hazel eyes and long red hair that reached almost to her waist. Her skin, pale as porcelain, had an almost translucent quality to it. Her features were perhaps too individual to be classed as beautiful, but she was certainly striking.

'Clare Towney?' Jess asked.

The girl nodded. 'I'm Clare.'

'Hi. I'm Jess Vaughan and this is my colleague Harry Lind. He's a private detective.'

Clare looked from Jess to Harry and then back at Jess. Her eyes narrowed a little. 'You didn't say that you were bringing someone.'

'You don't have to talk to me if you don't want to,' Harry said. 'If you'd rather see Jess alone . . .'

Clare studied him for a moment, but then gave a shrug and stood aside. 'It doesn't matter. You'd better come in.'

Jess stepped into a room that was overstuffed with furniture and knick-knacks. The wallpaper was old-fashioned and flowery, the large pink blooms more suited to a bedroom than a lounge, and the grey carpet had one of those busy patterns that would give you a headache if you stared at it for too long. The curtains, heavy and pulled partly across, blocked out most of the afternoon sunlight. From the room beyond came the sound of a tele-vision.

Clare gestured vaguely towards a dark corduroy-covered sofa.

'Thank you,' Harry said, moving a cushion and settling into a corner. 'We'll try not to take up too much of your time.'

Jess took the place beside him. She waited until Clare had sat down in an armchair before she began. Without going into too much detail, she swiftly explained about the article she'd been planning on writing and how she'd gradually become more interested in the original trial. 'And then, of course, I talked to Ralph Masterson and he gave me the impression ... well, that he wasn't entirely convinced of your uncle's guilt.'

'Really?' Clare said. She looked bemused.

'He didn't mention that we'd talked?'

Clare shook her head, but her gaze met Jess's for only a second before flicking down towards the floor. 'I haven't seen him in years. We moved away after the trial.'

'I see,' Jess said. She was about to probe a little further when a female voice, a slightly scared-sounding voice, piped up from the room beyond.

'Who is it? Who's there?'

Clare jumped up and went over to the open door that separated the two rooms. 'Don't worry, Mum,' she said gently. 'It's only ... it's only some friends from work. You watch your programme. We won't be long.'

'Is it the man about the boiler?'

'No, Mum. He came last week, remember? The boiler's fine. There's plenty of hot water and everything. I'll only be a few minutes, yeah?'

Clare walked back, sat down again and crossed her legs. She was wearing a floaty sleeveless summer dress that made her look faintly ethereal. Her feet with their pearl-coloured toenails were bare. She looked over at Harry and gave him a tentative smile. 'I'm sorry about that. She gets nervous when there are strangers in the house.'

'It's all right,' he said, sitting forward and smiling sympathetically. 'We understand.'

Jess watched her closely. The way she'd addressed her apology solely to Harry made her suspect that Clare Towney was the type of girl more comfortable in the company of men than women. Or was she just trying to get one of them on side? As soon as the thought crossed her mind she felt a twinge of guilt. Having an uncle like Donald Peck couldn't have been the easiest thing to deal with, and now the past was coming back to haunt her again. 'It must have been tough for you, the trial and everything.'

Clare put her hands on her lap and twined her fingers together. 'I try not to think about it.'

'But you never had any doubts?'

'Doubts?' she echoed.

'About your uncle's guilt,' Jess said.

Clare shook her head. 'She was there, wasn't she? That poor little girl was there in his house.' She glanced over at Harry. 'I don't mean to be rude, but I'm not quite sure what . . . I mean, I don't understand why you're involved in all this.'

'I've been retained by Sam Kendall,' he said. 'Do you remember her? She was one of the girls who went to your uncle's house with Minnie that day. She's been receiving death threats.'

'Really? Oh, that's terrible.'

'But not as terrible as what happened to Becky Hibbert,' Jess said.

Clare blinked hard. 'But that doesn't have anything to do

with ... She was killed by her boyfriend, wasn't she? That's what it said on the news.'

'Maybe,' Jess said. She left a short pause before she continued. 'You worked with Becky, didn't you? That must have been awkward.'

'We usually worked different shifts. I do mornings – one of the neighbours comes in to sit with Mum – and she did afternoons. I hardly ever saw her.'

'But you heard about the article I was writing? Even if Becky didn't tell you herself, one of your workmates must have mentioned it.'

Clare hesitated, a look of indecision passing over her face. She probably wanted to deny it but had no way of knowing if Jess had already talked to the staff at the supermarket. 'I may have heard a rumour.'

'And how did that make you feel?'

'What do you mean?'

'Well, if I was you I wouldn't have been happy,' Jess said. 'Here's this girl, who some might say was partly responsible for what happened to Minnie Bright, bragging about how she's going to be in a glossy magazine as if the whole horrible affair was something to be proud of.' Jess was only guessing, but it was a guess based on Becky's response after she'd first approached her. 'After everything you've been through, that can't have been easy to deal with.'

Clare gripped her knees tightly and stared hard at Jess. Her hazel eyes flashed with suspicion. 'Are you accusing me of something?'

'No,' Harry said firmly, shooting Jess a warning glance. 'Of course not. We're just trying to talk to everyone involved in the original case. We're not singling anyone out and we're certainly not throwing any accusations around. We're here to try and establish whether Donald Peck's conviction was safe. If you have any doubts, any doubts at all, then we'd like to hear them.'

'I don't,' Clare said. 'My uncle was a sick man. He had serious problems. You must be aware of his record.'

Harry nodded. 'So you don't share any of Masterson's reservations?'

'I wasn't aware that he had any. Like I said, I haven't seen him for years.' Clare gave a weary sigh. 'Look, I was fourteen when all this happened. I barely knew the guy and I certainly wasn't privy to his thoughts on whether my uncle was guilty or not.'

As Jess glanced around the room, her gaze alighted on the sideboard by the door. On it was a framed family photograph, a picture of Clare Towney when she was six or seven standing in a garden with her parents. At least she presumed they were her parents. The woman had a look of Clare about her – the same striking red hair, the same wide eyes and mouth. The man, in his early thirties, had blander, less memorable features.

'Is that your mum and dad?' Jess asked.

Clare, looking startled at the question, followed Jess's gaze. 'Yes.'

'So your dad, he's . . . er, not around any more?'

'No,' Clare said. 'He cleared off shortly after that picture was taken, cleared off and never came home again. Mum spent the next twenty years waiting for him to walk back through the door. Even when we were in Devon, she still thought he'd . . .' She gave a small, bitter laugh. 'He couldn't take it, you see, having a brother-in-law who was the local perv. It's not the greatest family connection, is it? Hardly something to brag about down the pub.'

'It must have been hard for the two of you,' Harry said.

'We managed. We had to. Now all I want to do is to put the past behind me and get on with my life. That's not too much to ask, is it?'

'No,' Harry said. 'Of course not.'

Jess could sense that Harry was about to end the meeting. He'd not been comfortable about coming here in the first place, and it was clear that since arriving, he'd heard nothing from Clare that had led him to suspect her of being anything more than a victim. She, however, wasn't so sure. Harry might be smart, but he was still a soft touch when it came to damsels in distress.

'So if there's nothing else?' Clare said.

Jess wasn't in a hurry to leave. She still wanted to talk about Lynda Choi and the light. If nothing else, it would be interesting to see Clare's reaction. Just as she was about to broach the subject, she sensed a movement behind her. Turning her head, she saw a woman standing in the doorway.

Stella Towney – for surely it had to be her – was a tall, gaunt woman in her mid-fifties. Her hair, cropped short, was a faded shade of red. With her hands pushed deep into the pockets of a long green cardigan, she gazed around the room with a look of bewilderment. Finally her brown eyes settled on Harry. She stared at him for a moment, and then, as if a flicker of recognition had dawned somewhere in the back of her mind, she inclined her head and smiled.

'Hello,' she said. 'How are you? Have you come to see Alan?'

'No, Mum,' Clare said, quickly standing up. 'Dad isn't here any more. You know that.'

'Hello, Mrs Towney,' Harry said.

Stella rocked on her toes, her gaze still fixed firmly on his face. 'He isn't home yet, you see. Has Clare made you a cup of tea? You should have a brew while you wait.' Her eyes shifted over to her daughter and then back to Harry again. 'He could be in the pub,' she said. 'Have you tried the Fox?'

'He's not in the Fox, Mum,' Clare said, her voice full of strained weariness. She took her mother's arm and led her gently back into the other room. 'Come on, let's get you sat down and then we'll find something for you to watch.'

Jess wondered if Stella remembered Harry from long ago, from the trial perhaps, or the police station. The woman was comparatively young to have developed dementia, but Jess knew that it could strike at an even earlier age. It couldn't be easy for Clare to cope with. Not only had she had to return to Kellston, but also, as an only child, she'd had to take on all the responsibility for her mother's care. Jess felt some sympathy. However, if she was putting on her cynical hat, she could see how easy it would have been for Clare to become bitter, to turn against others, to maybe even want some payback for the cruelty of her own ruined life.

When Clare came back, Harry immediately rose to his feet. 'We should be going,' he said. 'Thank you for talking to us. We appreciate it.'

388

Jess, left with no other choice than to follow suit, reluctantly stood up too. 'Yes, thank you.'

Clare smiled thinly, walked across the room and opened the front door. 'I'm sorry I couldn't be of more help. As you can see, I've got more to worry about at the moment than what may or may not have happened in the past.'

'Well, if you think of anything that could be useful,' Jess said, holding out a small piece of paper with her name and number written on it, 'you can call me any time.'

Clare Towney gazed disdainfully at the offering before eventually reaching out and taking it from Jess's hand with the tips of her fingers. As if she couldn't wait to get rid of it, she immediately turned and dropped it on to the sideboard. 'Goodbye.'

'Goodbye,' Harry said.

Jess gave her a nod.

They were barely out of the door before it was shut firmly behind them and the bolt pulled across. Jess squinted as they walked in silence along the short driveway, past the bins and into the street. It seemed extraordinarily bright outside after the gloom of the semi-curtained room.

'So, what do you think?' she said, keeping her voice neutral. She was irked by Harry's unilateral decision to leave but determined not to show it. After everything he'd done for her, it would be churlish to pick a fight now.

'I think she's struggling. It must be stressful trying to hold down a job and take care of her mother at the same time.'

Jess glanced up at him. 'Yeah, but maybe that's not all she's struggling with.'

Harry's blue eyes met hers. 'Meaning?'

'How about a guilty conscience for starters?'

'And how do you figure that one out?'

Jess held his gaze and smiled. He might believe that Clare Towney had nothing to hide, but she thought otherwise. 'Just call it feminine intuition.'

'Is that something to be relied upon?'

'Oh, Mr Lind,' she sighed. 'You've still got a lot to learn.'

46

DI Valerie Middleton had spent almost fifteen minutes on the phone, fifteen minutes of wheedling persuasion and implied threats in order to finally convince Chris Street that it was in his best interests to hand over Monday's security tapes from the Lincoln. She had known that she was on dodgy ground, that she probably couldn't force him to comply without going through the more usual time-consuming legal channels, but she wanted those visuals as fast as possible.

Eventually, a compromise had been reached and Street had agreed to release the footage from the external cameras only. What went on *inside* the Lincoln probably wasn't something that he'd relish being viewed by the police. Still, it was a result. Livesey had been working the door that night so everything he'd done and everyone he'd talked to would have been caught on camera.

It was now over half an hour since Street had relinquished the tapes. Valerie and Swann were sitting side by side in the incident room going through them carefully. There was the usual motley crew drifting into the pool hall – shifty-looking youths, hustlers, dealers, even a couple of toms hoping to pick up some business – but no one out of the ordinary.

Livesey was a wide, solidly built man with the kind of face only a mother could love. He was virtually chinless, with small eyes, a fleshy mouth and a nose that had clearly been broken on more than one occasion. His head was shaved and his bald pate gleamed in the fierce security lights. Dressed in a dark suit and tie, he looked bored and sullen. For long periods of time there was nothing for him to do. He leaned against the wall, smoking cigarettes and fiddling with his phone.

'He's either texting,' Swann said. 'Or he's checking out the hot babes on the internet.'

'And you'd know all about that.'

'Yeah,' he said, smirking. 'I do a lot of texting.'

Valerie raised her eyes to the ceiling. 'Well, there were no texts sent from the mobile he left in the flat. And the one and only call he made to Becky Hibbert that night was at five past twelve, shortly after he got to the Mansfield. That's kind of late to ring, isn't it?'

'Depends on the hours you keep, I suppose.'

'But why not call earlier and let her know he was coming?'

'Maybe he didn't want her to know. Or maybe he only made his mind up at the last minute.'

Valerie stared hard at the grainy image of Livesey. 'He doesn't look like a man with murder on his mind. More like he's trying to choose between a bag of chips and a kebab.' She placed her elbows on the table and tried not to yawn. It had been after one o'clock before she'd got to bed last night.

After dinner at Adriano's, she and Simon had gone on to a wine bar. It had been an enjoyable evening – he was good company – but she'd drunk more than she should have and woken up with a hangover. The remnants of a headache still tugged behind her temples.

'Fast-forward it,' she said to Swann. 'Let's see what happens at closing time.'

The Lincoln theoretically closed at eleven but it took another half-hour for the pool hall to empty. The punters came out in twos and threes, some with that glazed look in their eyes as if they'd been tugging on a joint for the past few hours, others more rowdy from the pints of lager they'd been knocking back. Livesey swiftly moved them on. The quicker he got rid of them, the sooner his work was done.

It was at twenty to twelve that a familiar face emerged from the open door of the Lincoln, lit a cigarette and went over to chat to Livesey. The man was clearly part of the security team. Valerie instantly became more alert. She sat up straight, a thin stream of adrenalin running through her blood. 'Well, fancy that,' she said. 'If it isn't the delightful Micky Higgs.'

'He wasn't on the rota for Monday night.'

'No, he must have swapped shifts with someone. Nice of him to mention it to us.'

'Lying toerag,' Swann muttered. 'He said he hadn't seen Livesey since Saturday. Now why would he tell a porkie like that?'

Valerie kept her eyes fixed on the screen. 'Exactly.' She frowned. 'And how come we didn't see him go in?'

'He must have got there early. Maybe he had a few games of pool before he started work.'

The conversation between the two men seemed casual at first, nothing more than a friendly chat between two co-workers, but after a couple of minutes everything changed. Livesey became more animated, his face tightening, his arms waving around. He turned away, turned back, and glared at Higgs.

'Not good news, then,' Swann said.

'Interesting.' Valerie leaned in towards the screen. 'Can't make out what they're saying, though.'

The heated conversation continued for a while, and then Dan Livesey suddenly stormed into the Lincoln. Higgs, with a smug expression on his face, finished his cigarette, chucked the stub on the ground and followed him inside. It was almost midnight when Livesey came out again, now wearing a long dark overcoat over his suit and looking like thunder.

'That is not a happy man,' Swann said.

'A man in the mood for murder, perhaps.'

Livesey strode down the path and turned right in the direction of the Mansfield. After that, the cameras lost him and he disappeared from view.

'Right,' Valerie said. 'Let's pull in Micky Higgs again and see what the lying bastard has to say for himself.'

It was twenty past four before DCs Lister and Franks finally managed to find Higgs and bring him into the station. As Valerie entered the interview room, with Swann behind her, Micky blatantly looked her up and down. He was a tall, good-looking, cocky sod who thought he could talk his way out of anything.

'Hello, darlin',' Higgs said. 'Have you missed me?'

She pulled out a chair and sat down across the table from him. He was wearing a white T-shirt that said *Fuck the Law*, which naturally endeared him to her. 'Like a hole in the head. And it's Inspector to you.'

Higgs grinned. 'You didn't need to send the plods, *Inspector*. You could have just given me a bell. I'm always happy to oblige.'

'Glad to hear it.'

Swann turned on the recording equipment and they went through the usual procedure of announcing who was present in the room.

'Hang on a second,' Higgs said. 'Shouldn't I have a solicitor?'

'You're not under arrest,' Valerie said. 'You're just helping us with our enquiries. We need to clear up a little … misunderstanding from when we talked to you yesterday.'

Higgs thought about this for a moment and then gave a lazy shrug. 'Go on, then.'

'It's about the last time you saw Dan Livesey,' Valerie said. 'Saturday night? Wasn't that what you said?'

'Yeah, Saturday. We were working together at the Lincoln.'

Valerie gave him a thin smile before opening a brown folder and sliding three black and white stills across the table. 'And yet here you are, large as life, chatting to him on Monday night.'

Higgs sat forward, frowned and stared at the pictures. He wasn't the slightest bit fazed at being caught out in the lie. 'Was that Monday? Sorry, I must have got my dates mixed up. The job's kind of boring, you know, one night's much the same as another.'

'Except Monday night wasn't the same as any other, was it?' Swann said. 'Your mate's ex-girlfriend, Becky Hibbert, got murdered. That kind of thing tends to make a night more memorable.'

Higgs sat back and folded his arms across his chest. 'Like I said, I just got my dates mixed up.' He gave Valerie a sly look. 'It was a genuine mistake. Can't get arrested for it, can you?'

'No,' she agreed, 'but we could do you for perverting the course of justice.'

'Only if you can prove that I did it deliberately.'

Valerie tapped her fingernails on one of the photographs. 'We've had a look through the security footage, Micky, and at about twenty to twelve you came out of the pool hall and said something to Livesey that got him mighty upset. You mind sharing it with us?'

Higgs unclasped his arms and raised his hands in a gesture of frustration. 'Ah, come on. Do you remember the details of every conversation you've ever had?'

'Don't waste my time,' Valerie said. 'Up until that point Livesey's perfectly calm, and next thing he's like a bull with a sore head. I'm presuming it was to do with Becky, because that's where he went next, straight to the Mansfield Estate.'

'Which could make you an accessory to murder,' Swann said. 'I mean, if you knew he was going there to kill her . . .'

'Hey,' Higgs said, suddenly not quite so cocksure. 'You're not pinning that on me. No fuckin' way. I didn't know what he was planning on doing, did I?'

Valerie was quick to take advantage. 'So just tell us what you said to him. That's all we want to know and then you're free to go. I'm sure, on this occasion at least, we can overlook your unfortunate memory lapse.'

Higgs looked from one to the other while he weighed up his options. In the end he came down on the side of self-preservation. 'I just tipped him the wink, didn't I?'

'Tipped him the wink?'

'Yeah. About what that filthy slag was up to. Someone had to let him know. She's supposed to be taking care of his kids, right? And if the Streets had got wind of what she was up to, they might have thought Dan was taking a share. He'd have been out of a job – and minus his kneecaps too. The only toms they allow to operate on the Mansfield are their own.'

'But I thought that was just a rumour,' Valerie said. 'I mean about her working as a prostitute.'

'Rumour or no rumour, he needed to know about it.'

'So why didn't you tell us all this yesterday?'

Higgs scratched at his head and scowled. 'You don't grass up a mate, do you? I had no idea he was going to ... How could I have known? I'm not a fuckin' mind-reader.'

Valerie could have pointed out that it didn't take a mind-reader to see what mood Livesey had been in, but she held her tongue. 'Okay,' she said, gathering up the photographs and putting them back in the file. 'You can go.'

'That's it?'

'Unless you've got something else you want to tell us,' Swann said. 'Like where Livesey could be hiding out, for example.'

Higgs rose to his feet, shook his head and grinned. 'He'll be well gone, man. Not gonna hang around and wait for you lot to pick him up, is he?'

'And you haven't spoken to him or seen him since the murder?'

'Why would I?'

They accompanied Higgs back to the foyer and watched in silence as he swaggered through the doors. As soon as he was out of earshot, Swann said, 'That piece of shit knows more than he's letting on.'

Valerie gave a nod. 'You bet he does. Let's put a tail on him and see what he does next.'

47

At ten past five, shortly after Harry had taken over the surveillance at Walpole Close, the electric gates slid smoothly open and a white Ford Mustang appeared with Aimee Locke at the wheel. Quickly he jumped into the driver's seat of the van and started the engine. He let a couple of cars go by before pulling out. It wasn't long before they hit the busier part of Kellston, where the traffic, heavy and slow-moving, meant he had no problem keeping her in sight.

Even as he edged along behind the Ford, Harry was aware that it was probably a waste of time. Ray Stagg would already have tipped Aimee off about the tail. It had been an error of judgement, he thought, going to the casino like that. He'd been hoping that Stagg wouldn't be around, or if he was that he wouldn't make the connection with Aimee Locke. Harry slapped his hand against the wheel. Damn it! He should have given the job to Warren or one of the others.

Halfway along the high street, the Mustang's indicator flashed left and the car turned into Market Road. As there was no business today, no stalls or traders or bustling crowds of customers, there was plenty of room to park. As she drew up beside a meter, Harry drove on past and pulled in further along the road.

He watched in the side mirror as she got out of the car. She was wearing a stylish cream linen suit and high heels. She took out her purse, fed the meter and then glided back towards the high street. He took a moment to admire her long, shapely legs before climbing out of the van and following her. She crossed the road at the zebra – cars screeching to a halt as soon as she appeared – and went into Boots.

Wanting to keep a safe distance, Harry remained on the corner on the other side of the road. He pretended to examine the display in an electrical goods shop while surreptitiously watching the reflection of the chemist's in the window. She reappeared in a couple of minutes, waited for all of three seconds for the line of traffic to stop, and crossed over again. He kept his back turned, continuing to watch her progress in the glass. Any moment now she would pass right by him on her way to the car.

No sooner had the thought entered his head than Aimee Locke was at his side. He had no time to stride away, no time to take evasive action. She gazed up at him with her cool grey-green eyes.

'Hello, Mr Lind. Thinking of buying a fridge?' Her voice was soft and husky, tinged with amusement.

There was no point in him trying to deny the obvious. He looked back at her with a wry smile. 'I guess this is what's known as being caught in the act.'

'I hope it's not too much of a blow to your professional pride.'

'Did Stagg tell you?'

'Did you expect him not to?'

Harry gave a shrug. 'I don't expect anything of Ray Stagg.'

Aimee Locke raised her blonde brows. 'You don't like him. Well, he's not to everyone's taste.' She continued to look at him, her eyes gazing directly into his. 'I think we need to talk.'

'Is that a good idea?'

'Was it a good idea for my husband to hire a private detective to spy on me?'

Harry didn't think there was a right answer to that one so he didn't bother trying.

'I'm going to the Green,' she said, moving away. 'You want to walk with me or would you rather follow on behind?'

He lifted his hands in a gesture of submission before falling in beside her. 'Your husband's going to want his money back.'

'My husband can easily afford whatever he paid you. I'm not going to tell him, and if you've got any sense you won't either.'

Walking along the high street, he pondered on what she'd just said. What exactly did it mean? There was no doubting that Aimee Locke intrigued him. As they made their way towards the Green, he noticed how heads turned, the men admiring in their glances, the women appraising. Up close she was even more beautiful than from a distance. Her skin, flawless and lightly tanned, was the colour of pale honey, and her curves could have been designed by Hollywood. It was vainglorious, he knew – especially after he'd just blown the job he'd been paid to do – but he couldn't help but bask in her reflected glory. Any male ego would be boosted by being in her presence.

'What are you thinking?' she asked.

'That I'm not as good at this job as I thought I was.'

'Don't worry,' she said in that husky, seductive voice. 'I would have known even without Ray tipping me off.'

Harry pulled a face. 'And that's supposed to make me feel better?'

She smiled. 'I didn't mean it like that. You think you're the first private detective he's hired? Martin always employs someone to follow me around when he's out of town. This time it was your turn.'

'And why does he do that?'

'Because I'm a scarlet woman. Because the minute he's out of the door I can't wait to jump into bed with any guy who gives me a second glance.' There was a weary acceptance in her voice now. 'He likes to control people, Mr Lind. It's the way he is.'

'So why don't you leave him?'

Aimee gave a mirthless laugh. 'You don't leave men like Martin Locke.'

The Green, Kellston's equivalent to a park, was a stretch of ground about the size of a football pitch laid to grass with a few spindly trees and bushes. She turned on to the main path and began to walk down the centre until she reached an empty wooden bench. She sat at one end and put her handbag down beside her. Harry sat on the other side of the bag.

'Are you married, Mr Lind?'

402

'No,' he said. 'And you may as well call me Harry.'

'But there's someone in your life? A partner? A significant other?' She smiled again. 'Isn't that what they're called these days?'

He didn't respond immediately. Valerie came into his head, but he wasn't sure how significant he was to her at the moment. He also wasn't sure what he was doing sitting here talking to Aimee Locke.

'Sorry,' she said, reaching into her bag and taking out a pack of cigarettes. 'None of my business, right?'

'It's complicated,' he said. She offered him a cigarette and he shook his head. She took one for herself and lit it with a slim gold lighter.

'In case you're wondering,' she said, 'there's nothing going on between me and Ray. We're just old friends. He looks out for me.'

'Well, it's always good to have friends.' He glanced around the Green. The last of the afternoon sun was slanting across the grass, creating a dark triangle of shadow in the far left corner. Two of the other benches were occupied, one by an elderly lady with a terrier, the other by a young woman with a toddler in a pram. 'Talking of which, would you mind if I asked you something, just to satisfy my own curiosity?'

She put the cigarette to her lips, inhaled, and then released the smoke in a long thin stream. 'Ask away.'

'Why did you lie to your husband about going to Adriano's on Friday?'

Aimee lifted her face to the sun and half closed her eyes. 'Because I didn't want a row.' She blinked twice and gave him a sidelong glance. 'He doesn't like Vita. In fact, he doesn't much care for any woman with a mind of her own. It was less bother to tell him I was going to work.'

'But by lying, you only fuel his suspicions.'

She sighed and took another drag on the cigarette. 'Only if he finds out. I thought it was worth the risk. I didn't think my shadow would start watching until Saturday, when Martin went away. That's how it usually works.'

Even through the tobacco, Harry could still smell her perfume, a light, exquisite scent that floated in the air. 'Vita Howard's a friend of yours then? Or were you seeing her in a more professional capacity?'

Aimee turned her head to look at him again, but she didn't give a straight answer to his question. 'Vita's a smart lady.'

'Apart from her choice in partners.'

'Oh, Rick's okay. He's actually quite charming. So he made a few mistakes in the past. Who hasn't? Are you telling me you've never done anything you've regretted?'

Harry flinched, wondering if Stagg had told her about the drugs deal. 'I suppose.' He paused, and then said, 'So why did you go on to Selene's that night?'

'Because I left my phone there on the Wednesday. I couldn't really go home without it. Forgetting it twice would have seemed more than careless.'

Harry didn't entirely believe the explanation. With the resources Stagg had at his disposal, he could easily have sent it back to her by courier. There was no need for her to travel all the way to the West End to pick it up. 'Wasn't Martin curious as to why you were home so early?'

Aimee dropped what remained of the cigarette and ground it into the grass with the sole of her shoe. 'I told him I had a headache.'

'What I still don't understand—'

He was interrupted by a squeal of brakes from the high street. Aimee flinched, her whole body stiffening. 'I shouldn't have come here with you,' she said. 'It was stupid, ridiculous. I just wanted to ... I don't know ... If he ever found out ...' Rising abruptly, she caught the edge of her bag and it tumbled off the bench, the contents spilling at Harry's feet.

He leaned over to help her gather up the items. There was a purse, lipsticks, tissues, a small black wallet, two sets of keys, scent and a comb. Together they swept them up and put them back into the bag. Finally, the only thing left was a silver mobile. She reached out her hand – it was shaking slightly – but then withdrew it again. 'Oh God, it isn't broken, is it? Please say it isn't broken. He's always telling me how clumsy I am.'

He heard the fear and panic in her voice and it startled him. Just what kind of a man was Martin Locke? He was starting to think that his first impressions had been right. Bending down, he picked up the phone and turned it on. The screen immediately lit up. 'It seems okay.'

'Are you sure?'

He went to the main menu and scrolled through a few options. 'Yes, it's fine. Don't worry about it.'

Relief spread across her face. She held out her bag and he dropped it in. 'Thank you,' she said. 'Thank you so much.'

'Aimee, is there something you want to tell me?'

She stood up, clutching her bag to her chest, and shook her head. 'No, no, there's nothing.' But still she didn't leave. She worried on her lower lip for a moment, as if trying to come to a decision. 'You can't help me.'

He stood up too and touched her lightly on the arm. 'Not if you don't tell me what's wrong.'

Aimee met his gaze for a second, looked away and then looked back. 'All right. But I can't talk now. If you really want to know what's going on, come to the house tonight. Come at nine.'

Harry stared at her. 'I can't do that.'

'No,' she said. 'Of course you can't. I'm sorry. I shouldn't have asked. I should never have asked.' Without another word, she turned and walked quickly away across the Green.

'Aimee!' he called after her, but she didn't turn around. He watched until she passed out of sight. For some reason his heart was beating hard in his chest. He couldn't possibly go to her house. It was out of the question. It would be unprofessional, a betrayal of his client's trust, a supremely stupid and foolish act. But still he glanced at his watch, checking how much time was left before nine o'clock.

48

Jess was alone in the flat, pacing from one side of the living room to the other. She was trying to get her thoughts in order and work out what to do next. The meeting earlier in the afternoon had done little to convince her that Clare Towney was quite as innocent as she made out. In fact the very opposite. But gut instinct was one thing, hard evidence quite another. How could she prove it?

From time to time she stopped and stared down at the street, wondering if her stalker was lurking in the vicinity. It spooked her to think of him out there somewhere, watching and waiting, his black soul full of murderous thoughts. She glanced up at the smoke alarm on the ceiling, tempted to stand on a chair and test that it was working. No, Harry had assured her that it was fully operational and she knew that she could trust him. There were also two fire extinguishers, one in the living room and one in the hall. He'd done everything he could to make her feel safe – but how could she feel safe while a madman was still at liberty?

Harry was currently over at Walpole Close, continuing his surveillance of the beautiful Aimee Locke. Now there was a woman who could get a man in a whole heap of trouble. She'd only have to bat her eyelashes and all good sense would fly out of the window. Even Harry, smart as he was, wasn't immune to her charms. Jess had seen the way he'd looked at her at the casino. Still, that was his affair and not hers. He was old enough and hopefully savvy enough to keep himself out of trouble.

She sat down at the table and immediately stood up again. Outside, the light was starting to fade, but there was still another hour before sunset. She was jumpy now, but knew she'd be much worse later. That was the thing about fear: it grew and flourished in the dark, its long tentacles reaching into the deepest part of the imagination.

Standing by the window again, Jess tried to figure out what she'd do if she was in Clare Towney's shoes. Well, she'd certainly get in touch with her partner in crime to let him or her know what had happened. So a phone call for sure – but maybe more than that. And unless Clare could find someone to sit with her mother, then the other person would have to come to her. Masterson was still top of Jess's list of suspects. He could have already been over to see her, but Jess doubted it. Wasn't it more likely that he'd come after dark and when Stella was in bed?

Jess, unable to bear the thought of sitting around doing nothing, decided to take a leaf out of Harry's book. She went through to the kitchen and searched until she found a flask under the sink. Then, while the kettle was boiling, she made herself a couple of ham sandwiches and wrapped them in foil. She filled the flask with coffee and dropped that and the sandwiches into a carrier bag along with a couple of sheets of kitchen roll. There was nothing worse than driving with sticky fingers.

Back in the living room, she pulled on her jacket, picked up her keys, the Minnie Bright file and the carrier bag and headed out of the flat. The first-floor landing was quiet, the office of Mackenzie, Lind all locked up for the night. She left the stair light on so that she'd be able to see when she came back. After resetting the alarm, she went out and secured the door behind her.

When she reached Palmer Street, Jess drove around the block several times until she was sure that she had no one on her tail. When she was certain she wasn't being followed she pulled in to the first available parking space she found. It was about twenty yards from the Towney house and gave her a clear view of anyone entering or leaving. 'And now,' she murmured as she switched off the engine, 'all I have to do is wait.'

An hour later she was still waiting. She had been through the file twice, rereading all her notes and scanning the press cuttings again. She'd had one cup of coffee and eaten one of the ham sandwiches. She had called Neil and put on a bright and cheery voice, pretending that everything was normal. On Saturday, when she picked him up from Euston, she'd have to tell the truth, but until then she preferred to leave him in happy ignorance.

With her gaze fixed on number 36, Jess wondered how private investigators coped with the boredom. The road was a quiet one and there weren't even that many passers-by. When someone did appear, she would grab her phone and pretend to be making a call. She didn't want to arouse any suspicion or draw unnecessary attention to herself.

At 8.30, just as the street lights went on, her mobile started ringing. She glanced at the screen. It was Sam Kendall.

'Hi there,' Jess said, glad of the distraction. 'How are you? How's things?'

'I just wondered if you had any more news.'

Jess had called her as soon as she'd heard about Becky's murder. She knew that Harry had contacted her too. 'Nothing yet. I think the cops are still searching for that Livesey bloke.'

'Right,' Sam said. 'Look, I've been thinking I might go away for a while. I know that Mr Lind doesn't reckon I'm in any danger, but ...' Her voice trailed off.

'Has something else happened? Have you had another note?'

'No, nothing like that. It's just that with Becky and everything ... Well, I'm going to get out of London, go and stay with my dad for a while.'

'It's a good idea,' Jess said. Although on the whole she agreed with Harry's assessment – the acts perpetrated against Sam seemed more malicious than murderous – how could either of them be certain? It was better to be safe than sorry. 'I'll stay in touch, let you know if I hear anything.'

'Thanks. I'd appreciate it.'

'Oh, just one thing before you go. I don't suppose you know a girl called Clare Towney?'

There was a pause. 'Who?'

'Clare Towney,' Jess repeated. 'She lives in Kellston. She's Donald Peck's niece.'

'No, I've never heard of her.'

'Or her mother, Stella Towney?'

'No, sorry.'

'Are you sure?'

Sam's response was fast and sharp. 'I said, didn't I? What is this, some kind of interrogation?'

'Of course not,' Jess said, surprised by her tone. 'I just thought . . . Well, it doesn't matter. You take care of yourself, okay? Have a nice time with your dad.' She said her good-byes and hung up.

Sitting back, she wondered why Sam had been so riled by the questions. It was probably down to stress and worry. There was a limit to how much grief anyone could take. On the other hand, how much did she really know about Sam Kendall? She'd only met her six months ago, and although her instincts were usually sound, she wasn't infallible. This case was so full of smoke and mirrors that it was impossible to know who to trust. Literal smoke in her case, she thought wryly.

She went over the conversation in her head. Could it really be true that Sam wasn't familiar with the Towneys? It had been clear from the story the girls had told the police fourteen years ago that all the local kids were aware of Donald Peck and his habit of exposing himself. So wouldn't they have been aware of his family too? Maybe, she thought, but not necessarily. Even if Sam had once heard the name, it could easily have slipped her mind. And Clare was four years older than the other girls, so they wouldn't have mixed in school or outside of it. No, Sam was proba-bly being straight. It was perfectly feasible that she had no knowledge of the Towneys.

For all that, a small doubt still niggled in the back of Jess's mind. It made her feel bad that she was questioning the honesty of a woman she viewed as a friend, but she couldn't afford to take anything for granted. If there was one sure way of deflecting suspicion it was to pretend to be a victim. With the slashing of her tyres and the threatening notes, Sam had effectively removed herself from any close investigation.

Jess shook her head. But that didn't make sense either. If Sam had been worried about the Minnie Bright murder being looked at again, she would never have raised the subject in the first place – or agreed to be interviewed for an article. Well, not unless she had a guilty conscience, or was one of those people who liked to take unnecessary risks.

The more Jess turned it over, the more confused she became. She put her notes aside and gazed towards the Towney house. Still no movement. Was she wasting her time? She had the feeling that she might be. By now it had grown too dim to read without squinting, and she put her notes on the passenger seat. She didn't want to switch on the internal light in case Clare looked out of a window and saw her. So all she was left with were her thoughts.

She turned them back to the Towneys, going over the afternoon meeting again, trying to recreate the conversation exactly in her head. It was only when she came to Stella's appearance that she paused and rewound for a few seconds. Stella had believed they were there to see Alan. Had that simply been the product of a muddled brain, or was there more to it? Was there a chance that after years of absence the husband and father had finally returned?

Perhaps Clare's partner in crime wasn't Masterson at all, but someone much closer to home.

Jess screwed up her face. It wasn't much of a theory, and unless she was going to camp outside the house for the next twenty-four hours, she had no way of proving it one way or another. How long *was* she going to wait here? Until ten, eleven, midnight? She wondered if Harry was having any more luck than she was. At least he had the comparative comfort of the surveillance van, with light and warmth and space to move around. She stretched out her legs, already beginning to feel her muscles stiffen.

Ten minutes later a black cab came slowly down the road. She held her breath, peering through the gloom as she tried to see the passenger in the back – could this be Masterson arriving? – but after a few yards the cab accelerated again, passed the Mini and disappeared around the corner. She released the breath in a sigh of disappointment and returned her attention to number 36. The curtains in the front were still pulled partly across, but there was a glimmer of light that must have been coming from the room beyond. After a while her gaze slid to the front garden, with its small square of easy-maintenance gravel and its huddle of bins that took up most of the available space. Suddenly her heart missed a beat as she was struck by an idea. Bins meant rubbish – and rubbish included old newspapers, papers that *could* have been used to provide the cut-out letters for the messages that had been sent to Sam Kendall.

'Why not?' she murmured. If Clare Towney had been responsible, she'd have had no real reason to dispose of the evidence elsewhere. She couldn't have thought that anyone would connect her to the threats. Jess felt a flutter of excitement in her chest. But when had the bins last been emptied? The recycling was probably collected fortnightly and the last note had been delivered about a week ago.

Well, there was only one way to find out. All she had to do was get out of the car, walk down the road and take a look. No sooner had the thought entered her head than she realised how risky it was. What if Clare heard her rooting about outside? What if one of the neighbours saw her? The dread of being caught in the act was more than enough to make her think twice. What the hell would she say if she was discovered? There were some journalists who wouldn't think twice about rifling through other people's waste, but she wasn't one of them.

She rolled through the options, trying to decide what to do next. Surely the end justified the means? If Clare had been responsible, then it would be foolish to pass up the opportunity of exposing her. The sensible thing, however, would be to wait until late, until after midnight perhaps, when there was less chance of getting caught. Yes, that would definitely be the smart thing to do.

She glanced at the clock on the dashboard. Another three and a half hours. God, she couldn't wait that long. Now that the idea was in her head she had to follow through. And she had to do it quickly before she changed her mind again. She got out of the car, closed the door as quietly as possible and set off down the street.

49

Jess crossed the road and strolled up to number 36. Glancing sideways at the house, she lost her nerve and kept on walking. The front room was probably empty, but the curtains were still partly open. What if Clare or Stella emerged from the back and looked out of the window? It was dark now, but there was an orange glow from the street lamps. And there were still the neighbours to worry about.

She kept on going until she reached the corner, where she stopped and gazed back down the road. Her eyes quickly scanned the surrounding houses. Most of them had their curtains closed, but there was no saying who might be watching from an unlit upstairs room. She lifted her phone to her ear and went through the routine of pretending to chat again.

Jess knew that the longer she lingered, the more suspicious she would look. She put the phone in her pocket and with her heart in her mouth set off back in the direction she had come. But the closer she got to the house the more nervous she became. *Come on*, she urged herself, determined not to bottle it this time. Thirty seconds, that was all it would take. Maybe even less. All she had to do was reach in and . . .

She was almost there. *Do it! You have to do it!* Her mouth had gone dry and she could feel a heavy thumping in her chest. The street ahead of her was empty. She glanced over her shoulder. There was no one behind her either. A couple more steps and she was standing right outside the house again. She could see in through the gap in the curtains to the thin light coming from the back room. All she could hope was that the two of them were watching TV. Hopefully, any noise that she made would be drowned out by the sound of the television.

Jess stared at the cluster of bins. She knew that the purple one was for recycling, and that, fortunately, was the one closest to the entrance. She took another rapid look around and then stepped on to the pathway, flipped open the bin lid and peered inside. It was satisfyingly full, a sign that it hadn't been emptied for a while. Inside, all mixed together, was a heap of papers and magazines, tin cans, plastic and glass bottles and depleted aerosols.

Tentatively she reached into the bin. The problem was in retrieving the newspapers without making too much of a racket. The first few, lying near the top, were easy, but the further she delved, the more the other stuff shifted around, the bottles clinking against each other, the noise sounding like thunderbolts to her overly sensitive ears. Convinced that she was going to get caught, her hands became slow and clumsy. A feeling of panic began to grow inside her, tightening her throat and making her heart race even faster. From somewhere far away came the sound of a car backfiring, and she almost jumped out of her skin.

For a moment, she stopped, holding her breath and listening for any signs of movement coming from the Towneys' house. Nothing. In one last manic push, she began to rummage again, grabbing every single paper she could and adding them to the pile at her feet. Then she bent down, swept the pile into her arms and set off for the car.

Even as she was walking away, she was waiting for the shout, for the opening of a door, for the denouncement that was bound to come. *Stop, thief!* She hurried forward, the fear growing, the adrenalin pumping through her body. By the time she got back to the car, she was in a cold sweat. She jumped in, threw the papers on to the passenger seat, switched on the engine and took off.

By the time she was approaching Station Road, Jess had started to calm down. What was she doing? Her original plan had been to keep watch in case Masterson or someone else turned up. Well, she was hardly going to see them if she was sitting in Harry's flat going through a pile of old newspapers. Surely the clever thing to do would be to return to Palmer Street and keep up the surveillance for the rest of the evening.

At the next opportunity she took a left and headed back. When she'd reached her destination, she drove cautiously around the block again. It wasn't a tail she was worried about this time, but any sign that her underhand activities might have been observed. But everything was quiet in Palmer Street. She pulled into the same space she had recently vacated and had a good look around. When she was sure it was safe, she got out of the car, went around to the boot and took out her torch.

Back inside the car, Jess quickly sifted through the copies of the *Sun*, throwing anything that had been printed after last Friday on to the back seat, along with all the gossip and fashion magazines and editions of the local paper. Then she started flicking through what was left. Ten minutes later, she was beginning to wonder if she'd got it all wrong. She was coming up with a big fat zilch.

And then, just as her hope was ebbing away, she found it: half a page that had been torn out of the paper. That in itself wasn't proof positive – it could have been ripped out for any number of reasons – but when she came across another page further on that had been similarly treated, she reckoned she was on to something. She felt that sudden burst of exhilaration that always came with a major break-through. All she had to do now was to get hold of the original version and see what headlines had been removed. If the letters matched those in the notes sent to Sam, then Clare Towney was bang to rights.

Jess had left the laptop back at the flat. If she was lucky, she might be able to find the back copies of the paper on the internet, otherwise she'd need to take a trip down to the library. But that would mean waiting until tomorrow, and she was too fired up to leave it until then. No, what she wanted to do was confront Clare right now and find out what she had to say for herself.

Before she had the chance to ponder on it and maybe change her mind, Jess got out of the car. She walked across to number 36 and rang the bell. A few seconds later the light went on in the front room.

'Who is it?' Clare said from the other side of the door.

'It's Jessica Vaughan.'

'What do you want?'

'I need to talk to you.'

'It's late,' Clare said with clear irritation in her voice. 'You'll have to come back tomorrow.'

But now that Jess had made the decision to confront her, there was no turning back. 'Oh, okay,' she said. 'Should I do that before or after I've been to the police?'

'What?'

'You're in trouble, Clare. You can talk go to me or you can talk to the cops, but this isn't going to go away.'

There was a short pause before Jess heard the sound of a bolt being pulled across. Clare opened the door and scowled at her. 'What is it? What do you want?'

Jess held up the newspaper, open at the place where part of the page had been torn off. 'Do you mind explaining this to me?'

A look of alarm passed over Clare Towney's face, but she was quick to try and disguise it. 'It's a paper,' she said. 'So what?'

Sure that on this occasion her instincts were right, Jess took a gamble. 'Not just any paper, though. This particular edition was cut up to create one of the notes sent to Sam Kendall. I found it in your bin.'

'You had no right—' Clare began, but then abruptly stopped. 'There's no proof that it's ours. Anyone could have put it there. *You* could have planted it.'

'That's true. But I'm sure the police will be testing it for fingerprints. Or did you wear gloves? Still, even if you did, your mother's prints will probably be present, which will prove that the paper came from this household. And then there's the envelope you sent the note in. If you had to lick it to seal it, they'll be able to retrieve your DNA.'

Clare glared at Jess and then at the paper she was holding. Suddenly her hand whipped out as if to snatch it off her. Jess smartly took a step back, waving the *Sun* in the air. 'Oh, you didn't think I'd bring the actual paper, did you? No, that one's safely under lock and key.' Suspecting that Clare might try to destroy the evidence, Jess had had the foresight to bring a different copy, tearing off the top of the page in a way that looked identical to the original.

Clare Towney had two choices. She could either call Jess's bluff, tell her to go to the police and try and prove it, or she could give in gracefully. Her eyes blazed with anger for a moment, but then the light went out of them and her whole body slumped, her shoulders drooping. Defeated, she turned and walked away, leaving Jess to follow her inside and close the door behind her.

'Mum's in bed,' Clare said as they crossed the front room, 'so we'll have to do this quietly.'

Jess, who had no intention of raising her voice, gave a brief nod. 'Of course.'

The room at the rear of the house was small but cosy, with a couple of easy chairs, a TV and a gas fire turned on low against the chill of the evening. Clare dropped into a chair, put her elbow on the arm and sank her chin into the palm of her hand.

Jess carefully closed the door to this room too and then sat down. She rolled up the paper, placed it beside her on the chair and waited. When it became clear that Clare wasn't about to start the conversation, she said, 'So, do you want to tell me why you did it?'

'Why do you think?'

Now that the time had come for at least some of the truth to be exposed, Jess felt that familiar tingle of excitement. 'Because you wanted to stop Sam Kendall from talking.'

Clare gave a wry smile. 'Got it in one. I heard Becky Hibbert chatting at work. She was bragging about how she and the other girls were going to be interviewed for a magazine and have their photos taken. She thought the past was something to be proud of, to show off about. She didn't give a damn about the trouble it would cause for other people.'

'You could have come directly to me. I'm not a monster, and I'm not in the business of causing people unnecessary suffering. If I'd have known your situation—'

'You're a journalist,' Clare said bluntly. 'And all the experiences I've had with journalists in the past have been bad ones. I didn't think you'd listen to me.'

Jess gave another small nod. 'Okay, but why choose Sam to threaten? Why not Becky or Paige?'

'Because we ... because I figured that Sam would probably be at the centre of the article. She's the thoughtful one, isn't she? She's the one with the brain. So I reckoned if I could scare her off, you wouldn't have much of a piece.'

Jess acknowledged to herself that this was probably true. Without Sam's contribution, and the knowledge she had of Lynda's suffering, the article would have been pretty thin. At the same time she wondered how Clare had known what type of a person Sam was. So far as she was aware, the two of them had never met. 'And so you decided to take matters into your own hands. Well, you and Ralph Masterson. He was helping you, wasn't he?'

Clare shook her head. 'No, it was just me. I did it on my own.'

'If you're not going to be honest, there's no point in continuing with this. I went to see Ralph, remember? He's not the best liar in the world.'

Clare pushed back a strand of long red hair from her face, then frowned and bit down on her lip. 'Okay,' she said eventually. 'But all he ever did was pick me up and drive me over to Hackney. He didn't . . . I mean, I was the one who made the notes and posted them and did the damage to her car. He had nothing to do with any of that. He only agreed to help because I persuaded him it was for Mum's sake, that she wouldn't be able to cope if all the bad stuff started up again. It would kill her, I know it would. She wouldn't understand what was going on.'

'So Ralph must feel very protective towards her?'

Clare stared at her for a second. 'I guess. They got to know each other pretty well over the years. My uncle was always in and out of prison . . . Well, you know what for, no point going into the details. But Mum would never turn her back on Donald, not even when he . . .' Clare briefly closed her eyes and swallowed hard. It was as if she couldn't bring herself to think about the act, never mind say the words out loud. 'Anyway, apart from me, Donald was the only family she had. Ralph understood that, tried to help and support her, but other people . . .'

Jess could imagine how other people had treated her. She

422

would have been a social pariah. 'So why did he tell me that he had no idea whether she still lived locally?'

'To put you off the trail, I suppose. He was worried about you making the connection between the two of us. It was a stupid lie. They've all been stupid lies.'

'And was he also lying about thinking that Donald might have been innocent?'

'Is that what he said?'

Jess gave a small shrug. 'He said that Donald never lied to him, that he always admitted to his crimes. But not on the last occasion, not when it came to Minnie Bright.'

Clare flinched, her face twisting a little on hearing the name. 'I suppose he doesn't want to believe that my uncle did it. It would mean that he'd been wrong about him for all those years.'

'Wrong?'

'You know, that he wasn't capable of violence.'

'Trying to protect his own reputation, you mean?'

Clare's brow furrowed again. 'Not exactly. I didn't mean it to sound like that. It's more that ... Well, he always believed that Donald wasn't a major risk, didn't he? He went out of his way to try and support him, to offer him some kind of friendship. If my uncle *was* guilty of murder, then it means that Ralph got it all wrong. Maybe that's hard for him to face up to.'

Jess could see how Ralph Masterson might struggle to come to terms with his own lack of judgement. At the same time, she found herself wondering if the relationship between Stella and Ralph had been more than friendship. If he had deeper feelings, was it possible that he'd stuck by

Donald Peck for Stella's sake? She was tempted to ask but decided that now was not the time.

Clare bent her head and buried her face in her hands. 'Oh God,' she murmured. 'What have I done?'

Jess lowered her own eyes for a second. The room that had seemed so nice and cosy when she'd first entered was now awash with pain and turmoil. Clare Towney looked very small and vulnerable, like a child lost in an adult world. Like Minnie Bright, she had been the victim of someone else's sins. Before Jess could start to feel too sorry for her, however, she gave herself a mental shake, refocusing her thoughts on what Clare had actually done. 'In the notes,' she said softly, 'you claimed that Sam was responsible for Minnie's death. Why was that?'

Clare slowly lifted her face. 'Because she was, wasn't she? All of them were.' There was a bitter edge to her voice now. 'They *made* her go into his house. They forced her. If they hadn't done that, then—' She stopped abruptly, pushing her fist against her mouth.

Jess didn't fill the silence that followed. She waited patiently until Clare was ready to carry on. There was a clock on the mantelpiece and she gradually became aware of its steady rhythmic ticking. The sound seemed to fill the room, to grow ever louder. It must have been a full minute before Clare spoke again.

'I wanted to scare her,' she said eventually, shifting her hand away from her lips. 'Really scare her. The way I was scared back then. No one's ever made them pay for what they did. A slap on the wrist, that's all they got. And none of them have ever said sorry for their part in it all.'

424

'You threatened to kill her.'

'I didn't mean it,' Clare said quickly. 'I just wanted her to know how it felt to be constantly afraid, to always be waiting for the next awful thing to happen – the next brick through the window, the next set of insults, the next pile of shit pushed through the letter box.' Her face grew tight and angry. 'I just wanted her to feel a tiny, tiny bit of what we had to go through.'

'Well, you certainly succeeded in that.'

Clare bowed her head again for a moment, her hair falling around her face like a curtain. 'I'm sorry. It was a terrible thing to do.'

'And then Becky Hibbert got murdered,' Jess said.

As if she'd been slapped, Clare's head jerked up, her eyes widening. 'I had nothing to do with what happened to Becky. I swear on my mother's life. I'd never ... I wouldn't ... I sent the notes. I did the stuff to Sam's car. I admit that. But I didn't—'

'I know,' Jess said. 'I believe you. You may be a lot of things, but you're not a murderer.'

Clare's eyes filled with tears. 'So what happens now? I can't go to the police, not tonight. I can't leave my mum on her own.'

Jess couldn't help but feel sorry for her despite what she'd done. 'Maybe it won't come to that.'

'What do you mean?'

Jess wasn't sure if she was doing the right thing, but she couldn't see that having Clare dragged through the courts and ending up with a criminal record was the way to go either. 'Well, I could talk to Sam and try and explain

425

everything to her. Maybe if you apologised and offered to pay for the damage to her car, she'd be prepared to let it go.'

Clare leaned forward, her hands gripping her knees. 'Are you serious? Do you really think—'

'I can't make any promises. It's not up to me.'

'No, no, I understand. But thank you.' As she forced a shaky smile on to her lips, a single tear travelled down her face. 'I swear I'll never do anything like this again.'

'I know you won't,' Jess said, rising to her feet. 'I'll be in touch. I'll let you know what she decides.'

They walked in silence through the front room. There was more Jess had wanted to ask – like what Clare's relationship with her uncle had been like – but she sensed that the woman was already close to breaking point. Anyway, there were some old wounds that were best left alone.

'Thank you,' Clare said again as she opened the front door. She looked as though she was about to say something more but then shook her head.

Jess stepped outside and turned. 'What is it?'

'It's nothing. It doesn't matter. I suppose I'm just glad that it's all out in the open now.'

'Sometimes it's better that way.' Jess tapped the rolled-up newspaper lightly against her thigh. The atmosphere in the house had been charged with too much emotion and she gulped in the cool night air gratefully. 'Do you still have my number?'

'Yes.'

'Well, call me any time. Or come round to Mackenzie, Lind. They're on Station Road, the high street end. I'm staying there for a while.'

Clare's face had a crumpled look about it, as if she was about to start crying again. 'Okay.'

Jess felt no sense of elation or triumph as she walked back to the car. She might have solved one part of the puzzle, but the discovery brought her no pleasure. She couldn't condone Clare's actions, but to some extent she could understand them. Panic and fear could do terrible things to a person.

When she reached the Mini, Jess glanced back towards the house. The door was closed. Clare was gone. Would she be all right? With a sigh, Jess unlocked the car and climbed inside. She threw the newspaper into the back, pulled her seat belt across and started the engine. But still she didn't drive away. For a while she simply sat there, wondering why it was that some people's lives were so full of misery. It was a while before she finally set off for the flat.

50

All he could do now was wait. He looked at his watch again, impatient for it to be over. Everything depended on timing, on phone calls, on traffic, on fate. No matter how well a job was planned, there was always that element of chance. He paced from one side of the room to the other. He had never been this worried, this anxious before. He wanted to view it as just another assignment, but he couldn't. There was too much riding on it. The past was slowly creeping up on him, like a cancer.

He looked down at the bed, at the gun, and tried to get his thoughts in order. What he had done had been wrong and he'd had to live with it for too long. What kind of a man abandoned his wife and daughter? A weak one. A cowardly one. And the worst thing was that although he felt guilty and ashamed, he didn't regret it. Not deep down, not where it really counted. No, he'd been relieved to get out of this place and make a new life for himself.

He stopped pacing and sat down on the edge of the bed. Playing happy families had never come naturally to him, not after what had happened to his mother. He felt a shrivelling inside as he thought about her suffering. It had been worth coming back just to spit on the grave of the man who had killed her. She had not died from a single blow, not cleanly or quickly, but only after years of abuse. His father had broken her down bone by bone.

He thought of Anna in Cadiz. She had never asked about his past, never tried to delve into the darkness of his soul. Perhaps she had her own secrets. Most people did. Small parcels of shame and pain, tied up with string and pushed to the back of a cupboard that was only rarely opened.

With his fingertips he traced the zigzag pattern on the duvet cover. There was no good way of explaining the path he had chosen all those years ago. Only that it had suited him, that it had met some inner need. He felt nothing when he fulfilled a contract. It was a job, nothing more, nothing less. And now, for the last time, he was about to kill again.

His gaze flicked over to his watch. Not long now.

51

Harry knew that the first thing he should have done after Aimee Locke had approached him on the high street was to call Mac, explain how he'd been rumbled and abort the surveillance. He should have shifted the van and gone back to the office. That was what business partners did. They kept each other in the loop. So why hadn't he followed the usual procedures? Why was he still here, still watching the house and still watching the time?

There was only five minutes to go before nine o'clock. Aimee was in trouble. He'd seen it in her eyes. And she had turned to him out of . . . panic, fear, desperation? Whatever the source, he felt unable to ignore it. He remembered the meeting with her husband and the bad feeling he'd had about the man. Martin Locke was at best a bully and at worst . . . Well, he was about to find that out.

Harry raked his fingers through his hair and pulled on his jacket. If he thought about it any more he'd probably talk himself out of it. There was no harm, surely, in spending a little time with her to try and find out what was wrong. It was, he knew, a disingenuous argument. His desire to help was rooted in something more than a vague concern for her safety. He was attracted to her. She was not just beautiful, but enigmatic too. It was a fatal combination.

He got out of the van and strode across the road to number 6. He peered through the high wrought-iron gates at the floodlit garden and the front of the house. Everything was quiet. He stared at the bell embedded in the right-hand pillar. Last chance to change his mind. He could still turn around, go back to the van and get the hell out of here. While he was considering this option, it occurred to him that he was in full view of the cameras. Was she watching him now, watching him dither like some teenage schoolboy on a first date? The thought of it was more than mortifying.

He quickly reached out and pressed the bell. There was a short delay before it was answered.

'Hello?'

'It's me,' he said. 'It's Harry Lind.'

She didn't say anything else. The next sound he heard was the smooth swoosh of the gates swinging open. Harry took a deep breath and started walking up the path. A chill breeze sent a rustle through the pink and white rhododendrons, making him jump. He turned and peered into the shrubbery, but all he saw was shadow.

Aimee Locke was opening the door as he arrived. Her face looked pale and drawn. She had changed out of the linen suit and was wearing a pair of slim black trousers and a silky blue shirt. There was a tiny gold cross on a chain around her neck.

'Thank you,' she said. 'Thank you for coming.'

Harry nodded as she stood aside to let him in. 'Are you all right?'

A faltering smile quivered on her lips. 'Come on through.'

Harry found himself in a large tiled hall with pure white walls and timber beams. A pale wood stairway curved grandly up to the next floor. At the base of the stairs a vase of lilies stood on a table, their heady scent permeating the air. As he followed her through to the rear of the house, he tried to keep his gaze fixed on the back of her head rather than on the seductive sway of her hips.

The living room, built on a grand scale, was designed to impress. The walls were a pale shade of green and were covered with abstract paintings. Harry had no idea of the artists or whether they were originals or not. There were numerous sculptures scattered around too. Everything was ultra modern – the furniture and the fittings – as if any hint of the past was to be avoided.

'Sit down, please,' Aimee said, gesturing towards one of the wide leather sofas.

As Harry walked across the room, he took in the large plasma TV and a bank of expensive-looking music equipment. A computer in the corner, linked to the surveillance system, showed a picture of the empty space outside the gates on its screen. Long white drapes, pulled closed against the night, ran almost the entire width of the far wall. Behind them, he surmised, were French windows leading out to the garden.

He sat down on the sofa, sinking into the plush leather. 'You have a lovely home.'

She looked around as if seeing it for the first time. Her soft lips parted in a sigh. 'The gilded cage,' she murmured.

Harry wasn't sure how to respond. He thought about it for a moment, and then said, 'Is it that bad?'

Aimee sat down in a nearby chair, glanced over at him and immediately stood up again. 'I need a drink. How about you?'

'No, thanks,' Harry said, thinking it best to at least try and keep a clear head.

'A small one?' she suggested, clearly not wanting to drink alone.

He gazed up into her wide grey-green eyes. They were the kind of eyes that could break a man's resolve in less than five seconds flat. 'Go on then, just a small one.'

Aimee glided over to the corner, where an ebony cabinet held enough bottles of booze to stock a nightclub bar. She didn't ask what he wanted but poured neat malt whisky into two thick-bottomed glasses. 'You must think I'm crazy,' she said, as she returned with the drinks.

She handed him one of the glasses, sat down again and crossed her legs. 'I mean, I don't even know why I asked you to come here.'

'Because you need help,' Harry said.

'Yes, but what kind of woman turns to the guy who is being paid to follow her around?' She took a large gulp of the whisky and frowned. 'That doesn't make any sense, does it? It's madness. You don't owe me anything, whereas—'

'I owe him everything?'

That faltering smile appeared on her lips again. 'Not everything, perhaps, but *something*.'

433

Harry carefully studied her face. Although he thought her fear was real, a small part of his brain was still trying to work out if he was being played. Aimee Locke might be a vision of loveliness but he wasn't blind to the possibility of ulterior motives. 'So what made you do it? What made you invite me here tonight?'

'Desperation,' she said.

'You want to start at the beginning?'

Aimee downed what remained of the whisky and jumped up again. She went back over to the drinks cabinet. 'I will,' she said. 'I just need another of these first.'

Harry took a sip from his own untouched glass. The whisky was golden and smooth as silk. He watched as she poured herself a large one. Her hands were shaking slightly. With her back still to him she moved in front of the computer, obscuring the screen. His gaze ran the length of her body and then back up again. From somewhere distant he thought he heard the soft purr of a car engine.

Aimee Locke turned suddenly and smiled at him. 'I'm sorry,' she said.

Harry wasn't quite sure what the apology was for. But he didn't have to wait long to find out. First came the sound of the front door slamming and then the heavy tread of footsteps across the tiled hallway.

'Aimee?' a male voice called out.

Harry shot to his feet. Jesus Christ! Martin Locke was back! He glanced over at Aimee. The expression on her face was of neither shock nor surprise. Her mouth was partly open, her eyes gleaming. With a sinking heart he realised that he'd been set up. She had brought him here so she could confront her husband with the living, breathing evidence of the tail he had put on her. God almighty! He was about to find himself in the middle of a very nasty domestic.

The door to the living room was open. Harry could feel his heart thumping as the footsteps grew closer. What to do? There was nothing he could do. And then suddenly the man was there. As the two of them came face to face, there was mutual confusion. Harry had only a few seconds to absorb the short, slim body, the white hair, the unfamiliar features of a stranger, before it happened. The noise wasn't loud but it was distinctive – the sound of a silenced gun going off. A small red rose blossomed on the man's chest and he crumpled to the ground.

Harry whirled around to the windows behind him. There was a wave of chill night air as the long drapes billowed out. Whoever had fired the gun had escaped into the garden. He turned quickly back but then found himself frozen. For all his years of experience, for all his police training, he was temporarily paralysed. Aimee Locke didn't move either. She didn't scream, didn't shout, didn't even cry out.

For a moment, Harry felt as if the world had stopped turning. His legs, made of stone, refused to move. The reality of what had just happened refused to penetrate his brain. But then, finally, the adrenalin kicked in. Rushing forward, he crouched down and reached out a hand to feel for a pulse on the man's neck. There was nothing. The kill had been quick and clean and professional.

'The police,' he yelled. 'Call the police!'

From the edge of his vision he was aware of Aimee coming towards him. He didn't realise until it was too late. There was a soft whooshing sound, a shifting in the air, before everything went black.

52

It was twenty past eleven when Jess left the Fox. After her encounter with Clare, she had felt in need of a drink, and one drink had turned into another until closing time had finally come around. She had spent the evening perched on a stool at the bar chatting to the landlady, Maggie McConnell. After a while the conversation had turned, inevitably, to Donald Peck and what he had done.

Maggie, who seemed to know everything about everyone, had filled her in on more of the details. 'I dread to think what happened to him when he was a boy. There were all sorts of rumours about what went on in that household. Social Services took the two of them into care, you know. Stella was just a toddler then, but he was about eight. She was adopted into a nice family but ... Well, nobody wants them when they're older, do they? And especially not the damaged ones.'

'I suppose not,' Jess had said.

'I think Stella felt guilty about it, that she was lucky enough to get a fresh start – and that she couldn't remember anything much about the past. She always loved Donald despite the things he did. She'd try and help him out, do a bit of cooking and cleaning for him, but she couldn't solve his real problems. Nobody could.'

Jess had sipped her glass of red wine and pondered on how some people seemed doomed before their lives had properly begun. 'So what was Alan Towney like? Did you know him?'

'Oh sure, I knew Alan.' Maggie had given a snort. 'That man didn't have the backbone he was born with. Upped and left the minute there was a hint of trouble. He wanted Stella to stay away from Donald, but of course she wouldn't. It caused all sorts of rows. He didn't like it, you see, being related – even if was indirectly – to someone like that.'

'So he just pissed off?'

'Yeah, that's exactly what he did. And he never came back or got in touch. Never sent the poor woman a penny either. She was left on her own with a kid to raise. It wasn't easy for her.'

Standing on the pavement outside the pub, Jess went over the conversation again. She was still wondering if it was possible that Alan Towney had finally returned home. Clare might have confessed to sending the notes, but somehow it was difficult to associate either her or Masterson with the actual words that had been written. The threats went beyond mere bitterness. There was something hard and nasty and vengeful about them.

As she was waiting for a car to go by, she glanced up towards the windows of the flat. They were in darkness, but the ones beneath were blazing with light. Her first thought was that Harry must be home and working in the office, but then a more sinister explanation occurred to her. She shivered in horror. What if it was the arsonist? What if he was splashing petrol around the rooms and preparing a fuse to set the place alight as soon as she got back?

No sooner had the thought jumped into her head than she realised how ridiculous it was. No self-respecting arsonist was going to announce his presence to the world by leaving all the lights on. She was stressing over nothing. But still she got out her phone and dialled Harry's mobile, just to be sure. It went straight to voicemail, so she tried the office number instead.

It had barely rung once before it was answered.

'Yes?' a male voice said with more than a hint of impatience.

'Is that Mac?'

'Who is this?'

'It's Jess,' she said. 'I'm outside and I saw the lights. I was just—'

'You'd better come up,' Mac said brusquely and immediately hung up.

Jess's heart sank. What the hell was going on? She crossed the road at a brisk pace, unlocked the front door and jogged up the stairs. As she walked through the empty reception area and into Mac's office, four heads turned to look at her. She recognised Mac and Lorna and Warren James, but the fourth – a lean middle-aged man in a business suit – was a stranger to her.

She only had to look at their faces to know that the news was bad. 'What's happened?'

There was silence for a few seconds, and then Lorna spoke up. 'It's Harry,' she said. 'He's been arrested.'

'What?'

'A couple of hours ago, over at Aimee Locke's house.'

Jess's mouth fell open. 'What? Why? I don't understand.'

'Join the club,' Mac said. He pushed back his chair and stood up, but then didn't seem to know what to do with himself. Abruptly he sat back down again. 'He's been arrested for the murder of Martin Locke.'

'But he can't. He . . .' Jess was so shocked that she felt her legs buckle. All the air seemed to fly out of her lungs. She reached out for the corner of the desk, trying to steady herself.

Lorna quickly took hold of her arm and propelled her into an empty chair. 'It's true, I'm afraid. They haven't charged him yet, he's still at the hospital, but they'll interview him properly in the morning. It's not looking good, though.'

'The hospital?' Jess murmured.

'The bitch smashed a bottle over his skull,' Warren said. 'She claims he turned up at the house, asked to wait for her husband and then shot him in cold blood.'

Jess's head was spinning. None of this made any sense. 'But why? I mean, why would she say that?'

Warren sat back, scowled and put his hands behind his head. 'Because she's a fucking liar and she's trying to stitch him up for murder.'

'The trouble is that her story, at least at the moment, appears to stand up.' It was the stranger who had spoken. Jess looked at him and he gave her a nod. 'Richard Morris,' he said. 'I'm Harry's solicitor.'

'Tell me,' she said.

Morris glanced over at Mac, as if checking for permission to speak freely.

'Yeah,' Mac said, rubbing at his face with his hands. 'Tell her. Maybe she can shed some light on this whole bloody nightmare.'

Jess tried hard to concentrate as Morris recited Aimee Locke's version of events. Aimee had, apparently, bumped into Harry on the high street in the afternoon. He'd introduced himself, shown her some police ID and claimed that they'd met before at a charity function. They'd sat for a while on the Green and had a brief conversation. Then, later that evening, at about nine o'clock, he'd turned up at the gates of the house, saying that there had been an incident at her husband's office and that he needed to speak to him. Having already chatted to Harry earlier in the day, she didn't feel any concern about letting him in. Martin was on his way back from the airport after a business meeting in Milan and she was expecting him home at any time. She had given Harry a drink and they had sat and made small talk for about ten minutes. She had asked him about the alleged incident, but he'd said that he'd prefer to wait until he could speak to her husband. There was no indication, according to her, that anything was amiss.

'It's all bollocks,' Warren said angrily. 'The bitch is making it up.'

Mac flapped a hand. 'Let him finish.'

Morris paused for a second and then continued. 'She claims that when she heard the front door open she went out to the hall to greet her husband and to inform him that

441

a police inspector was waiting to talk to him. When they came back in, Harry had moved from his chair to a position just in front of the French windows. He was holding a gun and he shot Martin Locke as soon as he saw him. Then he ordered Aimee to turn off the security cameras. After that, he walked across the room, crouched down beside the body and checked for a pulse.'

'Jesus,' Jess said softly.

Morris gave a light shrug of his shoulders. 'Aimee Locke claims she was terrified that she was going to be next. While Harry was leaning over the body of her husband, she grabbed a bottle from the drinks cabinet and hit him over the head. Then, while he was out cold on the floor, she ran out into the street and called the police.'

Jess, feeling as dazed as if someone had just smashed a bottle over her own head, looked at the others. Her gaze flew from Mac to Lorna to Warren and then back to Morris again. 'But why should anyone believe her?'

'They found forged police ID in his jacket pocket.'

'Planted,' Warren said.

'And two phones,' Morris said. 'One that everyone knows about, that he used on a regular basis, and another, a pay-as-you-go, that contained over sixty pictures of Aimee Locke taken over the past few weeks and a large number of texts declaring his love for her. The police think that he might have developed some kind of an obsession.'

'That's ridiculous,' Jess said. 'He wasn't ... he wouldn't ...'

'Unfortunately, his prints were all over the phone. The police also ran a test for gunshot residue on his hands and clothes. They were positive. All in all, it's not looking good.'

'But we know he's innocent,' Lorna said, reaching out to touch Jess gently on the arm. 'We've just got to prove it.'

Richard Morris looked at his watch and stood up. 'I'm sorry, but I've really got to go. I'll call you in the morning, Mac, after I've talked to Harry again.'

Mac and Lorna both rose to their feet and escorted him to the door. While they were saying their goodbyes, Jess shifted across to the seat next to Warren. 'Surely the cops can see that Harry's been set up? This is crazy.'

Warren shook his head and sighed. 'The cops believe what they want to believe, babe. If they've got enough rope, they'll go ahead and hang him.'

'No way,' she said vehemently. 'They can't pin this on him.'

Mac came back to his desk and glared at Jess. 'So is there anything you want to tell us?'

Lorna sat down and shot him a warning glance. 'Don't take it out on her, Mac. None of this is her fault.'

'I'm not saying it is. But she's seen a damn sight more of him than we have recently. What can you tell us about Harry and this Aimee Locke?'

'I don't know any more than you do,' Jess said. 'I mean, I went with him to the casino at Selene's last night, but then Ray Stagg threw us out and—'

'He did what?' Mac snapped.

Jess was surprised that Harry hadn't told him, but then again, he probably had his reasons – one of them being that he didn't like being pushed around by the likes of Ray

Stagg. When Stagg had ordered him to leave Aimee alone, Harry would have been inclined to do the very opposite. 'Well, he asked us to leave.'

'Did he know Harry was there to watch Aimee Locke?'

Jess could see where there this was going and had to think quickly. She didn't want to land Harry in it. 'I've no idea,' she lied. 'But the two of them have had run-ins in the past, haven't they? And I don't imagine Stagg much cares for private investigators hanging around his establishments – they might see something he doesn't want them to see.'

Mac gave her a long, cool stare but didn't press the point.

'That'll be why he didn't mention it,' Warren said, backing her up. 'If he couldn't be sure that his cover was blown, then why abandon the surveillance? There were only a couple of days to go anyway.'

Jess stepped in with a question of her own. 'What's with this stalking thing? I don't get it. It was Martin Locke who hired Harry to spy on his wife. You must have the paperwork for that.'

Mac gave a weary shake of his head. 'Yeah, we've got paperwork all right, but we haven't got Martin Locke's real signature. That's another major problem. It seems that it might not have been him who came to the office last week but someone else entirely. And he paid with a cash cheque that can't be traced.'

Jess gazed down at the desk and drew in an uneasy breath. A someone, she realised, who must have been part of a carefully laid plan.

'And the only person who saw him was Harry,' Lorna said. 'So there's no proof that anyone was actually here at all. So far as the police are concerned, he could be making it all up.'

As Lorna's words sank in, Jess suddenly jerked up her head. 'I saw him,' she said. 'At least I think I did.'

Three pairs of eyes turned expectantly towards her.

'You were here?' Mac asked.

'Not in the office, no. I'd parked the car at the Fox and I was waiting for the lights to change so I could cross the road. I noticed a man, a middle-aged guy, pacing up and down outside. He kept stopping by the door and staring at the name plate. I thought he was a nervous client trying to pluck up the courage to go in.'

Mac opened a folder that was lying on his desk and pulled out a cutting from a magazine. 'Is this him?' he said, pointing a finger at a photograph of a thin, white-haired man standing in the middle of a group of businessmen outside a City office.

Jess shook her head. She didn't need to think twice. 'No, this other guy was younger, in his fifties. He was broader, too. And his hair was grey, not white.'

'Would you know him again?'

'I think so,' Jess said. 'But I couldn't swear to it.' She racked her brains, thinking back to last Friday and trying to summon up an image of the man she'd seen. 'He had a tan, I remember that. He was tall, about the same height as Harry. And he was wearing a very smart grey suit.'

Mac slipped the picture back into the file. 'Trouble is, you didn't actually see him come in.'

'But her description tallies with the one Harry gave,' Lorna said. 'It has to be the same guy.'

Warren hunched forward, placing his elbows on the desk. 'Now all we've got to do is find him. Shouldn't be too difficult. How many middle-aged grey-haired guys can there be in this city?'

'Very helpful,' Mac said drily. He rubbed at his eyes, which already looked red and sore. 'I think we should call it a day. Let's all go home and get some sleep. We'll see where we stand after Harry's been interviewed in the morning.'

Jess still had plenty of unanswered questions, but she could see that now wasn't the time to be asking them. She said her goodbyes and trudged despondently upstairs. After opening and closing the door to the flat, she pulled the bolts firmly across. Harry wouldn't be coming back tonight. She put on the light and gazed around. A cold fist of fear suddenly clenched around her heart. If the treacherous Aimee Locke got her way, he might *never* be coming back.

53

Harry's head ached, partly from the blow from the bottle and partly from the interview, which had been going on now for over two hours. He had spent the night in hospital before being brought to Cowan Road in the morning. It had been a sleepless night, but that had been down to the shock of what had happened and the throbbing pain of twenty-two stitches criss-crossing his skull rather than any serious concern about Aimee Locke's accusations. He had always had faith in the law – he'd dedicated years of his life to it – and a solid belief that the truth would eventually come out.

That faith, however, was starting to recede. The two officers sitting in front of him, DI Wall and DS Henson, were less than convinced by his story. He could see it on their faces, in the way they glanced at each other. They had that look in their eyes. He remembered it well from his own days in the interview room. They already thought they'd got all the evidence they needed to hang him out to dry.

'So, this man who you *claim* came to your office last Friday. Describe him to me.'

Harry stared across the desk at DI Wall. He was a thin-faced, hungry-looking guy in his mid-thirties. Hungry for success, that was. Results meant promotion and promotion meant respect, more money and more opportunities. Harry had met his type before. A fast-track university graduate who was climbing the greasy pole as quickly as he could.

'Haven't we already covered this?'

Wall's eyes narrowed a little. 'So I'd like you to go over it again. You got a problem with that?'

Harry gave a shrug. He knew how it worked. You asked a suspect to repeat his story over and over again in the hope that holes would eventually start to appear. He repeated the description of the man he'd thought was Martin Locke for the third time.

'And he paid with a cash cheque. Is that usual?'

'Not unusual,' Harry said. 'Plenty of people like to keep their private business private.'

'And there are no cameras in the office?'

'No,' Harry agreed, inwardly cursing the fact that they hadn't decided to install them until after 'Locke' had made his visit.

Wall opened a file and took out a photograph of the corpse of Martin Locke. He slid it across the surface of the table. 'And it definitely wasn't this man?'

'No,' Harry said. He stared down at the photograph, reliving the moment when Martin Locke had walked into the room. Those seconds of confusion, of bewilderment, and then ... He drew in a breath.

Wall left the picture sitting there. 'How do you account for the gun residue on your hands?'

'I can't,' Harry said. 'It must have been placed there after

I'd been knocked out. All he had to do was wrap my hand around the gun and discharge it again.'

'He?'

'Whoever shot Martin Locke.'

'And the phone? And the fake ID? Did he put your prints on those too?'

Harry recalled his encounter on the Green with Aimee Locke. 'As I said earlier, I picked up both of those items when Aimee Locke dropped her handbag.'

'But why should she go to all that trouble when she could have done it after you'd been knocked out?'

Harry gave a shrug. 'How should I know. To save time? To make sure the prints were convincing ones?' He had another theory too, which he didn't voice out loud. Aimee Locke, he had realised belatedly, was the kind of woman who liked to live dangerously. It must have given her a kick to let him pick up the fake ID, to take the chance of him flipping open the wallet and seeing what was inside.

Wall and Henson exchanged another of their sly looks. DS Henson was an older man, probably smarter than his boss but with the sense not to flaunt it. It was he who said, with a slightly lascivious edge to his voice, 'She's a good-looking girl, isn't she?'

Harry could hardly deny it. 'I suppose.'

'Keen on blondes, are you?'

Harry stared back at him. He presumed that they already knew about his relationship with Valerie. They would have been doing a good bit of digging over the last twelve hours. 'As much as any other man.'

Henson grinned. 'I prefer brunettes myself. So when did

you first set eyes on the lovely Aimee Locke?'

Harry sighed, feeling his head begin to throb even harder. 'We've been through all this. Apart from the picture that Martin ... that the man who *claimed* to be Martin Locke showed me, the first time I saw her was at Adriano's last Friday.'

'And afterwards you followed her to her place of work and then back to her home again.'

'Yes.'

'And then you went to the casino on Wednesday night?'

'Yes,' Harry said. 'That was what I'd been hired to do.'

'Of course,' DI Wall said. 'By the mysterious man who said that he was Martin Locke.'

Harry could see what they were thinking, that he'd made up the story about the fake client in order to give himself an excuse to follow Aimee around and track her movements for most of the day and night. 'Yes,' he said again.

Wall raised his eyebrows, as if he didn't believe a word. He left a short silence and then said, 'Right, let's go over this encounter you had with her in the afternoon. You're claiming that *she* approached you on the high street, said that she knew you were a private investigator and that she knew what you were doing.'

'That's exactly what happened.'

'And why should she confront you like that?'

'Because she was tired of her husband hiring someone to follow her around every time he went out of town.'

'And then she suggested a cosy chat on the Green?'

Harry nodded. 'She said she wanted to talk to me.'

'Wouldn't it have been smarter to just walk away?'

'In retrospect.' Harry had spent half the night wishing he had done just that. 'But I was curious as to what she had to say.'

'Curious?'

'Yes.'

DI Wall steepled his fingers and gazed at Harry thoughtfully. 'And what did she have to say?'

'Not much. She seemed scared of him, though, frightened of what he might do next.'

'And so you agreed to a second chat at her house that night?'

'No,' Harry said. 'I didn't agree to anything. She asked me if I'd come at nine o'clock, but I didn't say I would. At that point I hadn't decided what I was going to do.'

'But at nine o'clock you turned up all the same.'

Harry shifted in his seat. 'I thought she was in trouble. That was the impression she gave me.'

DI Wall's eyebrows shot up again. 'And is that common practice, for you to try and help your clients' partners, the people you're supposed to be gathering evidence against? It seems somewhat contradictory, if you don't mind me saying.'

'It wasn't exactly professional, no. But I believed that she was afraid of him, terrified even.'

'So you thought you'd try and save her from this terrifying husband of hers,' Wall said caustically. 'Very gallant, I'm sure.'

Richard Morris, Harry's brief, looked up from the notes he was making. 'My client is simply trying to explain the reasons for his actions.'

Harry was starting to sweat. The room was hot and he could feel the perspiration lathering his forehead and trickling down his spine. He'd always thought that only guilty people sweated, but now, with his own future in the balance, he knew better.

'Let's move on to the photographs on the phone and the text messages,' Wall said.

'I don't know anything about them.' Harry could see where this was all going. They were trying to build up a case based on the fact that he'd developed an obsession with Aimee Locke, an obsession that had led him to murder her husband.

Wall gazed at Harry from over the top of his fingertips. 'You don't seem to know very much about anything.'

'Inspector!' Morris warned.

Wall smirked and leaned back in his chair.

Harry was trying to keep calm, but with every minute that passed his situation was growing increasingly dire. If nobody believed him, he could be spending the next twenty years of his life in the slammer. 'Look, I did *not* murder Martin Locke. Why don't you talk to Ray Stagg? Ask him what he was doing last night.'

'We already have,' Henson said. 'He was at his club with hundreds of witnesses.'

Harry's hopes slumped even further. He'd been convinced that Stagg must have been the killer. Hearing about the alibi was like another nail in his coffin. Frustration finally got the better of him, and he leaned across the desk, glaring at the two officers. 'For Christ's sake,' he snapped. 'Can't either of you see that this is one almighty stitch-up?'

Richard Morris laid a restraining hand on his arm. He looked across at the two police officers. 'Gentlemen, my client's tired. He's also suffering from a very nasty injury. Might I suggest we take a break now?'

54

DI Valerie Middleton was sitting in the incident room going through the file on the Becky Hibbert killing. Her eyes gazed blankly at the information in front of her. Hard as she tried, she simply couldn't concentrate. Harry's arrest the previous night had knocked her for six. She didn't believe he was guilty, not for one second, but she was still angry at him. Raising her head, she looked across the desk at Kieran Swann.

'How could he have been so stupid? I mean, what did he think he was doing going to her house?'

'We don't know the whole story, guv. I'm sure he had his reasons.'

Having spotted Aimee Locke in the foyer, Valerie had a fair idea of what those reasons might be. The woman was a tall, leggy blonde with a pouting mouth and a figure to die for. Even in her widow's weeds – a simple black dress with matching jacket – she somehow managed to ooze sex appeal. 'Yes, I'm sure he did.'

'She won't get away with it,' Swann said. 'Everyone knows that Harry isn't capable of murder.'

'Try telling that to Bill and Ben.' DI Wall and DS

Henson had been drafted in from another station because of Harry's previous connection to Cowan Road and his relationship with her. 'From what I've heard, they've got him right in the frame.'

'Yeah, well, don't believe all you hear. It's early days yet.'

But Valerie didn't feel reassured. In fact, she felt the very opposite. Her stomach was twisted in a knot. With so much evidence pointing towards Harry's guilt, she didn't trust Wall and Henson to get to the truth. She slapped a hand down on the desk, fear and frustration finally getting the better of her. 'Jesus, if she wanted her husband dead, why couldn't she arrange for it to be done somewhere else? Why at the house? Why not at Locke's office, or in the street? And why the hell did she have to involve Harry?'

Swann's eyebrows shifted up at the outburst. It wasn't often that he saw her so rattled. 'You know why not. Who's the first person we look at in situations like these? As Martin Locke's nearest and dearest, she'd be top of our list of suspects. This way there's a ready-made scapegoat. If she can make a convincing argument for being stalked by Harry, for being the unwelcome focus of his affections, then it's only one small step to him bumping off her husband.'

'One *small* step?'

'Well, you know what I mean. It gives him a motive. Stalkers are single-minded, obsessive, and their sense of reality isn't the same as anyone else's. With all the texts and photographs found on the phone, Harry's being made to look like a fantasist, as if he was convinced that he and

Aimee could walk off into the sunset together if it wasn't for the minor impediment of her husband.'

Valerie put her elbows on the desk and cupped her chin with her palms. 'Now you're really cheering me up.'

'Sorry.'

'So what do we know about the black widow?' Her eyes brightened a little. 'Maybe we should do a bit of digging of our own, see what we can find out.'

Swann pulled a face. 'Come on, guv. If Redding gets the merest sniff of you poking around, he'll have your guts for bloody garters.'

Valerie knew he was right. Her relationship with Harry meant she wasn't supposed to get involved in the case. It was strictly off limits.

Swann glanced around the room to make sure no one was listening before leaning towards her and saying softly, 'But I could give David Mackenzie a call.'

'Mac?'

'Get him up to speed with how things stand. Tell him what we know, fill him in on a few details. I'm sure he'll be keen to do some digging of his own.'

Valerie bit down on her lip and stared at him. What he was suggesting was more than risky, and if they got caught they'd be facing, at best, a disciplinary hearing. At worst, they could end up fired. But what was the alternative? Aimee Locke had spun a web of such complexity that it would take more than the likes of Wall and Henson to unravel it.

She was saved from making a decision one way or another by the arrival of DC Joanne Lister.

'Sorry to interrupt, guv, but uniform have just brought in a kid called Gary Banks. He was arrested on the Mansfield with a bag full of Es.'

Valerie frowned. 'Well, they can sort it, can't they?'

'They're still waiting for the duty solicitor to get here. The thing is, Banks wants to talk to you first. He claims he knows something about the Becky Hibbert killing.'

Gary Banks was seventeen, a short, skinny youth with silver piercings in his lip and eyebrow. He was dressed in jeans and a T-shirt and was sitting back with his arms folded across his chest. There was a stiffness about the pose, as if he was trying too hard to look nonchalant.

'I'm DI Middleton,' Valerie said, pulling out a chair. 'And this is DS Swann. I understand you have information about the Becky Hibbert murder.'

Gary looked warily from one to the other. 'Might 'ave,' he said.

Valerie gave a sigh. 'Don't waste my time, Gary. Either you do or you don't.'

He gazed sullenly back at her. 'What's in it for me?'

Swann leaned forward, a sneer on his face. 'What's in it for you, son, is that you don't get done for wasting police time on top of everything else.'

'I ain't wasting no one's time.'

'So?' Valerie said.

'I wanna make a deal,' Gary said.

Swann gave a snort and glanced at Valerie. 'Do you hear that, guv? He wants to make a deal.' He shifted his gaze back to Gary. 'You think you can give us some bullshit story and we'll just let you walk out of here? I hate to break the bad news, but it doesn't work like that.'

'It ain't no bullshit, man! I saw her and her mates. And I saw him. I saw that guy you're looking for. I was on the estate that night.'

Valerie recalled the group of boys that Becky and her friends had passed on their way home from the pub. She was suddenly gripped by the conviction that finally they were about to get the break they needed. 'Look, if what you tell us turns out to be the truth—'

'It is the truth. I swear it.'

'As I was saying,' Valerie continued, careful to keep her voice neutral. 'If what you tell us turns out to be the truth, then when your case comes to court we can let the judge know how helpful you've been. It's the best we can do, I'm afraid.'

Gary thought about this for a while. He stared hard at the table before slowly lifting his eyes to them again. 'It ain't enough,' he said.

Swann pushed back his chair and stood up. 'Suit yourself. How many Es was it you had in your possession? You'll have plenty of time to figure out if you made the right decision when they send you down.'

'Okay, okay!' Gary said, his eyes growing wide and fearful. For all his bravado, he was still a seventeen-year-old boy looking at his first stretch inside. 'I'll tell you what I saw.'

Swann sat back down. 'Good choice.'

Gary ran his tongue along his upper lip, making the piercing jiggle. Then he reached out for the plastic cup in front of him and took a large swig of water. His hand was shaking as he put the cup back on the table. 'You got a fag?'

Swann inclined his head towards the NO SMOKING sign on the wall. 'Sorry, mate.' He left a short pause before adding, 'But maybe later, when you've given us the facts, we could nip out into the yard for five minutes.'

Valerie, who knew there'd be no nipping anywhere, gave Swann's foot a swift kick with her own. She didn't approve of empty promises. 'So, Gary, you saw Becky Hibbert on the night that she was murdered?'

'Yeah,' Gary said. 'We was just hanging, me and some mates.'

'And what time was that?'

Gary gave a shrug. 'Dunno exactly, 'bout midnight? Anyhow, we was walking towards the gate and they're coming the other way. Three of them, like. A bit pissed up, I reckon, laughing and shouting and that.'

'Did you speak to them?' Swann asked.

'Nah,' Gary said. 'We didn't say nuthin'. They was old, man. You know what I mean?'

Valerie raised her eyes to the ceiling. If he thought twenty-four was old, he probably had her down as geriatric. 'Go on.'

'So, we pass 'em and go on out the gate. I didn't see none of 'em again. We split for a while, twenty minutes or so, and then we come back. We're just down the road and that Livesey guy walks past and goes on to the estate. He works at the Lincoln, right? I've seen him around.'

Valerie gave an encouraging nod. 'And?'

'And I'm watching him, right? I mean, not really watching, but it's kind of quiet and I'm leaning forward with me

459

elbows on the wall having a smoke. I see him walk across to Haslow and he gets out his phone.'

For the first time, Valerie was certain that Gary was telling the truth. How else could he have known about the call Livesey had made shortly after going on to the estate? 'Okay,' she said casually, not wanting him to realise how important this could be in case he started talking deals again.

'Well, then he stops near the door and hangs around a while.'

'How long is a while?' Swann asked.

'I dunno. A few minutes. Five, maybe. Like he's waiting for someone. Pacing up and down like he's getting impatient. And then he goes inside. Next thing he's up on the tens. I can see him walking along. There's lights up there.'

'When you say *next thing*,' Valerie said, 'what do you mean exactly? Think carefully. As long as it took him to go up in the lift, or was there a delay?'

'Yeah,' Gary said. 'Pretty quick, I reckon. Well, as quick as them lifts ever are. And then, like I said, I see him walking and he stops about halfway along and he rings the bell of her flat.'

Swann leaned forward again. 'How can you be sure it was her flat? In fact, how can you even be sure that he was on the tens?'

Gary shrugged his skinny shoulders. 'I know them towers, man. I know a dude who lives on the tens. It's got two boarded-up flats on the corner, right?'

He *was* right, Valerie realised. She could remember walking past them on her way to Becky Hibbert's place. 'So he rings the bell. What happens next?'

'He stands there for a while. But there's no light on so he must figure there's no one in. He turns around and comes back down. He took the steps this time. I could see him as he turned the corners. Then he comes out and—'

'Straight out?' Valerie asked. 'There wasn't any delay?'

'Yeah, straight out. Then he hangs around the entrance again, doing that pacing thing.' Gary picked up the cup and took another gulp of water. 'After that he comes back along the main drive, out the gate and walks past us again. He's looking well pissed-off. You know, like someone's just done him over. Not happy, man, not happy at all.'

Valerie frowned. If Gary was telling the truth, then the chances of Dan Livesey being their murderer were slight. Even if Livesey had met Becky in the foyer of Haslow House he'd barely have had time to kill her. If he had some-how managed it, why on earth would he go on up to her flat afterwards? He'd want to scarper as quickly as he could. And he couldn't have done it on the way out, not if Gary was right about watching his progress down the steps. Anyway, even the most stupid of killers didn't normally pace around in full view after they'd just bumped off their ex. 'Why didn't you come forward with this information before?'

Gary shifted his shoulders again, the gesture speaking a thousand words. Residents of the Mansfield never volun-teered information unless they had to. Or unless there was some advantage to be gained from it.

'Anything else?' she asked.

Gary shook his head. 'Nah, he just got in the car and left.'

'A car?' she snapped. 'You said he was walking. Where did this car suddenly appear from?'

Gary pulled a face, as if he was undeserving of this sudden change in tone. 'It was up the road, parked on the corner near the Lincoln.'

'What kind of car? You remember the colour, the make?'

'I dunno, do I? Dark-coloured. Black or blue. Nuthin' fancy.'

'No chance of you remembering any part of the registration, I suppose?'

Gary hesitated, perhaps wondering if he should try and make something up, before eventually shaking his head again. 'Sorry.'

'And then he just drove off?'

'Nah, he wasn't driving. He got into the passenger side, didn't he? Some other geezer was driving.'

Valerie tried to rein in her impatience. It wasn't easy. 'You're sure the driver was a man?'

Gary lifted a hand to his mouth and chewed on a dirty fingernail.

'Is that a yes or a no?' Swann said.

'It was kinda dark. I thought it was a bloke, but . . .'

Valerie wondered if it could have been Micky Higgs. She waited, but it soon became apparent that they weren't going to get anything else out of him. After thirty seconds she gave a nod to Swann and rose to her feet. 'Okay, Gary, thanks for your help. We may need to talk to you again at some point.'

'But you'll put in a word, right?'

'So long as you've been telling us the truth.'

462

Swann stood up too and followed Valerie to the door.

Gary stared after him. 'Hey, man, what about that fag you promised?'

'Huh?' Swann said, glancing over his shoulder. 'What fag was that?'

'Shithead,' muttered Gary under his breath.

Swann grinned as he went out into the corridor and closed the door on one very unhappy Gary Banks.

'What do you reckon?' Valerie asked as they headed back to the office.

'Well, he's a scumbag dealer, hardly the most reliable of witnesses.'

'Except he did know about the phone call. And he hasn't really got a reason to lie about the rest of it. Unless he's trying to cover up for Livesey, I think his story could be true.'

'Which means?'

Valerie stopped at the base of the stairs and turned to look at him. 'Which means that Becky was probably already dead by the time Dan Livesey got to the estate.'

55

When Jess emerged from Cowan Road, Mac was waiting for her in the dark blue Freelander. She climbed in beside him, sat back and shook her head. 'God, I thought I was never going to get out of there.'

'They put you through the wringer?'

'That's putting it mildly. I thought they were going to arrest me too. They kept going on about Adriano's and the casino, as if it was mighty strange that I'd been with Harry on those two occasions and not someone from Mackenzie, Lind.'

'And what did you tell them?'

'The truth,' she said. 'That he asked me along to the restaurant because no one from the business was available and he'd have stood out like a sore thumb eating on his own. And that he asked me to go to the casino to take my mind off the fire.' Her mouth twisted in exasperation. 'They didn't seem convinced, though. Because I'm staying at his flat, they seem to think that something must be going on between us. And if something's going on, then obviously I must be covering for him.'

Mac took an unopened pack of cigarettes out of his

pocket. He stared at it for a moment before ripping off the cellophane. 'I'm supposed to have quit,' he said. 'Don't tell Lorna.'

Jess, who had also given up a few months ago, stared longingly at the pack. What she craved more than anything else at the moment was a heady burst of nicotine. 'Your secret's safe,' she said, 'so long as I can have one too.'

They smoked in silence for a minute, puffing guiltily on their cigarettes. Mac was the first to speak again. 'So, what else did they ask you?'

'They kept going on about Harry's *feelings* for Aimee. I told them that he didn't have any. It was a job, nothing else.'

'And did they believe you?'

'No,' she said. 'They kept asking what he'd said about her, how he'd behaved around her. Did I think he was attracted to her.' Jess took a long drag on her cigarette and tipped the ash out of the open window. 'I mean, for God's sake, she's a smart, sexy blonde. What heterosexual man isn't going to find his pulse racing? But there's a difference between a spot of lust and a psychotic plan to dispose of a husband.'

'And did you say that?'

'What?'

'That she set his pulse racing.'

'No,' Jess said, frowning. 'I'm not completely stupid.'

Mac looked at her. 'Well, that's something.'

Jess knew that she wasn't Mac's favourite person, but they had no choice other than to work together if they were going to get Harry out of this mess. 'How did your interview go?'

'They questioned me about Harry's past relationships and whether he made a habit of obsessing over clients.' Mac made a sound halfway between a sigh and a grunt. 'They're also going to go through the business diaries, check when and where Harry was working over the past few weeks. They're trying to compare the times and places with the photographs that were taken of Aimee Locke.'

'Well, whoever set this up would have made damn sure that Harry didn't have an alibi for any of those times.'

'Exactly,' Mac said. 'And with the security system turned off after the shooting, the killer was able to walk out of the Locke house without being caught on camera.'

'Although it begs the question how he got in there in the first place.'

'Which is another problem,' Mac said. 'So far as the police are concerned, the security footage proves that no one other than Aimee Locke went in or out of the house all day. Well, not until Harry arrived. Which makes his story about a mystery killer hiding behind the curtains sound somewhat less than convincing.'

'Jesus,' Jess murmured. 'So what now?'

'Now we try and find out who the fake Martin Locke is. Got any ideas on how we might do that?'

Jess took a final drag on the cigarette, gazed at it regretfully and then dropped the butt out of the window. It was hardly admirable to add to the litter already on the streets, but the ashtray in the Freelander was clearly out of bounds. 'As it happens,' she said. 'I have. But it rather depends on where Ray Stagg is at the moment.'

Mac gave a nod towards the station. 'He's in there. I saw him arrive about ten minutes ago.'

'So he should be a while yet.'

'What are you thinking?' Mac said.

'Ray Stagg's business partner is called James Harley-Cunningham. Do you reckon you can find out what kind of car he drives?'

Half an hour later they pulled into the small parking area to the side of Selene's. A prominent sign declared FOR STAFF ONLY, along with a threat to clamp any trespassing vehicles. The only other car there was James Harley-Cunningham's racing-green Morgan. It was a beautiful motor, of which its owner, no doubt, was extremely proud.

With what had happened to Aimee last night – or rather to her husband – Jess knew that all the staff would have been told to be alert to any visits from the press. Reporters had probably been sniffing around already, hoping for a juicy titbit on the glamorous grieving widow and the horrors that had befallen her. There wasn't a chance of getting through the front door and seeing Harley-Cunningham face to face, and so they would, metaphorically speaking, have to get in through the back.

'You think this'll work?' Mac said dubiously.

Jess took out her mobile. 'Only one way to find out.' She dialled the number and lifted the phone to her ear.

Her call was answered by a woman with a cut-glass accent. 'Good afternoon. This is Selene's. How may I help you?'

'Oh,' Jess said, acting flustered. 'I'm just outside the club.

467

I'm dreadfully sorry, I really am, but I appear to have reversed into someone's car. It's a Morgan. Does it belong to anyone you know?'

There was a brief intake of breath. 'Hold on a moment.' Jess could hear a light muttering in the background as the information was passed on. Then the woman came back on the line. 'Wait there,' she ordered. 'He'll be right with you.'

Jess got out of the Freelander and waited.

Thirty seconds later, James Harley-Cunningham came hurtling out of the building. He was in his late twenties, a tall, slim, slightly effeminate-looking guy with tousled brown hair and wide brown eyes. From the look of sheer horror on his face, anyone would have thought that it was a loved one that had been hit rather than his car.

He glared at Jess as he approached the Morgan. 'What the . . .' he began. His gaze fell on the rear of the car and his expression gradually changed to one of confusion. Quickly he walked around the vehicle, closely examining first one side and then the other.

'Sorry about that,' Jess said. 'I just needed a chance to talk to you in private.'

'What?'

'My name's Jessica Vaughan. I'm a friend of Harry Lind's.'

He gave a shrug, the name obviously not meaning anything to him.

Jess gave him a thin smile. 'He's the poor sap who's currently being held for the murder of Martin Locke.'

'And what's that got to do with me?'

'Well, you're Ray Stagg's business partner, aren't you?

Surely you realise that he's involved with Aimee Locke. The two of them planned the killing together and put Harry in the frame.'

'Don't be ridiculous!' Harley-Cunningham said, placing his hands on his hips. 'I've got nothing to say, okay? Just bugger off and find someone else to harass.'

Jess smiled sweetly back at him. 'So how does it feel to be an accessory to murder?'

He had turned, intending to head back towards the entrance, but stopped dead at her words and whirled around again. 'What the hell are you talking about?'

'It's only a matter of time before the police work out what really happened. Withholding evidence is a serious offence.'

'I'm not withholding anything.'

Jess slowly shook her head. 'Are you trying to tell me there's nothing going on between Ray Stagg and Aimee Locke? Because we both know that's not true. Still, maybe you don't care if he takes you down with him. You're still young. A few years in the slammer shouldn't entirely ruin your life.'

Harley-Cunningham scowled at her. 'Are you threatening me?'

'I'm just telling you how it is. Ray Stagg's a villain through and through. He made his money through drugs and prostitution and God knows what other sordid enterprises. But maybe you don't care about that either.' She paused, aware that she was sailing close to the wind, but carried on regardless. 'The cops are going to care, though. And when they pull this club apart – which they will –

469

you'd better hope that Stagg hasn't been stashing anything he shouldn't on the premises.'

It had been a shot in the dark, but it definitely hit home. Harley-Cunningham visibly paled. He shifted from one foot to the other and refused to meet her gaze.

Jess realised she was on to something and quickly pressed home her advantage. 'Maybe you're in on the drug pushing too. It must be a profitable sideline.'

'There's no dealing in this club!' he snapped.

'Are you sure of that? Only rumour has it that the place is swimming in the stuff.' She left a short pause and then added, 'Or is Stagg taking all the profits for himself?'

'There's no dealing here,' he said again, but this time without much conviction.

Jess could sense that his resolve was weakening. She also had the distinct feeling that the honeymoon period between the two business partners – had there ever been one – had long since expired. There was no love lost between Harley-Cunningham and Stagg. 'The sooner he goes down for what he's done, the sooner you'll be free of him. Make the right choice, James. Don't let him walk all over you.'

Harley-Cunningham thought about this for a while, but he didn't reply.

'You see that guy over there,' Jess said, gesturing towards the Freelander. Mac had shifted the car close to the gates and was currently enjoying his second cigarette. 'He's a retired cop. Harry Lind used to be a cop too. The police don't like people screwing over their own. They tend to take it personally.'

'What is it you want from me? I've already told you I

don't know anything. Aimee Locke's an employee, that's all.'

'So maybe there's something else you can help us with. We're trying to track down a man in his early fifties: tall, short grey hair, suntan, smartly dressed. He's probably Irish. Could be ex-army. Does that ring any bells? Have you seen anyone like that with Ray Stagg?'

Harley-Cunningham opened his mouth, then closed it again and glanced around warily as though someone might be watching.

'James?'

'I'm not sure,' he said.

'Not sure if you've seen someone like that, or not sure if you want to tell me?' Jess took a step closer to him and lowered her voice. 'Look, no one's going to find out that you talked to me. I give you my word. Just give me a name and I'm out of here. You'll never see me again.'

While he weighed up his options, Harley-Cunningham scratched nervously at his chin. The seconds ticked by. 'There may have been a man like that,' he said eventually. 'He used to come into the casino. He gambled pretty heavily, usually lost more than he won.'

'And you definitely saw him with Stagg?'

He nodded. 'A few times, but not recently, not for ... I don't know, three or four weeks.'

'And his name?'

Harley-Cunningham pushed his hands into his jacket pocket, stared briefly down at the ground and then raised his eyes again. 'Raffles,' he said.

'Raffles?'

'That's what Ray called him.'

'Is that some kind of nickname?'

'I've got no idea.'

Jess didn't think he was lying. It was a shame he couldn't give her more, but it was better than nothing. 'Okay, thanks for that. I'll leave you in peace.' She started heading back towards Mac, but had barely gone a couple of yards when he called out to her.

'Wait! There's something else.'

Jess felt her heart miss a beat. She turned and walked back to him. 'What is it?'

Harley-Cunningham's pale face was now flushed with pink. Having dipped his toe in the water of betrayal and found it not entirely disagreeable, he'd obviously decided to take the plunge. 'I don't know if this is important, but a while back I overheard Ray and Aimee arguing in his office. It was something to do with her father.'

'What about him?'

'I'm not sure. I was passing by the door and only caught a snatch, but it was pretty heated. The two of them were going at it hammer and tongs.'

'Has he ever been here, her father I mean?'

Harley-Cunningham shook his head. 'I always thought her parents were dead. That's what she told people. That's why I thought it was odd. Maybe it's nothing.'

'Maybe,' Jess said. She waited, but it soon became clear that he had nothing more to say. 'Okay. Thanks again.'

It was then that Harley-Cunningham's courage deserted him. He raked his fingers through his hair and screwed up his eyes. 'Christ, if Ray ever finds out that I—'

'He won't,' she said firmly. 'You've done the right thing. Don't worry about it.'

By the time Jess reached the car, Harley-Cunningham had already scuttled back inside the club. Climbing into the Freelander, she sat back and smiled. 'I don't think James is altogether enamoured of his business partner.'

'Hard to believe,' Mac said drily.

She gave him a quick summary of the conversation and the information she'd managed to extract. By the time she'd finished, Mac was looking at her with a new-found respect.

'I'm not even going to ask how you got him to talk,' he said.

'Best not,' she agreed. 'So have you ever heard of this Raffles bloke?'

'No, but I'll call Swann and get him to do a PNC check. Something might come up on the computer.'

'Who's Swann?'

'DS Kieran Swann. He works alongside Valerie at Cowan Road. He rang me earlier, suggested we pool our resources.'

'I didn't think Valerie would be allowed to get involved.'

'She isn't – at least not officially. But what the powers-that-be don't know, the powers-that-be won't grieve over.'

Jess raised her eyebrows but kept quiet while Mac made the call. It was short, only lasting a minute or two. When he'd finished she said, 'So what next?'

'Now we chase up that other lead.' Mac quickly punched in another number on his phone. 'Lorna?' he said. 'It's me. Yeah, I'm still over at Selene's. We're just leaving now. Can you do me a favour and get Warren to dig out a birth certificate for Aimee Locke?' He paused and nodded. 'Yeah,

473

the file's in my top drawer. We need to find out who her father is.'

As they set off back through the West End, Jess wondered if they'd finally turned a corner. But she couldn't allow herself to hope too much. They could be on the right road, or they might be heading straight down a long blind alley.

56

DI Middleton and DS Swann were huddled in a corner of the incident room. Valerie had a poky office of her own, but when there was a major investigation on the go she preferred to be in the thick of things. To date there hadn't been much progress on the Becky Hibbert case. Livesey was still on the run and they weren't any closer to finding him. Although Valerie knew that she should be putting all her energies into finding Becky's killer, her mind was preoccupied by an entirely different murder.

'So what do we know about Aimee Locke?' she said softly to Swann.

'Sod all, basically, other than that she's been working at the casino for the past three years. And she hasn't got a record, not so much as a parking fine.'

'And Martin Locke?'

'Yeah, he's kind of interesting ... or should I say *was*. Stinking rich, of course, and thirty years her senior. Made most of his money from insurance. He also gave a lot of it away to charity, and we're talking hundreds of thousands.'

'Maybe she decided to bump him off before his bank account got too depleted.'

'Or just grew tired of sharing an old man's bed.'

Valerie wondered at Swann's ability to bring everything down to sex. 'Do we know how much she stands to inherit?'

He shook his head. 'Not yet, but I'm sure it's more than adequate to keep her in mink bikinis for the rest of her life. That house must be worth half a million for starters.'

'I saw Vita Howard in the foyer earlier.'

'The solicitor?'

'Yes, and she's backing up Aimee's story. Well, part of it. Apparently Aimee's been to see her several times over the last month concerned about the text messages she was receiving. Vita advised her to report it.'

Swann stared at her. 'She told you that? For God's sake, guv, you shouldn't even have been talking to her. If Redding finds out, you'll—'

'Of course I didn't talk to her. Jerry Cooke told me. He got it from a PC who overheard Vita Howard mention it to Wall.'

'Right,' he said, looking relieved. Then his face dropped as he realised how fast the evidence was stacking up against Harry. 'So Locke's got a solicitor to back up that part of her story.'

'It doesn't prove anything. Only that Aimee exploited her friendship with Howard to make it seem like she was being stalked. There has to be a way of proving she's a liar. What about this Raffles bloke that Mac called you about?'

Swann glanced down at his notebook. 'Yeah, I ran a check on him. His real name's Paul Rafferty. He's a known con artist, been at it for years. Tends to target rich older widows and try to charm them with his tales of heroic army exploits. Truth is, of course, that he's never been out of civvies in his life. He's a bit of a gambler too, which would fit in with him hanging round Selene's.'

'But no address, I suppose.'

'No, nothing current. He tends to move around. He could be anywhere. But Mac's put the word out. He's been in touch with all his contacts, offering a generous reward to anyone who can find him. With five grand up for grabs, I shouldn't think it'll be too long before he gets a bite.'

'Let's hope so.' She glanced at her watch and groaned. 'God, if we don't get a break soon, Harry's going to end up in the dock.'

'It won't come to that.'

But Valerie didn't share his confidence. Wall and Henson were gunning for a result and the evidence had been laid out on a plate. It was only a matter of time before they decided to go ahead and charge him. She was still stressing over this when she became aware of someone hovering. She looked up to see Simon Wetherby standing beside her. 'Hi, what are you doing here?'

'Sorry to interrupt. I heard about Harry Lind. I'm really sorry. Are you okay?'

She smiled, pleased to see him. At times like this, every friendly face was welcome. 'Okay might not be quite the word.'

'No, I don't suppose it is. But I was wondering if I could help, if you needed a hand with anything.'

Before Valerie could reply, Swann leaned across and said, 'You solved all the crimes on your patch, then?'

Simon laughed. 'Not quite.'

Swann's voice took on a nastier edge. 'Well you don't need to worry about us. Best get back to sorting your own problems.'

Valerie glared at her sergeant before looking back at Simon. 'Don't mind him,' she said. 'He was born without the politeness gene. It's good of you to offer. I appreciate it. I'll let you know if anything comes up.'

Wetherby gave her a nod. 'I know you might not be in the mood, but if you fancy a chat later, give me a call. We could grab a drink at the Fox.'

'Thanks. I may well do that. I'll see how it goes.'

She watched as he walked away and then turned to Swann. 'Jesus, what's with the attitude? He was only offering to help.'

'Yeah, well, we don't need his help.'

'Maybe you don't, but I'm not sure if Harry would agree.'

Swann gave a dismissive wave of his hand. 'I don't trust him. And the fewer people know about what we're doing, the better.'

'He's not going to go blabbing to Redding.' She suspected that Swann's antagonism towards Simon Wetherby was down to a misplaced sense of loyalty to Harry rather than any real worries about the superintendent. So far as Swann was concerned, she and Harry were still an item and no other man had the right to try and muscle in. Annoyed, she found herself thinking about Jessica Vaughan again. It was okay, apparently, for Harry to move Vaughan into his flat without so much as a word to her about it, but far from okay for her to go for a drink with Wetherby. She was still dwelling on the unreasonableness of this when Swann's phone started ringing.

'DS Swann.' He listened for a moment and then put the receiver against his chest. 'It's DC Lambert, guv. Higgs and Fielding have just met up with Kirsten Cope at Connolly's. Cope's handed over a jiffy bag. Looks like it may have money in it. Do you want them picked up?'

Valerie's expression instantly changed. 'You bet I do.' Perhaps, finally, they were going to get the break they needed in the Becky Hibbert case. She shot up from her chair, the adrenalin starting to pump through her body. 'You and DC Franks take Higgs and I'll interview Paige Fielding with Lister. We'll leave Kirsten Cope until the end. It won't do any harm to let her sweat for a while.'

57

Paige Fielding had told her story and she was sticking to it. The five thousand pounds found in the jiffy bag was a loan from Kirsten.

'It's a lot of money,' Valerie said.

Paige shrugged. 'So? We're old mates, ain't we?'

'And you need the money for what exactly?'

'The van's packed in. I need a new one to get me gear to the market.'

'Why cash, though? What's wrong with a cheque?'

Paige folded her arms across her cheat and smiled slyly back at her. 'Got an overdraft, luv. No point putting it in the bank. And Micky, well, he just come along to make sure I got home safe. Lots of scumbag muggers on the Mansfield. You may have noticed.'

'So does Kirsten Cope often lend you money?' DC Lister asked.

'No,' Paige said. 'Course not. It's an emergency, ain't it?'

Valerie inclined her head and gazed at her. 'Must be good to have such generous friends.'

'Like I said, it's just a loan. She ain't givin' it to me.'

'Take a while to pay all that back.'

Paige gave another of her lazy shrugs. 'So I borrowed a few quid. Weren't a crime last time I checked.'

'There was money found in Becky's flat,' Valerie said. 'Did Kirsten give *her* a loan too?'

'Are you kidding me? Kirsten wouldn't lend nothin' to Becky. You know where that came from. She was ... y'know ... making a bit on the side.'

'Really?' Valerie said. 'Only it does seem rather a coincidence that first we find cash at Becky's place and now you've suddenly come into a considerable sum too.'

'Yeah, well, that's all it is – coincidence.' Paige leaned across the table towards Valerie. 'Now, are you gonna charge me with summat or can I go?'

Valerie knew that she wasn't going to get anything more out of her. The girl was too savvy to be intimidated by the law or to make any stupid mistakes. Paige was lying, but there was nothing she could do about it at the moment. 'You can go.'

Paige rose to her feet, smiling smugly. 'About time too.'

Valerie and Swann met outside Room 3 and quietly exchanged notes on their respective interviews. Micky Higgs, unsurprisingly, had backed up Paige's story about the loan from Kirsten.

'What do you reckon?' Swann said. 'You think the two of them could be blackmailing her?'

Valerie peered through the small window in the door. Kirsten Cope was nervously tapping the tabletop with her fingertips. Her face was tight, her mouth set in a thin straight line. Fear was written all over her. 'I wouldn't put it past them. Question is: what's the terrible secret? It has to be pretty damning to merit five big ones.'

'Maybe Harry was right. Maybe this does all go back to the Minnie Bright case.'

Valerie felt a tightening in her stomach. 'Christ,' she murmured. 'If that's true, we could be about to open a whole can of worms.'

Swann took a sheet of paper out of the file he was carrying and passed it over to her.

'This just came through.'

'Not that surprising,' she said, reading through it.

'Not surprising at all.' Swann looked towards the door again. 'So how are we going to play this? You want to be good cop or bad cop?'

Valerie rolled her eyes. 'You've been watching too much TV again.' But as he opened the door and they stepped inside she murmured, 'Bad.'

Kirsten visibly jumped as they entered the room. She was one of those Barbie doll girls, all fake tan, long blonde hair, cleavage and lip gloss. If wearing too much pink had been a criminal offence, she could have been arrested. She was dressed in skinny pink jeans, a skimpy white vest and a long pink cardigan.

Valerie made the introductions and she and Swann sat down.

'Shouldn't I have a solicitor?' Kirsten asked anxiously.

Valerie frowned as if she didn't quite understand. 'We're not charging you with anything, Ms Cope. You're just here to help us with our enquiries.'

'What enquiries?'

'We're investigating the murder of Becky Hibbert.' Valerie pursed her lips, assuming a stern expression. 'Unless of course you feel that you *need* a solicitor. If that's the case, we can stop right now.'

Kirsten thought about this before shaking her head. 'No, but I don't know anything. How could I? What's Becky's murder got to do with me?'

'You were a friend of hers, weren't you?'

'Not really. I mean, not recently. I haven't seen her for a long time.'

'It must have been a shock, though, her being killed like that?'

Kirsten's eyes darted between the two of them. She raised a hand to her mouth and gnawed on a fingernail. 'Well, yeah, I suppose.'

'Were you aware that five hundred and twenty pounds was found at her flat?'

'Was it?'

'That's a lot of money, don't you think, for someone like Becky to have. Do you have any idea where it might have come from?'

There was a distinct hesitation before Kirsten shook her head again. 'Why should I? Like I said, I haven't seen her in years.'

'So it didn't come from you?'

'No,' Kirsten said too quickly. 'It's got nothing to do with me. Nothing. Why would I give her money?'

'You gave money to Paige Fielding. Five thousand pounds, in fact. Quite a considerable sum.'

Kirsten squirmed in her seat and glanced away. 'She

483

called me up, said she needed it.' She looked back at Valerie, but only for a second, before her gaze dropped down to the table. 'It's only a loan. She'll pay me back.'

'That'll take a while.'

'I suppose.'

'And she didn't tell you what it was for?'

Kirsten chewed on her lip while she tried to come up with an answer. 'Bills and stuff,' she said eventually.

'Bills and stuff?'

'Yeah, I think that was it. I'm not sure. I don't remember exactly.'

Valerie could see the lie imprinted on her face. Paige and Micky Higgs might have got their story straight, but they hadn't bothered, or maybe hadn't had the time, to share the details with Kirsten. 'You don't remember why you lent someone five thousand pounds?'

Kirsten Cope didn't answer.

'So what's with the jiffy bag full of notes?' Valerie persisted. 'It seems a funny way to go about things. Why didn't you just give her a cheque?'

Kirsten, who wasn't anything like as glib as Paige, was still struggling to come up with answers. 'Er . . .'

Swann, sliding into his good cop routine, rode smartly to her rescue. 'Maybe she needed it in a hurry, huh? Couldn't wait for a cheque to clear. Was that it?'

'Yeah,' Kirsten said, nodding. She gazed gratefully at Swann, batting her lashes in a way that was probably supposed to turn his legs to jelly. 'That's it. That's why.'

'Well,' he said, glancing at Valerie. 'That's cleared that up.'

Kirsten looked relieved. 'So is that it? Are we done now?'

'Not quite,' Valerie said. 'There is something else I'd like to talk to you about.' She left a deliberate pause, and then said, 'Minnie Bright?'

Kirsten's whole body stiffened, her eyes growing large at this unexpected turn of events. 'Minnie? What? I—I don't understand,' she stammered.

'Oh, I think you do,' Valerie said. 'We're not stupid. There's no point in lying any more. It's time to tell the truth.' She was winging it, following her instincts and watching Kirsten's responses carefully. One wrong word and she could blow it completely. 'Paige has given us her version, so why you tell us yours?'

'Paige? What? I don't . . . I haven't . . .'

Valerie smiled coldly back at her. It was the oldest trick in the book, playing one suspect off against another. Paige would have laughed in her face – she wasn't so naïve – but Kirsten had little experience in dealing with the law. She might have grown up on the Mansfield Estate, but the last time she'd been in any trouble was when she was ten years old. 'She's told us why you really gave her the money. And why you gave money to Becky too.'

'She's lying!' Kirsten spat out, a red flush spreading across her cheeks. 'You can't believe anything she says!'

Valerie felt that familiar tingling sensation, the feeling she always got when she was on the brink of a breakthrough. She only had to look at Kirsten to see how close to the edge she was. One more push was all it would take. 'I'm afraid she's told us everything. It's over, Kirsten. There's no use denying it. The secret's out.'

For a moment Kirsten looked like she might be prepared to put up a fight. Her eyes blazed and her hands clenched into fists on the table. She glared back at Valerie, baring her teeth. Then her face suddenly crumpled, and tears slipped from her eyes and slid down her cheeks. 'It was him,' she wailed, giving in to her fear. 'He made me do it! It wasn't my fault.'

Valerie and Swann exchanged a quick glance.

'Hey, it's okay,' Swann said, leaning across to pat Kirsten paternally on the arm. 'It's over now. It's out in the open. We know what he did. You don't need to worry any more.'

But Kirsten could barely speak for weeping. She had her head in her hands and was racked with sobs. 'It . . . it wasn't my fault,' she repeated. 'He said he'd take care of me. He . . . he said that if I did as I was told, you wouldn't send me to jail.'

It took ten minutes and two glasses of water before she finally started to calm down. Valerie asked if she'd like a solicitor now, but she refused. 'No, no, I don't want anyone else here.'

When Kirsten had recovered some of her composure, Swann said, 'Let's start at the beginning, shall we? Why don't you tell us in your own words what actually happened.'

Kirsten wiped her face with the palms of her hands. 'I was sixteen,' she said, her voice small and shaky. 'That's when he first came to see me. He said he'd heard that the police were looking into the Minnie Bright case again, that her mum wanted us punished for making Minnie go into the house.' She gave another light sob and gazed at Swann

486

pleadingly. 'It was only a game. We didn't mean ... we didn't know that she ...'

'Of course you didn't,' Swann said in a kindly tone. He passed another tissue across the table.

Kirsten dabbed at her eyes before she continued. 'I was scared, you see. He said we were all old enough now to go to prison, that it could be ... could be years before we got out again. He said he didn't think it was fair. He said he wanted to help me.'

'And how was he planning on doing that?' Valerie asked.

A red flush stained Kirsten's cheeks again. 'He said he knew people, high-up people like judges and lawyers, MPs and that ... and that if I was nice to them, if I ... well, they'd make sure the case stayed closed. He said it was the only thing to do. And he said I mustn't tell the others, mustn't tell *anyone* else. It had to be our secret.'

Valerie winced inwardly. How many times had she heard stories similar to this one – young girls exploited through fear or need, used and abused by predatory men. For the first time that afternoon, she felt sympathy for Kirsten Cope. 'Go on.'

'He got me a flat and everything. He was nice at first, really kind. So long as I did what I was told, it was all okay.'

'And when you didn't?'

Kirsten gave a shudder, the response more descriptive perhaps than any words could have been.

'How long did this go on for?' Valerie asked softly.

'A couple of years. Until I was eighteen.'

When she was no longer young enough or fresh enough, Valerie thought, to satisfy the perverted needs of the men

487

who were abusing her. 'And then? Did he leave you alone, or . . .'

Kirsten gave a quick shake of her head. 'He said I was his, that I'd always be his. He said he'd saved me from jail and so I owed him. I was starting to get some work then, just small parts, but he reckoned I could make it big. He found me an agent and everything. He said, if I played it smart, I could be the next Jordan.'

Valerie was aware of Swann's gaze flicking instinctively down to Kirsten's chest. The D-cup breasts, swollen with silicone, jutted beneath her skimpy T-shirt. 'And he took a share of your earnings, I presume?'

Kirsten shrugged. 'But things got better then. I mean, he couldn't . . . he couldn't hurt me any more. Not in that way. He couldn't leave any bruises, see? Not if I was filming or having photos done. It was all going good,' she said bitterly, 'until that reporter woman turned up.'

Valerie baulked at the girl's definition of 'going good' but knew that it was unfair to make judgements. Kirsten Cope had been controlled and manipulated from an early age. For her, the new situation must have been a hundred times better than the old one. 'Jessica Vaughan,' she said.

'That's her. She came sniffing round but I wouldn't talk to her. He said I mustn't. She'd found out, you see, about what I'd done, about how we'd escaped going to jail, and that was what she was really going to write about.' Kirsten's voice rose an octave, becoming thin and whiny. 'She was going to get the story splashed all over the Sundays. It was going to come out about . . . about . . .' Kirsten buried her face in the tissue, snivelling loudly.

Valerie had no time for Jessica Vaughan – she could well believe that the woman had been looking for a scandalous angle – but she was also aware that there had never been any suggestion of the girls being prosecuted. Kirsten had been played, just like they were playing her now. 'Do you have any idea how she found out?'

Kirsten blew her nose and nodded. 'He said it was Hannah Bright stirring up trouble again. That the two of them were in it together. He said we had to stop the other girls from talking or all of us would end up in the dock. She'd have twisted our words, see, tried to make out that we'd *forced* Minnie to go into the house. And then she'd have written about all the other stuff too, about the judges and—'

'Okay,' Valerie said, interrupting before Kirsten had the chance to start weeping again. 'So you reckoned that if you could stop the other girls from talking to Vaughan, this whole problem would just go away.'

Kirsten balled up the tissue, put it on the table and pushed it away from her. 'I told them it would ruin my career if the article was written, that no one would want to employ someone who'd been connected to the murder of a child. No one knows, see, 'cause I changed my name and everything. I gave them a thousand each, but then when Becky was killed, Paige rang me up. She guessed there was more to it, that there was other stuff I didn't want coming out.'

'And she wanted more to keep her mouth shut,' Swann said.

Kirsten nodded again. 'Five grand.'

'But you didn't try to pay off Sam Kendall,' Valerie said. 'Why not?'

'He said he'd deal with her.'

Valerie was still waiting for Kirsten to reveal his name. She hadn't used it, not once. Could it be Higgs? Or Livesey? And wasn't there a boyfriend? Some footballer, she thought, although he didn't seem a likely candidate. Whoever was pulling Kirsten's strings was dark and sadistic and willing to kill. When Kirsten had first embarked on her revelations, Valerie had felt a slightly shameful feeling of relief – at least this had nothing to do with the safety of Donald Peck's conviction – but now a few doubts were starting to surface.

Swann must have been thinking along the same lines, because he suddenly said, 'Tell me about the call that Lynda Choi made to you on the night she died.'

Kirsten screwed up her face. 'She was drunk, not making any sense. She was rambling on about a light she'd seen. A light that had gone on in the house on the day that Minnie was . . . you know.'

'Rambling on?'

'Saying that it couldn't have been the Beast and it couldn't have been Minnie and so there must have been someone else in there. But there wasn't. Everyone knows that sick bastard killed her. She kept going on and on like I was thick or something and just didn't get it.'

'Why was she so sure that it couldn't have been Minnie?' Valerie asked.

'I don't know.'

'She didn't explain? That seems a bit odd seeing as it was

490

the reason she called you in the first place.'

'I told you,' Kirsten said. 'She was pissed, wasn't she? Completely trolleyed. I couldn't understand half of what she was saying.' Her forehead creased up as she tried to recollect exactly what Lynda had told her. 'Pictures. Something to do with a picture she'd found in an old newspaper. And then she started saying about how she was going to go to the cops to tell them all about it.'

'And you didn't want that,' Swann said. 'Because you were scared she'd draw attention to the case again.'

'I suppose,' Kirsten admitted. 'Yeah, I tried to calm her down and talk her out of it. That was why the call was so long. I said she'd be in trouble for lying all those years ago, that she was better off keeping her mouth shut. I mean, it wasn't going to make any difference now, was it? Not after all this time.'

'And then Lynda conveniently drowned.'

Kirsten scowled at her. 'That wasn't anyone's fault. It was an accident. I didn't want anything bad to happen to her. But she was drunk, wasn't she? She must have slipped and fallen in the water.'

Valerie gave her a thin smile. 'But then Lynda's brother went though her phone records and started asking difficult questions. If you hadn't lied, he wouldn't have got so suspicious.'

'He was just trying to cause trouble for me,' Kirsten said, her tone growing peevish again.

Valerie wondered at the girl's ability to make everything revolve around herself. A consequence of the years of abuse, or part of her natural character? It was impossible to tell. She watched Kirsten closely as she made her next statement. 'And so you got Micky Higgs to sort it out.'

There was no reaction to the name other than genuine puzzlement. 'What?'

Valerie had been hoping for an indication that Higgs might be their man, but Kirsten's response told her otherwise. 'You didn't?'

'I barely know him,' Kirsten said. 'I never met him before today.'

'So why did he threaten David Choi?'

'Maybe Paige told him to.'

'And why would she do that?'

'I dunno. You'd have to ask her.' Kirsten wriggled in her seat. 'Well, I may have said something. You know, like Choi was looking to blame me for what happened to Lynda. I don't remember exactly.'

'Try harder,' Valerie said. For an actress, Kirsten was a pretty bad liar.

'Okay,' she admitted grudgingly. 'I told her he was threatening to go to the police. And I'd already lied about talking to Lynda that night. All they had to do was check the phone records and . . . Well, I didn't need the hassle, did I?'

'And Paige offered to help you out?'

Kirsten gave a barely discernible nod of her head.

'For a small fee, I'm presuming.'

'Five hundred pounds.'

Swann let out a sigh 'What a mess, eh?'

Anger flashed across Kirsten's face. 'If it hadn't been for Hannah Bright, none of this would have happened. Why couldn't she leave it? It wasn't our fault. We didn't want Minnie to get hurt. We didn't—'

'Shall I tell you something about Hannah Bright, Kirsten?'

Valerie glanced at Swann, knowing what was coming next. A piece of information that was about to shatter Kirsten Cope.

'What?'

'She's dead, love. Hannah took an overdose more than twelve years ago. She was never trying to have you prosecuted. He's been lying to you. He's been lying to you from the first day you met.'

'No,' Kirsten said, shaking her head furiously. Her eyes darted wildly around the room.

'It's true,' said Swann, sliding a sheet of paper across the table. It was the same document he'd shown Valerie at the door.

Kirsten stared down at the copy of the death certificate. Then, leaning forward she wrapped her arms around her body and started to rock. 'He's going to kill me,' she whispered, as if the full ramifications of what she'd done were only just beginning to sink in. Her blue eyes grew wide as saucers. 'When he finds out what I've told you—'

'He won't be killing anyone,' Swann said firmly. 'He'll be banged up, Kirsten. He'll be banged up for a bloody long time.'

Kirsten stopped rocking and looked across the table at him.

'I promise,' he said. 'But first you have to state his name for our records, love. You have to say it out loud.'

There was a pause, a very long pause, but finally she did. Valerie felt the shock run through her like an earthquake tremor. Her mouth fell open. And then, after a moment, she heard a soft, distinctive hiss escape from Swann's lips.

58

Jess's initial surge of excitement at positively identifying the mugshot of Paul Rafferty had quickly subsided. Even if he was still in London, it would be like searching for a needle in a haystack. 'Where do we start looking?' she'd asked Mac.

'We don't,' he'd said. 'We get other people to do it for us.'

For the next hour, Mac, Lorna and Warren were on the phone to every contact they had.

The old principle of never grassing up a fellow villain didn't hold for long when money was involved, and with three grand up for grabs, the phones were soon ringing off the hook. After several false leads, the news they were hoping for was finally delivered at ten past two. A high-class escort called Jennifer Jay had spotted Rafferty in a hotel bar in Chelsea. After giving her strict instructions to keep him in her sights, Mac grabbed his car keys and turned to go.

'I'll deal with this,' he said.

Jess put a hand on his arm and frowned. 'You're going on your own? What if he does a runner?' She was worried that if Rafferty took off and went to ground, they might never find him again.

'He won't,' Mac said. 'Not when I've explained what his

options are. As he's still in London, I'm betting he doesn't have a clue about the shooting. When Stagg hired him to play the part of Martin Locke, I doubt he mentioned anything about the fact that the guy was going to be brown bread by the end of the week.'

'Probably slipped his mind,' Warren said.

Mac gave a grunt. 'I'm sure it did. And our Mr Raffles is going to have loose bowels when he finds out what he's really got himself involved in. He's a con man, not a hardened criminal. Faced with a choice between being done for impersonating Locke and being an accessory to his murder, I sure as hell know which one I'd choose. I don't think I'll have too much difficulty persuading him to hand himself in.'

Jess let go of his arm. 'So what are you standing around here for? Get over to Chelsea and start persuading.'

Mac raised his eyes to the heavens and headed for the door.

After he'd gone, Jess turned to look at Lorna and Warren. 'Do you think he'll manage it?'

'Sure he will,' Warren said. 'Harry's his business partner. He doesn't want to waste time visiting him in jail when he could be bunking off to play a sneaky round of golf.'

'I'll pretend I didn't hear that,' Lorna said as she returned to the reception area.

Jess paced over to the window and back again. It could be hours before they heard anything. What if Rafferty didn't play ball? What if he was too scared of Ray Stagg to give evidence against him? She went back to the window and gazed down on the street. People were going about their business like there was nothing wrong: shopping, waiting for buses, nipping into the pub for a quick one. Meanwhile, Harry was staring down the barrel of a gun, wondering if he was going to spend the next fifteen years behind bars. She started pacing again.

'Can you stop doing that,' Warren said. 'You're making me nervous.'

'Sorry,' she said, pulling out a chair and sitting down beside him.

Warren handed her a sheet of paper. 'Here, take a look at this.'

'What is it?'

'A copy of Aimee Locke's birth certificate.'

Jess quickly scanned through the details. Born in Kellston twenty-nine years ago on 4 October. Mother: Karen Sage (née Lester). Father: David Sage. She glanced up at Warren. 'What am I looking for exactly?'

'It's the father who's interesting.'

'Father's occupation: bookmaker,' she read out. 'So he was a bookie. What's interesting about that?'

'Because it's not the truth. Far from it in fact. Kieran Swann ran a PNC check for us earlier. It seems our Mr Sage has quite a colourful past. He used to work for Lennie Blackwood.'

Jess shook her head. 'Never heard of him.'

'Before your time, hun. Before mine, come to that. Lennie was a south London gangster with a short fuse. Nasty piece of work by all accounts. Got his head blown off over twenty years ago.'

'So Sage was a villain too.'

'More than that. He was Lennie's disposal man.'

Jess looked at him. 'Does that mean what I think it means?'

'Yeah, Sage was Lennie's personal hit man, and very good at it he was too. He's still wanted on four counts of murder, and they're just the ones the cops know about. He disappeared back in the mid-eighties and hasn't been heard of since. Rumour had it he was swimming with the fishes, but maybe the rumours were wrong.'

Jess thought back to her conversation with James Harley-Cunningham. 'Which could explain the row between Aimee Locke and Stagg. Maybe he wasn't too keen on the idea of using Sage.'

'Or maybe he wasn't that keen on bumping off her husband at all. I mean, Ray Stagg's a villain, we all know that, but he's a damned careful one. You get involved in something like this and the law's bound to come sniffing round.'

'Yeah, well I'm sure the lovely Aimee can be very persuasive.' She dropped the certificate back on the desk. 'But we can't prove anything, can we? It's just conjecture.'

Warren shifted in his seat, as incapable as Jess of staying still. Frustration was biting at them both. 'Except who better to get rid of an unwanted spouse than a true professional. Sage fits the bill perfectly. No mistakes, no botch-ups, satisfaction guaranteed. And with the added bonus of him being the one man who's never going to grass her up.'

'God, that's a weird thought.' Jess felt a thin shiver travel down her spine. 'Can you imagine it? Getting your dad to murder your husband.'

'Maybe it was payback time.'

'What do you mean?'

'Well, if he did just disappear all those years ago, maybe she figures he owes her.'

'One hell of a bill,' she murmured.

Warren picked up a pen and tapped it against the desk. 'Anyway, conjecture or not, it's something else to throw at the cops. Anything that might cast doubt on Harry's guilt has to be useful.'

Jess glanced at her watch, hoping that the traffic wasn't too bad and that Mac would make it to Chelsea before Raffles melted into the crowd. 'If this Rafferty does come clean about being paid by Stagg, do you think they'll let Harry go?'

'Hopefully,' Warren said. 'But you can never tell with that bloody lot.'

'You don't sound too enamoured of the boys in blue.'

Warren pulled a face. 'Really, what gave it away?'

'But you work with two ex-cops.'

'The clue's in the *ex*,' he said. Then he grinned at her and heaved out a sigh. 'Oh, don't mind me. I'm just sounding off.'

Lorna put her head round the door. 'That's not all you'll be doing if you don't get a shift on. You're due at the Turner surveillance in less than fifteen minutes.'

'Christ,' he said, shooting up out of the chair. 'Is that the time?'

'And don't worry,' Lorna said. 'I'll give you a call as soon as we get any news.'

Warren laid a hand on Jess's shoulder as he passed. 'Stay

cool, babe,' he said. 'In a few hours' time this whole nightmare could be over.'

Or just beginning, she thought. If Rafferty didn't come good, Harry would be charged with murder.

59

Harry sat in the holding cell with his head buried in his hands. How had it come to this? No matter which way he turned, no matter how hard he struggled, he could see no escape from the intricate web of guilt into which he'd been drawn. And what made it worse was the knowledge that he'd been the master of his own downfall. He had stepped willingly into the trap laid by Aimee Locke, and now he was going to pay the ultimate price. *Will you walk into my parlour? said the Spider to the Fly.* And like an idiot he had done exactly that.

'Bloody fool!' he muttered.

Why had he gone to that goddamn house? It was a decision that would haunt him for the rest of his life. His future thrown away in a moment of recklessness. Anger merged with his shame and humiliation. He'd been photographed, fingerprinted and had a DNA sample taken. His name was chalked on the board outside the cell. He was no longer Harry Lind, ex-cop, private detective. He was defined now only by his alleged crime: *Murder.*

Racking his brains, he tried to think of anything, anyone who could help him. He replayed the events of the past week, rolling through the visit to Adriano's, to the casino, to the conversation on the Green. A week, that was all it had been, since the man who called himself Martin Locke had walked into the office. Seven days before his life had begun to disintegrate.

It was hours now since his last interview. He was expecting the door to be unlocked at any moment, for the charges to be laid against him. His solicitor, Richard Morris, was trying to remain optimistic, but Harry could see defeat in his eyes. It was over. The case would go to trial and he would stand in the dock and . . .

Harry thought of his father and how he would feel. His only son convicted of murder. He let out a low groan. He should have made that phone call after he moved into the flat. He should have gone to visit him. Now the only visiting would be done by Henry Lind in the grim surroundings of a prison. And it was not only his father he had let down. There was Mac to consider too, the one person who had offered him a second chance after his police career had been blown to hell. Not to mention Valerie. What would she be thinking? Did she believe in his innocence, or was there a tiny seed of doubt nestled in the back of her mind?

He shook his head. No, there was no point in torturing himself this way. Whatever the future held, he had to find a way of coping. But the words *life imprisonment* cut like a scythe across his good intentions. The breath caught in his throat. He thought of Donald Peck, continuing to protest his innocence until desperation drove him to place a noose around his own neck. He wondered how strong he himself would be when faced with the ultimate challenge.

His mind drifted back to that day fourteen years ago, to the shabby terrace in Morton Grove, to the rickety creaking staircase that led up to the bedrooms. One foot in front of the other until he reached the landing. Grey light coming in through a small window. The delicate pattering sound of rain against glass. A brief pause before his hand reached out to turn the handle, to push open the door ... and then the sudden wafting stench of death.

It was then, suddenly, that Harry remembered what he'd done next. The room had been dim, the curtains pulled partly across. He had looked for a light switch but there hadn't been one, only an old pull cord that had frayed and broken and been tied up high.

'Jesus,' he murmured, a shiver running through him.

And instantly he knew what Lynda Choi had been so distressed about. She must have found a photo of the bedroom in an old newspaper. She must have realised what it meant. The cord was way out of reach of Minnie Bright's tiny hands. And if Minnie hadn't turned on the light, then ...

Harry jumped up, walked across the cell and hammered on the door. 'Hey!' he called out. 'I need to see someone. I need to see someone now!'

60

It was getting on for five before the news came through that Mac was on his way to Cowan Road with Paul Rafferty. Jess was relieved, but she knew that Harry wasn't off the hook yet. The law would need to be convinced that Rafferty's story was true before even considering the release of a major suspect. Too restless to wait any longer in the office, she decided to continue her pacing upstairs.

Out on the landing, she saw that the cameras had finally been installed. They must have been there when she'd come back with Mac, but she'd been too preoccupied to notice them. They were fixed high up on the wall, their tiny red lights blinking. It was an odd feeling to know that she was under scrutiny, that her every expression, every movement was being recorded.

She climbed up the stairs and went into the flat. Once inside, she didn't know what to do with herself. How was she going to pass the next few hours without going completely crazy? She put the kettle on, intending to make a cup of coffee, but then changed her mind and opened a bottle of red wine instead. Caffeine was only going to add to her jitters. Alcohol probably wasn't the answer either, but at least it might calm her nerves.

Taking the bottle and a glass through to the living room, she looked around. What now? She needed a project to keep her occupied. The Minnie Bright file was on the coffee table, but she instantly dismissed the idea of reading through it again. She was too distracted to be able to concentrate. No, what she needed was something more physical, some way of exhausting all her nervous energy.

It was then that her eyes alighted on the cans of paint stacked up in the corner. Harry had started the decorating but hadn't got round to completing it. On a couple of walls the old colour was still clearly visible beneath the new layer of white. Now there was a project! It would also be a way of repaying him for everything he'd done for her. She poured herself a glass of wine, took a couple of swigs and set to work.

First she moved the furniture to the centre of the room and covered it with the dust sheets. Then she prised open the lid of one of the cans, poured a couple of inches of paint into the tray and slid in the roller. Starting with the left-hand wall, she began working fast and furiously, the sheer physical effort draining her mind of everything but the task in hand. She realised too late that she should have changed her clothes, but as her jeans and shirt were already spattered with paint, there wasn't much point in doing it now. With luck, it would all come out in the wash.

An hour later, her arm aching, Jess stood back to view her progress. Yes, it was already looking much better. When Harry got back – not *if*, she insisted to herself, but *when* –

the newly decorated living room would be ready and waiting. She was about to resume work when there was a light knock on the door.

'Hi, it's only me,' Lorna called out.

Jess rushed over and opened the door. 'Is there any news?'

Lorna shook her head. 'I'm sorry, luv, nothing yet. Mac's still down at Cowan Road.'

'Okay,' Jess said, swallowing down her disappointment.

'I just wanted to let you know that I'm off home now, but I'll give you a ring as soon as I hear anything.' Just as she was about to go, Lorna stopped and stretched out her hand. It contained an A4 brown envelope. 'Oh, I almost forgot. This was dropped off for you about ten minutes ago.'

Jess took the envelope and looked down at her name scribbled on the front. She didn't recognise the handwriting.

'I told her I could ring up and get you to come down, but she said it didn't matter.'

'She?'

'A pretty girl, long red hair. She said not to bother, that she was in a hurry.'

'Okay, thanks,' Jess said. It must have been Clare Towney. She couldn't think of anyone else who fitted the description.

'I'll see you tomorrow then,' Lorna said. 'Take care.'

'Bye, Lorna.'

Puzzled, Jess walked back across the room. Clare had already admitted her part in the threats that had been made against Sam Kendall, so what was so urgent about whatever was in the envelope that it had to be delivered by hand? Well, there was only one way to find out. She dragged the dust sheets off the sofa, dropped the envelope on to a cushion and went through to the kitchen to wash the paint off her hands.

When she came back, she wandered over to the window and looked up and down the street. There was no sign of Clare. She sat down on the sofa and ripped the envelope open. It contained about fifteen sheets of paper, neatly typed and stapled together. She sat back and started to read.

On the surface there was nothing different about that dull August day in 1998, and yet it was to change all our lives for ever. Shall I tell you about it? There's a part of me that wants to, that longs to, but another part that's simply too afraid. I've kept it hidden for so long, and if I open the box all kinds of demons might fly out. I'm not sure if I can cope with that. There's something else I'm worried about too, another fear that can't be pushed aside: I'm terrified of being judged. Even as I write these words I'm aware of how cowardly they sound. But that's who I am. I'm a coward and a liar, and because of me a ten-year-old girl died.

Jess paused for a moment, the hairs on the back of her neck standing on end. Oh God, she had got it so wrong! It hadn't just been a few threats that lay on Clare Towney's conscience. What she held in her hands was a confession, an admission that Clare had been responsible for Minnie

Bright's death. She carried on reading until she got to the end of the first section.

That was the last time any of them saw Minnie Bright. It was forty-eight hours before her crack-addicted mother reported her missing, and a few hours more before the police entered the house and found her small twisted body hidden under a bed.

She stopped again and took another large gulp of wine. Her hands were shaking as she put the glass down on the coffee table. How did Clare know all this stuff, what the girls had said, what they'd done that day? Part of it could have come from the trial transcripts and the newspaper reports, but she had the feeling that Clare must have spoken to one of the girls. Or maybe someone else had.

That someone else was soon revealed as she hurried through the next few pages. They detailed exactly what had happened – and the events that had led up to it. By the time Jess had finished, her head was reeling. She leaned forward, burying her face in her hands. The story was tragic and pathetic and terrible.

She laid the confession down, unsure about what to do next. Why had Clare chosen to give it to her? Why not hand it straight to the police? If Harry had been around, she could have talked to him, asked for his advice, but he was facing his own dreadful problems. Well, the only other thing she could do was to try and contact Clare. Except she didn't have a number for her. Damn it! And then she was suddenly assailed by a colder, more disturbing thought.

What state of mind must that girl be in now? She could be about to do something stupid.

Jess jumped to her feet, grabbed her jacket and car keys and headed for the door. She was almost there when she remembered the wine she'd had. She looked back over her shoulder at the half-empty bottle. Hell, was she over the limit? She didn't feel drunk, but then Clare's confession was enough to shock anyone into a feeling of sobriety. Perhaps she'd better get a cab instead. She was still trying to decide when the buzzer went. She snatched up the receiver.

'Hello?'

'Is that Jess? It's DS Kieran Swann.'

'Come in,' she said, pressing the button. 'I'm on the second floor.' While she waited for him to climb the stairs, she wondered what he wanted. It must be news about Harry. It had to be. She knew that Swann had been helping out behind the scenes, making checks for Mac and feeding him information.

She stood by the open door, shifting impatiently from one foot to the other. She needed to try to find Clare, but she was desperate to know Harry's fate too. As he rounded the corner of the stairway, Swann smiled at her. She smiled back, recognising his face. She must have seen him when she'd been down at Cowan Road.

'Hi,' she said. 'Come inside.'

'Thanks,' Swann said. 'Mac said I'd find you here. This won't take long. It's about Harry Lind. I just need to go through a few things with you.'

Jess's shoulders slumped in disappointment as she closed the door. 'So they're not letting him go?'

'It's early days yet.'

'But what about Rafferty? I thought . . .'

'The legal wheels turn slowly, I'm afraid. But every bit of evidence helps.'

'Of course.' She gestured towards the sofa. 'Take a seat. I'm sorry about the mess. Would you like a tea or a coffee?'

'Thanks, a coffee would be good. Black, no sugar, please.'

Jess went through to the kitchen and switched the kettle on. While she spooned some instant coffee into a couple of mugs, she tried to think of anything she could tell him that might help the cause. Nothing came to mind. Her heart sank as she realised that he wouldn't even be here unless things were looking bleak for Harry.

She was halfway across the living room, a mug in each hand, when she suddenly stopped dead. Damn it! She had left Clare's confession lying on the coffee table and Swann had picked it up. He was hunched forward, carefully reading through the pages.

'What are you doing?' she snapped, even though she knew it was too late.

He stared up at her, his smile not quite as friendly as before. 'Is this what I think it is?'

Jess put the two mugs down and sighed. 'I was going to bring it along to Cowan Road, I swear I was. I only got it half an hour ago. I wasn't trying to hide anything. I just . . . I just wanted to talk to Clare first. I'm worried about her, about what she might do.'

Swann glanced down at the confession, then looked up at her again and shook his head. His eyes had grown cold. 'And have you?'

'What?'

'Have you talked to Clare Towney?'

'No,' she said. 'I was on my way out to try and find her when you arrived.'

'Good,' he said.

Jess frowned. 'I don't know what's good about it. She must be in a right state.'

'Good for me, I meant,' he said softly.

Jess didn't understand. At least not for a few seconds. It took that long for her brain to slot the pieces together. 'Jesus,' she murmured, her blood running cold as she realised who she was really speaking to. 'You're not Swann, are you?' She glanced down towards the confession, to where Clare had named her partner in crime. 'You're Wetherby. You're Simon Wetherby.'

He brought his palms together in a slow handclap. 'Oh, well done, Jessica. It took a while, but you got there in the end.'

Jess felt her throat go dry. An icy stream of fear ran down her spine. She realised where she'd seen him now: not at the police station, but outside the Fox with Valerie Middleton. And now he was here, the man who'd strangled Becky Hibbert, the man who'd tried to kill her too. She looked towards the door, but she was way too slow. Wetherby was already on his feet, blocking her path.

'I don't think so,' he said.

As he loomed over her, Jess had an instinctive desire to scream, but she clenched her jaw. She knew it would be pointless. The windows were closed and the office downstairs was all locked up for the night. Nobody would hear her cries, and Wetherby would be tempted to silence her for ever. No, her only chance was to play for time. 'So it was you,' she said, attempting to keep her voice steady.

'Sit down,' he ordered.

She did as she was told, dropping into an armchair still covered by a dust sheet. 'It's too late, you know. I've already sent a text to Mac, telling him about the confession.'

Wetherby sat down on the sofa and grinned back at her. 'You disappoint me, Jessica. If you're going to lie, then at least make it sound convincing.'

She gave a shrug, her shoulders so tight that the movement was barely perceptible.

'Believe what you like.'

'You haven't told anyone. And you won't.'

Jess glanced towards the sheets of paper lying on the coffee table. 'It's a sordid little story.'

'But sadly not one that you'll be revealing to the world.'

'Perhaps not,' she said, 'but what about Clare? She could be down at Cowan Road even as we speak.' If she'd been hoping to rattle him, she was sorely disappointed. The slight shift of his brows suggested only mockery.

'The only person she's told is you.'

'How do you know that?'

He sat back, his expression calm and collected. 'Because she called me. She told me what she'd done. How else do you think I knew about the confession? That's the thing about Clare: she's very loyal. Even after all these years, she still can't let go of the feelings she once had. I guess she wanted to give me the chance to get away, to make a run for it.'

'But you decided to come here instead.'

'Naturally,' he said. 'I didn't think you'd do anything straight away. People like you don't make rash decisions. You like to weigh up all the options first.'

'People like me?'

'Hacks,' he said with contempt. 'Grubby little journalists who spend their lives poking into things that are none of their business.'

Jess's brain, edging on hysteria, was grasping for clarity. If he was here, if he'd come to collect the evidence against him, then that could only mean that Clare was no longer able to repeat it. Had he killed her? Would he have had the time? It was only half an hour or so since Lorna had delivered the envelope.

'You're looking worried,' he said.

He was sitting there watching her closely. She knew what he was planning, what he intended to do. Her stomach lurched with fear. Panic seeped into her veins. He couldn't allow her to live – not after what she'd read – but he didn't seem in any hurry to finish the job. 'So, what now?' she asked.

'I was thinking we might wait,' he said. 'Just until it gets dark.'

Jess understood what he meant. He wasn't going to kill her here. He was going to take her somewhere else, perhaps the same place he'd taken Dan Livesey. Maybe somewhere out in the sticks, like Epping Forest. She could imagine walking through the trees with a gun aimed at her back. If she just disappeared, it would be a while before it turned into a murder inquiry. Time he could use to cover his tracks.

She glanced towards the windows. The day was fading, the sky turning a smoky shade of grey. How long before sunset? She looked at her watch. Less than an hour before darkness fell. Less than sixty minutes before they set off on the final journey. Nausea rose up from her stomach, carrying a fear like she had never known before. There was still time to save herself, but only if she could keep him talking.

'You were lucky,' she said. 'Keeping the truth hidden all these years.'

'Lucky?' His pretty mouth crawled into a cynical smile. 'None of it's been down to luck, babe.'

'Clever, then,' she said, pandering to his vanity.

Wetherby seemed happier with this assessment. He glanced down towards the confession and then back up at Jess. His eyes glittered with a curious mix of triumph and scorn. 'You've read it,' he said. 'It was an accident. We didn't mean to kill her.'

'No,' she said. 'But you were happy for someone else to take the blame.'

'Donald Peck was a pervert. He deserved to rot in jail.'

'Even for a crime he hadn't committed?'

Wetherby barked out a laugh. 'It was only a matter of time. He made Clare's life a misery. Can you imagine what it's like to be the niece of the local flasher? Being an outcast in your own community because your uncle isn't capable of keeping his dick in his pants? We did society a favour by having him banged up.'

Jess stared at him, her guts turning over. 'Really?' she said. 'Or was it just to hide the fact that you were sleeping with a fourteen-year-old?' Everything in the confession was

514

revolving in her mind: how Clare had met Wetherby in Connolly's all those years ago, how they'd started an affair, an affair that could only be conducted behind closed doors – and those closed doors had been in Donald Peck's house. 'She stole the spare key off her mother, didn't she? So the two of you could meet in private when Donald went off on his regular visits to see Ralph Masterson. Except it all went wrong when the girls decided it would be a laugh to make Minnie Bright break into the house.'

Wetherby sat back, his expression amused, his lips sliding into a leering smile. 'We were in bed when she came in. We didn't even hear her at first. It was only when she came upstairs that we realised someone else was in the house.'

'It must have been a shock.'

He tilted his head back, gazing at the ceiling. 'Yes, it was unfortunate.' Slowly, he lowered his head and focused his gaze back on Jess. 'But you know it wasn't deliberate. We never meant to hurt her. We heard a noise, opened the bedroom door and there she was, staring straight at us. The stupid kid started screaming. Clare just wanted to shut her up. She grabbed her, but Minnie struggled and . . .'

'And?'

'She fell down the stairs. She was dead by the time she hit the bottom. There was nothing we could do about it.'

Jess closed her eyes. Nothing except admit to the truth. She blinked her eyes open again and stared at Wetherby. 'So you decided to lay the blame on someone else, to hide her under the bed in the spare room, to take some hairs from Donald Peck's hairbrush and place them on her body, to wipe all the prints from the doors and windows, to make it

515

look like no one else could have been responsible.'

Wetherby shifted forward, placing his hands on his thighs. 'What choice did we have? And there wouldn't have been a problem if you'd just left it alone. But you couldn't, could you, Jessica? You had to keep on digging.'

While he was talking, Jess was trying to figure out whether she could make it to the door. But even if she did, even if she managed to get it open and made a dash for it, he would probably catch up with her on the stairs. And she could imagine what would happen next. One hard push and she would roll down those steps as fatefully as Minnie Bright had rolled. She would be another 'accident'.

'You see, it was your fault that Becky Hibbert had to die,' he continued. 'She had a loose mouth and it was only a matter of time before she started talking about the light.'

Jess gave a nod. 'The light Lynda saw when she went back that day.'

'It was Clare who turned it on when we were hiding the body. It had got dark, you see. It was raining. She pulled on the cord as we went into the room. It wouldn't have mattered if Lynda Choi hadn't seen, but ...'

'No,' Jess said, although she didn't really understand. She knew that Donald Peck couldn't have turned it on – he was still on his way back from Masterson's – but she didn't see why Minnie couldn't have done it.

'Becky didn't understand the relevance,' he said. 'But it was only a matter of time before you did.'

Jess was still trying to work out how to respond when her mobile started ringing. The sound sliced through the tension like a knife. Wetherby jumped up, walked across

516

the room and grabbed it off the table by the window. He held it up for a second. 'Ah,' he said, 'Mr Mackenzie. He must have some news for you.' He jabbed at a button, disconnecting the call. 'It's a shame you'll never get to hear it.'

That was when Jess tipped over into panic. Launching herself out of the chair, she made a dash for the door. But Wetherby was too fast for her. He had his arms around her body before she'd even covered a few feet.

'You're going nowhere, bitch,' he hissed in her ear.

Jess twisted her right elbow, digging it hard into his ribs. He pulled in a breath. She kicked out wildly, aiming at his shins, his ankles, his feet, and eventually managed to wriggle loose. But she only got as far as the table before he was on her again. This time he brought her down to the floor, his weight hard on her back, the impact emptying her lungs. Before she knew what was happening, he'd flipped her over. She saw his eyes, full of hate, blazing into hers. She felt his fists slam into her, battering her ribs. Her arms flailed as she twisted to the side, smashing against the open paint can. It tipped over, the white paint spilling over their arms, their shoulders, their chests.

'Bitch!' he raged again before bringing his fist down against her face.

The pain shot through her jaw and almost knocked her out. Her head was reeling, her brains like cotton wool. His fist came down again, this time glancing off her cheek. She heard the crack of a tooth, could feel the blood in her mouth. It was only instinct that made her carry on, a primitive urge for survival. In a last desperate bid to escape she jerked her knee upwards and caught him squarely in the balls.

Squealing like a pig, he rocked back, cradling his groin in his hands. She could hear his breath coming in short, fast pants, his mouth uttering obscenities. She had one final chance. Lunging towards the coffee table, she grabbed the wine bottle, drew back her arm and smashed it hard against his skull. Red wine spilled down his face, mingling with the blood. He made a low moaning noise before his eyes rolled back in his head and he lay still.

Jess crouched on the floor, stunned by the blows. The room stank of paint, of wine, of sweat and fear. Her lungs were heaving. Pain racked every part of her body. She doubled over, thinking she was going to be sick, but only a thin, dry retching came from her throat.

She wasn't sure how long she remained like that. Time seemed to stretch out, to become indefinable. It might only have been minutes before she heard the sound of a key in the door, of voices, of people coming into the flat. And then there was an explosion of noise and activity, of people rushing past. Suddenly Harry's arms were around her, gently pulling her up, holding her close.

'Jess? Jess? Are you okay?'

She leaned in against his chest, relief flooding through her. Through the thin cotton of his shirt she could feel his heart beating.

'Jesus,' he said, his chin resting on the top of her head. 'I go away for one night and you trash the damn place.'

She tried to speak, but no words came out.

Eventually, when her trembling had stopped, he lifted

her chin and gazed at her face. 'You hit him with a bottle, Vaughan. That wasn't very original.'

Jess looked into his eyes and forced a faltering smile to her lips. 'Well, hun,' she croaked. 'If it's good enough for Aimee Locke, it's good enough for me.'

Epilogue

It was three days since Kirsten Cope had come clean about the past, opening up a Pandora's box of lies and deceit, murder and betrayal. Valerie was still seething about the way she'd been used and manipulated by Simon Wetherby. He had inveigled his way into her life, his only desire to keep a check on the progress of the investigation into Becky Hibbert's killing, his only motive one of self-preservation. She remembered standing on the steps of the courthouse with him and shuddered. He had strangled Becky only twelve hours before.

Detective Superintendent Redding cleared his throat, and Valerie, who'd been gazing at the office floor, glanced up. 'Sorry,' she murmured. 'I was just . . .'

'It's all right. This is a difficult time for all of us.'

Valerie nodded. She wasn't the only one having to address the consequences of her actions. Fourteen years ago, a jury had sent an innocent man to jail. And that jury had based their verdict on the evidence provided by Redding and his team. Today, his face looked almost haggard. Did he feel guilty about the mistakes he had made, or was his only concern the protection of his own career? Already the wheels of spin were in motion, the facts being twisted, all the blame being shifted squarely on to Wetherby's shoulders.

'So, you interviewed Michael Higgs again this morning?' Redding asked.

'Yes, he's told us everything.' Like Paul Rafferty, Higgs had no intention of going down as an accessory to murder. 'Apparently, on the day before Becky was killed, he was approached by a man claiming to work for the Streets. I'm presuming it was some lowlife of Wetherby's acquaintance, but Higgs didn't know that. And, of course, he was suitably impressed by the thought of playing with the big boys, even if it was only to act as their messenger.'

'Messenger?'

'Yes, this man told him that all he had to do was be at the Lincoln the following night. At some point in the evening he'd receive a phone call telling him what to say and who to say it to. In return, he'd receive a hundred pounds and the undying gratitude of Terry Street.'

'Who could refuse?'

'Who indeed. Anyway, Higgs, being the pragmatic sort, decided that rather than hanging around all night, he might as well change his shift and get paid twice. Wetherby must have called him right after he'd murdered Becky Hibbert. Higgs had never met him, so he didn't recognise the voice. He was told to inform Dan Livesey that his ex was currently moonlighting as a prostitute and that the Streets weren't happy about it. As you know, the Streets run all the girls on the Mansfield and they don't like amateurs invading their patch.'

'And Livesey was supposed to sort it out?'

'Exactly. So he goes rushing off to the estate, mad as hell that the mother of his kids is working as a tom. I imagine that he's none too happy either that he's suddenly become the focus of the Streets' attention. But when he gets there, Becky's not home, or if she is, she's not answering the door. He waits around for a while and then takes off.'

'Which is when Wetherby picks him up?'

'Well, we don't know for certain, but it seems the most likely scenario. Forensics are still checking over his car, and hopefully we'll pick up some traces. Wetherby needed a scapegoat, and Livesey fitted the bill perfectly. He probably killed him before going on to his flat. He wanted to make it look as though Livesey had done a runner, so he took his passport and cleared the place out.'

Redding's eyes closed for a moment. It was bad enough knowing that a murderer had run rings around them, but when that murderer was a member of the force ... His next statement had a sharp accusatory edge. 'I don't understand how he got on and off the Mansfield without being caught on camera. I thought the CCTV footage had been checked.'

'It was,' Valerie said defensively, aware that her own professionalism was being called into question. 'He didn't go in or out by the main gate. According to Micky Higgs, there are other ways to get on to the estate, especially if you don't mind climbing over a few walls.'

'And that didn't occur to anyone?'

Valerie knew what was going on. Redding was trying to cover his own back, but it wasn't going to be at her expense.

'Dan Livesey was there at the right time. He was Becky's ex, he was angry with her on the night on question and he subsequently disappeared. We had every reason to view him as a major suspect.'

Redding's face tightened a little. He straightened the folder on his otherwise empty desk.

Valerie ploughed on. 'Higgs and his girlfriend, Paige Fielding, both backed up the rumours about Becky working as a tom. They had their own reasons for wanting us to believe it. They didn't want us to look too closely at the money we found in Becky's flat. Kirsten Cope was a useful source of income, and after Becky was murdered, they could see a way of tightening the screws. Ms Cope wasn't going to want to answer any awkward questions about why she'd been doling out cash to Becky Hibbert.'

Valerie sat back, trying to keep her cool. She might have been fooled by Wetherby, but then so had everyone else. Despite her reservations at the time, she was relieved now that she'd inserted a possible connection to the Minnie Bright case into one of her earlier reports. That, at least, was one decision that wouldn't come back to haunt her.

'Wetherby still refuses to talk,' Redding said.

'Yes, I heard.' Simon Wetherby was sticking with a *no comment* response to every question that was asked. He would either deny everything when the case came to trial, or opt for an insanity plea. Was he mad? He was certainly sick, sick and twisted. But he was also clever. He was one of those psychopaths who moved easily through society, charming and entirely plausible.

'Well,' Redding said brusquely. 'Keep me informed.'

Valerie stood up and left the office, closing the door carefully behind her. 'Bastard!' she muttered under her breath as she stormed along the corridor. Part of her rage was directed at Redding, the rest at Wetherby. There was nothing worse than being used. She walked through the incident room, went into her own office and closed the door with a lot more force than she'd used on the superintendent's.

It was a couple of minutes before Kieran Swann knocked and put his head round the door. 'Safe to come in?'

Valerie was still fuming. 'What do you want?'

He held up a plastic cup of coffee. 'I thought you might be in need, guv.'

'Only if it's got half a pint of whisky in it.'

Swann came in and put the coffee on her desk. 'That bad?' Without being asked, he pulled out a chair and sat down on the other side of the desk. 'Want to share the grief?'

'Redding's doing what he always does – covering his own back.'

'Hey, everything was by the book. And anyway, he's the one with the problem. This all started with the Minnie Bright investigation. If that hadn't been such a botch-up, none of this would ever have happened.'

Valerie shook her head. 'You thought Peck was guilty too. Everyone did. Wetherby knew exactly what to do to make sure there was no doubt about it.' She took a sip of the coffee – it was thin and watery and tasted of plastic – before putting the cup down on the desk. 'Do you think Kirsten Cope knew that he'd murdered Becky?'

'I'm not sure,' Swann said. 'She's not exactly the sharpest

knife in the drawer, but she knew his capacity for violence. It must have crossed her mind.'

Valerie was quiet for a moment. Then she said, 'I went for a drink with him on Wednesday.'

'So what? He was a colleague. There's nothing wrong with that.' Seeing her expression, his mouth dropped open. He stared hard at her. 'Ah, Jesus, you two didn't . . .?'

'No, of course not!' But at the same time, she was aware that she might have done. She'd been charmed by him, and she'd welcomed the attention, especially after all that business with Jessica Vaughan and Harry.

'Well, then,' he said. 'What's the problem?'

'The problem is that I talked to him about the Becky Hibbert murder.'

Swann gave a shrug. 'So what?' he said again.

She gazed back at him. 'So we're not supposed to discuss ongoing investigations with anyone who isn't involved with the case. He was digging for information and I told him everything he wanted to know.'

'You think Wetherby's likely to mention it?'

'I've no idea.'

'He won't,' Swann said, smiling. 'It would only make him look more devious. You've got nothing to worry about.'

Valerie smiled thinly back at him. Nothing apart from her own bad judgement. That was something she and Harry had in common. She'd been taken in by Wetherby's slick charm and he'd been ensnared by the seductive Aimee Locke. They had both made mistakes and would have to live with the consequences. But as she thought about it, her mouth gradually widened into something less cynical. Her relationship with Harry would never be easy, but that was no reason to walk away. Perhaps, despite their differences, they weren't such a bad match after all.

The sun was shining in Cadiz, the thin morning rays warming his body as he strolled beside the sea. He was home, and relief flooded through his bones. Even as he'd been checking in at the airport, as he'd been boarding the plane, he'd been holding his breath and praying. Everyone's luck ran out some day.

From where he was walking he could see the bar with its tables and chairs set out for the morning customers. It would be another couple of hours before they opened for business. He couldn't see Anna, but he knew that she was inside, drinking her usual cup of black coffee while she read through the local paper. There would be no news of Martin Locke in it, no news of a murder in London. Spain had its own problems, its own murders, its own secrets and lies.

It was a few days now since he had stood in Kellston High Street, waiting until his daughter had parked her car and walked away. Then, as arranged, he had made his way down Market Road and climbed into the back of the unlocked white Ford Mustang. Fifteen minutes later, lying down on the seat, he had passed, unobserved by the security cameras, straight into the garage of the house in Walpole Close.

He thought about the long, brittle hours he had spent with Aimee while they waited for the man called Lind to arrive. He had asked no questions and she had said nothing either. Her eyes had looked at him with pure contempt. He had abandoned her when she was a child and there could be no

527

forgiveness. They were strangers, linked by blood but not by love.

Anyway, it was over. Done and finished with. He had no idea of what was happening in London. He didn't care. It didn't matter. His daughter's fate was no longer any concern of his. It was time to get on with his life. The bill had been paid, the debt discharged. He was free.

Jess counted the houses in the alleyway that ran behind Morton Grove until she came to number 14. There was a high wrought-iron gate fixed into the wall, and she peered through its bars at the terrace behind. It looked very different now to how it once had; the house had been smartened up, the trim neat and fresh, the windows gleaming. Even the yard was immaculate, strewn with pots of yellow daffodils.

Jess wasn't really sure what she was doing there, except she felt that the fate of Minnie Bright had somehow got lost in everything that had happened recently. One little girl who was never going home. Who was left to remember her? In her mind, she could hear the voices of the girls egging Minnie on, urging her to haul her skinny body through the tiny bathroom window.

Jess drank in the cool, damp air. It was three days since Simon Wetherby had turned up in Station Road, planning on silencing her for ever. Since then she'd been putting the pieces together. She understood now the relevance of the light, the reason why Paige and Becky had changed their minds about talking to her, and Kirsten Cope's part in it all. She knew too how Wetherby had managed to get her new phone number to torment her in the supermarket: Clare had got it from Masterson and passed it on to her old lover.

What had started as a casual conversation on a cab ride home had turned into an unearthing of terrible lies, terrible deeds. Becky Hibbert had been strangled, Dan Livesey murdered too. And what about Lynda Choi? Perhaps no one would ever know the truth about what had happened to her that night.

Jess thought of the girl with the long red hair. Clare Towney had carried her guilt around for fourteen long years. Now she was dead too. One single step as the tube train slid smoothly into Bethnal Green station. Had the driver had time to realise, time to avert his gaze? And what of Clare – what had she thought of in those final few seconds? Her mother, perhaps, her mother's scared, bewildered eyes?

Jess raised her own eyes to the cloud-filled grey sky. It was time to move on, to put it all behind her. She had bridges to build in Pimlico. Neil was still resentful about being kept in the dark, still annoyed that she had chosen to go it alone. And perhaps he was right. The best relationships were based on honesty and trust. After giving the house one last glance, she set off down the alleyway and didn't look back.

Harry peered at his face in the mirror, searching for signs that it had changed. He felt different on the inside, altered in a fundamental way. His experiences had taught him a valuable lesson about what was important and what wasn't. He thought of the small holding cell and shuddered. He was lucky, he'd got a second chance and he didn't intend to throw it away. Next weekend he was going to see his father, and in the meantime he was going to put his head down and concentrate on work.

Jess and Mac had saved his skin and he would never forget it. Paul Rafferty had been paid generously by Stagg to impersonate Martin Locke. He'd also been paid to leave the country immediately afterwards. But by a stroke of good fortune, Rafferty had latched on to a rich American widow and decided not to use his ticket to Spain. Rafferty's greed had proved to be Harry's get-out-of-jail card.

He found himself wondering why Ray Stagg had chosen him as the scapegoat. There were hundreds of private detectives in London. Had it been pure chance, or something else? Perhaps it was simply that Stagg understood his weaknesses. By throwing him out of the casino, by ordering him to leave Aimee alone, he had ensured that Harry would do the very opposite. He frowned into the mirror. Or maybe it was to do with the past. They had made a deal once, a deal that still rankled with Harry and that maybe played on the other man's mind too. Had Ray Stagg been worried that one day he'd be made to pay?

Harry would probably never know the answer, but there was one thing he was sure about. When the case came to court, Stagg and Aimee Locke would try and tear each other's throats out. If there had been love, it would turn to hate. If there had been loyalty, it would quickly turn to betrayal. Each would blame the other but both would end up behind bars.

Of David Sage there was still no news. He had probably slipped out of the country on the night of Locke's murder.

Having evaded justice for the past twenty-six years, there seemed little chance of the law catching up with him now. Would he have any sleepless nights about the part he had played in his daughter's downfall? Somehow Harry doubted it.

He turned away from the mirror, left the bedroom and went through to the living room, where he gazed for a while at the bare floorboards. Another job to complete. Yesterday he had taken up the paint-smeared carpet and rolled it out into the hall. Perhaps he would sand down the boards and leave them bare.

Although she hadn't been with him for long, the flat seemed curiously empty without Jess. He kept expecting to see her seated at the table or curled up on the sofa. And then he wondered if it was specifically Jess he missed or simply having someone else around to share the good times and the bad. Valerie had called, suggesting they meet up for a drink. It was time for him to work out what he really wanted.

Harry gave the living room one final glance before he locked up and went downstairs. As he entered the office, he was surprised to find the reception area buzzing with extremely attractive women.

Mac was standing at the desk with Lorna.

Harry walked over. 'Hey, what's going on here?'

'We talked about it,' Mac said. 'The honeytrap venture, right? We're checking out some likely candidates today. You're going to sit in on the interviews, aren't you?'

Harry looked over at the women. A cool, classy blonde with eyes you could drown in met his gaze and smiled. His lips were on the verge on responding when an image of Aimee Locke's swaying, seductive hips appeared in his mind. He patted his partner softly on the shoulder. 'You know what, mate. I think I'll pass on this one.'

Harry walked over to his office, opened the door and closed it firmly behind him.

STRONG WOMEN

Roberta Kray

Jo Strong is the youngest widow in the East End. Running her late husband's jewellery shop, mercilessly bullied by her evil mother-in-law, she is trying to get her life back together again.

But then the fourteen-year-old daughter of one of the East End's most notorious gangsters is kidnapped, and Jo finds herself in a deadly race against time to rescue the girl – before it is too late. And to get her back, she'll have to join forces with damaged but handsome bad boy Gabe Miller, a man who has a dark past of his own . . .

'A Cole-esque, addictive read . . . expect a healthy dose of the kidnapping, blackmail and murder that no East End novel would be complete without' *London Lite*

978-0-7515-4108-3

THE VILLAIN'S DAUGHTER

Roberta Kray

Small-time villain Sean O'Donnell walked out on his family almost twenty years ago and hasn't been heard of since. Now his daughter, Iris, has returned to the East End to find out just what happened. But it isn't going to be easy. Everyone close to Iris seems to be keeping secrets.

When the mysterious Guy Wilder offers to help Iris uncover the truth, he changes everything. As the son of the local criminal matriarch, though, Guy has plenty of problems of his own . . .

'There can be few people better placed to write about East End gangsters than Reggie Kray's widow Roberta, and her unique insight into the murky world of organised crime shines through'
News of the World

978-0-7515-4143-4

BROKEN HOME

Roberta Kray

Hope Randall leads a quiet life, but that peace is about to be
shattered. When a stranger turns up on her doorstep, bringing news
of a half-sister she never knew she had, he's going to change her
world for ever. Connie's in deep trouble and the mysterious Flint
needs Hope's help in finding her.

Returning to London, Hope is forced to confront old demons – and
new ones. To find her sister, she'll have to toughen up and fast. But
when she enters the dark underworld of the East End, it's not only
the notoriously savage Street family she'll have to worry about:
there's also a psychopath on the loose, attacking working girls.

If Connie's going to be saved, Hope may have to get close to
the enemy . . .

978-0-7515-4474-9